D1175510

A Subtle Grace
(O'Donovan Family #2)

A Novel

By Ellen Gable

Full Quiver Publishing
Pakenham, Ontario

This book is a work of fiction. Although the setting for this novel takes place in late 19th century Philadelphia, most of the names, characters and incidents are products of the author's imagination. Any similarity to actual events or persons living or dead is used fictitiously.

A Subtle Grace

copyright 2014

by Ellen Gable

FQ Publishing

PO Box 244

Pakenham, Ontario K0A 2X0

ISBN Number: 978-0-9736736-9-2

Printed and bound in the USA

Cover photo by James Hrkach

Cover design: James and Ellen Hrkach

Scripture texts are taken from the 1881 Douay Rheims/Latin Vulgate Edition of the Holy Bible

NATIONAL LIBRARY OF CANADA

CATALOGUING IN PUBLICATION

Gable, Ellen

A Subtle Grace

Dedication

to my mother, who always made me laugh
Elizabeth May Gable Power
"Betti"
1934 - 2007

and to my father, an aspiring author
Francis Henry Gable Jr.
"Frank"
1928 - 1978

St. Agnes, Virgin and Martyr,
Pray for us

"Then veil my too inspecting face,
Lest such a subtle, shimmering grace
Flutter too far for me..."
"A Something in a Summer's Day"
Emily Dickinson

"Everything is grace."
St. Thérèse of Lisieux

1

Kathleen Emma O'Donovan's initial reaction upon entering the birthing woman's bedroom was to wince, scowl and gasp, all at once. The grunting and moaning happened to be coming from the mouth of her otherwise prim and proper mother, known in polite society as Caroline O'Donovan.

The nineteen-year-old girl's second thought, mindful that she already had an overabundance of siblings of the male gender, and none yet female, was *Please God, let this be a girl.*

She held onto her mother's trembling hand and squeezed as the woman grunted through a painful contraction. Mama's mouth pursed as she endeavored to remain quiet.

Kathleen's father, who was formally known as David John O'Donovan, owner of O'Donovan Mercantile, had spent the previous hours pacing in the hallway. Remaining obedient to the midwife's orders, he was as present as men were allowed to be for a birth, a spectator only evidenced by his heavy footsteps and shadow passing.

Mrs. McHugh, the midwife, was a large woman with thinning gray hair pulled back in a severe chignon. She gave her scripted response to Papa's occasional query: "Yes, Mr. O'Donovan, she is fine, just birthing a baby."

"Mama, go ahead and cry. Scream, if it helps."

Kathleen's mother shook her head and winced; her green eyes widened and her nails dug into her daughter's palm.

The girl released her mother's hand momentarily to wipe the woman's forehead with a cool cloth. The soft glow of the oil lamp illuminated the numerous gray strands in her mother's copper hair.

Mrs. McHugh knelt on the foot of the bed in between the birthing woman's legs. The woman's sleeves were rolled up and her hands positioned under Mama's bottom like she was about to catch a ball.

"One more push, Mrs. O'Donovan!"

Kathleen's heart raced with excitement. Another little person was about to make his or her entrance into the world!

"Come on, Miss Caroline, the baby's almost here. Push!" Their longtime servant, Jane, a middle-aged stout woman, bellowed. Kathleen had never heard the servant, whose tone was normally mild-mannered and pleasant, speak so forcefully. "We can see the head, just one more push!"

Kathleen craned her neck and watched her mother push the child from her body and into the hands of the midwife. Kathleen held her breath as the dark-haired baby began to whimper. Mrs. McHugh cut the cord and pronounced, "It's a girl, Mrs. O'Donovan."

Splendid! A sister. I finally have a sister!

The baby cried, her loud wails high-pitched, as the midwife handed her to Jane who rubbed, cleaned, then wrapped the baby in cloth linens.

Her mother relaxed against the propped up pillows, her damp red hair plastered against her face and forehead. "Is she...all right?"

"Yes, Mrs. O'Donovan. She's fine...a wee bit small, but fine. A beautiful baby girl."

With wide eyes, Kathleen stared at her baby sister. She could hardly breathe at the wonder of this new life. It was difficult to comprehend that this little girl did not exist until nine months ago.

Frantic banging on the door and her father's voice made Kathleen stifle a smile. "Is my wife all right? May I come in?"

"One moment, Mr. O'Donovan. Your wife is almost..."

This time, her father opened the door without waiting for permission. Kathleen stood up and greeted him with an embrace. "You've finally got another daughter, Papa!"

"Thanks be to God. How is Mama?" he muttered, leaning his head to one side as he studied his wife across the room.

"Fine. Come, sit by her side."

Mrs. McHugh held a basin under her mother's bottom and out slid the large and bloody placenta.

Kathleen's father, a squeamish man, winced and turned away. Kathleen put her hand on his back and nudged him forward until he stood at the bed side. He kissed his wife's forehead, then lowered himself to sit on the edge of her bed. His salt and pepper curly hair was disheveled. Her mother gazed at her father with bright and glassy eyes; her father stroked her mother's face.

"Miss O'Donovan?"

Kathleen turned to face the midwife. "Yes, Mrs. McHugh?"

"Help me determine if the afterbirth is intact. If any of it is retained, it could lead to infection or other maladies."

Kathleen left her parents and crouched down beside the midwife. The girl had forgotten that she'd told Mrs. McHugh she would be entering the Ingersoll Training School for Nurses in September.

"No reason you cannot start your training now, with your baby sister."

"Of course."

The midwife picked up the afterbirth and laid it out flat on a metal tray. "This is what gave your sister nourishment for nine months." Kathleen was in awe of this necessary part of the birthing process.

"Do you think anything is missing?"

In actuality, Kathleen was unsure, so she made an educated guess. "No?"

"Correct."

"Would you like to hold your baby sister?" Jane asked.

Kathleen glanced at her mother, her eyebrows raised and her smile wide.

"You hold her first, Kathleen. I've been carrying her for nine months."

Kathleen sat in the arm chair at the foot of the bed and Mrs. McHugh gently placed the baby in her arms. She carefully held her sister; she was indeed quite small, perhaps less than six pounds. She nodded and stared in awe at the most beautiful baby she had ever seen – and with her dark hair, small round face and deep eyes, the infant was so different from blond-haired, green-eyed Kathleen. Her newborn sister was trying to stuff her fist inside her mouth.

"Mama, Papa, what name have you chosen?"

"We've decided on Maureen," answered her mother,

"Gaelic for Mary."

Kathleen nodded. "And her middle name?"

"Caroline," her father responded with near reverence.

"Mama, she's exquisite. The most beautiful baby I've ever seen!"

Papa whispered, "Your goddaughter is most lovely, isn't she, Kat?"

"Yes, she..." Kathleen stared at her father, then glanced at her mother. "My...goddaughter?"

Her mother nodded. "We want you to be your sister's spiritual guardian."

For a moment, Kathleen couldn't speak, then she said, "How wonderful!"

"Then you accept?" her mother asked.

"Of course I accept!"

"Time for little Miss Maureen to nurse." Jane was holding her arms out. Kathleen handed the baby to the servant, who placed her in her mother's arms.   Kathleen and her father were escorted out by Jane who proclaimed, "It's called labor for a reason...Miss Caroline needs her rest."

"I didn't get to hold my daughter yet."

Jane laughed. "No, you certainly did not, Mr. David. But I will come and get you when she's done nursing."

"I don't expect I shall be sleeping," he replied.

In the hallway, Kathleen embraced her father again.

"Can you believe it? A girl, a daughter?"

"No, I can't, Kat, although I'm very grateful your mother and the baby are all right."

"And I had an opportunity to study the afterbirth. Even Mama didn't get to do that."

"You're excited about starting college?"

"Yes, I suppose I am. I know I want to help others, especially children, and I do find the medical field fascinating." Her father nodded and smiled.

"Isn't she a fortunate girl to be born into this family?"

Her father cocked an eyebrow. "You think so?"

"I do. Goodnight, Papa." She kissed his cheek and turned toward her bedroom.

"Kat?"

She swung around. "Yes?"

"I'm very proud of you for being with your mother."

"No need. I wanted to be there. Why can you not be with Mama?"

"The midwife and Jane think I will get in the way."

"You were worried about Mama?"

"I was. She nearly died after birthing John. I don't know what I would do if she...well, let's not talk of such things."

"Mama did very well, Papa."

"She most certainly did. Goodnight, Kat."

"Goodnight."

***

Seventeen-year-old William O'Donovan leaned against his bedroom door and listened to his father and sister conversing in the hallway. He had been praying for the last two hours as he watched his father's shadow pacing past his doorway, and as he heard the muffled sounds of his mother's moaning. Kat had been hoping for a girl for years. When he heard "daughter," he burst out laughing. *A girl! Extraordinary!*

John, his sixteen-year-old brother, stirred in the bed beside the window. "Turn the lamp down. I'm trying to sleep."

Will sat on the side of his brother's bed and patted John's back. "We've got a new sister."

John rubbed his eyes then opened them wide. "Really?"

"Yes."

"Is Mama fine?"

"I believe so."

"Good." He sat up, rubbed his eyes again and yawned. "Why aren't you asleep?"

"I've been praying."

"Ah. Praying *again*. Why do you pray all the time?"

"It gives me peace. I like to pray."

John sat on the edge of his bed, his legs swinging. "You think we might be able to see the baby?"

"Not sure. Would you like to?"

"Yes, although I suppose we ought to let Mama rest. It is, after all," John squinted at the clock on the mantel, "2:40 a.m."

"Yes, we should wait until tomorrow," Will agreed. "I wonder who she looks like."

"Hmmm..." His brother's eyes were returning to their closed state. "I hope you will be extinguishing the light soon."

"In a moment."

John rolled over and went to sleep.

Will knelt by his bed and silently recited a prayer of thanksgiving. *Thank you, Almighty Father, for the safe arrival of my baby sister.* He made the sign of the cross, then turned down the oil lamp, his mind turning over myriad thoughts. In a few weeks, he would enter his last year of secondary school and a time of decisions as to where he would attend college. He laid his head against the pillow.

Despite his brother's snoring in the other bed, Will relished sharing a room with him. Most upper class children enjoyed the luxury of having their own private space or bedroom but, as far back as he could remember, he and John had shared a room. Growing up, John seemed like his other half. It could be because they both bore a striking resemblance to their father. People often mistook the boys for twins. Instead, they were "Irish twins," so called because they were born in the same year — he in February and John in December. Nonetheless, there were subtle differences between them. Will's chin bore a distinct dimple; John's didn't. Will could sing on key; John couldn't. Will was more of an outgoing sort; John less so.

Will relaxed against his pillow, wondering what his sleep would hold. His dreams usually were a hodgepodge of silliness. Occasionally, though, he dreamt of a beautiful dark-haired woman. He could picture her face so distinctly, even when awake. More peculiar was that the dream always happened in the same manner: the woman would reach out to embrace him, Will would step toward her and she'd vanish.

Closing his eyes, the last clear thought before he drifted to sleep was, *Heavenly Father, thank you for my family.*

2

I witnessed another human being coming into the world.

Kathleen's head sunk deeply into her feather pillow as she stared upward. Her oil lamp, as always, was dimly lit and projected a small yellow-white circle onto the ceiling. From as far back as she could remember, Kathleen had despised the blackness that surrounded her at night. She felt safer when there was light, even a flicker. If she woke and the oil lamp had gone out, she felt like she was suffocating. When the light came on, she could breathe again. It was foolish to be afraid of the darkness; nonetheless, the fear remained.

She tossed back and forth as sleep eluded her. How could she possibly rest after what she had just witnessed?

While she looked forward to college, she wished that her non-married state had not necessitated her choosing a college at all. She would have preferred to be married by now, but thus far, no eligible bachelor — at least none of whom Kathleen approved — had shown serious interest.

The clock downstairs struck quarter past three. Her younger siblings hadn't wakened during the night – Mama had kept fairly quiet during labor – but in the morning, all of her brothers would be excited to discover that they had a new sister.

After five brothers, it seemed like having a sister was an impossible dream. For a moment, Kathleen thought of her own vocation, confident that it was marriage and motherhood. Her "coming out" reception last year when she was eighteen was a tremendous success. Why, then, was she not married yet? Two of her friends from high school had already married. Kathleen was beginning to think she might become — heaven forbid — an "old maid."

It was essential that Kathleen meet her future husband immediately to stave off this terrible fate. As far as the motherhood aspect of her vocation, after seeing firsthand what happens to a woman during the birthing process, Kathleen doubted that she would have as high a tolerance for pain as her mother obviously possessed.

Shaking that thought from her mind, Kathleen recalled holding her sister for the first time. She had so much to share with little Maureen: that she was very, very fortunate to be born into this family, especially blessed to have parents who, despite their wealth, rarely surrendered to their children's whims, were firm when they needed to be, and were devout, loving and kind.

They valued her as much as her brothers, as evidenced by their allowing her to register for and attend college.

Kathleen turned up the oil lamp, got out of bed and sat at her desk. She reached inside the top drawer for her journal.

At the front of the book she kept the tintype portrait of her mother and her "real" father, Papa's brother, Liam, at his wedding to her mother. Mama had given her the photo when she was twelve, explaining that her first husband had died and that she had married his brother. Over the years, she had learned that Liam was a fine, godly man who had died in a carriage accident before Kathleen was born. Staring at his face, she concluded that he was a handsome man with light hair, a trait Kathleen had obviously inherited from him. Mama had told her that when she was a toddler, her blond hair was almost white.

Kathleen concluded that her real father and Papa did not look related, although her mother told her that the two brothers' voices sounded identical. Kathleen wished there was a way she could hear Liam's voice, instead of merely seeing his face in this photograph.

She picked up the pen, dipped it in ink and began to write in her journal:

August 16, 1896

This is one of the happiest days of my life! I am officially a big sister...again! Maureen Caroline O'Donovan made her entrance into the world this day, or shall I say, morning, as she was born at two a.m. I am the only O'Donovan child who possesses this wonderful information. Even more wonderful: I am to be Maureen's godmother! I am extremely pleased by this news! Who will they ask to be her godfather?

As regards the birth, Mama moaned and grunted. She

was in dreadful pain, but finally the baby came out. I cannot even imagine how painful it is to push a baby out down there.

She lifted up the small holy card she used as a bookmark, a picture of St. Agnes holding a lamb, two doves hovering nearby. *St. Agnes, where is my sweetheart? Please send him to me soon!*

After reading her inspiring story a few years previous, St. Agnes, virgin and martyr, had become Kathleen's favorite saint. In the fourth century, Agnes' virginity was preserved despite the young saint being stripped naked and taken to a brothel to be violated by a group of men. The saint was saved when most of the men could not go through with the heinous act. The man who wanted her to forcibly marry him was struck blind. She was eventually martyred.

Kathleen paged through the earlier entries of her journal until she came to January 20th of last year, on the eve of St. Agnes' Feast Day, where she'd written down a prayer/poem to St. Agnes.

January 20th, 1895
  Now good St. Agnes, play thy part,
  And send to me my own sweetheart,
  And show me such a happy bliss,
  This night of him to have a kiss.

On that January day a year and a half ago, she had recited the prayer, then had finally fallen asleep. Indeed, she *had* dreamt of a man.

His face was blurry like an Impressionist painting, except with less detail. The man leaned in to kiss her, but his lips only gently brushed against hers. Immediately, Kathleen knew that this was her beloved. She couldn't explain how, but she could tell that his heart was pure and true and good. All of a sudden, the man vanished and in his place was a blue and green hummingbird hovering above her. How would she recognize her sweetheart if she could not see his face?

She left her journal open on her desk. Against the wall near the window was her hope chest filled with linens and various items she would use as a married woman. Someday soon, she hoped. The soft light of the oil lamp made the yellow background of her wallpaper seem like warm amber and the pink foreground like burgundy.

The moon was full, the night clear. As she leaned against the window sill, she stared at the stars in the night sky, twinkling against a blue-black darkness. It was silent except for a few crickets chirping below her.

The O'Donovan house was situated outside of town and Kathleen was grateful they didn't live in Philadelphia or Germantown proper. While she liked certain aspects of the city, it was too noisy, dusty and claustrophobic.

Images from baby Maureen's birth replayed in her mind. When Tim was born nearly five years ago, Kathleen was fourteen and had listened to her mother's anguished sounds. Her imagination had conjured up all sorts of wretched images. It was much less horrifying to be present at a birth than to simply overhear one, which is why, in her opinion, her father ought to have been inside the room as well.

With a sigh, Kathleen put on her robe and quietly crept down the back staircase to the basement kitchen. She heard voices, then muffled laughter. At the bottom of the steps, she saw that her father was sitting at the long table in the middle of the large kitchen. Jane was standing beside him, her hands on her hips. One lone gas lamp beside the stove illuminated the area. Beyond the stove were the pantry and another staircase leading up to the foyer and main staircase.

"Couldn't sleep, Kat?" Her father was still dressed in his suit. He stood as she approached the table.

"No, I couldn't."

Jane also remained in her day clothes — a white and gray blouse and a gray skirt — although she had already removed her mobcap. She was a stocky woman, with gray and brown hair pulled back showing a slightly wrinkled face. The servant was a kind soul, who wore a constant smile that made Kathleen always want to be in her presence. Jane spoke of her late husband, Kip, a former O'Donovan servant, with great affection.

"Come sit beside me, Kat." Her father patted the chair next to him. A smile tugged at the corner of his mouth.

Jane was staring at the table under the wide window where twenty newly-canned jars of pickled beets were lined from one end of the table to the other like sentinels guarding a fort. "I ought to bring those jars to the pantry," she said, "but I'll wait until tomorrow, if you don't mind, Mr. David. I didn't get a chance to do it because Miss Caroline went into labor."

"Leave them till tomorrow. Those jars aren't going anywhere."

"No, but if one of those boys knocks into the table, there will be a red mess to mop up."

"Yes, but the boy responsible will be cleaning it up."

Jane nodded. "If there's nothing else, Mr. David, I'm going to bed. The ice wagon will be making a delivery at seven a.m."

"Of course, Jane." The servant patted Kathleen's back, then quickly ascended the back stairs.

"You were worried tonight, Papa."

"Was it obvious?"

She nodded and leaned close. "Mama has been through this many times."

"I know, but..."

"I was praying, Papa."

"Thanks, Kat. I'm relieved, to say the least."

"Papa?"

"Hmmm?"

"Why are men not allowed to be present during birthing?"

"Mrs. McHugh and Jane want to help your mother without me getting in the way."

"I'm sure you would have kept out of the way."

"No doubt."

They sat in silence. Papa was a handsome man, even at 42, with his finely chiseled face and his curly gray-brown hair. His kindness, his devout faith and his devotion to their family made him a most special man. She smiled fondly as she recalled, at age six, proclaiming to her mother that she would marry Papa. Her mother had laughed. "Little girls cannot marry their fathers, sweet."

"The baby is exquisite, Papa."

"I know. God has blessed your mother and me many times."

"And...I am honored to be Maureen's godmother!"

Her father smiled, then winked at her.

"Papa?"

"Yes?"

"Pray tell...who will you ask to be her godfather?"

"Will."

"Wonderful! This will mean so much to Will."

"Your mother and I are very proud of you and Will. You both take your faith seriously and are consistently helpful around the house."

"You've been a most loving and kind father."

"Thank you, Kat. Every time a new child is born, I feel like God is giving me another opportunity to be a better father."

"I don't think there could be a better father than you."

David lowered his head, then he reached across the table and took her hand in his. "It's a shame that Lee — Liam, your...father — never got to know you."

Kathleen wasn't sure how to respond so she remained silent.

"And that you never got to know him." He paused. "You're much like him in many ways."

"Really?"

"Yes." He tilted his head toward her. "So what do you think of having another sibling?"

"I cherish it, Papa. I'm especially happy that I now have a sister. I cannot believe it!"

"It's one more little person to help with."

"I don't mind..." She winked. "Most of the time."

David pushed his chair back and stood up. He kissed the top of her head. "I'm going to try to sleep. Mass in the morning."

"I know. I'll just enjoy the silence for a while."

"A rare commodity."

"Indeed."

Her father's footsteps on the back staircase were heavy and fading. Closing her eyes, she wondered what it would be like to be married and have a family of her own. Would that time come soon?

Kathleen made her way upstairs for a quick trip to the privy, then crawled into bed, hoping to catch a few hours of rest before dawn.

3

Despite the late night, Will rose early. He knelt beside his bed and quietly recited morning prayers, especially one of thanksgiving for his newest sibling. Rising, he blessed himself and stood by the window, careful not to wake his snoring brother. The sun was just appearing, casting an orange glow on the drooping oak tree in front of the house, its full green leaves swaying with the warm breeze. Will enjoyed this view, one to which he had wakened for most of his life. He remained at the window until the sun was completely above the horizon, then he returned to his desk and opened his Bible. After reading for a short time, he got up and entered the hallway. No sounds yet from his baby sister, but he was anxious to see her. When would everyone else be awake?

***

Kathleen woke to the delighted squeals of her younger brothers, Tim, five and Kevin, ten. They giggled and shrieked as they banged on Kathleen's door.

"Kat, Kat, we have a baby sister, we have a baby sister!"

She sat up, stretched her hands in mid-yawn, and glanced at the clock on the mantel. Seven o'clock. She groaned as she removed her night cap. She would have liked at least another hour of sleep. This morning, her room was a bright blast of yellow with the sun beaming through her light-colored drapes onto the yellow and pink-patterned wallpaper.

"Yes, yes, I know, boys." She swung open the door to find Kev and Tim bouncing in front of her. They were dressed in their robes, although in their excitement, the garments were hanging off their shoulders. It seemed like yesterday that Kev and Tim were toddlers. Kev was dark-haired like his older brothers Will and John, while Tim and Pat were fair, with light brown hair.

"Papa said we can see her now! Come on, everyone's there. We're waiting for you!"

"Very well."

Kathleen joined her youngest brothers in the hallway and

further down could see the older boys, Will, John and Pat standing outside their parents' room. Pat, at 13, was already nearly as tall as both Will and John, and much taller than Kathleen who stood five feet two inches.

Tim and Kevin each grabbed one of her hands and pulled her toward her siblings. The top of Kevin's head now came to Kathleen's shoulders.

As the younger boys drew her closer to the older boys, Will turned. "Finally awake, Kat?" He cocked an eyebrow and smiled.

"I was up most of the night, you ninny."

"Remind me to ask you the details."

"Remind me not to tell you. That's private, Will."

His eyes widened, as if he hadn't realized that birthing was an intimate affair. "I suppose you are correct."

"Kat, you finally have a sister," John said.

"It's about time. I've been waiting my entire life!"

Pat placed his arm around her shoulder. Kathleen found it hard to believe he was already nearly as tall as Will and John.

"Who does she look like, Kat?" His voice cracked and had already begun to sound deeper.

"Like Papa, dark-haired, but tiny. You'll see for yourself in a moment."

Pat's mouth turned slightly in a grin. When Patrick smiled, he reminded Kathleen of John and Will, despite his light brown hair and Mama's green eyes.

The door swung open. On Papa's face was a smile so wide that Kathleen was certain it reached from ear to ear.

"Is everyone present?" Her father's eyes swept from child to child, counting. "Kat, Will, John, Pat, Kev, Tim, yes, everyone's here. Time to meet baby Maureen. Your mother has finished feeding her and Jane is dressing her."

"Can I hold her, Papa? Please, Papa?" Tim asked. "I want to hold Mo-reen first."

Her father's eyes brightened. "You shall be the first, Tim, to hold baby Mo." As he corralled his children into the room, her father winked at Kathleen because she had been the first to hold her, even before her parents. She returned his wink with a knowing grin.

Kathleen could not believe her mother's transformation from sweaty, flushed and exhausted to fresh, radiant and rested. She was indeed a beautiful woman.

Each child took turns sitting in the big arm chair beside their parents' bed and fawned over the new baby. Baby Mo slept through the entire sibling introduction. However, when it was Kathleen's turn, her little sister opened her eyes. "We've already met. I'm your big sister, Kathleen, but you can call me Kat, since everyone else in this family does, not to be confused with the feline household pet." She kissed the top of Maureen's dark hair which smelled of baby soap.

Will leaned close and whispered. "Kat, will you teach our dear sister the ways of defending herself against her boisterous brothers?"

Kathleen's eyebrows lifted. "Whatever do you mean, Will?"

He held his arm out and pointed at the small scar near his elbow.

With a chuckle, she said, "Oh, that. I haven't bitten you or John in many years."

"True...and I admit we were being too rough with you, but for goodness' sake, that hurt!"

"You wouldn't let me go, you were hurting *me*...I did what I had to do."

"Yes, you did."

"Kat?" She turned to find her father leaning close to her and whispering. "Please make sure the younger boys wear the proper attire for Mass this morning. Your mother and the baby will be staying home."

"Of course, Papa."

***

Dressed in a pale green cotton dress with matching gloves and hat, Kathleen walked her two youngest brothers to the larger carriage and waited until Jesse, their servant, arrived to help her and the boys get in. While she waited, she gazed at the home she'd always found so beautiful. The O'Donovan house was a gray stone mansion with two white marble pillars; dark green shutters were open on this sunny warm day. Wrought iron railings and a small covered porch led to a spacious foyer inside. Trimmed bushes and yellow, purple and orange daylilies painted the front bottom of their stately home.

As the entire family could not be made to fit in one carriage, Will and John took the Columbus two-seater buggy. Kathleen, Papa, Tim, Kev and Pat went in their Cabriolet carriage driven by Jesse. A man of few words, Jesse was a Native American who wasn't much older than Kathleen. He was a gentle young man who never complained and worked hard. His long hair was kept in a ponytail and he wore brown leather moccasin boots. He had come to live and work with their family a year ago after Jim Fraser, their longtime hired hand and driver, had passed away from a heart attack.

The carriage roof had been removed on this comfortable and bright day and Kathleen lifted her head to enjoy the warmth on her face. Despite the bright sun, the gentle bouncing of the carriage seemed to be making it hard for Papa to keep his eyes open. Beside her, Tim and Kevin were trading marbles. Pat had won the coveted seat beside Jesse.

Papa lifted his head and stared at the landscape, his eyelids heavy. He finally made eye contact and Kathleen winked at him. Papa laughed under his breath.

"I'm tired too, Papa."

"You're younger than I am."

She shrugged. Kathleen's excitement about the birth was stronger than her fatigue. She couldn't seem to keep still; she wanted to shout out to everyone, "I have a new sister!"

The carriages stopped in front of St. Vincent de Paul Church which had been their parish for the past five years. They occasionally attended Mass at St. Peter and Paul Basilica in Philadelphia, but this church was closer and Papa had shared that he wanted his children to experience the faith life of a smaller parish. Admittedly, St. Vincent's was less grandiose than the cathedral but, at first glance, its Italian Renaissance architecture and pilasters made it look more like a European library than a church.

Her father got out first and assisted Kathleen onto the stepping block beside the carriage. Will, John and Jesse helped the rest of the children.

Kathleen took Tim's hand and walked behind her father

into the church as her remaining siblings followed. Inside, her father and brothers removed their hats.

The family made their way to the front and the second pew on the right. They each genuflected. John filed in first followed by Kathleen who knelt down and thanked God for her little sister. Will knelt beside her.

The Mass began with the hymn "Faith of Our Fathers."

The priest made the sign of the cross. "In Nómine Patris et Fílii et Spíritus Sancti."

After prayers in Latin and Scripture readings in English, Father Morrissey stepped up to the ambo and began to speak. The white-haired priest possessed deeply set wrinkles and jowls as well as kind, gentle eyes.

John tapped her and whispered. "Hey, Kat, that high 'n mighty police chief's son, Karl, is here."

Kathleen immediately straightened and nonchalantly glanced over her shoulder. Karl Wagner was looking forward and listening to Fr. Morrissey.

"He's been staring at you since we came in."

Kathleen's eyebrows lifted. "Really? He's not looking now."

She again glanced at Chief Wagner's pew. Next to the middle-aged police chief was young Karl Wagner, the most strikingly handsome man she ever had the pleasure to lay eyes on. *When did he become so handsome?* The last time she saw him must have been about seven years ago, before he went away to boarding school. Karl was now over six feet tall, with dark, wavy hair, dark eyes and a tanned complexion.

As she was staring, he looked at her, holding her gaze longer than necessary. *Did he just wink?* She gasped. Flustered, she turned away.

"He's got nerve," John whispered.

"Stop, John." Despite her protestations, she was most curious about Mr. Wagner.

"I've heard that he's trouble."

"You mustn't listen to gossip."

"Shhh, Kat," Will said under his breath. "This is the Holy Sacrifice of the Mass, not a social gathering."

She scowled at John. He shrugged.

Kathleen found it hard to pay attention. It didn't help that Mr. Wagner stole many glances at her.

When Mass ended, the family started toward the door.

"Mr. O'Donovan?" Police Chief Wagner called to David when they reached the church entrance.

"Yes, Chief Wagner?"

"I hear congratulations are in order."

"Yes, the newest addition to our family was born this morning around two a.m."

Police Chief Wagner shook her father's hand.

Kathleen had always admired Chief Wagner. He was a man of means, an upper class gentleman who, despite an inheritance from his parents, had served the community as a police officer for many years. He had become police chief last year. Like his son, the man was tall and broad-shouldered, but with graying black hair and a midsection that suggested he drank and ate in excess.

"Mr. O'Donovan, you probably haven't seen my son, Karl, in many years."

David smiled and offered his hand. "No, I haven't. Good day, Mr. Wagner."

"The pleasure is all mine, Mr. O'Donovan," the young man said. Kathleen thought his manner most pleasing and his voice deep and masculine.

David stepped aside to allow Kathleen to come forward. "And may I present my daughter, Miss Kathleen O'Donovan."

Karl Wagner nodded and smiled widely. Her heart pounded in her chest; her fair skin felt warm with a blush.

For a moment, it seemed like no one else was there. Kathleen offered a shy smile.

"Miss O'Donovan, I am so pleased to see you again after all these years." He turned to her father. "Mr. O'Donovan, I have been admiring your beautiful daughter since she arrived this morning."

Tim yanked on Papa's coat. "Billy is waiting for me at the front. I want to tell him about my baby sister."

"One moment, Tim. Yes, well, you —" Her father was interrupted by yet another well-wisher. "Congratulations, Mr. O'Donovan," a middle-aged man said.

"Yes, thank you." Her father touched her shoulder to leave.

Before Kathleen turned away, she offered Karl Wagner another coy smile, then allowed her father to escort her down the aisle. Behind her, Kathleen felt the young Mr. Wagner's eyes on her and her heart fluttered in her chest.

Outside, in the warm August air, the O'Donovan family fielded questions from fellow parishioners.

"Who does she look like?"

"Is Mrs. O'Donovan well?"

Her father answered the questions politely, although Kathleen could tell he was distracted. Kathleen was likewise distracted and a quick perusal of the young Mr. Wagner told Kathleen that he continued to stare in her direction.

John leaned in and whispered. "I do believe that he is quite enamored, dear sister."

"Cease your chattering. Really."

John continued. "Don't look now, Kat, but it looks like he's coming this way."

"John...that's ridicu..." Kathleen was interrupted by young Mr. Wagner's presence and her mouth opened slightly. She quickly closed it and held her hand to her chest to quiet her thundering heart.

"Excuse me, Mr. O'Donovan." Karl did not look, smile or wink in Kathleen's direction. Instead, he faced her father.

"Yes?"

"May I please have a word with you, sir?"

Papa sighed, but patiently answered, "Yes, you may."

Mr. Wagner and her father walked off in the distance.

"If he's asking father to court you, he doesn't waste any time, does he, Kat?" John asked. "What's his rush?"

"Don't be absurd. He wouldn't be asking Papa that." But even as she said the words, part of her wondered whether John was correct.

Margaret, her friend, standing beside her new husband, Stephen, waved to her from across the street. She nodded and returned the gesture. They made such a handsome couple.

Her father stood thirty feet away with his back to Kathleen while the young Mr. Wagner was facing her. From time to time, the gentleman glanced in her direction, as if he wanted to make sure she was watching, then he focused his attention on her father. Papa shook his head, turned and walked toward his family. The young man stepped away and began walking alongside Chief Wagner.

"What did he want?" Kathleen asked.

Her father ignored her. "I want everyone in the carriages."

"Papa, I want to sit next to the driver this time," pleaded Tim.

On the way home, Kathleen had to control her desire to ask her father the reason Mr. Wagner wanted to speak to him. To do this, she daydreamed of the dashing and handsome Mr. Wagner. She wondered what it would be like for him to kiss her and felt a warm blush thinking about it.

4

Patience was a virtue that Kathleen had always lacked. So that evening, after supper, when she still had not yet heard the details of what Karl had discussed with her father, she went to her parents' room.

The door to their room was slightly ajar. Kathleen reached out her hand to knock, then pulled it back when she heard her mother's voice. She leaned her ear close to the door.

"We don't know this young man very well. He's been away for so long."

"That is why I said no. He informed me that he has finished college and will likely be taking a job as a police officer in Philadelphia in the near future."

"I would feel more comfortable giving our permission if we knew his family better...or if we knew him better."

"I agree, although he's moving too fast for my liking. When a young man asks to court my daughter, I expect him to be nervous about it. Karl seemed too confident, haughty even."

"And we ought to speak with Kathleen. She is putting enormous pressure on herself to be married...especially since Margaret wed earlier this year."

Knocking, Kathleen didn't wait for an answer and opened the door. Her father stood beside the bed; her mother was sitting up in it.

"Baby sleeping?" Kathleen asked.

"Yes, quite soundly." The small bassinet was quiet on the other side of the bed.

Kathleen's head lowered. "I was eavesdropping."

Her father's mouth opened in surprise, then he frowned and stood up. "Have a seat."

Her mother spoke, her voice soft, but laced with concern. "Kathleen, this young man has expressed an interest in courting you, but we know little about him. He tells your father that he has finished college."

"I could easily get to know him if we courted, Mama."

The older woman sighed.

"Kat, a man ought to be able to provide for a woman. He hasn't yet procured a job. Besides, it would be more acceptable if he became acquainted with our family first. Then perhaps after six months or a year, we would agree to allow him to court you."

Kathleen exhaled then curtly said, "By then I will be an old maid and he will be married to another young lady. Is it your wish for me to be an old maid?"

Her mother frowned. "Kathleen, you're acting juvenile."

"Juvenile? Please, Mother."

"Kat, we want you to be happy," her father spoke softly.

"Well, if you wanted me to be happy, you would allow me to get to know him in a courting relationship."

Her mother sighed and her father stepped forward and took hold of Kathleen's hand. "If you like, I shall invite him to come to our home perhaps in a few months' time."

Kathleen turned her back to them. They really *did* want her to remain unmarried.

"Kat, listen to reason."

"I'm nineteen years old. You treat me like a child."

She heard her father exhale. He whispered to her mother, then said, "Kat, turn around."

Kathleen slowly turned to face them. Her father placed his hands on her shoulders. "We shall invite him to dinner in two weeks. Allow us to see how he interacts with the family. We shall give our consent then, and only then. Is that acceptable?"

"That would be perfect, Papa. Thank you!" She hugged first her father, then her mother.

The baby chose that moment to let out an ear-piercing scream. Mama tried to nurse her, but the baby turned her head away.

"It's time to try Papa's method of calming a child," her father said, in a high-pitched voice. He picked up his violin and after a moment or two of tuning, he began playing.

"How wonderful," Kathleen said between baby screeches. "You haven't played in months."

He winked. As the melody became apparent, it took her

breath away. The piece of music was *"Oft in the Stilly Night,"* Papa's favorite song. Magically, the baby stopped her loud crying. Soon, baby Mo was closing her tiny dark eyes.

Returning to her bedroom, Kathleen closed the door, then leaned against it. A smile passed over her lips. She was so happy, it seemed like her heart was bursting. First, a new baby sister. Then, a most handsome and charming man had asked to court her.

An unusually cool breeze slipped in through the window and caressed her face like a silk handkerchief. She breathed in deeply and decided that it would be impossible to wait two weeks until she saw Mr. Wagner again. Even the name spoke beauty and class to her. She imagined herself on the arm of Mr. Wagner. Other girls would be envious. After all, *she* had captured his attention.

Just then, the hallway outside her room became filled with the sounds of thundering footsteps and giggling boys. She got up, opened the door and stepped into the hallway. "Rrrooom." Tim swept past her and knocked her against the wall.

"Timothy James O'Donovan, get back here and apologize."

The boy turned and frowned. "For what?"

"For shoving me into the wall."

"Sorry, Kat," his sweet voice answered.

Kathleen backed up into her room, picked up her journal and headed upstairs. In the attic, there were smaller rooms that had previously been used as servants' bedrooms. Papa had once told her that when he was a child, his parents had twelve full-time servants. After her grandparents' death, when Papa became the head of the house, he decreased the number to three full-time and one part-time and eventually moved the servants to the larger bedrooms on the second floor. Over time, the attic rooms had become storage areas.

Being in a house with so many brothers, it was difficult to read, or study or accomplish anything sometimes. So, journal in hand, Kathleen opened up the first door on the left, a small eight by ten room with a slanted ceiling.

She sat down to write in her journal.

August 16, 1896

I overheard my parents speaking about the dashing and handsome Mr. Karl Wagner and his desire to court me. At first, they insisted I wait a whole year! They finally agreed to invite him to dinner in two weeks' time. Why is it that I am flattered and excited upon hearing the news that this particular man wishes to court me? The notion of matrimony excites me, especially the thought of being married to such a handsome, confident and charming man. Mr. Wagner is the first man who has ever really noticed me! St. Agnes, thank you for sending me my sweetheart!

5

"The obligation of a godfather and a godmother is to instruct the child in its religious duties, if the parents neglect to do so or die." Will read and re-read the section on Baptism in the Baltimore Catechism, then he knelt down and recited his evening prayers. Earlier, his parents had asked him to be godfather to baby Mo. Today, he would begin praying for his youngest sister as a spiritual father prays. "Heavenly Father, bless her with strong and devout faith." He made the sign of the cross and stood.

Scowling, he stared at the empty bed near the window. After the family rosary, Papa had told everyone to go to bed. He knew John couldn't be doing homework, since it was still summer holiday, so what *could* he be doing?

He turned down the oil lamp until the only light in the room was from the moonlight.

Shortly thereafter, as he was drifting off to sleep, he heard the bedroom door quietly open then close, the rustling of clothes coming off and his brother slipping into the other bed.

***

Dr. Luke Peterson rode his modest carriage to the O'Donovan home just outside of Germantown. Mr. O'Donovan had sent him a letter by courier stating that his wife had just given birth. He requested that Luke call upon the family for his wife's postpartum examination.

While riding down the laneway, Luke enjoyed the apple trees and red maples that lined the road. Seeing the house in the distance, he surmised that Mr. O'Donovan must be a wealthy man. However, as he rode closer to the house, it seemed that although it was a very stately looking home, it was a plain, understated wealth. A field and some outbuildings were in the back and a forest of lush evergreen and deciduous trees populated either side of the house. The building looked to have been built early in the century.

He pulled his carriage in front of the house and immediately a young Indian man greeted him and offered to take his horse and carriage around to the barn. Luke thanked him, picked up his bag and stepped down from the carriage.

Facing the house, he pushed his glasses up on his nose and stared at the painted script above the front door: "*As for me and my house, we will serve the Lord.*"

A middle-aged servant met him on the porch.

"Good afternoon."

"Good afternoon. Permit me to introduce myself. I'm Dr. Luke Peterson."

"Pleased to make your acquaintance, Dr. Peterson. My name is Jane. I'm the O'Donovan's head servant and housekeeper. Please do come in." Jane had salt and pepper hair pulled back under a servant's cap and wore a gray and white blouse and skirt. Her eyes were bright and welcoming.

"Mr. O'Donovan will be down presently."

***

Kathleen's door was open. She had just finished brushing her hair and was about to pin it up when she heard her brother shout, "I got it!" She turned to see Tim run off down the hall with her journal.

"You little sprat! Give me back my journal!" Kathleen yelled. She raced down the hallway and nearly ran into her father as he was coming up the stairs.

"Whoa, Kat. Where are you going in such rush?"

"He stole my journal! Make him give it back."

"Tim," he called. Her brother had already made it to the end of the opposite hallway before he turned.

"Return your sister's journal immediately," David called.

The boy's head lowered, but he didn't move.

"If you don't return Kat's journal, I shall place you on manure duty two days this week instead of one afternoon."

Tim sighed, then walked toward his sister and father. He stood with his hands behind his back.

Jane was on the stairs. "Mr. David, the new doctor's here to look in on little Miss Maureen."

"Thank you, Jane." Papa checked his pocket watch.

"This is his first time here, Mr. David, and you ought to meet him in the foyer rather than have me bring him up."

"Of course. Although it probably won't be his last visit,"

David responded. "Not with the various injuries that take place here on a weekly basis."

***

Luke waited in the foyer as a cacophony of children's voices swept down from the second floor. A man in his forties, with curly dark hair laced with gray, descended the stairs. Luke immediately recognized him from somewhere, but he couldn't recall where, perhaps the post office?

"Dr. Peterson?" Mr. O'Donovan held his hand out and Luke shook it. "Permit me to introduce myself. I am David O'Donovan."

"It's a pleasure, Mr. O'Donovan."

"My wife is upstairs," he said, then led him up the marble staircase.

***

Kathleen scowled at her little brother. "Give me back my journal or..."

"Make me!"

"You'll get manure duty, like Papa said."

"So? Make me."

"You, you!" She reached out and grabbed onto his hands to try to retrieve the book from behind his back.

"Stop it, you two," she heard her father say behind her. Kathleen sighed and, although frustrated, she straightened. She looked up to see a youthful man with glasses carrying a black oval-shaped bag.

"Dr. Peterson, may I present two of my children, Miss Kathleen O'Donovan..."

"It's...um...my pleasure," the young man said, nodding toward her. Dr. Peterson's pale complexion flushed; he cleared his throat, then squared his shoulders.

"Nice to meet you, Dr. Peterson," Kathleen said.

Papa pointed. "And this is Tim who, as you can tell, is a major instigator of pranks in this house."

Dr. Peterson leaned down and patted Tim's head. Tim scowled. Her youngest brother hated when grown-ups did that. Kathleen already liked the new doctor for annoying Tim. She quickly grabbed her journal from her brother.

"Doctor, my daughter will be studying at the Ingersoll

Training School for Nurses in September."

The doctor raised his eyebrows and his mouth formed a wide grin. "Th...that is outstanding, Miss O'Donovan. Please do...uh...let me know if I may be of assistance in your studies."

"I will, thank you most kindly." As Kathleen studied Dr. Peterson, she found it hard to believe that he was a full-fledged physician as he couldn't be much older than she. He was average, if not pleasant, looking with dark blond hair reaching to just above his shoulders. He had brown eyes behind small wire-rim glasses, was about as tall as Papa, and his face was smooth and beardless. *Is he even old enough to shave?*

"And, in here, you will meet the newest addition to our family, baby Mo...Maureen...as well as my beautiful, but fatigued, wife." David motioned for the doctor to come into the room. Kathleen returned her journal to her desk, then remained at the doorway of her parents' bedroom, tilting her head as she listened.

"Caroline, this is Dr. Luke Peterson, the new physician who has taken Dr. Mayfield's place."

"I'm pleased to meet you, Dr. Peterson."

"Thank you, Mrs. O'Donovan. Do you wish me to examine you as well? The midwife informed me that it was a textbook birth, but I would be glad to provide you with a postpartum examination at no charge."

Mama stared in the distance, then appeared to be forcing a smile. Kathleen wondered whether Mama was hesitant because the doctor was young – and male – but after a moment, her mother nodded.

Her father cleared his voice. "I shall be downstairs in my office, if you need me," he said to his wife. "Dr. Peterson, it's been a pleasure."

"Thank you, Mr. O'Donovan."

Dr. Peterson accompanied David to the door and, when the man left, he began to close the door when Kathleen asked, "Mama, may I remain here with you during the examination?" She was interested in how the doctor would examine the baby. As well, she sensed her mother was not comfortable with the new doctor.

"If it's acceptable to the doctor."

"Dr. Peterson, may I remain here with my mother?"

"Of course, especially since you will be a nursing student soon."

The doctor pulled a stethoscope out of his bag, rubbed the bottom of it and listened to her mother's chest. He then held onto her hand and looked at his pocket watch. Then, keeping her mostly covered, he seemed to be touching Mama's abdomen. Finally, he asked her a few questions.

"So this is your seventh child, Mrs. O'Donovan?"

"Yes, my seventh."

"So gravida seven..." The doctor scribbled a note in his book.

"Oh...and, yes, I've also had two miscarriages." She spoke so softly that Kathleen had to strain to hear her.

"Gravida nine, para seven... you've given birth to seven children." Dr. Peterson also whispered. He had a pad of paper and a pencil and appeared to be ready to write something down.

Again, her mother's voice was whispering so she had to strain to hear. "I... forget that I didn't give birth to him."

Mama looked at Kathleen and smiled. Kathleen returned the gesture, but she wondered what had gotten into her mother, who leaned closer to the doctor and whispered again.

"Oh, I see." He turned and glanced at Kathleen, who offered an awkward smile. Mama said something about *not* giving birth to *him*. What else had she said? Then, as if she had been hit over the head, she remembered: *Will*.

Kathleen had a vague memory of Will coming to their family when she was about four. Will's natural mother had been a servant who had died and her parents had taken in and adopted Will. She recalled once when she asked her mother about Will and how much he looked like Papa, her mother had muttered, "Well, sweet, you know how sometimes people who spend a lot of time together resemble each other."

At the time, that made sense to Kathleen, but whenever she looked at Will and John, there was no denying that they actually *looked* like brothers; more so than John and Pat, or even John and herself.

As far as Kathleen knew, Will had no knowledge that he was adopted and Kathleen wondered why her parents hadn't informed him before now. After all, Mama had told her years ago that Papa wasn't really her father, that Papa's brother, Liam, was her natural father.

Truth be told, Will seemed so much a member of their family that she never actually thought of him as "adopted."

The young doctor continued his duties, but Kathleen made a mental note to ask her parents about Will.

"Now, Miss O'Donovan, I'm ready to examine your sister. Would you like to be my assistant?"

Kathleen's eyes brightened. "Yes, I should like that very much."

Dr. Peterson walked to the bassinet, leaned in and carefully picked up baby Maureen. "Let's see how this beautiful little lady is doing."

He gently removed the baby's blanket as if he was performing an intricate surgical procedure. Baby Mo was just waking, stretching her neck and opening her mouth to nurse. She began to whimper and the doctor whispered, "Shhh, little one. I shall only be a moment, then you can be cuddled in your mother's arms." Remarkably, the baby quieted. He quickly rubbed the bottom of the stethoscope on the palm of his hand. Kathleen stared as she wondered why he was...then her expression softened to a smile when she realized that he was warming the stethoscope before placing it on her sister's chest. A simple but kind act that she recalled he'd done for her mother as well. Still, despite this kindness, when the doctor placed the stethoscope on baby Mo's chest, her little arms startled and she began to whimper. Dr. Peterson tenderly caressed her sister's arm. "Shhh."

He listened to the baby's chest. He examined her, lifting her arms, opening her diaper and refastening the pin, moving her legs. He then wrapped her tightly in the blanket. "Mrs. O'Donovan, shall I hand the baby to you or to her sister?"

"She needs to nurse, so I shall take her."

This new doctor was nothing like Dr. Mayfield, who was perhaps the most ancient person Kathleen had ever met. Even from the time she was young, Dr. Mayfield possessed bushy white eyebrows and hair white as cotton. Dr. Peterson seemed to have a great amount of patience and tenderness that the older physician had lacked.

Although Kathleen had never liked being examined by old Dr. Mayfield, he was, after all, elderly and not able to see very well. She couldn't conceive of being examined by such a young man, physician or not, as he was far too close to her age and it would create a most awkward situation.

Kathleen shrugged. She was likely the healthiest O'Donovan family member. Aside from the occasional cold, the last time she could recall being sick was when she was fourteen. Another good reason that she might make a most suitable nurse.

***

Luke descended the staircase, his hand resting on the smooth railing. He thanked God that there was thick carpet on these beautiful Italian marble stairs. With so many children, no doubt that feature saved a few boys from a fall. Jane handed Luke his hat and riding gloves. "Good afternoon, Dr. Peterson."

He tipped his hat. "Good afternoon, Jane."

Above the door mantel was a simple wooden crucifix and beautiful script: *Céad Míle Fáilte*. He stared and studied the words. He knew Latin, but not this language. Although he recognized *mile*, which he assumed to be a thousand, he didn't understand the rest.

"A thousand welcomes."

Luke turned to see David staring upward. "It means a thousand welcomes in Gaelic."

"Beautiful."

"My late father's idea."

Luke nodded.

"How are Caroline and the baby faring?" David asked.

"Very well. Your wife is doing well and your baby is a healthy, but small, little girl."

"Splendid." David handed Luke several bills. "This is for today, Dr. Peterson."

Luke counted the money, ten one dollar bills. "Mr. O'Donovan, this is too much. I only charge three dollars for a postnatal home visit."

"This is what we would pay any doctor for a house call. Just because you're young doesn't mean we shouldn't pay you the same."

Luke grinned. "If you insist. But..."

"No buts."

"It is much appreciated, sir."

"Please call me David. And one other thing..."

"Yes, David?"

The older man held out a second envelope. "This contains $20. As a physician, you will probably become aware of unfortunate families who might need this. Please give this away to anyone who needs it."

"I don't understand."

"Over the past ten years, I gave Dr. Mayfield $20 each month. He would hear of families who couldn't afford to pay for basic medical needs or food. This envelope is for you to use at your discretion."

Luke opened his mouth, but couldn't speak. Finally, he muttered, "Thank you, sir. I shall be a good steward of your charity."

"Good day, Dr. Luke."

"Good day, David."

Luke walked to his carriage, dropped his medical bag onto the seat and got in. He tipped his hat to David.

As he rode home, he thought back to meeting Miss O'Donovan and immediately felt like a silly schoolboy. When he saw her the first time, the breath caught in his throat and he nearly gasped. He was sure he had blushed. She was lovely, with holly green eyes, a slightly turned up nose, smooth skin and silky golden hair that cascaded over her shoulders. The fact that she was studying to be a nurse meant that, like him, she must be interested in anatomy and helping others.

Of course, the way her expression brightened when he asked her to be "his assistant" was endearing.

Luke straightened and clicked the reins. He was overwhelmed by the kindness and generosity of David O'Donovan. The man was obviously well off, but seemed different from the elite of Philadelphia society. Even more surprising, he overheard the man speaking of chores to his children. Upper class children with chores? This family was not the typical wealthy family.

Normally, Luke wasn't comfortable with those in the upper class. In fact, he avoided fancy medical dinners that necessitated the protocol of wearing certain clothes for different affairs. Despite his status as a medical doctor, he had no desire to be an 'upper class gentleman.' He was quite satisfied with second, or middle, class.

For the moment, he considered David's wife. He was astonished to learn Mrs. O'Donovan was thirty-nine years old. Except for a few grays in her red hair, she didn't look much older than thirty. A beautiful woman. It was no surprise that her oldest daughter was so lovely.

When Mrs. O'Donovan spoke of forgetting that she hadn't given birth to her oldest son, Luke admired her a great deal. Luke surmised that either Mr. O'Donovan had been married previously or the couple had adopted the boy. Her attitude reminded Luke of his aunt and uncle's kind treatment of him as one of their own when he went to live with them after his sister died.

Luke veered around a branch in the road with his modest carriage. He stopped, got out and kicked the branch off the road.

Before continuing, Luke patted the envelopes in his breast pocket. As much as he tried to refuse the extra money, Luke was thankful for the man's generosity. He knew what he would be putting this $10 towards: a new three-spring Phaeton carriage with lamp holes and one extra spring. He had already saved $50 and with this additional $10, he would be able to purchase it free and clear. Last week, he took a test ride and he nearly said yes to the salesman who offered to allow him to buy it on credit and drive the rig home. Luke, however, preferred to deal strictly in cash. A few of his patients did not adhere to the same policy, but Luke didn't mind waiting for his fee, and sometimes he received produce or handmade items in payment. Of course, this was one of the reasons he liked living in a small town on the outskirts of Philadelphia. People felt more comfortable asking to barter and he felt more comfortable getting to know these new acquaintances.

Miss Kathleen O'Donovan's lovely face again came to mind. Lovely did not adequately describe her and Luke's attraction had been immediate. She wore her hair down and her face was devoid of face paint common in upper class girls. And those green eyes...he sighed. Her animated speech carried the hint of a song, even when she was remonstrating with her younger brother. It reminded Luke of those parents who disciplined their children with a slight smirk on their faces.

Luke pulled up in front of his house and steered the horse into the stable beside it. He unhitched the mare from the carriage. The animal trotted over to the feeding and water trough.

He took out his pocket watch. Five p.m., nearly dinner. He could almost smell the meal: was it beef? His schedule was light this afternoon. Otherwise, there was little to do this beautiful day.

A large industrial carriage passed and the hustle and bustle of Germantown proper made Luke want to escape from the noise.

Beside the carriage, leaning against the side wall of the stable, was his shiny bicycle. His aunt and uncle, who had raised him, could barely afford basic necessities and yet they had bought this brand new bicycle for his graduation from medical school. He almost insisted they take it back; he wanted to tell them they shouldn't have spent the money on him. Instead, he graciously accepted it. And it was the only manner of transportation he normally used in town since it was faster to prepare than hitching the horse and carriage.

His aunt and uncle's generosity had been evident from the first week he went to live with them. Six-year-old Luke, still grieving the death of his younger sister, had remained quiet and withdrawn. A few weeks after he moved in, his uncle had bought a small telescope for Luke. The telescope, which they could ill afford, became the source of Luke's healing. Over the next few years, he had spent hours peering through it, studying the stars. Later, he borrowed astronomy books from the library until he could identify all the constellations.

He silently recited a prayer of thanksgiving. Luke couldn't imagine his life without them, their simple faith and charity. His only regret was that he lived two hours away from them. He had little choice as this small Germantown practice was the only opening when he graduated. As much as the doctors at the University of Pennsylvania had urged Luke to focus his talents on surgery, he had declined. That was where the money was, they had informed him, but Luke wasn't interested in money, nor was he interested in surgery. He felt called to be a family physician.

On the street, a mixture of noises greeted him as he walked to his front door. The clopping of a horse and carriage quickened as the rig sped past. The whistle from a nearby rubber factory squawked like a high-pitched crow letting workers know it was quitting time. Across the street, through an open door, the blacksmith hammered the hot metal, blue sparks flying.

Facing the house, he liked that it was Italianate in style, missing a tall structure in the middle, but with a spacious porch in the center that led to the house's large entrance and, to the right, his office door.

Entering the foyer, Luke saw that two envelopes had been placed on the table by the door. The tantalizing scent of pot roast hung in the air and he could hear the distant sound of Mrs. Bradley whistling an upbeat tune in the kitchen.

One of the letters was from Aunt Edna. The other was an invoice from a medical supply company. Luke strolled through the hallway and entered the sitting room to the right.

He sat down and read the letter. He was delighted to find out that Uncle Henry was feeling better and that Aunt Edna had been featured in an article in the local newspaper. He took the folded newsprint out. The headline was: "Local Woman To Organize Quilting Bee." He chuckled.

Luke moved to the chair at his roll-top desk and spent the rest of the afternoon composing a letter to his aunt and uncle.

***

Shortly after the new doctor left, Kathleen tapped her father's shoulder as he stood on the porch. He turned and smiled.

"Papa...that doctor?"

"Yes?"

"He's awfully young. He looks like he's in secondary school."

Her father scoffed. "I can assure you he is older than he looks, Kat."

"Well, he does seem like a kind and pleasant gentleman, the studious sort, with the spectacles and all. And he asked me to be his assistant."

"That was very thoughtful."

"Indeed." Kathleen recalled the whispered conversation between her mother and Dr. Peterson with her mother admitting that she had given birth to six babies. "Papa, may I ask you a question? Mama is resting and I wanted to ask an awkward question."

"Awkward?"

"I overheard Mama whispering to the doctor. She said she had given birth to six babies, not seven. I remember Will coming to our family when I was about four, right? So he would have been about two?"

He nodded and pressed his fingers to her lips. "Try not to say that loudly, Kat. Will does not know." He stared with a blank "I've been caught" expression.

"Why haven't you told him that he's adopted?"

"Well..."

"He looks so much like you and John. How is it..."

"Kat...."

Her father was pulling at his cravat and avoiding eye contact.

"Papa?"

"Hmmm?" He stopped and turned toward her.

"Does Will know any of this —"

"No." Her father sighed and spoke softly. "Your mother has some items from Will's real mother. It never seemed the right time...to tell him."

"Where was Will's father in all this? Why didn't he step forward to take care of his son? Did he die as well?"

"Well...uh...I..."

"Whatever it is, Papa, you and Mama must tell him soon.

He has a right to know."

"We shall tell him very soon." He took her hand in his. "Kat?"

"Yes?"

"Please do not mention any of this conversation to Will."

"Of course not, Papa. The information needs to come from you and Mama."

***

In bed that evening, Kathleen pondered the information about Will. And how could two non-blood siblings look so similar? Stranger things have happened in the world, she concluded. And there was *one* obvious difference between Will and John. Will most definitely had a dimple in his chin. Perhaps from his natural parents? Either way, it didn't matter. Will was a member of their family regardless of his humble start in life. Kathleen trusted that her parents would tell him in their own time.

"Will, let's play house."

"I don't like playing house. Can't we play war? Or chase? John can play too."

"Yes, let's play chase. I like to run!" Kathleen sped off and around the tree as she looked back to see Will catching up to her.

6

The following Saturday was the occasion of the parish fundraising cookout. As was his usual custom, Will woke early and prayed while it was still dark. Papa had asked him to drop off a shipment to the post office after daily Mass, which was at six a.m. He had packed the shipment in the Columbus carriage the night before, then left at 5:40 a.m. as the sun rose on this warm and sunny day.

At Mass, Fr. Morrissey read the Gospel of Matthew (4:19):

And Jesus, walking by the sea of Galilee, saw two brethren, Simon, who is called Peter, and Andrew his brother, casting a net into the sea (for they were fishers). And he said to them: Come ye after me, and I will make you to be fishers of men. And they, immediately leaving their nets, followed him.

After Mass, Fr. Morrissey reminded the few parishioners present about the fundraising cookout taking place later in the day. The priest didn't have to remind the O'Donovan clan, since Will and his siblings had been looking forward to the event for weeks.

Will remained after Mass because he desired the quiet solace of the Church as he prayed in front of the Blessed Sacrament.

In the darkness, with colored light streaming in through the stained glass windows to his right and to his left, he could only see the twinkling of the tabernacle candle, as well as a few votive candles to the right of the altar.

Bowing his head in prayer, he recalled the words that Fr. Morrissey had read from the Gospel, "Come ye after me and I will make you...fishers of men." Will continued to pray, but the words of Jesus kept returning, "Come ye after me and I will make you fishers of men." As he remained in the church, these words filled his mind. He genuflected and went to the Columbus carriage outside. Fr. Morrissey and another priest were standing in front of the church. He nodded to them and

Fr. Morrissey responded, "Will, I expect your entire family to attend the church cookout."

"We will be there, Fr. Morrissey."

"Good."

On the way home, he felt anxious but couldn't understand why. Perhaps a hearty breakfast was all he needed.

***

The day was hotter than it had been in the past week, so Kathleen planned to wear a blouse with long sleeves and a hat that extended over her pale skin. She despised that she burned so easily, but if she wore her bonnet and stayed out of the sun, she should be able to avoid a sunburn.

St. Vincent de Paul Church was in desperate need of a new roof after lightning had struck the dome earlier this year. Sackcloth and linen had so far kept the elements from disrupting church services, but the past few weeks' worth of rain necessitated changing the linen to protect the sanctuary. The men on the parish council came up with the idea to hold a cookout in late August and bring baked goods and sundry items to sell.

With Jane's assistance, Kathleen had baked an angel cake and a peach pie. Her father had contributed three books to the literature table. Parishioners brought cakes, cookies and pies.

***

Luke was enjoying the sunshine and had just finished giving Mrs. Cathcart solicited medical advice on how she could remove a plantar wart from the bottom of her foot. He noticed two carriages arrive. Mr. O'Donovan stepped out and assisted Kathleen, another blond girl, a young teenager and two small boys down. The other vehicle had two very similar looking teenagers. David gathered his family together as each one emerged from the carriage.

***

Kathleen was dressed in a light green-patterned skirt, a dark green long-sleeved bodice, white gloves and a matching green hat. She remained in front of the church with Alice as she scanned the crowd to see if her friend, Margaret, had arrived without her husband.

What Kathleen enjoyed most about these functions were the interactions with other parishioners. Normally, her family only had the opportunity to see these people at Mass. Since parishioners were encouraged to bring friends and relatives to the event, she brought her cousin, Alice, Aunt Elizabeth and Uncle Philip's only child, who was twelve. Despite the fact that she was seven years younger, Alice was nearly as tall as Kathleen, and dressed in a green-colored dress. With their fair hair and facial features, it was no wonder that people often thought they were sisters.

"Kathleen!" Margaret, her bright-eyed, effervescent friend was waving frantically to get the girls' attention. Kathleen and Alice walked over to the young woman who was dressed in a blue cotton dress and matching hat, her light brown hair pulled up fashionably in the back. "I'm so happy you came. Hello, Alice!"

"Hello, Margaret."

"Where is Stephen?" Kathleen asked.

"At home with a cold."

"I'm dreadfully sorry he's ill."

"He shall be fine, I am sure."

"You look so well...and happy. Married life suits you," Kathleen said.

"I am very happy." The young woman paused. "Kathleen, there are many bachelors attending. This is a most appropriate setting to find a prospective beau."

"Have I not told you about Karl Wagner...wait till you hear."

"Do tell."

"He has asked Papa's permission to court me within moments of meeting me!"

All three girls squealed.

"Karl Wagner is the son of the police chief and a most eligible bachelor. At first, my parents wanted me to wait a year. Can you imagine such an unreasonable request?"

"No! An entire year to court? Why, Kathleen, you're older than I am!"

With a sigh, Kathleen said, "Karl is so handsome. He's..." The girl glanced to her right and noticed Karl riding up in a carriage. "...right over there." She pointed discreetly.

Both Alice and Margaret gasped in delight. Margaret spoke first, whispering. "Good gracious! He *is* handsome!"

Karl stepped down from the carriage. He was such a snappy dresser, the suit perfectly pressed, his hair expertly combed. He scanned the grounds. Kathleen immediately looked away. She didn't want to appear too eager. Whispering to her cousin and friend, she said, "I wonder who will bid on my baked goods."

"I dare say that every eligible bachelor will be bidding on them," Margaret said.

"I do agree," Alice giggled.

Kathleen, Margaret and Alice remained near the front of the church to chat with the other young women. An impromptu square dance had begun as one of the men began playing the fiddle and a parish council member called moves. It started with only women dancing, but gentlemen had arrived to take part, including her brother, Will, who enjoyed square dancing. What surprised her was the skill of Mr. Wagner, who seemed to execute every dance step and move with ease and perfection. A few times, he caught Kathleen's eye and winked.

Every time Karl looked at her, Kathleen thought she might faint. His dark eyes were so piercing.

"Isn't that the new doctor over there?" Margaret was pointing off to a place about forty feet away, in front of a tree. Dr. Peterson was clapping with the music and smiling as he watched the dancers. The caller motioned for the doctor to join the dancers. He held his hand up to politely decline, but the older man would hear none of it and pulled Dr. Peterson into the group.

Why is he refusing to dance?

He smiled awkwardly, shook his head and Kathleen could understand his reticence once the dancing resumed. In contrast to Karl's precise and graceful dancing, the young physician appeared to have three feet. The poor man could not keep with the flow of the dancing and Kathleen felt sorry for him. He soon bowed out and another gentleman stepped in to take his place.

Karl had also left the dancers and walked toward her. Kathleen's whole body started to shake. *Calm down,* she told herself. She squared her shoulders and turned toward him as he approached her and tipped his hat.

"Miss O'Donovan, I am delighted to see you here. And who are these lovely young ladies beside you?"

"Permit me to introduce my cousin, Miss Alice Smythe."

"It is a pleasure, Miss Smythe. I can see that beauty runs in families."

Alice, who wasn't normally one to react so, nearly swooned.

Karl smelled of a hint of musk cologne. As he stood close to her, Kathleen could see that his clean-shaven face had no flaws or imperfections.

"And may I introduce my friend, Mrs. Margaret Quinn."

"An equal pleasure, Ma'am," he said, then he faced Kathleen, his dark eyes staring intensely. "Miss O'Donovan, I am greatly looking forward to dining with your family tomorrow evening."

Kathleen giggled in response.

"And...I wanted to inform you that I shall be bidding on your baked goods later today, and I shall be winning, no matter what the cost." He winked and leaned closer to her.

"Thank you very much..." was all she could mutter. Somehow, it didn't matter to Kathleen how much he bid or paid or how much money it raised for the church roof. What mattered was his intention to do so.

***

Luke spent most of the afternoon dispensing free medical advice. Instead of telling the ladies and gentlemen to come back to his office on Monday, he patiently answered each question. He was new in town and was happy that most people had welcomed him so graciously. He had been watching and enjoying the square dancing when he had been forced into the circle of dancers. Luke was no dancer, he realized that, but the worst aspect was that Kathleen O'Donovan had been watching. She was so lovely that he could barely think any rational thoughts when he was near her. After he bowed out of the dance, a tall, handsome gentleman spoke to her. The young woman was obviously enamored with that man.

David saw Luke and came over to him. Luke nodded. "Good day."

"How are you this fine day, Dr. Luke?"

"Fine, lovely day for a barbeque."

"It is."

"Who's the gentleman talking to Kathleen?"

"Karl Wagner, the son of the police chief."

"He is standing rather close to your daughter, isn't he?"

David squinted. "You're correct." He approached the pair and greeted Karl with a handshake, then pulled his daughter back away from the man. Kathleen scowled.

When he was speaking to David earlier, Luke had a fleeting thought to ask the older man for permission to court his daughter, but nervousness got the better of him and he decided to wait.

During the course of the next few hours, the three times Luke attempted to get close to Kathleen, Karl Wagner used his body to block him. Of course, the man was tall and strong and kept every male away from Kathleen, even, it seemed, her brothers. Disappointed, Luke looked forward to the auction.

Later, as the baked goods were auctioned off, he had intended to bid two dollars for the angel cake (one of his favorites)...and he knew that was an exorbitant bid, but he was willing to sacrifice the extra money he was saving towards his new carriage. However, Karl, who had spent nearly the entire afternoon talking to Kathleen, ignored the starting bid of ten cents and came back with his own bid of $10. Luke shook his head in disappointment. With handsome, rich and charming men like that, Luke wondered whether he should even bother asking David for permission to court Kathleen.

7

"I love you, my dearest, and I want you to be my wife,"
Karl whispered to her, then leaned down and gently kissed
her forehead.

"Come on, Kat, it's time to wake up for Mass!"

Kathleen wished she could remain in her delectable dream.

"Kat!" Will's voice was slightly high-pitched; he was obviously annoyed. She opened her eyes, sat up and removed her night cap. Excitement welled up within her. It was Sunday and Karl was scheduled to visit their house for supper. She jumped out of bed and began to dress. She would spend extra time this morning in an effort to look as beautiful as possible.

Soft knocking was followed by Izzy's voice. "Miss, do you need help dressing?"

"One moment, Izzy." Putting on her robe, she opened the door. Jane's daughter, Isabelle, also known as Izzy, was smiling. Her long brown hair, flawless olive skin and dark eyes made her the most beautiful girl Kathleen had ever known.

"Yes, Izzy, thank you. I especially need some help in picking out the most alluring dress I have."

"Alluring, Miss?"

"Of course. Mr. Wagner will likely be at Mass, then he will be delighting us with his presence at dinner."

"How wonderful." Izzy's dark eyes brightened. "Miss Kathleen, we will find you the most *alluring* dress you have."

Immediately, Izzy flipped through her summer dresses. She dropped several on the floor. "Sorry, Miss."

"That's fine." Izzy could be unusually clumsy. Jane teased her daughter, saying she often tripped over her own shadow.

After picking the other gowns up, Izzy lifted up a deep blue and white-patterned bodice. "Alluring?"

"It's perfect! I've only worn this dress once and received many compliments! Izzy, you're indispensable!"

"Thank you, Miss."

Later, Kathleen and Izzy entered the hallway. Will and John were standing outside their room several feet away. Upon seeing Kathleen, John remarked, "Look what the cat dragged in." He smiled at Izzy.

"Why are you dressed like..." Will stopped. "Ah, yes, Karl Wagner." He sighed. "Kat, there's something about him...."

"Stop. Why do you insist on acting in such a manner?"

Will lowered his head.

Papa entered the hallway, his eyes wide. "Kat, you look lovely." She moved closer to him and he leaned down and kissed her cheek. "What's the special occasion? You don't usually dress so...formally for Mass."

"It's Karl."

"I see." Papa's eyebrows lifted.

In the Cabriolet, Kathleen was glad for the sun and warmth. Her bonnet kept her hair in place for the short jaunt. She could hardly remain still. She giggled at a clever joke by Kevin; she tapped her foot against the floor of the buggy. She felt breathless at the thought of seeing Karl again. The vehicle hit a hole in the road and Kathleen bounced in her seat. It was a perfect day with a blue sky and a warm breeze.

As the carriage stopped, her younger brothers spilled out ahead of her leaving Kathleen inside. Jesse came down as well, but first assisted Tim from the driver's seat. Papa grinned on seeing her, waiting to be escorted out.

"Come, Kat, I'll assist you down."

"Thank you, Papa. Honestly, you'd think my brothers were ruffians, the way they treat a young lady." Just then, Kathleen could see from the corner of her eye a man approaching. She avoided looking up, instead focusing on her father's smiling face.

"I'm sorry, Kat," Will said, as he came into view. Kathleen's heart sunk. It was only Will. "I should've assisted you from the carriage."

"It's all right. Papa was here."

"Thanks, Papa," Will said.

Inside the church, Kathleen scanned the congregation for Chief Wagner and his son. Neither Karl nor his father was present. In their pew, she knelt beside her family and lowered her head. She tried to quietly recite a prayer, but all she could muster was *"Please, God, let Karl come today; even if he misses Mass, let him come to dinner today..."*

She sat back, turned her head and looked carefully about the congregation. Still no Mr. Wagner.

"Kat, stop gawking." Her father's stern voice made her skin flush warm with embarrassment and she released a heavy sigh.

Mass began as Fr. Morrissey faced the altar and made the sign of the cross. "In Nómine Patris et Fílii et Spíritus Sancti. Amen."

After Mass, it seemed like Kathleen had attracted the attention of every eligible bachelor in the parish. No less than four different gentlemen stepped forward to speak with her. Miss O'Donovan this, Miss O'Donovan that. Kathleen wished that Karl would've been flustered, but the man hadn't even taken the time to attend Mass. *Well, he must have a good reason.*

She had just excused herself from the group when she heard a man clearing his throat behind her. Could it be Karl? Why was he late? Her mouth widened in a smile in anticipation. She turned to find Dr. Peterson. Her smile faded, her face blanching with disappointment.

"Uh...Miss O'Donovan, you are... looking lovely today," he said, as he tipped his hat.

She forced a smile, then cleared her throat. "Thank you, Dr. Peterson. I didn't realize you attended this parish."

"I sometimes attend Mass at the Cathedral, but I shall be attending here because it's closer to home." He pointed down the street toward his house.

"I see."

"Good day," she heard him say as she rushed off to meet her family at the carriage.

***

Luke nodded to the O'Donovan family and quickly exited the foyer of the small church. Just what was it about Kathleen O'Donovan that transformed him from an academic scholar to a stuttering fool? All he wanted to do was to say hello.

However, he overheard Will speaking about Karl Wagner's wish to court Kathleen. He was disappointed for the usual reasons, although not surprised. As he had discovered at the church cookout, Karl Wagner possessed an overwhelming personality. The man was handsome, but exuded an air of superiority. Luke shrugged. Perhaps he was jealous and wanted to see Karl in a bad light. He brushed those thoughts aside.

***

Upon arriving at home, Kathleen emerged, this time with both Will and John assisting her, out of the carriage. She surmised that they must've been given orders from Papa. Despite the beautiful, sunny and warm day, her lips were pressed together in a scowl. With her shoulders slumped and her heart disappointed, she walked across the landing, facing the ground. Inside, Jane greeted her.

"Miss Kathleen?"

"Yes, Jane?" she asked, not bothering to look up.

"Your father received a message from Mr. Wagner. Can you please hand this to him?"

"Oh?" Kathleen straightened and looked up. Jane was holding out an envelope. Kathleen snatched it from her.

"Pardon me, Miss Kathleen, but that is addressed to your father."

"Oh, yes." Kathleen rushed onto the porch and gave it to her father. "Papa, it's a note from Karl Wagner."

"Thank you, Kat." He followed her into the foyer, opened it, read it, then handed it to her.

Dear Mr. O'Donovan,

I was not able to attend Mass earlier today because my father and I have been assisting in the extinguishing of a fire in nearby Cheltenham. I hope to accept your cordial invitation to dine at your house later this evening, but I shall be arriving later than five o'clock. Please advise your wife and family that I look forward to the evening ahead with great anticipation."

Respectfully Yours,
Karl M. Wagner

Kathleen's whole demeanor lifted. Her eyes sparkled and she giggled. She could scarcely wait until the dashing and handsome Mr. Wagner came to their house. How would she count the minutes?

***

Will could not stand to be in the same room with his sister as she danced about with excitement. He rushed into the dining room for lunch and bumped into Jane as she was coming through the doorway to beckon the rest of the family. "Mr. Will, so sorry, but you ought to slow down. I know you like my cooking, but the food will wait for you!"

"I'm sorry, Jane. I couldn't stay and watch Kat dancing around the room because of Karl. She's acting rather foolishly."

Jane shook her head. "I don't think I'd call it foolish, Mr. Will. Perhaps flighty or giddy."

Will's recent anxiousness had made him less patient than usual. For the past few days, Will reflected deeply on the Gospel reading where Jesus calls his disciples. Was it possible that God was calling him?

The family descended upon the dining room like a herd of cattle. Tim and Kev bumped into him as they pulled out their chairs to sit. Baby Mo was in Mama's arms and was whimpering. John, Pat and Papa were engrossed in a conversation about the Phillies' recent loss.

Will studied his father and two brothers as they spoke of baseball. He wished he could become more animated at the news of a sports team's loss, or wins, but sports were merely something to pass the time. For him, prayer and the sacraments gave Will greater joy.

***

When the doorbell rang, Kathleen seemed to float toward the foyer. Her father touched her shoulder. "Jane will answer the door, Kat." She stepped back and waited beside her father, tapping her foot to contain her excitement.

Karl Wagner stood tall; his smiling handsome face made

Kathleen breathless. He looked past Jane and Papa and winked at her. Her father stepped forward. "Mr. Wagner, welcome to our home. Do come in."

Karl strolled in comfortably, as if he had been visiting their home for years. He shook the older man's hand and gave his hat to Jane.

"I want to apologize again for not being able to attend Mass. The fire near Cheltenham was a tragedy. The unfortunate family lost everything."

Her mother brought her hand to her mouth. "That's dreadful."

"My father gave them a most generous donation, so let's not dwell on that tragedy. Instead, there is much to be thankful for, at least from my perspective."

"I would also be most willing to donate to the family.'

"Dinner will be served in ten minutes, Mr. David." Jane left and headed down the stairs to the kitchen.

Tim and Kev rushed into the foyer and knocked into Mr. Wagner. He gasped, then frowned, but said nothing.

Kathleen felt her face redden with embarrassment. "Papa, please talk to the boys."

"Yes, fellows, if you're going to run around, do so outside. Mr. Wagner, I apologize for my rambunctious sons."

"Apology accepted, Mr. O'Donovan. Boys will be boys."

Why couldn't her foolish little brothers behave themselves this one time? Earlier today, she had taken all of them aside and told them to act prim and proper around Mr. Wagner. She should have known they would not listen. Will and John were conspicuously quiet in the corner and Kathleen was certain she noticed a slight smirk on John's face. She sighed. She glanced at her mother, who smiled sympathetically.

Her parents escorted Mr. Wagner into the parlor. The first thing he appeared to notice was the small photograph of Kathleen from last year's high school graduation sitting on top of the piano. He picked it up, smiled then returned it to a different place on top of the piano. "Nice photograph, but it does not truly capture your beauty." Kathleen blushed.

At dinner, Mr. Wagner picked up his fork and began eating with gusto. Papa cleared his throat. Karl placed his fork down and bowed his head along with the rest of the family. During the meal, he was very animated in conversation. Kathleen was embarrassed that her father asked him so many questions, but Mr. Wagner seemed eager to talk about himself. Kathleen enjoyed listening to him. She found out that he was an only child. He said that he hoped to follow his father's footsteps and become a police officer. Kathleen sighed. She already felt safe and protected in the presence of a future policeman.

***

Later that evening, Will knelt down to pray. Was he virtuous enough to consider the holy vocation of priesthood? How could he know for sure whether God was calling him?

Almighty Father, give me a concrete, irrefutable sign.

John walked through the door just as Will was blessing himself and standing up. "I do believe you pray too much, Will. I think I shall start calling you 'Father Will.'" John laughed.

Will's mouth fell open. "Do not jest about that. The priesthood is a holy vocation."

"What are you getting all high and mighty for? It's just a joke. Besides, you do pray too much."

"I don't think a person can pray too much."

John sighed. "What is wrong with you?"

"Nothing...I'm distracted...I apologize."

"That Mr. Wagner..." John said, in a high-pitched feminine voice, "...Kat seems quite taken with him."

Will shrugged.

***

After Karl left, Kathleen asked to speak with her parents in their room. "Papa, Mama, may I court Karl? You had an entire evening to spend with him."

Her parents glanced at each other, hesitated for what seemed an extraordinarily long time. Then her father said, "Yes, you may. But you must follow the rules of never being alone with him, and consent to being properly chaperoned."

"Of course! Thank you, Papa, Mama!"

8

Mrs. Ellen Bradley was a small woman with a large personality. Like Luke, she wore tiny spectacles; she had brown hair with graying temples which she kept fashionably in a chignon. For a woman in her fifties, her body seemed a healthy weight, except for the usual postmenopausal thickness around her middle. Her face was surprisingly devoid of wrinkles. She could be talkative but, for the most part, she whistled as she cooked and cleaned. The woman had been Dr. Mayfield's housekeeper for ten years, and it was now Luke's good fortune that she had decided to stay on.

When Luke initially moved in a month ago, he sat down to his first home-cooked meal in months. He had enjoyed a healthy first plate, followed by a full second plate.

Luke thanked her for tonight's dinner. Lamb wasn't his favorite, but he was taught to eat what was placed in front of him.

"Only one serving, Dr. Peterson?"

"I've had a long day and I'm very tired."

"Hmmm," she said, her hands on her hips. "I must remember not to serve lamb again."

"Now, now, Mrs. Bradley, I'm not a fussy sort."

"Look, Dr. Peterson," the woman said, her hands folded in front of her, "feeding Dr. Mayfield was like trying to make a child eat liver. I enjoy cooking and I want you to savor it."

"Thank you very much."

The woman pointed at him. "You like beef pot roast, chicken, turkey, steak, hamburger, fish and pork. Yes?"

"Yes, I like all those."

"You don't like lamb or liver?"

"I don't like them, but I will eat them."

"Tsk. No lamb or liver then as well."

Luke had already gained a few pounds. The extra weight on his slim figure made him appear less fragile and more robust. Mrs. Bradley always seemed to be putting food in front of him whether it was mealtime or not.

Shortly after she washed the dishes, Mrs. Bradley bid Luke goodnight and left.

The house, a spacious two-story building, was in need of renovations, although the price of the home and the housekeeper were just right.

The physician's house was a mixture of old and new, with a telephone installed in the examining room/office, as well as running water and a flush toilet nearby. He sat at the long table in the spacious kitchen and looked out the window. Like the house, the side and back yard needed some tender loving care. The grass was overgrown in places, although the oaks and maples flourished.

Dr. Mayfield's hired man had been elderly and retired at the same time. Luke hadn't yet had time to interview a man to take his place. Hopefully that would happen soon.

In preparation for bed, Luke toured the first floor, turning down gas lamps and chandeliers, starting in the kitchen. From there, he opened the door to the medical storage room which led into the examining room/office. This section of the house was the only section currently equipped with electricity. His desk lined the wall at the front of the house beside the window. A stack of unfiled papers sat in a disorganized array and he made a mental note to tidy up in the morning.

Luke walked through the waiting room and locked the separate outside office door that patients, in theory, were supposed to use. Many people still used the front door, since there was an entrance to the waiting room from his foyer as well.

The foyer led to one of Luke's favorite rooms in the house, the parlor, which was to the left of the front staircase. Bay windows and an old-fashioned stone fireplace gave the room a rustic feel.

The bathroom was situated conveniently on the far side of the staircase closer to the dining room and kitchen. He turned off the gas sconces on the wall just before turning right and entering the reading room. It was smaller, with one sofa, an oversized chair, two end tables and a small bookcase. There weren't any pictures on the wall yet, just a simple crucifix and an antique image of the Sacred Heart hanging on the wall above the sofas. At a future date, he would find time to pretty up the place. He turned off a gas sconce in the hallway before returning to the parlor.

A bookcase filled with pleasure reading lined the far wall. He stood in front of it and picked up "David Copperfield." He opened it to the last place he read, a tintype serving as a bookmark. The book open on his lap, he took his glasses off and pinched the bridge of his nose, then returned the spectacles to his face. An acute case of myopia, or nearsightedness, from the age of five necessitated the glasses, although they gave his youthful face legitimacy and, for that, he was grateful.

He picked up the tintype. On the back of the photograph were the printed words, "Kaplan Photographers, 1877." His father, the son of Swedish/German immigrants, was tall and thin with a square jaw and perpetual stern expression. His mother, a Lenape-Delaware Indian, was sitting on a high back chair beside him, her long black hair in a fashionable chignon. She wore a modest long-sleeved gown and, in her expression, the hint of a smile. Sarah, his sister, who would have been three, sat on his mother's lap. Her image was blurred because she had probably moved. Luke and Zach stood in front of their father; Zach, although younger, was slightly taller than Luke. Luke's father and sister were fair-haired, like him. Zach's hair and skin tone were more like their mother's.

Luke cherished this photo because it was the only image of his original family, a family that had been relatively happy...until that summer day in 1878 when his sister had tragically died.

"Mama, wake up. Please wake up." Six-year-old Luke pulled the covers down. Mama's black hair was tangled and she smelled bad. She roused enough to shake her head and cover herself. The top of her black hair poked out. It was the only part of her he had seen for the past week.

"Mama, please."

"Go downstairs. Leave her alone!" Luke's father had not said a kind word to him in the past week. Most of the time, Luke was ignored, but he was glad. No attention was better than angry words.

Neither he nor Zach, however, had eaten much in the past few days and both had stomachs that were hurting from hunger. His relatives and neighbors had brought food earlier in the week, but it had been eaten immediately. That morning, in a desperate search for food, Luke had waited until his father had left before sneaking outside to the crab apple tree. The tiny apples would not be ripe, but they were food and he picked as many as he could. He forced a few down — they were sour — but gave most of them to his five-year-old brother, who had devoured them.

Grief had taken up residence in the Peterson house and refused to leave. Didn't his parents understand that he was sad, too?

Luke shook his head. Eventually, his aunt and uncle arrived and took Luke home with them. They had wanted to take Zach as well, but his father wouldn't permit it. Luke missed his brother and his parents. Tragically, both his mother and father died in a fire less than a year later, and Zach eventually went to live with another aunt.

Because of his own family situation, Luke now longed for a normal, happy life. What this house needed most wasn't prettying up; it was the hopeful sound of children.

When he thought of marriage and children, Kathleen O'Donovan's pretty face naturally came to mind. Disappointment welled up in him. He had recently heard that Kathleen was now courting Karl Wagner. He straightened, resolved. God would send him a wife. Until then, he must be patient.

He returned the book to the shelf and decided he would spend the rest of the evening stargazing with his telescope.

As he ascended the stairs, frantic pounding on the door made him turn around and return downstairs. Opening the door, he had no time to speak before a young girl with face paint and a red dress blurted out, "Doctor, we need you! One of our girls is bleeding. Come quickly."

"One moment." He quickly fetched his medical bag. Of course, he need not have asked from where she had come; the colored face and low cut attire meant that she was from the local brothel. With a sigh, he closed his door. The girl ran off and Luke was torn between quickly getting his bicycle or running after her. In the end, he decided to follow the girl who was now was racing across the street, lifting her dress to keep it from becoming soiled with the dirt and mud of the road.   *Almighty Father, grant me purity in my heart, eyes, mind and body no matter what I see. Grant me charity and respect for those less fortunate.*

They passed a slow moving carriage and ran two more blocks. The saloon's lights, men's loud voices and piano playing distracted him for the moment as he followed the girl. A dog frantically barking nearby urged him on.

This would not be his first errand of mercy at this particular place of "business." Tonight, Luke already suspected what was wrong as it was a common problem with prostitutes and he quietly said a prayer for the girl, who had likely become with child and had tried to terminate the pregnancy.   Rarely did these working girls carry a baby to term if they could avoid it.

While he would never participate in the killing of an unborn child, nor condone it in any way, Luke tried not to judge these girls, many of whom were younger than the O'Donovan girl, some forced into this way of life.   These young women certainly didn't receive respect from the men who used their bodies. *If every man would stop visiting houses of ill repute*, he thought, *perhaps these girls could earn a respectable living elsewhere.*

At the door of the brothel, the girl swung around and waited for Luke to reach her, then she yanked on his arm and pulled him toward a staircase just inside the door. He passed a few young prostitutes and turned his head out of respect. At the top of the staircase, the girl released his arm and raced toward the right, down a corridor, then up another set of narrow steps to a small room. A young woman lay on a simple wooden bed, blood seeping from under her bottom — the only clothing her shift, which had been pushed up to her waist.

Luke studied the girl's pale face, her eyes closed, her skin ashen. *Jesus, Mary and Joseph, help her.* Setting his bag down, he felt her forehead with the back of his hand; she was warm. Her breathing was labored and her pulse was weak.

He finally noticed the middle-aged woman dressed in a dark violet dress and made up with heavy face paint – who he remembered was the brothel's madam – and directed his questions to her. "How long has she been bleeding?"

"Since this morning. I came in and discovered that she had tried to..."

He nodded. Judging from the amount of blood on the bed and the weakness of her pulse, she was near death and he would not be able to help her.

"Why did you not come for me sooner?"

The older woman shrugged. "I thought we could stop the bleeding by giving her natural elixirs."

Luke cringed. He knew that if the girl had been brought to the hospital earlier today, physicians might have been able to save her with immediate treatment.

"I don't need to tell you not to call the police, Doctor."

Luke sighed. The local police rarely did anything about prostitutes anyway — usually treating them like they were invisible, unless there was a question of feticide — and rarely was the crime prosecuted. "Unfortunately, ma'am, there is little I can do for this girl. She barely has a pulse and continues to hemorrhage."

The woman sighed heavily, then whispered words to the girl who had led him here. Both retreated from the room, leaving Luke alone with the poor girl on the bed. He wished that he could do something for her, but all that could be done now was to make her as comfortable as possible. He tried to put some laudanum to her lips, but she was unresponsive. With a sigh, he pulled a small blanket up to her chin and sat quietly. *No one ought to die alone.* He remained by her bedside, praying, until he determined the girl had passed on. He covered her face with the blanket and recited a final prayer for her troubled soul, ending with "Requiescat in pace."

Tragic waste of a human being, especially one as beautiful as this girl.

As he was preparing to leave, a scantily clad blond girl came into the room. "Is she...gone?"

"Yes, I'm sorry, she is."

The girl, who looked like she could be Kathleen

O'Donovan's sister, bit down on her lip to keep from crying, then turned and quickly left the room.

Luke then made his way to the staircase, colliding with a broad-shouldered man coming up the steps.

"Watch where you're going," he heard. Luke glanced up and gasped. The man did not recognize him.

Luke walked home, his shoulders slumped. *Should I inform David that the man who is courting his daughter spends time in a house of ill repute?* Good men sometimes gave in to the temptations of the flesh. Luke recalled the young red-faced gentleman who had presented himself at his office last week with a venereal disease. Luke had felt sorry for the man, who was married with two small children.

Shaking his head, he sighed. No, he resolved that David must be made aware of Karl's presence at the brothel.

***

Will stirred and opened his eyes. The dark-haired woman had monopolized his dreams again. He sat up, trying to make sense of it all. Dreams weren't the only reason he was tossing and turning all night. He continued to feel restless. He knelt by his bed, recited his morning prayers then strolled over to the window. It was a cloudy, dreary day. Summer holidays would soon end. While he enjoyed the respite from academics, Will looked forward to returning to the routine of school; perhaps that would cure his anxiousness.

He put on his robe and headed downstairs to the kitchen.

"Good morning, Mr. Will." Jane kneaded dough in front of her at the large rectangular table. As usual, she didn't look up.

"How do you do that, Jane?"

"How do I do what?"

"Know who's coming down the stairs without looking up."

"The sound of your footsteps. You sound much like your father, but quicker. Your footsteps would indicate you are heavier than you are."

"Ah. What can I eat that doesn't need preparation?"

"Bananas and apples on the table under the window." She continued kneading. "If you can wait about an hour, there will be warm cinnamon bread."

Will's mouth watered. "I'll take a banana until then."

The door opened behind him and their part-time servant, Mrs. Lucy O'Grady, strolled in.

"Morning, Lucy."

"Morning, Jane. Top of the mornin' to ye, Mr. Will."

"Good morning, Lucy."

As he ate his banana, Will smiled at Lucy. The woman was not a typical servant. Like Jane, she was a widow; unlike Jane, who only had two nearly grown children, Lucy had a brood of children at home. She worked at the O'Donovan home only three days a week. Her oldest daughter, 12-year-old Colleen, looked after the younger children. Lucy was taller than Papa with hair redder than Mama's.

Sounds of a firearm being discharged came from the back yard area. "Who's shooting out there, Jane?"

"Your father is trying to get rid of a coyote that's been sneaking into the henhouse and killing chickens."

"Ah." Will pushed the last bit of the banana in his mouth before climbing the back staircase, picking his feet up to minimize the noise. On the second floor, he headed to his room, picked up his Bible, then made his way to the far end of the east wing, to a room he used when he needed privacy.

He opened his Bible to the Gospel of Mark.

"And Jesus saith to them: Come ye after me, and I will make you to be fishers of men."

He stopped reading and lifted his head. The apostles knew for certain that they were being called since Jesus physically called them. But what about him? "Do you want me, Lord? And if so, why would you want such an imperfect man?" he asked out loud.

A sign. Yes, he had asked God for a sign and had not received it, unless he considered John's calling him "Father Will" to be one.

He pursed his lips and shook his head. He was not convinced that necessarily indicated a "sign" from God. And why was he so restless of late? When he received a definitive sign, he would discuss the matter with his father. Until then, Will would continue to prayerfully reflect.

9

Kathleen's first day of college was less than ideal. In fact, it was a disaster. She was taken to school by her father as if she were a child. She wished she could have gone with Will and John by train, but she couldn't, since it wasn't "proper" for young ladies to be traveling alone in Center City.

The next incident was a rather tragic spilling of her inkwell, just moments after she had opened it in class. The black fluid had ruined the top of the desk and provoked an angry lecture from the elderly teacher, whom she learned was an experienced Civil War nurse, Elva Schmidt. Everything about the woman was harsh: her tone of voice, her constant frown, her dull clothing. Even her name had a hard ring to it the way the teacher spoke it, as she always pronounced the "t" at the end. She had warned the students that nursing was not for the faint of heart.

"The qualifications required to be a successful nurse are necessarily of a high order, and this applies not only to the trained nurse, but to all who wish to adopt nursing as a calling. In the first place, she must be not only physically, but constitutionally, strong. She must be not only well-formed, but must have certain powers of resistance. A girl, for example, who is subject to sick headaches...will never make a good nurse."

Kathleen was prone to headaches, but only around the time of her monthly. Would that make a difference?

And last but not least, Nurse Schmidt had said, "a good nurse should not be clumsy." She then stared at Kathleen, who wished she could crawl under a rock.

At the end of the day, Kathleen carted three heavy textbooks to the carriage when Papa arrived to take her home. She chattered the entire ride home about the stern looking teacher and the fact that there were only seven other women in her class, all spinsters twenty-five and older.

"Do you think you will like college?"

"If it's anything like the first day, unlikely. And, I dare say,

Nurse Schmidt and I did not start off well. We shall see."

***

Kathleen beamed as she anticipated seeing Karl again. It was a beautiful Sunday morning and she and her family were traveling in two carriages to attend Mass. She also couldn't wait to tell him about her wretched first day at college and the extensive reading she had already accomplished in only four days.

As Kathleen was getting down from the carriage, she saw Karl come forward. He had a wide grin stretched across his face. He tipped his hat. Kathleen's heart raced. His smile made her swoon.

"Good morning, Miss O'Donovan. You look lovely."

"Thank you, Mr. Wagner."

"Would it be acceptable to speak with you after Mass?"

"Yes, of course."

Karl joined his father at the entrance of the church and went inside.

"Kat, are you all right? You looked flushed." Will leaned his head towards her.

"I'm...fine, Will. Just a bit warm, that's all."

Mama was holding the baby and staring at her. Her father was just lifting Tim down from the carriage. Tim pulled on his father's coat sleeve and whined. "Gotta go pee, Papa."

Her father rolled his eyes. "I told you not to use that word, Tim. Say you need to use the toilet or go to the bathroom."

"Gotta go to bafroom."

Kathleen then offered to walk the others into church while he took Tim to the privy inside. Her mother accompanied her as the others ran ahead.

During Mass, Kathleen stifled a giggle as Karl glanced at her from the pew across from her and winked.

Her father nudged her, then motioned for her to kneel. He leaned close and whispered, "Holy Mass is no time for giggling, Kat. Pay attention." She nodded and attempted to concentrate for the remainder of Mass.

Afterwards, the group exited the church to find Karl Wagner leaning against their Cabriolet. He smiled broadly.

What an extraordinarily handsome man he is.

Karl approached the O'Donovans, directing his comments first to David. "Mr. O'Donovan, I've been waiting to speak to you. I would like to request the honor of your daughter's presence at a cookout I'm hosting next Sunday."

"Mr. Wagner, the usual protocol is to send a written invitation. I have not received one yet."

"Of course, sir, and you shall receive an invitation this week...however, I wanted to ensure that your beautiful daughter would be attending."

"It is a cookout, you say?"

"Yes, sir. And there will be many from the neighborhood and friends of mine in attendance."

"Ah. Well, I would be happy to give my permission as long as you extend an invitation to my sons, Will and John as well....unless you wish to invite me."

Karl frowned, but immediately forced a smile. "I can assure you, Mr. O'Donovan, that since we are now a courting couple, I will not allow your daughter out of my sight. She will be under my constant scrutiny."

"I appreciate that. However, either I shall be attending the cookout or my two oldest sons will be. Those are the conditions for my daughter to attend."

Kathleen was certain that her fair skin was as red as a strawberry. Her father's insistence on Will and John attending meant either he didn't trust her or he didn't trust Karl. After all, hadn't Karl explained the cookout would be an outdoor affair and that there would be many people around? She and Karl would *not* be alone. Papa was just being unreasonable.

"Very well," he said, his mouth slightly curved. "I would be happy to also extend a most hearty welcome to Will and John." Karl's pinched expression told Kathleen he was annoyed, but she understood.

It also irked her and she would inform her father in no uncertain terms that she was frustrated at his treating her like a juvenile. She was, after all, nineteen years of age, not twelve.

In the carriage, Kathleen gave her father and her entire family the silent treatment.

Pat poked her. "Still daydreaming about Mr. Handsome?"

She sighed and ignored him.

"Kathleen, we simply don't know Mr. Wagner well enough," her mother's soft voice said.

She kept silent, pursing her lips, refusing to make eye contact.

Her father then spoke. "Kat, this is what parents do. They protect their daughters."

That was it. "You don't trust me," she pouted, tears glistening her eyes.

"We trust you, Kat. We just don't know Karl enough to trust him yet. Sending Will and John to keep an eye on you..."

"Karl will protect me. He's older than Will and John. The cookout will be held outside with many people. We won't be alone."

"Kat..."

With her back still to him, she said, "If you don't trust Karl yet, then why did you say yes to him courting me?" She turned and stared at both her parents. Her mother lowered her gaze to the baby in her lap. Her father seemed to be considering this question. After a few seconds, he responded, "Because you seem to be quite enamored with him and we want you to be happy. In this, we trust *you*."

She folded her arms in front of her chest and turned to look out the window.

***

Luke had planned to mention to David that he had seen Karl at the brothel, but the only time he had an opportunity to speak with the older man was at Mass earlier. The sacred place was not the appropriate venue to be discussing sordid matters. However, as each day passed, Luke felt compelled to inform the older man about seeing Karl at the whorehouse. Miss O'Donovan deserved better than Karl Wagner.

The upcoming week would be busy with Luke attending a three-day medical seminar at the University of Pennsylvania. Saturday afternoon might be an ideal time. This weekend he would visit the O'Donovan house and speak to David.

***

Later that day, Will turned the knob to his bedroom door and it was locked. Frowning, he called to his brother. "John?

Why have you locked the door?"

He heard John clearing his throat, footsteps, then a click as it was being unlocked. The door opened wide. John's face looked flushed and he was avoiding eye contact.

"So?"

"So what?"

"Why on earth did you lock the door?"

"I was resting."

"You can do so without locking the door."

John finally made eye contact with Will. Will stared at his brother. John glared back at him. "Tim and Kev were racing up and down the hallways and kept barging in. I wanted privacy, that's all."

John's eyes had a strange glassy look, and his expression reminded him of the time he tossed a baseball in the house and broke their mother's crystal vase. *Guilt.*

Will shrugged and sat down at his desk. He opened his science textbook and began reading.

"Will?"

Will turned in the chair and faced his brother. "Yes?"

"I'd like to move to the bedroom across from the bathroom."

"Move? What do you mean?"

"We both need privacy. You like to pray late into the evening and I like to sleep. I've already talked to Papa."

"But we've *always* shared a room."

"I know, but it's not as if I'm moving to another city."

Will gave the slightest nod, though in truth, it would seem that way to him.

John left, the door easing slowly shut with a click.

Will's feelings aside, John had made an excellent point. Will was a night owl *and* an early riser. There were times that he wanted to pray but John wanted to read.

Separate rooms seemed a good decision.

***

It rained the following week. Nursing classes were tedious and difficult. If Kathleen thought Nurse Schmidt cross and harsh the first week, she had been mistaken. In retrospect, the woman had been overly kind those first days. Since then, on more than one occasion, Nurse Schmidt had asked Kathleen for answers to questions and Kathleen, giving the wrong response, was harshly reprimanded.   Evenings were spent poring through books searching for answers to any possible questions her teacher might ask.   And, while she found the information fascinating, the stress was giving her headaches.

Saturday morning could not come quickly enough for her. When it did finally arrive, it was a bright, crisp autumn day. Still, Kathleen remained annoyed that it had been necessary for John and Will to accompany her. Is that what Papa meant when he said they should never be alone?   It was preposterous.   They would be surrounded by dozens of people. Besides, how did her father think she would be able to develop any sort of relationship with the man who might be her husband one day without time away from others?

10

Kathleen's excitement was frustrated by the anger festering inside her at having to attend Karl's cookout with two younger chaperones. Kathleen tried appealing to her mother, but as always, Mama firmly supported Papa.

***

John rode in silence as Will attempted small talk with Kathleen, who sat in the middle. "The leaves on these trees are starting to turn color already, Kat."

His sister's answers were short and non-engaging, but at least she was speaking with them. Despite Kat's anger, Will wholeheartedly agreed with Papa regarding the necessity of their presence.

***

Earlier in the day, Luke had planned to send a note to David asking if he could visit. Then, four separate emergencies occurred one after the other, and Luke had no time to get away nor think of anything but setting two broken bones, treating a second degree burn and stitching up a long, deep leg laceration.

***

They rode up to the Wagner house, and Kathleen straightened her body, craning her neck to get a better look. One could see the entire homestead from the road and although the size of the property was modest compared to her father's land, the house rivaled their own. It was a narrower home, three stories high, all red brick with brown shutters and a tall chimney on the left side of the house. People were milling about and, for a brief moment, Kathleen felt nervous. She was so focused on seeing Karl that she forgot there would be many friends, classmates and unfamiliar people who had come by train for the weekend.

At the front of the house, Karl was standing with a group of four men. As soon as he noticed their carriage, he stepped away from the group and greeted them. John got out first and, although he lifted his hand up to assist his sister out of the carriage, Karl rushed forward and took her hand and assisted her down. He smiled and her pulse quickened. He was wearing a dark blue waist coat, white shirt and black cravat with breeches in a shade of lighter blue. He held his arm out for her and she took hold of it.

"I would like to introduce you to some of my friends," Karl said. She nodded.

In the next hour or so, Will and John stuck with her like shadows. Everywhere she went, they accompanied her. She was Mary; Will and John were her little lambs. She supposed they were only following her father's orders, but this was, after all, an outdoor affair. What did they expect Karl would do outside with at least fifty people milling about? And did *they* not trust Karl? Karl was as bothered as she was with their presence. He didn't say anything, but he frowned a few times when he noted their proximity. She sighed as he glanced at her brothers, now standing under a tree close by and enjoying cobs of corn.

"I am angry that my father made Will and John come."

"Well, my dear, I would be glad to distract them so we could have time alone."

"Really? How?"

"Trust me."

Kathleen liked how he took control of a situation. That made him seem especially masculine and assertive. He seemed to be everything she wanted and needed in a future husband: handsome, confident, authoritative.

Karl strode over to a few young ladies and whispered something to them. They giggled and nodded.

Returning to Kathleen, he said, "I told them to wait five minutes, then saunter over to the boys, walk them to the other side of the tree and flirt with them."

Kathleen laughed, although she wondered how Will and John would react to the attention of these beautiful young women.

They engaged in small talk, but as the minutes ticked by, Kathleen wondered whether she should not have complained about her brothers. When she saw the two young women approach Will and John under the tree, she laughed out loud at the expressions on their faces. Both boys looked flustered and she could see Will pulling at his collar. One honey-haired girl, a giggly sort, led John around to the other side of the tree. The dark-haired girl motioned for Will to come away from the tree, but Will did put up some resistance when he shook his head so she stayed.

Karl held out his arm and Kathleen took hold of it. He felt strong and muscular under his jacket. He smelled clean and she blinked her eyes because she seemed a bit dizzy.

"Are you ill, Miss O'Donovan?"

"Not at all, Mr. Wagner."

They walked around to the back of the house. A male servant brought a tray with glasses of beer. Karl took one and offered a glass to Kathleen.

"Thank you, but no."

He drained the glass then quickly emptied another. The male servant waited patiently while Karl took a third glass. "That's all." He waved away the servant. To Kathleen, he said, "I was thirsty. Are you sure you don't want a drink?"

"No, thank you."

Karl looked down at Kathleen and smiled. It wasn't the usual happy expression that made her pulse race; it was a different sort of smile that made her slightly uncomfortable.

"This home has been in my father's family for three generations, or so I'm told," he said. They strolled along the side of the home, which was edged with peonies, roses and various fragrant flowers.

"So, Miss O'Donovan, we haven't really discussed it but don't you think we ought to be calling each other by our Christian names?"

Kathleen stopped walking. "Really?"

"Yes. I will call you Kathleen and you may call me Karl."

She couldn't imagine why there would be any harm in that. "Yes, that would be fine."

They stepped onto the back porch and entered the house through the basement kitchen. Two female servants were preparing food at the large wooden table in the center. Their eyes widened at the surprise visitors. "Mr. Karl, so sorry about the mess..." the teenaged servant said.

He ignored her and directed his comment to Kathleen. "Would you be interested in a tour of my home?"

"That would be delightful."

They took the stairs in the middle of the kitchen up to the main floor. He took her from room to room, showing her the beautiful parlor at the front of the house, then the dining room. It was not as large as the O'Donovan dining hall, but it was a fair size with high ceilings, a ceramic gasolier and pink, green and blue flowered wallpaper design.

On the flat surface of the mantel was a shiny silver box. Kathleen tiptoed to see the top of the container which had an etching of Atlantic City, her favorite place in the whole world. "How lovely."

"It was my mother's. My father bought it for her in Atlantic City just before she died."

"Atlantic City is my favorite city! Papa takes our family to the shore every summer for a week. We stay at the Seaside House Hotel!"

Karl picked it up off the mantel and handed it to her. "It is yours."

Kathleen stepped back and held her hand up. "I cannot accept this...it's your mother's precious box."

"I insist." He turned her hand over, placing it in her palm.

"What about your father? He would want to keep this, wouldn't he?"

"I don't think so. He has many items to remember her."

"I don't know what to say....thank you from the bottom of my heart."

"My pleasure."

They stood in front of a large portrait. "My grandmother, my father's mother."

Kathleen stared at the portrait of the pretty elderly woman. "Are there any portraits of your mother?"

"Unfortunately not. She passed away when I was six."

Kathleen didn't respond, but she felt overwhelming sadness for him. She couldn't imagine growing up without the nurturing influence of her mother. She felt melancholy for Mama (whose mother had died when she was a baby) and her real father, Liam, who never had an opportunity to know Kathleen.

"Come this way," he said, as he escorted her out of the room and across the hall.

He approached a doorway and held the door open for her as she entered.

The room had light pine wainscoting and cherry wood baseboards, a desk near the tall window and a long red couch lined the west wall of the room.

Near the couch, he pointed to a large photograph of a young boy dressed in a military type suit. The child was perhaps four or five. In one hand, he held a crossbow and under the other arm was an arrow. As Kathleen studied the photograph, it dawned on her that the little boy might be Karl. "Is this you?"

"The one and only," he smiled.

Karl was *so* handsome.

Jane's voice echoed in her mind, "Handsome men could be more trouble than they're worth, Miss Kathleen." Then she considered that her father and brothers were handsome — and devout — men.

"Yes, my father believed in educating me early in the fine art of the crossbow. I learned how to fire my first gun at three."

"Three?"

Karl stared at the photo. He didn't smile, nor frown. A few awkward moments passed so Kathleen decided to share her experience with college.

"Karl?"

"Yes?"

"I haven't yet had an opportunity to tell you about my first two weeks at nursing college."

"You're attending college?"

"Yes, at the Ingersoll Training School for Nurses."

Karl's mouth pursed. "Why are you doing that?"

"I find the medical books quite fascinating and — "

Cutting her off, he asked, "Shall we return outside?"

"Yes, very well." Kathleen blushed. Admittedly, she was disappointed that she didn't tell him more about the difficulties of college. Perhaps another time.

***

"You are only seventeen? You seem so much older," the young brunette said to Will. She was blushing, very lovely, with deep, intense brown eyes.

All of a sudden, he realized that he hadn't seen his sister in several minutes. Will then turned toward his brother.

"John, have you seen Kat?"

He shook his head.

Will's heart started to thunder in his chest. His father had given Will and John the job of keeping a close eye on their sister and he could not see her anywhere. But...they were also in a yard full of people. Karl and Kathleen couldn't be too far.

"As I was saying..." the young brunette said to Will.

"Pardon me, Miss, but my brother and I need to...check on our sister." The girl frowned and nodded to her friend; the two walked off.

Will turned to John. "Perhaps I'm overreacting, but we need to find Kat immediately."

"What could he possibly do with a hundred people milling about?"

"I don't know."

As they were winding around to the back of the house, Will saw Kat with Karl, the two standing under a tree beside the barn. Will sighed with relief.

***

Kathleen pressed her lips together in frustration when she saw her brothers rushing toward her. She and Karl had been involved in pleasant conversation about Karl's hobbies when her brothers rudely interrupted them.

Will spoke first. He blinked a few times, then sighed and whispered. "Kat, are you all right?"

"Why shouldn't I be?" She paused. "Really, Will, what is wrong with you?" Kathleen couldn't keep from scowling.

"Nothing, I...nothing."

"I shall return momentarily." Karl disappeared inside the house.

Kathleen scowled again. "William O'Donovan, are you trying to ruin my day?"

"No, I'm not. I'm just trying to..."

"Trying to what?"

"Well, look out for you, protect you."

"And what sort of protection do I need in the midst of all these people? Besides, Karl and I already went inside the house...in fact, we've been inside for the past twenty minutes."

"Are you daft? Why would you go inside his house alone?"

"Will, I told you, there are people all over the place." She paused. "Weren't you otherwise occupied with two young ladies?"

"I was not otherwise occupied. The girl and I were having a pleasant conversation."

The rest of the afternoon passed at a snail's pace with Will and John staying close by. Karl didn't say anything, but his forced smiles told Kathleen that he was getting annoyed and he sighed each time he saw them.

"My brothers are such pests."

"They are just following your father's orders and they are trying to protect you."

"Protect me? From whom?"

"Your family doesn't know me and, if I had a daughter like you, I would also want to protect her."

"I suppose you are correct. Would you ever think of coming to call on me at my home?"

"Yes, I certainly enjoyed my last visit at your home."

"And I would very much enjoy your calling on me anytime."

"Then it is settled. Shall I send your father a note?"

"Yes, please do."

"What about next weekend?"

Kathleen pursed her lips as she thought about upcoming plans. "This weekend, my father is out of town from Thursday to late Saturday evening. I shall be home on Saturday afternoon as most of my family will be visiting my Aunt Elizabeth for the day so perhaps you may visit next Sunday?"

Karl's eyebrows lifted and he smiled. "Yes, I will certainly ask your father for permission to call on you next Sunday."

After the luncheon, Kathleen bid goodbye to Karl and she, Will and John got into their carriage and began the short trek home.

"I shall count the minutes until I see you again, my dear."

He kissed her hand.

"Will you be attending Mass tomorrow?"

"No, I shall be out of town."

Karl was winking at her as they rode away. She felt as if her whole body was blushing. She lifted her hand to wave and wished that she didn't have to wait seven more days to see Karl. The silver Atlantic City box sat in her lap and she caressed the etching on top. She knew exactly what she would keep in this box.

***

Kathleen was convinced more than ever that her teacher, Nurse Schmidt, despised her. It didn't matter what she did. Kathleen was always wrong. Even when she wasn't wrong. The woman was making Kathleen's college experience most unpleasant.

Making matters more unpleasant, each day she arrived home, hoping that a formal request had been delivered to her father from Karl, but it hadn't. Why had he not sent her father a letter?

Before her father left on his business trip this Thursday past, she asked, "Papa, have you received a message from Karl? He asked if he could call on me this Sunday, here at home."

"I don't think so, Kat."

"Would that be fine with you?"

"If he sends a proper request, I will say yes. I'll insist that he remain here for dinner as well."

"Wonderful, Papa! Thank you!" She hugged her father and kissed his cheek.

Studying her face, he said. "You like this man very much?"

"Yes, Papa, I do. Perhaps he will be my husband."

"Don't put the cart before the horse, Kat. You must get to know him better before you make that kind of decision."

"Oh, but I *do* know him. I spent an entire afternoon with him." She paused. "And he gave me a beautiful box from Atlantic City," into which Kathleen had already placed her favorite tiny seashells.

Her father raised his eyebrows. "It takes more than an afternoon to get to know someone...but yes, if he contacts me, he shall be permitted to call on you this Sunday."

***

Luke enjoyed a leisurely stroll on this sunny, breezy day to the Germantown post office to inquire if his latest delivery from the medical supply company had arrived. He was told by the company that he would save 50 cents if he picked it up from post office instead of having it delivered to his office. It was a small order of glass vials, so it would be easy to carry. Luke tipped his hat and nodded a greeting as he walked by a mother pushing a baby carriage.

After picking up his package, he stepped onto the porch in front of the post office. David pulled up in his small Columbus carriage and tied the reins to the post.

"Good day, David."

"Good day, Dr. Luke."

"A pleasant day, don't you agree?"

David looked up and around. "Extremely pleasant."

"Might I inquire how your daughter, Kathleen, is doing?"

"She is quite well." David's eyebrows narrowed, then he smiled broadly. "As are the rest of my children. Perhaps you have heard by now that Karl Wagner is courting my daughter."

"Yes, sir." Luke tried to smile although he was sure it came off as a grimace. Although it was outdoors and others could hear, Luke felt an urging inside to share the information about Karl's visit to the brothel.

"David?"

"Yes?

"Well...I..."

David tilted his head. "Yes?"

As Luke was trying to form the correct words to bring up the most awkward topic, behind them, the postmaster called, "Mr. O'Donovan, I just received a parcel for you and I need a signature."

"Pardon me, Luke. I'll need to get that...I'm actually late for an appointment and must leave immediately. Good day, Luke."

"Uh...David?"

The man turned. "Yes?"

"Might it be permissible to visit you Saturday afternoon and speak to you about an important matter?"

David shook his head. "I shall be away until Saturday evening. Perhaps Sunday after Mass?"

"I...well, yes, of course."

"Must go. Good day, Luke."

"Good day, David."

With a sigh of relief, Luke left. He bought today's edition of the Philadelphia Bulletin from a newsboy on the corner. Knowing that many of these street urchins often had no other income, Luke gave the boy five cents — instead of two — and returned home.

11

Although it had rained for the past two days, Saturday was a warm and beautiful autumn day. Kathleen looked up from her novel and lifted her face to the sun. This was her favorite place to be on a warm, bright day: in a comfortable outdoor chair, enjoying a good story. This book, *Eight Cousins,* was a particularly fascinating tale. She empathized with Rose, the main female character and liked Uncle Alec, Rose's guardian. She especially agreed with Uncle Alec's idea of less restrictive clothing for Rose because he did not favor corsets or high heels, two items Kathleen could also do without.

Of late, Kathleen had come to appreciate Saturdays more than ever. The difficulty of the study load at college and the harshness of Nurse Schmidt frustrated her on a daily basis. She didn't know how much more she could endure of that wretched teacher's treatment.

In any case, her father wasn't expected to return from his business trip until this evening. Her mother, Jane, Izzy and some of her younger siblings had gone next door to Aunt Elizabeth's house. Lucy did not work on weekends, so the house was quieter than usual.

Knowing Alice wouldn't be home to miss Kathleen's lack of attendance — her cousin and uncle were away for two days in New York City visiting the Statue of Liberty — Kathleen had looked forward all week to spending the day alone since she almost never had the opportunity to be home without little children under foot. Unfortunately, Will and John had also decided to remain home. Still angry with Will for being overprotective, she continued to give him the cold shoulder.

And where was that written request from Karl? If it didn't come today, would her father permit Karl to call if it came the same day?

She basked in the heavenly warmth on her face. As was her custom on Saturdays, she wore her hair down and unpinned since she wasn't expecting any visitors.

Lazy days also meant the comfort of no corset.

The oak tree's leaves swayed and the water in the pond rippled with the wind. Suddenly, she startled at the sound of gunshots echoing from behind the house. Will and John were shooting at targets in the back field, preparing for their hunting trip with Papa next weekend.

In the distance, a carriage clopped up the laneway, but it was too soon for her mother and the others to return home. She held her hands over her eyes to shield the sun and get a better look. When the carriage came into view, she practically jumped up and squealed. It was Karl! She dropped her book on the chair and ran out to greet him.

"Karl, I'm so happy to see you!"

He was smiling as he pulled the carriage to a stop and got out. "I'm dreadfully sorry that I have not sent my request to your father before now. I've been busy and haven't been able to mail it. I have missed you terribly, so I figured that I should just deliver the note myself. Is your father at home?"

"No, he isn't. Remember, I told you he's away until late tonight."

"Oh, yes...of course. I...forgot..."

"But I've asked Papa and he has already said it is fine for you to call on me tomorrow."

He leaned close to her and Kathleen felt lightheaded. "Where is the...rest of your family?"

"Most of them are at Aunt Elizabeth's house."

Shots rang out from behind the house and Karl jerked.

"Except for Will and John; they're in the back field. Our male servant, Jesse, is working in the barn on the other side of the field."

"Ah, of course." Karl blinked like there was something in his eye. Then he smiled at her and she felt a hot blush creeping up her neck to her face. What was it about him that made her blush when he merely looked — or smiled — at her?

"Well, I should be...going. Please give this note to your father when he arrives home." Karl turned to get back into his carriage.

"Must you leave so soon?"

He turned to face her, his eyes bright, his mouth curved in a smile. "I suppose not."

"Perhaps we could take a short walk. It's a beautiful day."

"I would like that, Kathleen. But before we do, might I trouble you for a glass of water?"

"Of course. This way." Kathleen led Karl into the front entranceway, placed his letter on the table by the door, then walked across the foyer and down the stairs to the kitchen.

At the sink, Karl downed one glassful of water, and all Kathleen could think was that he must be frightfully thirsty to drink so quickly. She remembered when she was a child, they had an old-fashioned pump. Now a few years before a new century, they had running water in the kitchen and bathrooms.

He handed her the glass. "Where...did you say the servants were?"

"Jane and Izzy went with Mama and the young children. Lucy doesn't normally work on Saturday. And I told you that Jesse is in the barn on the far side of the shooting range."

"And your brothers?"

"In the back field." As she turned to lead him toward the staircase, she felt him take hold of her hand and pull her into the pantry. "Karl...uh...what are you doing?"

"Exploring. Didn't you ever explore new rooms when you were a child?"

Kathleen stepped back. "Uh, sometimes...I...suppose. But this is merely the pantry. Quite a boring room."

He shook his head and ignored her.

"Karl, we should be... returning... upstairs."

"Yes, of course." Daylight streamed in and lit up the room like an electric light. At first, Karl faced the shelves filled with canned vegetables, fruit, jellies, pickled beets and cucumbers. He then closed the door; it creaked as it left the two of them alone and in the dark.

Kathleen felt a chill and began to shake. "Karl, it's dark. You need to open the door," she said, her voice skirting on the edge of panic. "Please."

"Oh, I do apologize, my dear." He opened it a crack so there was a thin bit of light shining through. Just when she began to calm down, his face came down on top of hers before she realized what he was doing. He kissed her, an open-mouthed kiss. She couldn't breathe and pulled back. "Karl...I don't think we should..."

"You don't think we should what?"

"Be in here, kissing, like that..."

"Like this?" He kissed her again with his open mouth. Pushing him away, she backed up and wiped her face.

"Please...stop! It's too dark. I need light."

"You don't need light when you have me." Karl leaned down close and whispered, "You and I were meant for one another."

"Wh...what do you mean?"

He cleared his throat. "I will be asking for your father's permission to marry you."

"M...m...marry me?" The way he kissed her...the way he...looked at her. All of a sudden, Kathleen felt nauseated.

"You do *want* to marry me, don't you, Kathleen?" His voice slithered with forced sweetness.

She tried to smile, but everything felt wrong. "We should go upstairs now, Karl."

He grabbed the side of her hair and kissed her, hard, opening her mouth and cutting her lip in the process. Kathleen backed away until her head knocked against the broom on the wall of the pantry. Her whole body shook. Her heart was thundering in her chest...surely Karl could feel it. He must know that this was upsetting her, but taking her shaking hand, he whispered, "I cannot wait any longer. You...are so, so lovely..."

"Cannot...wait...for...what?" she stuttered, as her heart continued to pound.

Karl closed the door with his foot and pinned her against the wall, squeezing her wrists and holding them over her head. "You're hurting me. Please...stop!" He kissed her again hard on the mouth. She yanked her head from side to side but he was too strong. Then a realization. *No, not that.* "Karl, please, stop...." She began to hyperventilate.

"Stop! Remain still. You know you want this as much as I do. This is what a good wife does." His voice sounded strangely high-pitched, unlike his usual deep voice.

Jesus, Mary and Joseph, please help me. "I...am not

your...wife..." Her voice made it sound like she was shivering, but Kathleen was not cold; instead, she was in the middle of a horrible, frightening nightmare and could not wake up.

"Ah...but you will be my wife...very soon."

No, I won't. I will never be your wife...not now...not ever.

For the moment, in the darkness of that small room, she willed herself to calm down, to do as she was told, and to try to figure out what she could do to get away from him. Perhaps she should try to reason with him. "Karl...p...please. Do you... not care for me?"

"This is how I show it."

He squeezed her wrists roughly and she began to whimper. If she yelled, would her brothers or Jesse hear her? No, she decided...they were too far away.

Her arms were throbbing where he gripped her wrists and held them over her head against the wall, the straw broom pricking her neck and back. She started to cry out and Karl kept her quiet by smothering her with a pressing open-mouthed kiss. She couldn't breathe.

All of a sudden, she heard the back door open then slam shut and her brothers' voices in the kitchen. Karl whispered, his spit spraying her nose. "Quiet...if they hear you, if they try to come in here, I will hurt them." He took her hand and moved it to the gun on his belt.

Kathleen bit down on her lip to remain quiet. She wanted so desperately to call out to her brothers but she didn't want Karl to hurt them. *Dear God, help me to escape this nightmare.*

***

Will turned the faucet on and poured each of them a glass of water.

John drank his glass. "I'm going to return to the field."

Will nodded, then decided that he would get two more boxes of shells that were stored on the top shelf of the cabinet beside the pantry door.

He thought it a peculiar place to store shotgun shells and bullets but understood his father kept the guns in his study and felt it prudent to keep most of the bullets and shells in a separate and hard-to-reach spot to protect the younger boys.

He reached up and took out two boxes then made his way back out the door and to the firing range. *I wonder where Kat is. She must have remained out front or gone to her room.* All of a sudden, he felt a chill, but shook it away.

Either way, she was still not talking to him. It wouldn't be the first time, but even for Kat, this was a long stretch of the silent treatment.

***

Karl pressed his hand tight against her mouth. Kathleen could not breathe. Will's footsteps became distant as he walked out, the door slamming behind him. He was gone and so too any hope of her escaping. Karl removed his hand from her mouth and Kathleen sputtered as she took a deep breath.

"You did quite well, my dear. I can see that a marriage to you would be most congenial. And you might even enjoy yourself."

Suddenly, she felt a tingling at her mouth, then before she could do anything, she vomited her lunch on Karl's jacket.

"Damn," he hissed angrily. "If you think this is the end..." He leaned in close. "This is not the end. No one knows we're in here and I may as well enjoy you while I have you. Do you know how hard it was for me to control my desire to take you? I wanted to take you the first moment I saw you."

Kathleen squeezed her eyes shut. She could not look at him.

When he released her right hand to take his jacket off, she carefully felt around in the dark on the shelf beside her. She grabbed onto a small glass jar. It sounded like he was lowering his trousers. *Dear God, please no.* Lifting the jar up, she slammed it into his head. It didn't break, but he grunted and the jar fell to the floor in a crash. Fluid and bits of glass and vegetable splattered both of them. "You little..."

Kathleen crawled around him and tried to reach for the door. He grabbed her arm and yanked her back. She cried out in pain. Her right shoulder was on fire, a piercing pain that made it difficult to breathe. He threw her down onto the floor, slapped her face and covered her with his body.

Bits of glass cut into her legs. His hands on her chest pressed her body so tightly to the bare floor that she couldn't breathe and she nearly lost consciousness. He lifted himself up on his elbows. When he came back down, Kathleen did what she always did when her brothers were hurting her. She bit through his shirt and into his shoulder as hard and as deeply as she could. He screamed long and loud, then rolled off of her. Standing up, he spit at her. "You little wretch!" He backhanded her across the face. "You should not have done that. See what you made me do?" Her mouth bleeding, Kathleen began to cry loudly.

He grabbed his coat and opened the door. "You have just made the biggest mistake of your life! I will return to finish what I started. If you tell anyone, I will kill you...that is a promise." She could hear him racing across the kitchen and banging the back door. Kathleen remained on the floor, weeping.

***

On his way to the back field to join John, Will felt a chill again. It was a warm afternoon, so why did he feel that way? He stopped. Now he felt the words, *Kat is in danger*. He scowled. Why in the world would Kat be in danger? The last time he saw her she was on the porch. Could she have fallen? Will shook his head and continued walking.

Will was on the far side of the clothesline when he heard a distant low-pitched scream. He yelled to his brother, who was about to fire his Marlin at the markers in the distance. "John!" The boy turned. "What?"

"Did you hear that?"

"Hear what?"

"A scream."

"No. Probably one of the chickens." John joined him.

"I know the difference between a chicken and a person, John. Is Jesse in the house?"

"No, he's in the storage barn over there," John pointed to the far side of the shooting range. "I just saw him bringing bales of hay inside."

All of a sudden, Will felt sick to his stomach. "Come on, let's return to the house."

***

Kathleen remained on the floor, biting her already swollen

lip to keep from crying while the cold from the tile seeped through her back. As she slowly sat up, she began to shake violently. Pulling her torn blouse together, her eyes scanned the mess of the room. The door was open and she could see the chaos of the pantry, cans dotting the floor. One broken jar of pickled beets lay smashed near the door, its deep red splattered about. The rancid metal taste of *his* blood burned her mouth and she vomited what was left in her stomach.

Her shoulder was on fire with pain. She attempted to stand, but felt dizzy and dropped back down to a sitting position. Her body was trembling so violently that her teeth were chattering. Using her left arm, she felt her right shoulder and there was a rounded protrusion on her upper arm. *Likely a dislocated shoulder.* The pain lessened when she held her right arm close to her chest.

Kathleen startled at Will and John's voices just outside the back kitchen door. Despite her injury, she crawled along the floor and pushed it shut with her shaking hand. The darkness surrounded her and she was finding it hard to catch her breath.

No one could find her like this. No one could know what had happened. What could she tell her family? Karl threatened to kill her if she told anyone. But she was injured and needed medical assistance. Seeing the mess in the pantry, she devised a story. She would tell them that she had been trying to get a can from the top shelf and she fell. Yes, that would work fine. She willed herself to stop shaking, inhaling and exhaling to slow her breathing and calm her shaking hands.

***

Will held the back door open and motioned for his brother to enter ahead of him. As he stepped into the kitchen, he felt a chill despite the warmth in the room. It was the third time in ten minutes he had felt this "chill."

"Will?"

"Yes?"

John had walked ahead of him and pointed at the floor near the pantry. As Will moved closer, he leaned down and discovered what looked like a smeared boot print and splattered blood. He made the sign of the cross. "Dear God in heaven. What is this?" Immediately he thought of his sister. "Where's Kat?"

"I don't know. I saw her out front earlier."

Will stepped in front of John and stared at the closed pantry door. The floor splatter appeared to come from the pantry. "Kat? Are you in here?" He tapped it until it swung open, daylight illuminating the room.

His sister sat on the floor. *Red fluid...dear God was that blood?* He gasped. "Kat, you're hurt!" Cans were strewn all over the place, brooms appeared as if they had been thrown to the opposite side of the room, Kat's blouse was torn and her eyes were watering, her head lowered, her lip and chin bloodied. She held her right arm close to her chest. Vomit was on the front of her blouse.

"What happened?" Will crouched down beside her. Behind him, John cried out, "Kat! Are you all right? All this blood!"

His sister's body was shaking as she blinked back tears. When she lifted her head, Will saw that her lip was swollen and there were bruises on her face.

"Oh, I'm...all right. I just...fell. I think...my shoulder might be...dislocated." She said something else, but her voice was shaking so much he could not understand her.

"What?"

"It isn't... blood; it's beet juice. I...broke a jar."

With a sigh of relief, Will said, "Thank God." He heard his brother releasing his own sigh. "I thought I heard someone yelling," Will said.

"I am hurt, though. Look," Kathleen, her voice still trembling, parted the torn blouse to show the bony protrusion on her shoulder. "I believe I have a dislocated shoulder."

Will scowled. "You're going to need a doctor, Kat."

"I know," she drew in a breath as she tried to stand up. "Can...you...help me?"

"Did you try to get up before? There's a red boot print outside the door."

"Oh...uh...I...please help me up." With Will on her right side and John on her left, they lifted her up to a standing position. She screamed as they brought her out of the pantry.

"It hurts terribly. I can't walk like this." Will stared closely at his sister's face. Her lip was swollen and bleeding, and there was a small cut on her jaw, a bruise beginning to form.

"Kat, was someone here?"

She paled. "It hurts, Will. Please help me upstairs."

Will faced his brother. "I shall assist her up to her bedroom. I think it might be less harrowing experience than both of us helping her."

"Yes, of course." John released her.

"John, go next door and fetch Mama and Jane, but ask Aunt Elizabeth and Izzy to watch the other children. Tell them there's been an accident and Kat is hurt. Bring Mama and Jane back, then ride out to the doctor's place as soon as you can." John raced outside. The back door banged shut.

Will accompanied his sister up the stairs, staying to her left side, careful not to touch her injured shoulder. With every step, she cringed or moaned. In her room, Will lowered his sister to her bed. "Kat, what can I do to help you?"

She shook her head. "Nothing."

"Then perhaps I should go and see if John needs help hitching the horse to the Columbus." He turned to leave.

From behind him, he heard, "It hurts, Will. Please don't leave me!" She pursed her lips and there were tears in her eyes.

He returned to her, pulling a seat beside her bed. "Very well. I shall stay with you."

Kat rarely became sick and she injured herself even less frequently, so Will wasn't accustomed to seeing her in such a condition.

"You must think I'm a baby," she muttered.

"Nah. I'm sure that shoulder hurts like the dickens."

"It does." She swallowed, then muttered, "Thank you, Will. Thank you."

Will was grateful that Kat was talking to him again, but at what cost?

***

Kathleen's whole body continued to tremble. Will remained by her bedside and she was thankful for her kind and caring brother. She did not want to be alone. Would that horrible man return and try to hurt her and her family?

All she could smell was *him*. Nauseated, she gagged. Will reached for the basin and held it under her chin. Each time she retched, she felt intense pain in her shoulder. Even worse than any physical pain was that every inch of her body felt soiled and she wished she could scrub her skin to remove that dreadful man's scent from her.

Will placed the basin on her nightstand, then tried to rub her back. She flinched. "Sorry," he said. "I didn't mean to hurt you."

"S...sorry for not speaking with you... this week."

"Don't worry about that now, Kat."

Of course, the doctor would be here soon enough. She dreaded that an outsider would have to see her like this, but if her shoulder was dislocated, it needed to be set. Would she have to go to the hospital? *Please God, not that.*

12

Luke finished the last stitch on the deep, long scrape that Billy Harkins had managed to carve on his arm. His mother had brought him in last week after the ten year old had fallen from a tree and split his head open.

"There you go, Billy." Luke reached into the glass decanter on his desk and pulled out a piece of stick candy. "For being still while I stitched your arm."

"Thanks, Dr. Luke." Billy excitedly took the candy.

Smiling, Luke watched the boy and his mother walk away.

Luke returned to the examining room and ran water over his hands. He dried them on a towel nearby, then sat at his desk by the window that faced the front yard. He scratched out a few notes on the Harkins boy's chart, then placed it with the other charts to be filed.

As he became well-known, Luke hoped more patients would trust him. However, some in the community preferred to travel into Center City, Philadelphia to be examined by an "older, more experienced physician." Luke expected that. At twenty-six, it didn't help that his fair skin, dark blond hair and scant facial hair made him appear more like a teenager.

His sparse facial hair was no doubt a combination gift from his maternal Native American grandparents and his paternal blond Swedish grandparents. Whatever it was, he'd be happy someday not to worry about taking the razor often to his face.

The clopping of a carriage in front of his house made him look up. He pushed the drapes aside and looked out. A young man of around fifteen or sixteen was in the driver's seat. He hopped down and ran toward the office door. Luke met him on the porch.

"Dr. Peterson?"

"Yes?"

"I'm John O'Donovan."

"Oh, yes, of course." This young man was the spitting image of his father.

"My sister is hurt."

"Hurt?"

"Yes, Kat fell and she said she thinks she has a dislocated shoulder."

Luke cringed. Shoulder dislocations could be quite painful. Depending on the type of dislocation, it could be a simple injury to repair. The poor girl must be in tremendous pain. "Just let me get my bag and I'll be along immediately." Luke picked up his physician's bag, then he considered what he might need. At his supply cabinet in his office, he unlocked it and took out one additional bottle of laudanum.

He told Mrs. Bradley he'd be doing a house call and wasn't sure what time he would be home. "If anyone needs a physician, I'll be at the O'Donovan house."

He quickly got into his buggy and rode to the O'Donovan's.

When Luke arrived, he got out of his carriage and handed the reins to Jesse. Luke approached John, who was standing on the porch in front of the house waiting for him.

"She's upstairs. Come this way."

"How did she get hurt?"

"She fell. We found her on the floor of the pantry. Her shirt was torn and her face is bruised."

Luke took a deep breath and headed toward the house. He was met by John's lookalike brother in the foyer.

"Are you the doctor? Kat's upstairs in her room. Mama asked if you might have something to help with the pain."

"And what is your name?"

"Will."

"Will, I have some medicine for pain, but I must first assess her injuries and determine if she has any broken bones."

Luke silently recited a prayer. *Almighty Father, guide my hands to heal her.* He followed the two brothers up the stairs as they took two steps at a time and, upon reaching the second floor, he heard a female weeping. Will and John turned right toward the tormented sound, then they stepped aside to allow him to enter the bedroom. For a moment, Luke stood quietly out of view and carefully leaned his head around the doorway. Kathleen was sitting on the bed leaning against her mother, a blanket draped over the young woman's shoulders. Kathleen appeared to be holding her right wrist with her left hand against her chest. Her face had a stream of tears down her cheeks. Her lip looked to be bruised and swollen; there was a cut on her chin.

Caroline whispered to her daughter. Jane stood on the other side of the injured girl and rubbed her back. Luke cleared his throat, then knocked quietly on the door's molding. The servant looked up and immediately motioned for him to enter the room. "Come this way, Doctor."

Kathleen's mother stood up. Leaning down, she spoke softly, "Dr. Peterson is here to help you."

Even though the woman had gotten up, Kathleen continued to lean toward her right, her shoulder drooping downward, her left hand grasping the right wrist against her chest. Her eyes were glossy with tears. "It...hurts..." Her raspy voice quivered with pain.

Luke shuddered. "I know, but I'm going to help you."

Crouching down beside the bed, Luke said her name and waited for her to make eye contact. "I'll need to examine you first to determine your injuries, then I shall give you medicine for the pain." The girl nodded.

He had already seen that her lower lip was swollen. As well, she had a small cut and bruising on her left jaw. He reached out to gently touch her face and her entire body shrunk back. As it did, she gasped in pain. For a girl who had merely fallen down, this seemed an extreme response.

Kathleen's skirt had been removed but her legs were covered with stockings, stained with what looked like blood droplets.

"Can you tell me where it hurts?"

"I think...I may have dislocated...my shoulder...here." Her left hand released her right wrist long enough to point.

Luke gently lifted the blanket off. Kathleen was in her shift. He knew that a shoulder dislocation occurs when the head of the upper arm bone pops out of the shallow shoulder socket. The round protrusion sticking out under the skin was an indication that it was probably a shoulder dislocation.

Leaving her arm close to her chest, he moved it in various ways, determining that it was not broken. He studied, then touched her right arm and shoulder in different areas. She winced. She did indeed have an anterior dislocated shoulder, the most common dislocation. The pale skin on her arm and wrists had already darkened with large patches of bruises. Luke frowned and shook his head. He glanced at her face. She avoided eye contact, her swollen lips pressed together as she was trying hard not to cry.

"Shhh," he whispered. "You are right. You have a dislocated shoulder."

Kathleen nodded. "Y...yes."

From the specks on her stockings, he suspected she might be hurt elsewhere. He picked up her stocking foot and studied it. "Are you injured anywhere else?"

"Most of that is beet juice, Dr. Luke." Caroline's soft voice behind him said. "Jane tells me it looks like someone has been murdered in our pantry."

Beet juice, of course. He nodded, thankful that her dislocated shoulder seemed to be her only physical injury, other than numerous bruises that colored her arms, wrists and chest. He frowned again. The location of those bruises didn't fit with the young girl's assertion that she fell.

He reached out again to touch her uninjured arm, and again she shrunk away from him.

Turning to Jane, he said, "Could you please bring me a small glass of brandy?"

"Yes, Dr. Luke."

"Oh...and Jane?"

"Yes, sir?"

"Has the pantry been cleaned yet?"

"No."

"I should like to take a look before it's cleaned up."

"Of course."

"Mrs. O'Donovan, she has a dislocated shoulder, but I hope to be able to set it properly without having to take her to the hospital. Has Kathleen ever had laudanum?"

We keep a small bottle in the bathroom. She uses it infrequently for...during her monthly."

"Has she ever had any ill effects from it?"

"No, but we've only ever given her a few drops at a time."

Luke reached inside his bag for a bottle of laudanum. The

standard adult dosage was thirty drops, but Kathleen was slighter and smaller than the average adult. He recognized laudanum's addicting properties, but a few doses for pain management would be necessary. Besides, he was going to need her as calm and as still as possible, with her muscles relaxed, to set her shoulder. He would only give her one-half the maximum dosage, wait a short while, then proceed to set her shoulder.

The horrid taste of the drug necessitated a strong drink. Respiratory difficulties were the most common side effect, but given Kathleen's youth, that was unlikely.

Jane quickly returned with a glass and a bottle of brandy. She poured an inch into the glass and handed it to him. He took the bottle of laudanum from his bag and squeezed fifteen drops into the brandy and handed the glass to Caroline.

"Have her drink this."

Caroline nodded and held it to Kathleen's lips. She complied and drank the mixture, then shuddered.

"It tastes wretched, but it will help with pain."

Before the medication took effect, he whispered, "Kathleen, I'm going to have to touch you. However, I shall do everything I can not to cause you undue pain."

She looked down, pursed her lips and nodded.

Within a few moments, the laudanum appeared to be working. Kathleen's head bobbed and her eyes were closing. What he had to do to her already injured body could be dreadfully painful. In the past four months, he had only set three anterior dislocations using Kocher's Method. He wasn't yet an expert at doing so and, with two of the three previous patients, he had inadvertently hurt them. He didn't want to hurt her; he only wanted to alleviate her pain.

"Mrs. O'Donovan, if you could help, it is necessary for Kathleen to be sitting upright, if possible."

"Yes, of course."

"Kathleen," he whispered, "I shall need to move you back against your pillows." She nodded and Caroline and Jane helped her to relax against her pillows, with her legs stretched out on the bed. Kathleen's head jerked to remain awake.

"I will need to have her as close to the edge of the right side of the bed as possible." While the women gently slid Kathleen over to the edge of the bed, Luke moved to the other side of the bed and studied her shoulder. After a quick examination of the rest of her body, he concluded that she may have gotten the dislocated shoulder from a fall, but the rest of these injuries were most definitely *not* from an accidental fall. From the way she shrunk back when he touched her, to the lack of eye contact, to the expression in her eyes, Luke firmly believed that someone had caused her this pain. As he looked down for evidence of rape, he sighed, relieved, when he saw no evidence of a torn shift.

He willed himself to focus. This was an anterior dislocation and the most common and not as challenging to set as the other types.

"Mrs. O'Donovan, please position yourself behind Kathleen so that she is leaning against you and not the pillows."

"Yes." Caroline lifted her skirt a bit in order to maneuver herself behind her daughter.

"Jane, please stand beside me; I may need assistance," he said.

"Yes, Dr. Luke."

Kathleen's eyes were closed, her chin now rested against her chest, her shoulders drooping.

"Mrs. O'Donovan, if you could gently hold her back straight."

The woman looked at him with a quizzical expression.

"Jane, may I demonstrate on you?"

"Of course, Dr. Luke."

"Turn around, please."

The servant turned around so that her back was toward Luke. He put his hands on the tops of her shoulders and gently pulled back so that the shoulders were higher. "Like that."

"Yes, I think I can do that, but won't it hurt my daughter?"

"Be gentle and it will be fine."

"Very well."

"Once I set her shoulder, she should have immediate relief." From *her physical pain*, he wanted to say.

He first said a silent prayer that he would be able to set her shoulder the first attempt, and thus experience minimum pain. This girl had already endured enough.

Luke then felt the girl's arm, and because she was semi-conscious, the muscles were relaxed. He started by supporting her right arm, with her wrist and palm facing up. He externally rotated until he felt resistance. Then he moved the humerus forward and internally rotated the arm until finally, the shoulder popped back into place. Kathleen moaned and released a sigh. Luke exhaled, felt her shoulder and, satisfied, he nodded. "The shoulder is now back where it should be."

"Thank you, Doctor." Caroline kissed her daughter's head.

Kathleen's cheeks were still wet from tears. Luke held onto the girl's arm and back. "Mrs. O'Donovan, you may release her and move now. Jane, please get some pillows for Kathleen to lean against."

Slipping a few pillows under Kathleen's neck and head, Jane and Luke slowly placed her on her back. Then he turned toward Kathleen's mother.

"Mrs. O'Donovan?"

"Please call me Caroline."

"Caroline, she'll need to wear a sling for a few days to ensure the shoulder heals well."

The three turned when they heard knocking. The two lookalike brothers stood in the doorway, leaning their heads inward.

"Papa's train. We need to pick him up at the station at 8:00. Shall we go or send Jesse?"

"We'll send Jesse when the time comes," Caroline said. "I'll need one of you to pick up the other children at Aunt Elizabeth's house."

"I would be happy to go," said John.

"Very well. Thank you."

"Where is Jesse now?" Luke asked Will.

"I believe he's working in the stable. Why do you ask?"

"Just wondering." Of course, Luke wasn't just wondering. Jesse was the only other male present in the household. These injuries didn't come from a simple fall. Perhaps the dislocated shoulder, but not the bruising on her chest, neck and wrists. As time had passed, dark yellow-green bruises now appeared like dark bracelets on Kathleen's wrists, which were easily seen. Luke was convinced that Kathleen hadn't received her injuries from a fall.

Across the hall, whimpering, then wailing, from the baby followed. "Go ahead." Luke said to Caroline. "Kathleen is sleeping and Jane can assist me." Facing the servant, he said, "Would you bring me a small basin with warm water?"

"Of course, Dr. Luke."

"And a metal tray if you have one."

Jane closed the door and Luke now remained alone with his patient. Kathleen moved her head side to side and began to cry in her sleep. Her eyes were closed, but she mumbled softly, "Stop, please make him stop. I bit him. He stopped. It hurts, my shoulder hurts..."

Luke gasped like someone slapped his face. She *had* been assaulted. "He stopped after you bit him?" he whispered into her ear.

She nodded in her sleep. A drug and alcohol-induced sleep had brought forth honesty.

"Who did this to you, Kathleen?"

"Can't. He.... said he...would kill me. Can't... tell," she slurred.

Damn.

While Jane was absent from the room, he examined her bruises more thoroughly. There were three purple and green bruises on her upper chest, one on her neck just under her chin, green and yellow bruises on both wrists and darkening bruises down each arm.

Jane finally returned with the basin and water and, sitting beside Luke, she pulled the blanket down to Kathleen's waist.

Usually, Luke could look upon most girls with detached professionalism. But he found it difficult to do so with this young woman since he was already quite fond of her.

If Kathleen were telling the truth, even a drug-induced truth, the man had stopped when she bit him. But not before the wretched excuse of a man terrorized this sweet young girl.

Luke squared his shoulders and faced his patient on the bed. He cleaned the small open wounds on her chin and neck.

A few times, she hiccupped in her sleep, as if crying through her unconsciousness. He carefully put the sling around her shoulder so her arm would be bent at the elbow with the palm facing her stomach.

Covering her, Luke packed his bag and joined the group in the hallway.

"How long will it take for her injuries to heal?" Caroline's concerned, pained expression was so different from the peaceful one she'd worn the first time he visited last month after the baby was born.

"Physically, within a few weeks. As I said before, she will need to remain quiet for her shoulder to heal." Luke paused. He was faced with a decision. Should he inform the police? Should he tell her parents what Kathleen had said in her sleep? He needed to examine the pantry first before he decided.

"She won't be able to attend college, correct?"

"Yes. Perhaps you can send the school a message and they will allow her to study here at home. I would be happy to assist."

"Thank you." The baby began to cry again, so Caroline excused herself.

Luke turned to the servant. "Jane, would you remain here with Kathleen while I examine the pantry downstairs?"

"Of course."

"Someone may need to stay with her around the clock, at least for the first day." Luke handed Jane a small bottle of laudanum. "She may have ten drops two more times, but no more. And she may be disoriented when she wakes...but this should help her with pain."

"Yes."

"How do I get to the basement kitchen?"

"Just turn right and take the staircase all the way down."

"Thank you, Jane. I'll return shortly."

Luke followed the stairs down to the kitchen and at the bottom of the steps, he nearly gasped. Just beyond the table in the center of the kitchen was what looked like blood, but what Luke now knew to be beet juice. A red smeared boot print facing the back door was clearly evident. Did Kathleen try to get out before her brothers found her? He crouched down and studied the print. This seemed to be a man's larger boot print. Perhaps Will's or John's? He stepped over the smears on the floor and peered into the pantry. The only light was the natural light pouring into the room. Stepping into the small room, he cringed. Cans were strewn all over the floor, a broom had been knocked from the wall. What had once been a jar of pickled beets lay in smashed bits.

Something did not seem right about this scene. No. Her injury did not happen as the result of a fall. He needed to tell Caroline his suspicions. First, he should find Jesse, the only other male present at the time of the incident.

He ascended the staircase to the foyer. Will seemed to be pacing the large hallway.

"Will, may I see your boots?"

The young man stopped to allow Luke to examine his shoes.

His boots appeared to be smaller than the print he found in the kitchen.

"That boot print in beet juice...was it there when you came into the kitchen?"

"Yes."

"Do you know where Jesse is at this moment?"

"In the barn on the far side of the shooting range." Will was pointing. "I'd be happy to get him for you."

"Do you know where he was when your sister...fell?"

"Yes, we saw him over at the storage barn on the other side of the shooting range. John says he was moving hay bales."

13

Luke was close to eliminating or confirming one obvious suspect. When Will brought Jesse to the hallway outside of Kathleen's room, Luke asked, "Is there a room I can use to speak privately with Jesse?"

Jesse stepped forward. "My room is the next to last one on the right in the east wing, down there, Dr. Peterson."

"Thank you." He escorted the young man down the hallway to the last room on the right. Jesse opened the door and allowed Luke to enter the room first. The simplicity of the room, the lack of furniture and belongings seemed out of place in a mansion. The wallpaper was of a modest brown and white design, there was a simple white shade over the window and, lining the east wall, a small bed with a brown and black Indian woven blanket hastily thrown on. One lone dresser and a chair flanked the bed. "How long have you been with the O'Donovans?"

"Not long. What do you want to talk to me about?"

Luke bent down and stared at the man's pants. Admittedly, the dark pants could easily hide red beet stains. But his shoes wouldn't be able to hide the color. "Lift your shoes up, please." Jesse did as he was told. Luke tilted his head to examine the bottoms of his moccasin shoes, but all he could see was hay and dirt. As well, these shoes were different and smaller in size than the boot print found near the pantry. Jesse could have changed his shoes, but there was one thing that would be hard to hide.

"Thank you. Would you please take off your shirt, and allow me to look at your shoulders?"

The young Indian man opened his mouth to speak but said nothing. He removed his shirt and Luke studied the smooth, muscular shoulders. No evidence of any recent injuries, although Jesse did have some deep striated marks on his back. "Thank you, Jesse. That'll do."

As the man was putting his shirt back on, Luke commented, "Nasty scars. Someone mistreated you."

"The important thing is they ain't doing it no more. The O'Donovans are good people, treat me well, pay me well."

"Yes, they are good people. Thank you, Jesse. And sorry to have bothered you."

"You didn't bother me, Doctor. Not sure why you wanted to see my back, though. Remember...this family treats me well."

"Of course." He paused, then he escorted Jesse to the hallway.

"Jesse?"

"Yes?"

"What tribe are you?"

"Munsee...part of the Delaware."

Luke leaned in close and whispered. "My maternal grandparents were from the Lenape-Delaware tribe."

"Didn't take you for an Indian, Doctor."

"I look more like my father's Swedish-German side of the family."

Jesse's eyes narrowed. "And you don't want people to know because of what you saw on my back...that's how some white folk treat us. As I said, Mr. David and Miss Caroline are not like that."

"I know, but I'm also a doctor. I don't think the bigoted members of our community would appreciate my Indian heritage and I'd certainly lose the few patients I have."

"Probably right, Dr. Luke."

Luke remained at the O'Donovan house for the rest of the afternoon and into the early evening. Several times he tried to broach the subject of Kathleen's injury with Caroline as he wanted her to know his suspicions. However, between the baby fussing and the youngsters' needing their mother, he decided he would wait and share the information with David.

He sat with Will and John in the hallway outside of Kathleen's room until suppertime, then the boys left to join the family downstairs. Luke had no idea what sort of effect the laudanum would have on her. She would already have to endure the emotional turmoil when she woke up and became fully conscious. Before he even thought about leaving, Luke wanted to ensure his patient wasn't in need of anything.

Jane approached him with a tray of food. He had been so worried about Kathleen that he hadn't had time to be hungry. He gratefully took the tray from her. "Thank you, Jane. This smells delicious."

"It's Mr. David's favorite meal, fried chicken and potatoes. I saved him a plate for when he returns home."

"Again, thank you."

"Thank *you*, Dr. Luke."

***

Kathleen opened her mouth for air but could not breathe. She tried to move but Karl held her down. His heavy body was lying on top of hers. He laughed, his fetid alcohol breath burning her face. "Please, stop, please!" she screamed and opened her eyes.

"Shhh. You're safe."

Keeping her eyes closed, she shrunk back against the bed. *Whose voice is that?*

"Who...who is... there?"

"Dr. Luke."

Kathleen shuddered. She didn't want to be near him, but she must try to act normally. She couldn't let him — or anyone — know what had happened to her.

Then she felt a throbbing pain in her shoulder as well as the soreness in her chest, neck and arms. The pain had lessened, but what she felt most strongly was a searing agony in her heart. She squinted as she opened her eyes, then gasped when she realized it was nearly dark.

"Do you need more pain medication?"

"I need light. It's dark. Please!" Her heart was racing and she began to tremble.

"Of course. I am lighting the lamp straight away." Within a moment, the room was lit with the subtle glow of the oil lamp.

"Where is my mother?" She kept her head lowered.

"She is taking care of the baby."

"And Jane?"

"Not sure."

"Is Papa home yet?"

"I believe Jesse just left to pick your father up from the train station." The doctor was quiet for a moment, then whispered, "Are you in pain?" He was close, she could almost feel his breath.

"Yes." She heard a glass clinking.

"Drink this." Her hand reached for the glass although she refused to look at him. *Why did they leave him alone in the room with me? Couldn't Jane or Will or John have stayed with me?*

Kathleen gulped and heard him say, "Slowly." She nodded and sipped the rest, then handed him the glass.

"You may leave now. I should like to be alone."

"Of course. I wanted to make sure you were comfortable before I left."

"I'm fine. You may leave."

"Kathleen..." she heard but did not look at him. "You did not receive your injuries from a fall." An accusation.

She raised her chin to glare at him. "How dare you..."

With a sigh, he said, "I'm a physician. I know what injuries sustained from a fall would look like and they would not look like this."

Her eyes downcast, she remained silent.

"Your injuries are not consistent with a fall. You have extensive bruising on your face, neck, chest and wrists. Someone caused these injuries."

Her eyes began to water. "Leave me alone."

"Very well." Her gaze once again focused on her lap, she heard him open the door, then said, "Wait." He turned as she looked up. "Have you told my mother yet...this suspicion of yours?"

"No, but I do plan to inform them."

"No! Do not tell....anyone...please!" Kathleen began to sob. Luke crouched down beside her. Softly, he said, "If someone has hurt you, you need to tell your parents and the police must be informed."

She shook her head. "Please do not tell them. Please. I wouldn't be able to bear it. *They* wouldn't be able to bear it." She was slurring and becoming too fatigued to speak.

But she would not sleep, would not rest, her head swaying and bobbing as she tried to stay awake. "Please, promise," she said, the ending s sound slurring.

"Yes, Kathleen, I promise...I shall not tell them." She laid her head back and drifted off to sleep.

***

Luke sat on a chair outside of Kathleen's room and berated himself for promising that he would keep her secret. The animal that attacked her needed to be caged, in prison. If only she had shared who it was.

Lying never came easy to Luke. He hoped that he wouldn't have to lie to Kathleen's parents, although if one considered the lie of omission, he was already guilty. The O'Donovans were fine, decent people and they deserved to know what had really happened to their daughter.

"Dr. Luke, how is my daughter?" David met him in front of Kathleen's room.

"She's resting presently."

"Will tells me she fell in the pantry."

"That's what she says."

"What in the world was she doing in there? She has no reason to be inside the pantry."

Luke remained silent.

"May I see her?"

"Of course. She's sleeping. You'll need to be careful with her shoulder, which was dislocated. I've set it in place, and she's wearing a sling, but she's going to be sore for a few days. She is bruised and in some discomfort. I've given her laudanum to help her sleep."

David drew in a breath as he listened. He then nodded, and opened the door. "Good. The lamp is lit. She has hated the dark since she was a baby." Luke well understood fear. He wouldn't admit it to anyone, but he had his own distinct fear of cellars...or maybe he was just claustrophobic.

David knelt beside his daughter's bed and kissed her forehead. She roused. "Papa?" she slurred.

"Yes, Kat, I'm here. You're not supposed to get hurt while I'm away."

"S...sorry." Her voice caught, as if she were going to cry.

"Don't be. I'm glad Dr. Luke took care of you." David sat on the edge of her bed, took hold of her hand and began humming a soft tune. Kathleen immediately relaxed against the pillow, her head falling to one side and her eyes closing. The young doctor quietly stepped out of the room and returned home.

***

The next morning, Kathleen opened her eyes as the sun trickled in through the bedroom window. It was tempting to turn her back to the light, to pull the covers over her head and to fall back to sleep. For days. For months. Forever.

When she reached for the covers, however, she couldn't move her right arm because it was held tight in a sling. Sitting up, she was greeted with throbbing in her shoulder. She moaned. Admittedly, the pain was better than yesterday. She had a vague memory of the doctor setting her shoulder. The physical injuries would heal easily. The searing torment in her heart and soul felt like they would last forever.

All of a sudden, the scent of *that horrible man* permeated the air. Looking down, she saw that her original slip was still in place, dried and smeared blood dotting the garment. She cringed. Was it her blood or his? She got out of bed and tried to take the sling off. However, every time she tilted her head to remove it, pain radiated from just below her shoulder. She'd have to leave this horrid piece of clothing on, at least until someone could help her.

"Miss Kathleen, do you need medicine?" Jane's gentle voice asked through the door.

"Come in, Jane."

Opening the door, the servant's eyes brightened. "You're up and about, Miss Kathleen!"

"Can you help me put on a new shift, please?"

"I'd be happy to assist you." Jane carefully removed Kathleen's shift.

Kathleen looked down and gasped. Turning towards the mirror, she stared. Purple, green and yellow bruises like paint colored her chest, neck, jaw and arms. *Dear God, could this get any worse?*

Jane helped her to wash, then Kathleen returned to bed. The servant gave her a bit of sherry with laudanum and within moments, she drowsily surrendered to sleep.

14

The beautiful dark-haired lady caressed the top of his head. Will looked up at the woman and she smiled. The woman held out her arms to embrace him and when he stepped toward her, she vanished without a trace.

Will roused and sat up in bed. The dreams with the lady were becoming more frequent. What could they mean, if anything?

Glancing at the clock on the mantelpiece, he saw that it was five a.m. Time to rise. Admittedly, Will enjoyed being able to move about the room without worrying that John would waken. John had already taken most of his belongings to the room across the hall near the bathroom.

He leaned on the sill and peered outside. It was dark, but the moon lit up a fine mist at the front of the house.

Will couldn't understand how anyone in the house could sleep, not while his sister was suffering. He only heard her moan once through the night, but it was enough to make his heart burn with anguish. Something didn't seem right about her accident. He couldn't clearly state why, although he thought he had heard a man's voice yesterday before he had found her in the pantry.

He prayed and petitioned that a merciful God would take his sister's pain away.

***

Luke blessed himself and knelt in the pew before Mass. He couldn't seem to rid himself of the memory of Kathleen lying in front of him, broken and bruised. Anger rose up in him and he said a prayer that God would help him to forgive the depraved man who hurt that poor girl. He was thankful that she had bitten her attacker and that the man had stopped before doing any further damage.

Within a few moments, David and most of the O'Donovan children genuflected and entered their pew. Kathleen and Caroline were not among them.

After Mass, Luke approached the O'Donovans. David greeted him warmly and held his hand out so that Luke could shake it. "Dr. Luke."

"Good day, David." He lowered his voice. "How is Kathleen feeling today?"

"As well as can be expected," David responded quietly. "I believe she has had two small doses of laudanum as you directed, but was awake when we were preparing to leave for Mass."

"I'd like to visit now, if that is acceptable with you. I shall follow you home in my carriage."

"Of course."

***

The neighing and clopping of the horse and carriage pulling up below her window announced the return of her father and siblings from Mass. Her shoulder and chest throbbed; her right arm remained in a linen sling. She glanced downward and cringed when the doctor's carriage pulled up below her window. Stepping back, she clutched the robe closer to her body. How could she ever face the doctor or any man again? He had told her that he suspected she hadn't fallen, that someone had hurt her, that there was "extensive bruising." She stretched her sleeves down over her brown and green bruised wrists.

Kathleen could not understand how she could have been so wrong about Karl. That man, who had seemed to be the most charming man she had ever known, was wicked, a rotten apple in a shiny and beautiful skin.

She should have known not to go anywhere alone with him. Papa and Will were right. And she was stupid and naive.

"Kathleen?" Her mother's voice sounded on edge.

"Yes?"

"Dr. Luke is here to see you."

What was Kathleen supposed to say? *Come right on in, Doctor, take a look at me again?*

"Kathleen? Did you hear me?"

She wiped her eyes and slowly walked toward the door. What if the doctor was standing there?

"Kathleen, Dr. Luke needs to see you."

Why does he need to see me, she wanted to ask. Instead, her fists clenched, she said, "Tell him to leave. I am fine." She tried to sound in control, but her lip began to quiver.

"Kathleen, you are injured, and the doctor needs to see you again," her mother said.

Then the doctor's voice. "Kathleen, I should like to examine your shoulder."

"Kat, please open the door," her father's worried voice said.

She sighed and unlatched the door with her left hand, then stepped back, her eyes staring down at the floor. She turned, her back facing them.

The doctor's voice. "It's good to see you up."

She didn't respond.

"Dr. Luke," Caroline said, "may I remain here?"

"Certainly," she heard him say.

Kathleen's hands began to tremble. How was she supposed to tell him that she never wanted him or any other man to touch her?

"Kathleen," her mother whispered. "He's here to help you. Why are you being so contrary?"

The young woman turned slowly to face her parents and the doctor. She avoided eye contact with Dr. Luke, instead focusing on her mother, her eyes filling with tears. She wanted to pound her chest. She wanted to shout that she didn't fall, that Karl had hurt her. Instead, she straightened as best she could and remained silent.

***

Luke sighed and internally recited a Hail Mary for Kathleen. *Almighty Father, give her grace.* Kathleen was hurting, like a wounded animal who didn't know she could trust her rescuer. Most importantly, Luke needed her to believe she could trust him to keep her secret.

He leaned down, but kept his distance. "Kathleen," he whispered. "I'm going to help you. I need to make sure that your shoulder heals properly. I promise that I won't do anything that isn't necessary."

She briefly made eye contact. The sadness Luke saw in her green eyes gripped his heart and his anger surfaced again. He pressed his lips together and pushed his rage aside. He wanted to take her in his arms and promise her that she would never be hurt like that again.

"Perhaps sit here on the edge of the bed," Luke suggested.

Kathleen did as she was told and Caroline sat quietly beside her daughter.

"First, I'm going to take off the sling. I'll need you to keep the arm in place like this." He showed her how to keep the elbow bent at a right angle, then slipped off the sling.

"I'm going to remove your robe, Kathleen." She didn't respond. He pulled it carefully over her injured shoulder and down her arm, then lifted the robe off her other arm.

Luke glanced at her face. Kathleen was staring at the closed door and avoiding eye contact.

Medically, it was important that her shoulder and right arm remain in the same position for healing. Luke had to force himself to glance away from the bruising on her jaw, neck, arms and shoulders, as the marks had further darkened to purple, blue and green. He looked at Caroline, who was staring and scowling at the bruises and other marks on her daughter.

Luke pushed the strap of her shift down gently. He felt her cringe. "I'm sorry, Kathleen. I wish I could make this easier for you. I know you are embarrassed and I am doing everything I can to preserve your modesty."

He felt her right shoulder. "Excellent. It is exactly where it should be."

"Will she have to wear the sling much longer?" Caroline asked.

"A week or so." A close examination of the small wound on her chin indicated there was slight redness and swelling. He leaned into his medical bag and picked up the natural healing salve. It smelled awful but aided the healing process, especially for a wound like this. Again, Luke was thankful for both medical school and the native customs handed down from his grandparents.

Kathleen stared ahead as he opened the vial. She blinked a few times then squeezed her eyes shut and frowned. "What is that wretched smell?"

"Sorry for the odor, but this is the best healing salve I

have." He gently applied a minute amount to the wound. "This will heal the wound in a day or so." He put the vial away. "Do you need medicine to ease the pain?"

Kathleen continued to stare straight ahead. With a slight shake of her head, she indicated no.

Luke was certain she continued to be in pain, but if she wasn't asking for medicine, he would not insist.

When he finished his examination, her mother assisted Kathleen with her robe, then her sling. When Luke stood up to leave, he heard Caroline say, "Thank you, Dr. Luke."

He turned and offered the subtlest of nods. Just then, Tim could be heard yelling. "I want Mama!!"

"Go ahead, Mama," Kathleen said. "I'll be fine." Caroline left the room and Luke closed the door.

Kathleen sat on the side of her bed, and he watched as she pulled the sleeve of her robe down over her left wrist. The sling hid the bruising of her right arm and wrist.

The discolored wrists might be easy to hide, but the bruises on her neck would not be. He took a deep breath and exhaled, then crouched down beside her. "Kathleen, you need to tell your parents what happened. Who did this to you?"

Her eyes glistened and she finally brought her gaze upward. "I can't..."

"You've never seen this man before?"

She looked away.

"They're your parents...as much as it would hurt them to know what happened, they would want to know."

She lowered her head. "Please do not tell them."

"I've already promised that and I am a man of my word." He stayed there, torn between wanting to comfort her and demanding to know who had assaulted her, torn between wanting to tell her parents and keeping his promise to her.

Luke's chest tightened as he closed Kathleen's door and walked toward the staircase. It bothered his soul that she had to endure, alone, the emotional upheaval of having been hurt. David and Caroline met him at the top of the stairs.

Caroline spoke first, although Luke could tell from their stern expressions that they were both concerned for their daughter. "Dr. Luke, would you please join us in the parlor?

Jane has prepared tea and sandwiches there."

***

Kathleen could hear her parents and the doctor murmuring in the hallway. That wretched salve, while soothing, smelled like excrement and made her eyes water.

Either way, she was relieved to be alone. When the doctor touched her, she fought to keep herself from cringing. When he moved the strap of her shift, she was sure that she would die of embarrassment. She had peered into the mirror earlier this morning at the black, blue and green marks like paint that stained her chest, neck, arms and shoulder. Karl took what was once beautiful and had made it grotesque.

***

Luke followed David and Caroline down the stairs and turned right, where they entered a medium-sized sitting room. This was a woman's room, one in which he imagined Caroline sewing, having tea or entertaining. The decor was soft and feminine, the wallpaper a mix of pastel flowers, the fireplace unlit, and to the left of the fireplace was a large photograph of the entire family, the baby included.

"When did you sit for that photograph?"

"Two months ago, the week after Maureen was born. It was delivered last week. Beautiful, isn't it?"

Luke's eyes were drawn to the eldest. Kathleen was smiling, a coy smile, the innocent expression of a girl who hadn't yet experienced love or the world. With a sigh, he nodded.

It was quiet and any further chatter involved talking about the weather, the crops, the trees, anything but Kathleen.

David finally stood up and closed the doors, then returned to the area in front of the fireplace. "Luke," David said, "We would like to discuss Kathleen's health with you."

"Very well." They whispered to one another, then David faced Luke.

"We don't believe our daughter fell."

Luke exhaled, then lowered his head. "What do you think happened?"

David scowled. "We're not sure, but we have noticed her

trying to hide the bruises on her wrists. A fall would explain her dislocated shoulder, but not the bruises on her wrists."

Caroline turned to her husband. "Jane and I also noticed bruising on her chest and neck."

David lifted a single eyebrow, then shook his head.

Luke steeled himself to formulate a response. He wanted to say that they were correct, but he couldn't. "David, Caroline, you need to speak with your daughter."

"Do you have information about Kathleen?"

"She has asked me not to share the information with you. I will not betray her trust...as much as I want to tell you what I know, I do not know everything."

Caroline began to cry; David put his arm around her. "I knew she hadn't fallen. Someone has hurt her, isn't that right?"

"Caroline, please. You must speak with your daughter," was all Luke could say.

David pulled his wife into an embrace. "We will find out who did this to her." He stepped away and turned toward Luke. "Who could have done this? And in our own house?"

"You should speak with your daughter."

"Jesse...did he do this?"

"I'm confident that Jesse had nothing to do with your daughter's assault."

"What makes you so sure?"

"I cannot say without betraying your daughter's confidence. You need to speak with her."

David took his wife's hand and pulled her along with him. He turned toward Luke. "Follow us upstairs." Luke followed as they hurried up the staircase to their daughter's room.

David knocked. "Kat?"

"Yes, Papa?"

"Your mother and I would like to speak to you."

She opened the door, her eyes wide, her face flush. When she saw Luke, she blanched, swallowed hard, then scowled at Luke.

"May we come in?"

She nodded and stepped aside to allow all three to enter. Closing the door, her father turned toward her. "Please sit,

Kat. You look uncomfortable."

She lowered herself to the chair by the window.

"Kat, you need to tell us what really happened."

Her eyes flew to Luke's with anger, hurt and betrayal thrusting forward. "I see you've been talking to the doctor."

"No, we have...not..." her father stuttered. "Well, that's not entirely true, but he would not tell us anything. He said that we should speak with you."

Her eyes again made contact, but this time they softened and she glanced away.

"Kathleen." Caroline knelt before her and had already picked up her left hand. "Let me see your wrist."

The girl yanked her hand back and in doing so, winced. "No."

"Kathleen, sweet, your injuries are not the result of a fall, are they?"

Her eyes watering, Kathleen finally wept. "Oh, Mama." Caroline embraced her daughter.

David, standing close to Luke, took on a rigid expression. He joined his wife and daughter. "Kat?"

Kathleen wiped her eyes and looked up. "Yes, Papa?"

"I'm going to contact the police."

Her eyes widened and she pushed her parents away. "No, Papa, no police! Please!"

David motioned for Luke to join him in the hallway as his daughter finally let loose a flood of tears. The older man whispered, "I want to kill the animal who did this to her."

Luke kept his voice quiet. "We don't know who it was. Only that she bit him to make him stop."

David cringed. "Damn." He sank back against the wall. "Was there a delivery? Someone who visited?"

"Whoever did this came to the house at some point yesterday. Jesse told me he was working in the storage shed on the other side of the shooting range." He paused to allow David to consider that. "Will and John were shooting cans out back. Whoever attacked her must have convinced her to allow him to come inside."

"Or forced her inside." David paused. "I am going to contact the police."

"We have no idea who perpetrated this crime. There's plenty of evidence that she was, in fact, assaulted, but no evidence of who did it without her admission. Surely, given what she has endured, she shouldn't be forced to do anything at this point."

"What else do you know, Luke?"

"When she was first under the influence of the laudanum, she said that the man told her he'd kill her if she told anyone."

"Dear God! That is more of a reason to inform the police."

"Kathleen asked that you not contact them."

"I don't care. I'm going to send for the police. Whoever did this must pay for his crime."

***

Astonished, Will could not believe what he had just overheard as he was coming up the back staircase. He didn't like to eavesdrop, but Papa sounded angry, even as he spoke in hushed tones. Will felt like he had been punched in the stomach. How could someone just come into their home and hurt his sister? And who could have done such a horrible deed? Then he recalled the cold chills, the feeling of the words *Kat is in danger*, the masculine shout. Kat *had* been in danger and Will had dismissed it.

***

Earlier today, it felt like the burden of her secret had eased. She knew her parents were upset, but Kathleen refused to share any details, most especially regarding who was responsible for her injuries, and she would continue to allow them to believe she had never seen her attacker before. Now maybe she could put this entire episode behind her. Perhaps now she could...Her entire body stiffened as she watched a police carriage ride up below her window.

Kathleen had told her parents most definitely *not* to contact the police. She repeated that command in the presence of her mother, to Dr. Luke and to her father. Police involvement would mean that she would need to talk about the incident and she would never speak about it. Now, the entire police department knew. She wouldn't be surprised if news of her injury appeared in the Philadelphia Bulletin this evening.

She had respectfully asked Dr. Luke to keep her secret and

he did. Within an hour of admitting to her parents what happened, the police had been contacted. *So much for honoring my request.* Filled with rage, she turned and scanned the room. Then she saw it: the small silver Atlantic City box Karl had given her. She grabbed it with her left hand and tossed it across the room, the metal gouging out a thick chunk of wall near her closet, the tiny shells inside shattering to pieces on the floor.

Kathleen was prepared when her father knocked on the door. "Kat? There is someone who wishes to speak with you."

"Leave me alone, Papa. I do not wish to speak with anyone."

"It's a police officer. He wants to speak with you about the..."

"I told you I fell!" she yelled through the door.

She heard murmuring in the hallway. An hour passed and, finally, the police carriage left.

A short while later, her father knocked softly. "Kat?"

She swung open the door so quickly that her father stepped back. "Who contacted the police?" Her tone was sharp and, she hoped, stinging his face.

He opened his mouth but said nothing.

"Who...contacted them?"

"I informed the police."

Her jaw clenched and her mouth pursed into a thin line. *How dare he?*

"Kat, don't you understand? That man — whoever he is — will likely harm someone else. He needs to be brought to justice. You have to..."

She turned her back on him, refusing to respond. She was so angry that she wished he would just leave, the room, the house, the country for all she cared.

He continued speaking, but she would not acknowledge his presence. "Kat, please." She felt him touching her shoulder and she flinched as if his hand were a hot coal, her shoulder aching as she did so. Her father released a long sigh. Footsteps indicated he had left the room, the click of the door closing behind him. Kathleen exhaled, as if she had been holding her breath. Walking slowly to the window sill, she lowered herself onto the comfortable arm chair.

It was nearly suppertime. The day had been sunny and warm, but her heart and her soul were drowning in a sea of hopelessness.

Kathleen laid her head back in the chair, fidgeting and changing positions frequently. Her shoulder was sore, but not painful. The myriad bruises on her chest, chin and arms felt tender to the touch. Despite the discomfort, she drifted off to sleep.

Karl's heavy body on top of hers made it impossible to move. He laughed at her, his hot breath stinging her face, his wet mouth covering hers, his hands on her body.

Kathleen opened her eyes with a gasp. Darkness had replaced the light in the room, so she stood up and made her way to the oil lamp by her bedside. She took off the glass top with her left hand, managed to light the match, but the wick wouldn't flame.

Frustrated, she began to sob. "I just want light in my room, why can't I have light in my room?"

The door opened and Will was by her side. "What's wrong, Kat?"

"I need light, Will. I need light now!"

He picked up the base. "Your lamp needs oil. I'll be right back."

"Leave the door open."

"Of course."

Kathleen prayed he would return quickly. She began to shake and she was having difficulty breathing.

Will seemed to be taking an extraordinarily long time. "Please, please, I need light."

Someone else came into her room and stood beside her. He touched her back and she flinched. "Kat, it's me, John."

"I'm sorry, John."

"What do you need?"

"My lamp won't light."

"I don't see your lamp."

Behind him, Will said, "Her lamp needed oil. I've already lit it for you, Kat."

As the room was bathed in a subtle glow, Kathleen felt her body relaxing. "Thank you, Will."

"Do you want me to stay with you? I can read to you or John can stay and we can play cards."

Kathleen didn't respond. Read, play cards? She shook her head.

Her brothers left and she trudged back to the arm chair by the window. She held her lips together to stop from weeping. She didn't want to cry. She didn't want to do anything right now but crawl into a hole and stay there for the next year.

The distant bongs of the grandfather clock rang in the foyer downstairs. Seven o'clock. Her eyes focused on the picture Izzy had painted of her. Kathleen was sixteen at the time and Izzy, at twelve, had brilliantly captured her innocence and natural beauty. Izzy, who could be clumsy, had a unique artistic talent. This was one of Kathleen's favorite portraits; she preferred it to any of the photographs of herself. Izzy made her look beautiful. Now? Kathleen no longer felt beautiful.

Her eyelids became heavy and she surrendered to sleep.

Karl, his hot rancid breath, holding her wrists, kissing her with an open mouth...Darkness, blackness wrapped around her heart and Karl's words "Kathleen, you are mine, and I will have you one day..."

She sat up in the chair, holding her palm to her chest to calm her thundering heart. The clock downstairs began chiming and she counted. Two o'clock. Kathleen took a small breath in and out and tried to relax her shoulders. The physical pain was minimal. Glancing at the oil lamp, she was thankful that it remained aglow.

Despite that, overwhelming sadness enveloped her. She angrily shook it away and fought the urge to cry. Instead, she carefully stood up and inched toward the door. Opening it, she stepped into the hallway. She needed to be anywhere but alone in her room. Passing her brothers' rooms, she found herself envious. They were sleeping soundly with no cares in the world; they had brothers around their age, friends for life, as Papa often called Will and John.

I wish I had a sister my age. Her thoughts turned to baby

Mo — her only sister — her soon-to-be goddaughter. Kathleen hadn't cuddled her or even held her since — she shook the thought away as she shuffled past her parents' bedroom. She wished she could wake them, but she refused to speak to her father.

Making her way down the hallway, she stopped at Izzy's doorway and knocked quietly. She opened the servant's door and whispered, "Izzy?"

"How may I help you, Miss?" Izzy asked, her words slurred with sleep.

"Would you mind staying with me in my room?"

"Of course." The girl put on her robe and followed Kathleen.

"Do you want me to sleep in the chair by your bed, Miss?"

"It's a large enough bed. I'd prefer that you sleep with me."

The servant took off her robe and draped it over the chair.

"Would you like help taking off your robe, Miss Kathleen?"

She nodded. At fifteen, Izzy was already taller than Kathleen. The girl removed Kathleen's robe, first taking the sling off, and gently pulling the sleeve over her right shoulder, then the bringing the sleeve over her left. Izzy replaced the sling. "There."

"Would you paint another painting of me, Izzy?"

"Yes, if you'd like that."

The two got into bed, with Izzy taking the side closest to the door and Kathleen taking the side nearest the window.

"Good night."

"Good night."

Within moments, Izzy fell into a deep slumber, but Kathleen, lying on her left side, could not get drowsy. She wished that she could sleep without seeing that man's face in her dreams, without feeling the pressure of his strong body on hers, without hearing his seductive, cruel voice.

A warm breeze blew the curtains in and out. Swish, swish. Tapping of rain against the house sounded like hands clapping. Kathleen relished the sweet scent of the earth washed clean. The sound of the rain on the roof lulled her and, soon she was drifting off to sleep.

Kathleen woke to the chirping of the birds outside her

window and the distant cawing of a few roosters behind the house. The sling still felt foreign to her, it pressed into her skin as she sat up. She walked to the window and stared at the new day. The muscles in her arms and legs felt stiff. Her stomach and back continued to be sore.

Her favorite part of the day was just before dawn, when the sky often took on a pink and orange intensity. These were the moments when the house was still — the whole world seemed quiet — and Kathleen could feast her eyes on the beauty of God's creation.

Yet as she sat and watched the sun coming up, thick black clouds were forming in the distance, and gray flickering below them suggested that it was raining several miles away. Her eyes began to tear, but she blinked them away.

Despite the threatening rain, the sun remained insistent. *Why, God? Why did you allow this to happen to me? Were you trying to punish me?*

Just beyond the dark clouds, rising in the sky, was the half arc of a rainbow.

"Read me another story, Papa. The story of Noah."

"Very well." Her father flipped through the pages of his Bible and came to the story of Noah. "Noah, make thee an ark of timber planks: thou shalt make little rooms in the ark, and thou shalt pitch it within and without...Behold I will bring the waters of a great flood upon the earth, to destroy all flesh, wherein is the breath of life, under heaven. All things that are in the earth shall be consumed."

"Papa, why did God want to make a flood?"

"People had become bad, Kat, but God didn't want to destroy everything in the flood so he told Noah to build the ark and put two of every animal in there."

"And the rainbow came because it was a sign of God's promise never to destroy the earth with water again, right, Papa?"

"Right, Kat." He kissed the top of her head.

"Am I going to have a little sister someday, Papa?"

"Perhaps. That will be up to God."

She placed both of her arms around his neck and kissed

the side of his face. It was prickly. "Papa, your face feels scratchy."

"Yes, it does, Kat. Off to bed with you."

In spite of the happy and nostalgic memory, anger churned inside her. She hated that her father had contacted the police against her wishes. Now the entire city of Philadelphia knew what happened to her.

The rainbow now stretched into a full arc across the sky painting bright colors of hope within its arc. Suddenly, a blue and green hummingbird hovered, eye level at her window. He was a beautiful bird who stayed for several long seconds, perhaps looking for food.

Her entire body softened when she thought of her little sister, beautiful, sweet Maureen. She wanted to march right down to her parents' bedroom and touch her sister's curly dark hair and soft skin and watch her sleep as if she hadn't a care in the world. She shook her head as she reflected.

"Miss," Izzy sat up and stretched her hands in mid-yawn. "Do you need any assistance this morning?"

"No," Kathleen said, turning toward the servant. "But perhaps you can ask my mother to send Jesse to the college with a note of my injury."

"Yes, Miss. I can do that."

"Thank you, Izzy." The girl stood up and reached for her robe. While she covered herself, Jane knocked on the door. "Miss Kathleen, is my daughter in there with you?"

Izzy opened the door. "I'm here, Mama. Miss Kathleen wanted me to sleep with her."

"That's fine. How are you doing this morning?" Jane's eyebrows were raised and she smiled at Kathleen.

Kathleen shrugged. Jane came into the room as Izzy left, turned off the oil lamp and stood close to Kathleen. "You should try to take a bath today, Miss Kathleen. Either Izzy or I can help you."

She nodded.

"I shall send Izzy up with your breakfast shortly."

15

At the whorehouse, Karl Wagner snickered. No matter how you measured it, prostitutes knew their trade well. But there was nothing like the thrill of the chase with good girls like Kathleen O'Donovan.

The woman stared at the bandage on his shoulder. "What happened there?"

"Well, a girl became too — shall we say — overwhelmed."

"I see." She smiled and left the room while Karl pulled on his trousers. His thoughts turned to Kathleen. She had been completely enamored with him and, no doubt, had fallen in love. He had been certain that she would go along with his desire to have her. After all, wasn't that what a dutiful wife was supposed to do? She wasn't yet his wife, but it had been leaning that way. He scoffed. Karl was accustomed to getting his way. Eventually, Kathleen would need to understand that.

Last week, when Kathleen told Karl that her father and her family would be away, it felt too much like an invitation. Arriving at the O'Donovan place, he could hear shots at the back of the house and, after questioning Kathleen, he realized that no one else was close. It would be the ideal time to take her. That, combined with her long blond hair cascading over her shoulders, her lack of corset...well, Karl could not wait another second. He should have gotten what he wanted in short order.

In fact, Karl had hoped that she would become with child. That would have been a fine occurrence. Scandal aside, she would have been forced to marry the father of her child. Instead, she decided to be an animal and bite him through his best shirt.

Immediately after the "incident," he hightailed it out of Germantown and back to Cheltenham where he was living in a boarding house beside the saloon in which he worked as a security officer. He couldn't tell Kathleen's "dear old dad" that he was currently working at a saloon, but this was the only job his father could get him since he flunked out of college and failed the idiotic policeman's examination. David would never have given permission for Karl to court his daughter with that knowledge.

Earlier today, he'd received a letter forwarded to him by his father and delivered by courier. He ripped it open and nearly jumped for joy. The letter was from David and explained that his daughter "had an unfortunate accident and had taken a fall..." and that she would be unable to have visitors for the next few weeks.

Perfect. David would never have sent him a note if he knew what had really happened to her. It was brilliant for her to say that she had fallen. She hadn't told anyone and had kept her part of the bargain.

His mouth formed a straight line. What should be his next step then? Her parents still thought of them as a courting couple. He was in no position to deny that or to break the courtship. The thin line of his mouth turned into a smile. He knew exactly what he would do.

***

The next morning, Jesse drove Will and John to the Germantown station. The two oldest O'Donovan sons took the train to downtown Philly to attend Roman Catholic High School, the new and modern secondary school recently built by funds from the Archdiocese of Philadelphia. Will, as a senior, attended different classes than John, a junior.

At school, Will had to endure the cruel words of his principal once again that morning when he was asked by Fr. McHenry, his Theology teacher, to bring a package to the main office. Monsignor Granger, the principal, happened to be present in the office when he looked up to see Will. Scowling, the priest demanded, "What do *you* want?"

"Fr. McHenry asked me to deliver this to the office."

"Then deliver it and be on your way. You act like you don't have a class to attend." Monsignor always seemed to regard Will with disdain as if Will were guilty for all that was wrong in the world.

"Yes, Monsignor. I apologize." Will set it on the counter and left. He had no idea why he was apologizing.

Back in Theology Class, young and enthusiastic Fr. McHenry spoke of the importance of young men discerning their vocation, that only the finest, most virtuous men are called to such an important and holy vocation. Will sat back in his seat. Only the finest, most virtuous? Certainly, he was not worthy of such an esteemed vocation. *Lord, where is that sign?*

When he returned home from school, he headed straight for Kat's room. He was worried and found himself praying for her throughout the day. He knocked and she told him to come in.

Kat was sitting at the window. She stood up and turned to greet him. "How was school today, Will?"

"All right, I suppose. Does your shoulder still hurt?"

"Not really."

"Do you miss college? You haven't been there in a week."

"No, I don't, but I wonder if Nurse Schmidt misses me. She won't have anyone to criticize if I'm not there."

***

The following Saturday, Will woke early, dressed and prayed. It was still dark when he rode to the parish church in Germantown. Will steered his carriage to the front and tied the reins to the post. This was the advantage of attending daily Mass, especially on a Saturday. Only a small number attended, so there were prime parking places for his horse and carriage.

He went inside and, dipping his finger in the holy water font, blessed himself. He walked toward the front and stopped midway, genuflected, then entered a pew. He knelt in the Lord's presence and silently prayed. *Lord, if you want me to consider a vocation to the priesthood, send me a concrete sign.*

After Mass, Will returned to prayer. He closed his eyes and bowed his head. The scent of burning candles and the silence lulled him. This was where he was most happy, in the true presence of Christ, just after receiving the Eucharist, when he and the rest of the communicants became living tabernacles.

A tapping on his shoulders startled him and he found elderly Fr. Morrissey standing in the center aisle beside him.

"May I speak with you in the sacristy, Will?" he whispered.

"Yes."

Will followed the old priest to the sacristy. Pulling at his necktie, he waited for the priest to speak. Why would the elderly priest want to speak with him?

Finally, Fr. Morrissey said, "My eyes aren't very good these days. Would you assist me in putting these items away?"

Will heaved a sigh of relief. "Of course, I'd be happy to help, Father."

As Will moved a few boxes, the elderly priest said, "Will?"

"Yes, Father?"

"Have you ever thought of becoming a priest?"

The question so jolted Will that his mouth gaped open, and he nearly dropped the box he was holding. But he remained silent as he couldn't come up with any rational answer.

The older priest didn't wait for a response. "Pray about it. Spend time reflecting on it. Remember that only a few are chosen."

"Yes, Father. Thank you."

Will had asked for a sign and received one.

***

Dinnertime brought the scent of hot biscuits, chicken and dumplings and a hint of apple pie wafting up from the dining room. No one cooked like Jane, and Kathleen needed normalcy as well as fine home cooking. She descended the stairs.

At the dining room table, her brothers were unusually loud. Before her injury, she was often annoyed with the constant hum of her rambunctious brothers, but now she found it soothing. She ate with her left hand since her right arm was still in a sling. The food was delicious.

Jane appeared in the doorway.

"Mr. David? Mr. Karl is here to see Miss Kathleen."

At Karl's name, Kathleen choked and sputtered as her stomach clenched. Her entire body began to shake uncontrollably. *He* was here? Now? *Dear God, no!* She felt a tingling at her mouth and immediately jumped up and hurried toward the back of the dining room and down to the basement kitchen. She made it to the trash bin at the bottom of the steps just in time.

Leaning over the bin, her stomach now empty of its contents, she began to weep.

"Kathleen, are you unwell?" From behind, her mother's voice was filled with concern.

She straightened and wiped her eyes with her left hand. Without turning around, she asked, "What did...Mr. Wagner...want?"

"I believe he dropped off a letter for you, but he also spoke with your father."

"Has...he...left...yet?"

"Yes. He told Papa to let you know that he hoped you were feeling better and to give you his letter. He asked if he could call on you but your father said no."

Kathleen did not respond.

"What is wrong?" Her mother's hands on her shoulders, Kathleen turned. With a long sigh, the girl said, "I am fine. The food must not have agreed with me."

"I am going to send for Dr. Luke."

Kathleen cringed. "That is not necessary. I'm fine...now."

Jane was soon behind her mother and was closing her nose with her fingers. "Phew. It smells like you retched in the trash bin."

"I did. I'm sorry, Jane."

"No need, Miss Kathleen. If you're sick, you need to get yourself upstairs to your room."

"I agree, Kathleen."

"Would you like me to bring your dinner up to your room?" Jane asked.

"No, thank you, Jane. I'm no longer hungry."

Her mother took Kathleen by the arm and gently accompanied her up two flights of the back staircase to her bedroom.

***

Luke would have arrived at the O'Donovan house sooner, but he had been otherwise detained delivering a baby boy for the Sadler Family, their second child and first son. He arrived at his house to find Jesse waiting for him. The young servant handed him a note from David indicating that Kathleen was ill, and asked him to come as soon as possible. Didn't that poor girl have enough to deal with without also being ill?

Upon arriving, Luke was met by David. The older man ran his hand through his graying curly hair. "Luke, before you go upstairs, would you mind coming into my study?"

"Of course not. Is Kathleen seriously ill?"

"She vomited, but I believe she is now resting in her room."

In his study, David picked up an envelope from his desk and handed it to Luke.

"What is this?"

"A letter from Karl Wagner to Kat. He has been courting my daughter for about a month."

"Right." Of course, Luke knew precisely how long Karl had been courting Kathleen: thirty-four days. He almost blurted out to David what he had been waiting to tell the man for weeks, that he had seen Kathleen's beau at the brothel. However, before now, Luke had been distracted with Kathleen's injury and treatment.

"He delivered it himself at dinnertime." He paused. "Actually, he tried to call on Kat, but I told him she wasn't feeling well."

David held the envelope out. It wasn't sealed.

"Have you read it?"

"Admittedly, yes, I have. It wasn't sealed, after all. Caroline asked Kat if she wanted to read the letter and she responded that she didn't." He handed it to Luke who held his hand up.

"I don't think I should..." It was addressed to Kathleen and Luke did not want to betray her trust and read it.

"Then I shall read it to you," David said. "'*My dear Kathleen, I was pained to hear that you have been injured in a fall. I send you my fondest wishes and look forward to seeing you very soon. Regards, Karl Wagner.*'"

Luke was perplexed. "Seems innocuous enough."

"Yes, I suppose. Kat had come down for dinner. Jane then announced that Karl was in the foyer, waiting to speak with her. All of a sudden, Kat's face became white as a sheet and she started choking on her food. Then she jumped up from the table and ran down to the basement where Jane says she vomited."

Luke blinked as he thought of the only possible reason for Kathleen's distress. His stomach twisted.

David frowned. "The only disturbing conclusion I can come up with is that Karl is responsible for her injuries. Why else would she react in such a manner?"

"Yes, I agree." In fact, the more Luke thought about it, the more it seemed likely. "David, how did the first letter arrive and when did it arrive?"

"I found it waiting for me on the table by the door when I returned home, the day Kat was hurt. He wrote asking permission to call on her on Sunday. I merely responded to his letter. I didn't know when the letter was delivered. I had assumed Friday."

Luke shook his head and sighed as David continued.

"Did Kathleen say how it arrived?"

"We haven't asked her. However, we did ask Will and John if they saw anyone deliver it and they said they didn't. But they were in the back end of the field. Will did mention that he may have heard a male voice shouting and questioned Kat about it, but she never answered him."

Luke pulled at his necktie and stared intensely at David as the two men came to the same conclusion. There was only one way it could have gotten there: Karl himself had delivered it.

The older man's expression hardened. "That wretched excuse of a man came into my home and tried to rape my daughter. Then he has the audacity to visit my home after the crime? Now I want to kill him."

Luke certainly understood. From deep inside him, he wanted to cause Karl bodily harm as well for hurting Kathleen. "David, Kathleen refused to speak to the police. She told me her attacker threatened her. Besides, Karl's father is the police chief. Without her testimony, the police are unlikely to further investigate."

"I think it's time to talk to Kat...except she isn't speaking to me. Luke, do you think you can convince her to confirm that Karl hurt her? That animal must be stopped."

"I'm not sure she will tell anyone right now. Let me see how she is feeling."

Luke hastily left the study and went upstairs to Kathleen's room. He knocked.

"Who is it?" Her voice sounded impatient.

"Dr. Luke."

No response.

"Kathleen?"

"Come in."

He opened the door and entered her room. She was sitting by the window, staring blankly out the window at the darkness. Her lamp glowed brightly as if it were midday.

"Good day, Kathleen. I hear you're not feeling well."

"I'm fine. The food didn't agree with me." Her tone was flat, unemotional.

"Are you?"

"Am I what?"

"Fine?"

She released a long-winded sigh and turned to look at him with a frown. "What do you want me to say?" she asked sharply.

Luke stepped back. He understood her anger. But if the perpetrator of this crime *was* Karl — which Luke was now convinced it was — then the man should be apprehended quickly and thrown into jail.

"Your father tells me he received a visit from your...beau, Karl." As he guessed, she blanched at the mention of Karl's name.

Kathleen began to tremble. Turning toward the window, she blinked several times, but her eyes were filled with unshed tears. Luke shifted from side to side as he waited for her to speak. Several minutes passed.

She finally made eye contact. "Leave me alone."

"Was Karl the man who hurt you?"

Her eyes glistened and she blinked the tears away.

"He is the one who...hurt you, isn't he?"

Instead of denying it, she sucked in a breath to keep from crying. For Luke, that was all the confirmation he needed.

Her attacker had indeed been the man who had been courting her for the past thirty-four days.

"I don't want my father or anyone to contact the police. I just want to forget the whole incident...and, if you don't mind," she said, her voice rising, "I should like to be left alone."

"Very well."

Luke closed the door and returned to the study downstairs.

David stood by the window, like his daughter had been in her room, looking outside at the landscape painted in darkness. He puffed his pipe, the smoke collecting near the ceiling above him.

"David?"

The older man turned as Luke approached him. "She didn't confirm nor deny it verbally, but her reactions to my questions lead me to believe it *was* Karl who harmed her."

David nearly slammed his pipe down on the desk. "I have his father's address here in Germantown. Perhaps I should send him a nice little note explaining that if I ever see him again, I will kill him. Besides, that animal should be locked up before he can hurt anyone else." He exhaled. "My daughter is not speaking to me. Perhaps I should have a chat with Chief Wagner about his son."

"I don't think that's prudent. Kathleen asked you not to contact the police."

"First of all, she's still not talking to me. Second, I'm not going to the police station. I will merely indicate to the chief that I'd like to speak with him."

Luke shook his head. "If you say anything to Karl's father, don't you think he might tell his son? Karl threatened Kathleen."

"I hope he informs his son that if he ever comes on my property again, I will kill him. That if I ever see him again anywhere, I'll kill him!"

"This isn't the answer, David."

"Come with me, Luke."

***

Luke sat beside David as the older man clicked the reins. Every muscle tensed thinking that perhaps the incident with

Kathleen might have been prevented. Luke had planned to tell David about Karl's visit to the brothel, but he kept putting it off. And now this poor girl was dealing with the aftermath of an assault and attempted rape. Sharing the information about Karl wouldn't prevent anything at this stage, since David already knew what sort of man Karl was.

However, Luke felt an overwhelming sense of responsibility that he was partly to blame for Kathleen's injury. Guilt filled every fiber of his being and he promised himself that someday he would make it up to Kathleen.

David rode up to Chief Wagner's house. Lights were lit in every room, and it was only when they stepped onto the porch that they realized Chief Wagner must be entertaining guests. Would Karl be there as well?

A middle-aged, overweight female servant answered the door.

"Yes?"

"We'd like to speak to Chief Wagner."

"Chief Wagner is occupied for the evening. If you give me a message, I'd be happy to give it to him."

David's face reddened with anger. "We need to speak with him right away." She sighed and opened the door to allow them inside. The foyer was spacious, although not as large as the O'Donovan foyer. The exuberant low-voiced laughter of men came from deep within the house.

"Wait here." The woman ventured off to a distant part of the first floor.

They waited as the laughter died down. Moments later, Chief Wagner appeared in the foyer. "David. And you're the new physician, correct? To what do I owe this pleasant surprise? Mary said it was an emergency. What's the matter?"

David crossed his arms and tapped his foot. "Your son is the matter."

The edges of Chief Wagner's mouth angled down in a frown. "What are you talking about?"

David stepped toward him. Wagner was tall and broad-shouldered and David only came up to the man's chin. "Your son tried to rape my daughter. She was fortunate enough to only sustain a dislocated shoulder, swollen lip, cut chin and numerous bruises as a result," he said sarcastically.

Chief Wagner's mouth fell open, his expression dazed. "What? That's preposterous!"

"He just paid me a visit."

"He is courting your daughter. He had every reason to visit."

"Look, I have an injured daughter who cannot sleep at night because of what your son did to her," he countered.

The man stiffened and shook his head. "My son is courting your daughter, David. And I should think that my son's visit meant he had nothing to do with it."

"My daughter was physically sick during his visit."

"Has she said who attacked her?"

"No."

"There you have it."

With a long sigh, David said, "Make sure he knows that the courtship is off. If he ever comes near Kat again, I will shoot to kill. Do you hear me?"

"David, you're upset. My son is guilty of many things, but attempted rape? I don't think so."

"Your son..."

Chief Wagner cut David off. His face hardened, his lips pursed together. "I'll thank both of you gentlemen to leave my premises."

He was shoving them both out the door, as David blurted, "Tell him if I ever see him again, I will kill him. That's a promise!"

16

The lack of money is the root of all evil. Karl chuckled as he thought of Mark Twain's words. He liked his job at the saloon, but he had spent most of his paycheck on prostitutes or whiskey. At this stage, there were only two options: get money from his father or thievery. As he wanted to keep his job, his father was the logical solution.

The day was clear, the wind cool. He waited until an hour before dusk and traveled by horse. Saturday was his day off from his saloon job and he decided to pay his father a visit, although it was preferable that he not know that Karl was coming. The best case scenario would be that his father not be at home since the man yelled and screamed the last time Karl asked him for money.

It was out of his way, but Karl decided to take a back route to his father's house, by way of the O'Donovan's because he could not stay away from Kathleen. He could still taste her on his lips and feel her trembling body under his. He had had beautiful women before, even forced himself on a few of them, but none were like *her*, with her wide green eyes, smooth pale skin and blond hair. She was meant to be his and he must see her, even if just for a moment.

Near the laneway of the O'Donovan property, Karl steered the horse into the forest, staying just enough inside the greenery to be unseen. Dusk had descended and it was becoming more difficult to see so the horse moved tentatively. There was a full moon tonight, providing enough light to find the way.

He finally arrived at the area of the forest near the O'Donovan's livery stable. He walked the horse a short distance away and tethered her to a tree. The mare needed water, but Karl didn't want to stop so he opted to give the animal an apple instead, then he crept to the area beside the stable. He could hear noises: the regular neighing of horses, but also men speaking — Kathleen's father and another male.

"Jesse, I'd like you to harness Gent and Red to the Cabriolet. I'll be picking up my wife and youngest children."

Karl smiled inwardly. It was Saturday, and that meant fewer occupants at the house. Were the female servants gone as well? This was just too easy.

He stayed behind the trees and sprinted toward the road and away so he could see the front of the house and Kathleen's window. Just a brief glimpse was all he desired. He turned and stared. Karl could only see her shadow; his heart began to beat quickly. Refusal or not, she was beautiful, perfect, still within reach. She just needed to understand her place and who was in control. Of course, this evening, he would settle on taking one particular item. He wouldn't be able to stay long, but knowing there were few people here, he must try to sneak into the house. But how?

***

Kathleen leaned forward in her chair. Her father had left to pick up Mama and the others from next door. Her mother had told Aunt Elizabeth and Alice that Kathleen was still recuperating from her "fall."

"Kat?" Will peered into her room. "Would you like to play chess? I can bring the board and pieces up here."

"I don't think so, Will. Thank you for asking."

"Do you want me to get a book for you?"

She thought for a moment. *My anatomy textbook.* She couldn't attend college, but she could certainly read her textbook. "Yes, Will. Do you see that thick book beside my desk?"

He craned his neck, then walked to the desk. "This one here?" he asked, picking up a heavy brown book. "Anatomy and Physiology for Nurses. Interesting."

"It is. But I cannot hold it because of this sling. Can you find a small table and set it in front of me, then I can turn the pages myself?"

"Of course. I would be happy to do so." He set the book back on her desk and went downstairs.

***

David and the rest of the O'Donovans would return soon. Karl must make his move now. He needed to find a way into the house, take what he was looking for and leave without being seen. He wanted only one thing and he would not leave the house until he had it in his hands. Karl rushed to the back of the livery stable.

There was a narrow pathway between the stable and another outbuilding. Reaching the edge, he could see the basement kitchen door. Chatter to the right made him jerk back and hide in the shadows. The young servant was giggling. Beside her was one of the lookalike older sons. The two passed him and headed toward the livery stable.

This was his opportunity. He sprinted across the grass, heard noises in the kitchen then realized he would need to approach the house from the front. By his estimation, the three servants, one or two of the older boys and Kathleen were the only ones present. He raced to the side of the building, staying below the windows, and finally landed on the front porch. He peered in and one of the older boys was carrying a small table up the stairs. When the young man reached the top and turned, Karl took his chance and crept inside. Looking around, he darted toward the right into the parlor. His eyes scanned the room until they rested on the small photograph of Kathleen atop the piano near the tall window.

Heart pounding, he grabbed it and bolted out, the door banging behind him. Skimming the porch, he rushed around the far side of the house and back to the forest, he hoped, without being seen. He ran, his heart racing a mile a minute. He wanted to stop and enjoy the photograph, but he needed to remove himself from the property. He could stare at the picture when he returned to the boarding house. How he wished he could have gone upstairs, surprised her and finished what he had started. But he could not risk it until he was certain he could get away with it.

***

Will brought the small table into Kat's room and set it in front of her arm chair by the sill.

"Thank you, Will."

"Don't mention it. My pleasure." He picked up the large textbook on her desk and placed it on the table in front of her.

Ellen Gable

"Can you reach the pages?"

"Yes, I think so."

"If you need anything else, please let me know."

Will went to his room next door. It was a beautiful autumn night. Gray dusk had settled into night and the moon shone bright. He squinted and leaned into the window. A flash of metal or...could that be a horse in their forest? Will followed the flash of metal until it disappeared. *Why would someone be in our forest?*

***

Karl arrived at his father's house a short while later. He hitched his horse to the front post and went inside. Mary, the servant, approached him in the foyer. "Mr. Karl? Are you here to see your father?"

"Yes. Where is he?"

"He is gone for the evening."

"Fine." Karl went upstairs to his room, packed some valuables to hock, and opened the door to his father's bedroom. He strolled to the bureau, his boots clicking on the hardware floor. Opening the top drawer, he reached in and took whatever cash was there, stuffing it into his pocket.

He was just getting onto his horse when his father's carriage arrived. Karl would have preferred to completely avoid the man, but he waited for his father to get out.

"Why are you here?"

"Can't a son come and visit his father?"

"You were leaving. You were not going to wait for me. What is going on with you and the O'Donovan girl?"

"Going on? We're courting."

"David O'Donovan and Dr. Peterson paid me a visit."

Karl tensed and clenched his fists. "And what did they say?"

"The doctor said little, but David told me you tried to force yourself on her."

Karl's jaw hardened. *She did not keep her end of the bargain.* "She was going to be my wife. I had every right to have her." He hesitated, staring at his father. "Surely, you'd expect me to show her who the man is, wouldn't you?"

"Perhaps...but she was not your wife...yet." The older

gentleman paused. "If it means anything, David admitted that she did not tell them who attacked her. He only suspects you."

Karl slowly exhaled. *The little wretch did keep her end of the bargain. Good girl.*

"He told me to inform you that the courtship is off."

Karl's hands balled into fists and he squeezed the reins. His heart was pounding and, for a moment, he could hear jumbled words coming from his father.

"How much did you take?"

"What?"

"How much money did you take?"

"What money?"

Shaking his head, his father said, "That's the last time you will ever get money from me. And the last time I shall help you. You are a spoiled, self-indulgent man. The world does *not* revolve around you."

"Fine. I shall head back to my lodgings. I don't have to commit suicide like Mother to escape your tyranny," he spat.

"No more! Do you hear me? Get out of here, Karl!" His father had already raised his hand in a fist.

Karl smirked. "Go ahead. Hit me."

With a scowl, the older man lowered his fist.

"Just as I suspected. You don't have the guts to hit me."

His father swung a punch at his jaw and Karl fell back onto the ground. "Go the hell back to wherever you're staying. And don't come back! Ever!"

Karl rubbed his chin, stood up and climbed onto his horse. He kicked the mare roughly with his spurs and she squealed. As he rode, his breathing slowed.

Well, no matter. He didn't need his father anyway. His most prized possession was the small photograph of Kathleen.

Upon arriving back at his room at the boarding house, the first thing he did was take out the small photo of Kathleen and stare at it. Caressing the frame, he recalled her frightened expression, how he could feel her fear the moment he closed the door of the pantry.

Even now, he could feel her fear and it was...exhilarating.

The O'Donovans were not the brightest people in the

world. He had gone into their home unnoticed and had succeeded in stealing this picture. As much as he'd like to do it again soon, he understood that he must wait. Besides, he would be able to keep Kathleen under his watchful gaze in other ways.

This picture would be his constant companion. And it would serve him well in between visits to Pearl. He sat back and enjoyed the photograph.

***

Will's opportunity to speak with his father came on Sunday when the family arrived home from Mass. It was a rainy, cool October day.

The more he prayed and reflected, the more natural the idea of his being a priest seemed. He had asked for a sign, and received one. Once he had made his decision, it was like the weight of the world had lifted from his shoulders and his soul was at peace.

A priestly vocation would mean giving up the possibility of a wife and children, which Will was content to do.

Will brought the carriage to the barn. Jesse met him at the entrance and helped him take the harnesses off Belle, then walked the mare into the stall.

In the kitchen, Will greeted Jane and Izzy. They were finishing preparations for the afternoon meal. "Mr. Will?"

"Yes, Jane?"

"Tell your Papa that lunch will be served in ten minutes."

"All right."

Taking the staircase up to the first floor, he noted that the door to his father's study was closed, which was a sign that his father was there. He rapped on the door three times.

"Come in, Will."

He opened the door and was greeted with pungent pipe smoke. Will cleared his throat as he adjusted to the odor, although the scent reminded him of when he was a small child playing here. The older man motioned for him to sit in one of the chairs in front of the fireplace.

"Jane said lunch will be served in ten minutes."

"Excellent. I'm hungry."

Will fidgeted in his chair.

"Is there something on your mind, son? With everything that is going on with Kat, I do not want to shirk my responsibility to you."

"You're definitely not the sort to shirk." Will breathed in deeply then exhaled. "I...want to tell you of a decision I have made."

"Decision? Sounds serious."

"It is." He paused. "I think...I am being called to a vocation."

"A vocation?"

"To the priesthood."

His father's neutral expression grew to a wide smile. Then the man nodded and he laughed out loud.

Will scowled. "Is something amusing?"

"No, sorry, son, it's not amusing. I'm very happy...but I must say that I'm not surprised."

"You're not?"

He shook his head. "If anyone is worthy to be a priest, it is you." His father relaxed against the chair. "This is exceptional news. And I can't tell you how happy it makes me."

"You speak of being worthy. I don't know if I'm worthy."

"Priests are human. And I can say without a doubt that your faith is stronger and deeper than most adults I know."

"You're saying that because you're my father."

"Perhaps."

"Then you're pleased?"

"I'm more than pleased. I'm honored that God would call a son of mine to the priesthood." Pausing, he turned toward his bookshelf and pulled out a book called *St. Augustine's Confessions.* "This was helpful to me in my own conversion. You may find it interesting in light of your vocation."

"Thank you, Papa."

"I will contact my friend, Monsignor Flaherty. He'll know how to proceed. And Father Morrissey will give you an excellent recommendation."

"This morning, he asked me if I had ever thought of becoming a priest."

"He must have been happy with your answer."

"His question surprised me, so I didn't know how to respond."

His father laughed. "Leave this with me and I shall schedule a meeting."

Will nodded, then stood up. His father patted him on the back and hugged him. "I love you, Will."

"I love you, Papa."

His hand on the knob, Will turned back to face his father.

"Papa?"

"Yes?"

"You can tell Mama, but I don't want Kat or my brothers to know, not yet, not until I'm sure."

"Very well. But I think *you* should tell your mother. She will be quite happy."

***

One week later, Luke emerged from his carriage in front of the O'Donovan house. It was a beautiful fall Sunday, with a warm breeze, bright sunshine, red and orange trees and a deep blue sky.

Luke handed his coat and hat to Jane, greeted Caroline and David, then went upstairs and knocked gently on Kathleen's door. She opened it and kept silent, stepping back to allow him to enter, but left the door open.

This week she was dressed in a pale blue blouse and a darker skirt. Luke concluded that she looked lovely in blue. Her quiet, somber demeanor didn't diminish either her inner or outer beauty. She still wore the sling, which Luke recommended leaving on for an additional week, just to insure the shoulder had healed well.

Taking the sling off herself, she carefully slipped her right arm out. He turned while she took off her blouse until she was dressed in only her shift and skirt. She sat on the edge of the bed. Luke noticed that she was not wearing a corset.

He sat on the chair and faced her. She rarely made eye contact. Luke wished he could share his feelings with her. However, this wasn't the time nor place to do so.

Luke started with the question "May I begin," then he began by visually examining the arm and shoulder. He realized his hands were trembling slightly, like a foolish schoolboy. He forced himself to focus on the task at hand. When he finished the visual examination, he moved her arm different ways to ensure that the shoulder had healed. Convinced it had, he allowed her arm to drop slightly and asked her to move it. She raised it, at first gently, then down again. He lifted the strap of her shift and noticed that the bruises on her neck and chest were merely faint reminders of her injuries. He tried not to dwell too much on her body and returned the strap to her shoulder. "You may leave the sling off now." She nodded.

Standing, he turned again to allow her privacy to dress. His eyes wandered and came upon the book on her dresser "Poems by Emily Dickinson." He had read some of Dickinson's poems and had liked them.

When a few minutes had passed and the sound behind him had ceased, he turned to face her. She was staring at a painting of herself, an exquisitely painted portrait of a younger, more innocent Kathleen.

Kathleen never seemed to want to engage in any conversation during his examinations. He understood why, but Luke decided to try speaking with her today, in an effort to bring her out of her melancholy. "Beautiful painting. Who's the artist?"

"Izzy."

"Really?" he said, with some astonishment. "She is very talented."

"She made me look beautiful."

Luke agreed, not that the artist had made her look beautiful — she *was* beautiful — but that Izzy had so perfectly captured her beauty and innocence, inside and out. The expression on Kathleen's face was not overly happy; it was merely content. In her eyes, there was a twinkle, like she wanted to play a prank. He stared, mesmerized.

Kathleen remained quiet for several minutes, then finally whispered, "I shall never be that beautiful again."

"You are very..."

She cut him off by choking back a sob.

"Kathleen..." He reached out to touch her shoulder and she flinched. "Please...leave me alone. Just leave me alone."

***

Kathleen straightened, wiping her eyes. She didn't want to be curt with Dr. Luke. He was, after all, only doing his job. There were, in fact, a few aspects of the doctor's personality that she found tolerable. Although she didn't look forward to his visits, he always asked permission to examine her, which the elderly Dr. Mayfield never did. He respected her modesty. He usually attempted to make the examinations more comfortable for her. He calmly and gently spoke to her. No matter what he did, there was always a measure of gentleness, not simply in his manner of touch but in his general demeanor.

"Miss Kathleen?" Jane's voice called through the door.

"Yes?"

"Will you be coming down for lunch today?"

Kathleen wanted to eat the noon meal with the family, but if the doctor remained, she preferred to eat alone. Opening the door, she said, "I think I shall have lunch in my room."

A short while later, Izzy brought a tray of food to the small table near her bed. The young servant turned and studied Kathleen. "Why, Miss Kathleen, your sling is off! How lovely you look and..."

Kathleen forced a smile. She may look normal, but would her heart ever feel...normal again? Karl Wagner had stolen her normalcy. She nodded and closed the door.

***

Luke joined Caroline and David in the foyer.

Will and John were ushering Pat, Kevin and Tim outside to play. At the sound of thunder, Will paused at the front door. "I think it's going to rain," he said.

Caroline responded, "That's fine, Will. Even a few moments of fresh air is better than none. When it starts raining, they can come back inside."

The boys nodded and joined their brothers outside.

To Luke, it seemed like the O'Donovans had become his second family. He felt comfortable in their presence and enjoyed spending time with them.

David accompanied Caroline into the parlor and motioned

for Luke to follow them. Luke glanced at the cradle and the sleeping baby. "How's little Maureen doing?"

"Doing well. For the most part, she's quiet unless she's hungry or her diaper needs to be changed...except for the evenings. She's rather fussy then." She paused. "How is Kathleen this morning?"

"Physically, she's healing well. It is no longer necessary for her to wear the sling."

"Wonderful," she replied.

David nodded. "Sometimes Kat seems devoid of emotion; other times it's the opposite and she begins crying. She still won't speak to me."

The baby began to whimper. Caroline picked her up.

"Do you mind if I speak with Luke in my study, Caroline?"

"Not at all. I shall be taking the baby upstairs."

The two men stood up as Caroline left the parlor, then Luke followed David to the study. The older man lit his pipe and offered a cigar to the doctor. Luke held up his hand to politely decline.

"It's been two weeks. All I can think of is murdering that poor excuse of a man. And it angers me that he's free. He ought to be rotting in a prison."

Nodding, Luke said, "I agree the man should be locked away." A downpour of rain splashed against the window.

Moments later, Luke heard loud squeals and rambunctious laughter. David chuckled. "Boys are a noisy sort."

He and Luke followed the commotion to the foyer where Will and John were ushering the younger boys inside, away from the rain, standing and dripping on the foyer's tile floor.

"Now, everyone stop right there," Jane said firmly. "Wait till we get a few towels to dry you all off."

Tim and Kev started to shiver. "I'm cold," said Kevin.

Then, from the left-hand side of his vision, Luke noticed the blur of Kathleen running past the group. Jane's eyes widened and she turned toward the door.

"What is Kat doing?" David stepped onto the porch, Luke following close behind.

Kathleen was standing in the rain, her back toward the house, her face upward and her arms hanging limply by her sides. David looked at Luke with raised eyebrows.

"She's going to catch a deathly cold out there, Mr. David," Jane said.

Luke didn't wait for Jane or David to give him permission. He sprinted across the lawn. When she heard someone approaching, she said, "The rain is so pure...it will make me pure again."

"Kathleen..."

She turned to face him, the rain rushing like tears down her face. Then she brought her hands to her face and began to sob.

A crack of thunder startled Luke. He quickly became wet, waiting, wondering how to proceed.

Behind him, someone tapped him on the shoulder. He turned to find Jane handing him an umbrella. He stepped forward and attempted to hold it over Kathleen. She shook her head, pushed the umbrella and backed away. Luke continued to hold it over himself.

"How can I ever forgive myself?" she yelled through the rain.

"Forgive yourself? Kathleen, you have no reason to forgive yourself." He wanted to say '*I wish I could have warned your father about Karl sooner...maybe this wouldn't have happened*,' but he didn't.

"I brought him into my house. I trusted him!"

"Kathleen..."

"It *is* my fault. I can't sleep. Every time I close my eyes, his face haunts my nightmares. It's my fault!"

"Kathleen, please come inside."

"I don't want to go inside. I want the rain to wash me away. I want to be the way I was before..."

He leaned forward and attempted to hold the umbrella over her again. This time, she didn't resist. Under the shelter of the wide umbrella, Kathleen looked up at Luke, her sad eyes intensely staring at him. Finally, Luke took off his coat and draped it over her and held his arm over her shoulder as he accompanied her toward the house.

Caroline, David and Jane met them on the front porch. They backed up into the foyer to allow Kathleen and Luke to come inside. The O'Donovan sons were now quietly staring at their sister. Jane took the umbrella from Luke. "Here are fresh towels to dry you off."

Luke moved aside to allow Caroline to care for her daughter.

David reached out to comfort his daughter. She flinched and stepped back. "Please...leave me alone," she whispered.

The older man lingered at the bottom of the staircase as Jane and Caroline assisted Kathleen upstairs.

Luke was worried about Kathleen, but his job here was finished and he needed to return home to finish paperwork and filing. As he turned to leave, he noticed that David remained in the foyer, staring up at the staircase despite the fact that Kathleen was safely upstairs.

"David?"

The man blinked then glanced at him. "Yes?"

"I should be departing."

"Yes, yes, of course," David said, audible stress in his voice.

He had opened the door to leave when David called Luke's name.

"Sorry, Luke. Here is your fee for today." David handed him money. Luke pushed it back in his hands. "You have already paid more than you should have. I will not take any more of your money." This time, the man did not insist.

***

Later that day, two quick knocks indicated that John was in the hallway outside Will's room. It still seemed odd for his brother to knock on a door to a room they had shared for 15 years. Will opened the door. "Come in, John."

John sat on the bed nearest the window, his "former" bed.

"Kat's in a bad way," his brother offered. "Is there anything we can do to help her?"

"Not sure."

"What is going on with her? I hear our parents and Dr. Luke whispering. She gets physically sick. I mean, she just fell, right?"

Will wasn't sure how to answer him, so he remained silent.

"Will?"

"Hmmm?"

"You know something, don't you?"

He nodded. "Kat wasn't injured in a fall. Someone hurt her."

"What do you mean someone hurt her? In our house? While we were here?"

"I overheard Papa and Dr. Luke talking about it."

"That's ghastly." John stared at him, but said nothing for the moment, staring past him at the window.

Then John spoke. "How...old was Michael Bayford when he got married?"

Will sighed as he put his books down and faced his brother.

"You mean that fellow that used to be an acolyte with us when we were younger?"

"Yes."

"I believe he was nineteen. Why?"

"Just wondering."

***

Jane and Mama dried Kathleen's hair and skin as the girl stood before them. Her dress was dripping rainwater onto the floor and would have to be removed. She started to whimper. Her mother pulled her close. "Shhh..." A door slammed from across the hall and, for a moment, Kathleen was distracted from her own ordeal. The baby began to cry. Mama sighed and left.

Kathleen sniffed and wiped her eyes. "Now, now, Miss Kathleen, you're gonna be fine." Jane, who was like a second mother to Kathleen, embraced the young girl, the servant's ample bosom a comforting cushion. Jane smelled of flour and spices, chicken and pastry and, for a brief moment, Kathleen was four years old again.

Jane patted Kathleen's back. She wiped the young girl's tears with her thumbs. "Let's get you out of these clothes and into a warm, dry nightgown."

The servant's clothes were now dark with wetness from Kathleen's embrace.

"I've gotten you wet. I'm sorry, Jane."

"Don't bother yourself with that. A little rain can't hurt my clothes, Miss Kathleen."

Kathleen pulled her right arm carefully through the sleeve

as Jane coaxed the other arm into the nightgown.

Quiet knocking was followed by her mother opening the door. Her mother crossed the room. Kathleen pressed her lips together to keep from crying. "Oh, my dear girl," her mother said. "I'm sorry. Izzy's walking the baby now."

"Miss Caroline, I'll help Izzy with Little Miss Maureen."

"Thank you, Jane."

Jane left and Caroline remained with her daughter, holding her hand.

Kathleen let go of her mother's hand and stared at the pouring rain outside. "I want to feel the way I used to, Mama."

"I know, sweet. I wish I could take away your pain." Her mother was now standing behind her. All of a sudden, she felt Mama's arms gently around her. "I love you, Kathleen." She paused. "What Papa did…"

"I do not wish to speak about him. I shall never talk to him again."

"He only did what we thought was best for you. I agree that he should have called the police."

Kathleen stiffened. She wanted to blurt out a less-than-charitable response, but remained silent in her mother's arms.

17

The rain splashed against the window as Will tried to focus on writing his religion essay. It was Tuesday and he had just returned from school. He sat hunched over his desk. A clap of thunder startled him.

Mama was extremely pleased when he shared the news of his possible vocation. She smiled more, despite the recent difficulties with Kat.

Two more Scripture citations. He straightened and reached into his school bag only to realize that his small Douay-Rheims Bible had not yet been returned to him. *Drat.* He didn't like lending his books to his fellow classmates, specifically for this reason.

Mama kept an antique King James, or Protestant, edition somewhere in the house, but that Bible did not include all the books from the original Latin Vulgate. He knew that the Douay-Rheims, which was the translation of the Bible from the Latin Vulgate, included those missing books.

Didn't Papa tell him once that their family Bible was a Douay-Rheims?

***

Kathleen sat at the piano, her fingers drifting aimlessly across the keys. No melody, just the muted hiss of raindrops against the front window in the parlor blended with the soft sounds coming from the piano. Kathleen had always enjoyed playing, but she never possessed a deep passion for music like the musicians in the symphony orchestras her father took her to see from time to time. She stiffened just thinking of her father and his betrayal.

Lifting her head, she gazed atop of the piano, at mostly small tintypes and photographs: her family down the shore, her maternal grandfather, Kev and Tim. Where was the...she stood and studied each photo. She turned toward her mother, who was sitting on the couch with Tim. "Mama?"

"Yes?"

"Where is my graduation photograph?"

"On the piano, is it not?"

"No. Do you know where it is?"

"No, I don't. That is where we keep most of our small photographs."

Kathleen lowered herself to the piano bench. The picture would surely turn up somewhere.

***

When Will descended the staircase, Pat and Kev were just returning home from school. In the parlor, Will was pleased to see Kat tinkering at the piano. His mother was sitting on the couch and was reading a book to Tim. The baby slept in the bassinet nearby.

"Mama, is the family Bible still in the china closet? And is it a Douay-Rheims?"

"I believe so, Will. Why do you need it?"

"I lent my small Bible to a classmate who hasn't returned it."

"I see. Well, it's in the china closet." She pointed.

He passed through the parlor and into the spacious dining room. This room, which was used for extensive family gatherings as well as the main family meals every day, was three times the size of the parlor. When the long table was removed, a hundred people could comfortably be entertained for special occasions.

Situated at the far end of the dining room was the oak china closet, which held various settings of china, as well as family mementos. Behind the glass doors, in the middle of the second shelf, was the ornate family Bible, brown in color, a large embossed cross on the front. He opened the glass doors, carefully picked up the book and left via the back entrance to an area adjacent to the stairs. His father stood in the foyer looking out at the sheets of rain pummeling the window. He turned when Will entered the foyer.

"What have you got there, Will?"

"The family Bible. I lent mine to a classmate and he hasn't returned it yet."

"Ah."

"I need to search for two Scripture passages. I would be

happy to return it to the china closet as soon as I'm finished."

"That's fine, son."

He ascended the stairs to his room, the book heavy in his arms. When he reached his desk, he realized the book was so large that there was barely enough room to fit on his desk. It took a few minutes, but he found both passages, carefully copying the quotes down on paper. He took his time to make certain that he wouldn't spill one speck of ink on the family heirloom. Once he finished, he closed the Bible and placed it on his bed. He wrote a few sentences, then paused. He promised his father that he would return the book immediately. He picked it up off the bed. Curiously, he opened it to the first page.

"Family Record - O'Donovan Family"

He turned the page.

Marriages
Liam Francis O'Donovan - Caroline Martin
October 7, 1876
Births
Kathleen Emma O'Donovan   July 15, 1877

On the next page, he found the entry for his parents' marriage:

Marriages
David John O'Donovan - Caroline Martin O'Donovan
May 14, 1877 (Episcopal)
January 8, 1879 (Roman Catholic)

On the next page:

Births

John Liam O'Donovan	*Dec 12, 1879*
William David	*1879*
Patrick Andrew O'Donovan	*Nov 11, 1882*
Kevin Michael O'Donovan	*Jan 19, 1887*
Timothy James O'Donovan	*Oct 10, 1891*
Maureen Caroline O'Donovan	*Aug 16, 1896*

Will lifted his head and read the births one more time. He knew that Papa was not Kat's blood father and that Mama's first husband, Papa's brother Liam, was.

But why were there two dates for his parents' marriage? And why was his family name not included? Why did this record omit his birth month and day and only have the year? He stared again at the names and dates, as if he might be able to decipher the reason. However, after reading and re-reading, Will could not fathom why his birth was out of order with the others, why his parents had two marriage dates and why his last name wasn't written in ink after his Christian names.

His mother would know the answer. This was her script. He clapped the Bible shut and, carrying it flush against his chest, he went downstairs. Mama was still reading to Tim, and Kat continued to play the piano. Kev was flicking marbles and Pat and John were playing chess at the table in the middle of the room.

"Mama?"

His mother looked up from the book. "Yes, Will?"

"I have a question for you...about the family history at the front of this Bible."

His mother frowned and blinked her eyes. Her already pale complexion turned white as a sheet. "Oh...yes. What is your question?"

"Why is my name listed second rather than first of the births of your marriage to Papa? And why no month or day listed? Why is my last name not included?"

"Speak slowly, Will." Mama forced a smile.

"Why do you and Papa have two marriage dates?"

Mama whispered to Tim and handed the book to him.

"Kathleen?" His sister stopped playing and turned. "Yes?"

"Would you be so kind as to finish reading this book to Tim?"

"Of course."

"Come with me, Will." Near the staircase, his mother put her hand on his shoulder. Mama wasn't an unusually small woman, but at five feet three inches tall, she was much shorter than Will's five feet nine inch frame. Today he seemed to tower over her. She pointed toward the study. "I think your father may want to participate in this discussion."

"What...discussion?" Will's eyes narrowed as he stared at his mother in bewilderment.

She knocked on the study door. "David?" Opening the door, she went in. She mumbled something to Papa, at which point, his father's eyes widened and he looked past her at Will.

"Yes, of course."

The older man set his book down and motioned for Will to follow them upstairs to their room. Will wondered what necessitated all the secrecy. Wasn't this just a mistake?

His parents entered their room first. His mother went to her dresser and removed a packet of papers. His parents carried on a whispered conversation, then Papa pulled an arm chair close and placed it across from them. "Take a seat."

Will sat in the chair and rested his elbows on the marble arms.

"Will..."

Papa tilted his head to the side and leaned forward. "We have some news for you." His father was stone-faced; his mother was avoiding eye contact.

"This is something that we have delayed too long. Now that you're seventeen, you should know — have a right to know — more about your background. I suppose we should have had this discussion years ago, but it never seemed the right time."

"Background?"

"Yes," Mama said. She was holding a small packet of papers in front of him. "These are from your...mother."

"My mother? What do you mean? You're my mother."

"Yes, Will, but I did not give birth to you."

"I...don't...understand."

She glanced at Papa, but kept silent.

His father spoke. "Your mother came to us when she was ill and asked us to take care of you."

All of a sudden, Will felt like he had been punched in the stomach. His parents weren't actually his parents? "Wait. Do you mean to tell me that I am adopted and that..."

"Will..." His father's lips were pressed together in a slight grimace. As the older man pulled at his collar, he opened his mouth to speak, then merely sighed.

"This can't be right, Papa. I look like John. I look exactly like *you*."

The man hesitated, then quietly said, "Yes, son, you do, because I *am* your real father."

"Wait a minute. I...I don't understand."

"Will, your real mother — her name was Missy — was a servant with my family for years. She then worked at a saloon...and I...well, we..."

Finally, Will understood. He sank back in the chair and covered his mouth. His parents' voices were a muffled jumble of words. He blinked several times to try to comprehend it all. Everything he had believed about his life was a lie. He had been conceived out of wedlock, the product of lust, a bastard.

Will held his hands over his ears and shook his head. Then he rushed out of the room, slamming the door behind him. Stumbling down the back steps, he ran through the kitchen and out the back door. He heard Jane's voice call to him. "Mr. Will, what's wrong?"

He didn't know where he was going, but he needed to be as far away as possible.

***

Will remained in the barn for hours. He could hear his father searching for him, but he did not wish to be found so he kept silent.

This was Papa's fault. His father and a servant? This was not the father Will knew. Papa was a devout, church-going man. How could it be that Will was not conceived within the legitimate bonds of marriage, but in a moment of lust?

Why had they waited so long to tell him? He tried to pray, but he couldn't. How could God allow Will to be conceived in lust, rather than in the loving embrace of a marital union? How could God be calling him, a bastard, to the priesthood? Will had obviously been mistaken. God could not be calling a man whose life began in an illicit manner to a holy vocation.

Will pounded at the hay, then one of the horses neighed, a cow mooed and the odor of fresh manure made his eyes water. The barn seemed the appropriate place for him now.

Many questions lingered. Mama was not the one at fault here. Her choices had only been good, loving ones. Papa, on the other hand, had made an immoral choice and Mama agreed to raise the consequence of that 'choice' as her own. How difficult that must have been. And yet Will never felt anything but love from her.

As the darkness in the barn closed in around him, Will realized that he must eventually leave his hiding place. He carefully emerged and headed to the basement kitchen. He wanted to sneak up to his bedroom via the back staircase. Unfortunately, Jane stopped him by reaching for his arm. "Mr. Will, your parents are looking for you."

He pulled his arm back and scowled. "I know. I do not wish to be found."

"Now, Mr. Will, it's not like you to talk like that."

He exhaled. "Well, it's not like my parents to lie to me for my entire life."

Jane opened her mouth, closed it and nodded. "Mr. Will, I don't know what's going on in that head of yours, but your parents did the best they could. Missy was sick and you would've ended up in an orphanage. They did the right and honorable thing for you."

"The right and honorable thing? Are you serious, Jane?" He leaned close to her face. "Being illegitimate is a right and honorable thing?" he asked in a raised tone.

"Hush, Mr. Will. Sometimes good people make mistakes. And sometimes God takes a mistake and makes a good thing. That good thing was you."

Will stepped back and folded his arms in front of his chest. Since the revelation of how he was conceived, he stopped believing that he was a "good thing."

"You best find your father and talk to him. I believe he has some papers and a photograph for you."

A photograph? Was it a picture of his real mother? And did Will want to see the picture of the former servant who willingly gave her body to his father?

"Mr. Will, your ma was a kind woman who loved your father. Your father didn't love her, but he was a different man back then."

"You knew *her*?"

"I did. She worked as a servant here for years. She came back to be a wet nurse for John since your mother was sick."

Will sighed. His "mother" had nursed John. Why didn't that console him?

"And she loved you very much."

He scoffed.

"Now, go on," Jane admonished. "I think your father is in his study. When you're hungry, I've got a warm plate of food for you."

Will's shoulders relaxed and he nodded. He didn't want to have this conversation with his father. He was angry that his father had lied to him, angry that he was conceived in a moment of lust. But Jane was right. His father deserved to be heard.

From the basement kitchen, he trudged up the staircase to the foyer then crept towards his father's study. He straightened, held his fist out to knock, then pulled back. Shaking his head, he knocked with three firm knocks. Will could hear his father's approaching footsteps. Opening the door, Papa said, "Will, thank God. Where have you been?"

"In the barn, behind the horse stall."

"John said he checked the barn. I checked the barn."

"Obviously not well enough. I was there. I heard you both."

"Come in, son." Will cringed. It now bothered him that his father called him 'son.'

David turned two chairs to face one another, then sat down in one. "I owe you an explanation, and I hope you can forgive our decision to wait so long to tell you."

"Tell me about *her*."

David pursed his lips and exhaled. "She was a servant who worked here for a few years. She left, I married Caroline, then I...well, I had stopped drinking, then started again. I don't really remember anything."

"That's just grand," Will said curtly.

"Son, please...I didn't know you were mine until Missy told Jane she was sick and needed us to care for you. Missy didn't want you to go to an orphanage."

"How noble," he said sarcastically.   Even Will was surprised at how cutting his tone was.

"Will, please." He turned toward the desk. His father picked up a packet of papers, a tin type and other miscellaneous items. "We promised Missy — your mother — that we would give these to you."

Will took the items from his father and, all of a sudden, he wanted to be alone. He stood up, his father's eyes following him.

"Will?"

He stared at his father, but remained silent.

"Your mother and I formally adopted you when you were three. You are very much legitimate now. We had your last name legally changed to O'Donovan."

He shrugged and turned to leave.

"Will?"

He turned and made eye contact.

"I love you, son."

Will left without responding.

Back in his room, Will placed the items on his bed and picked up the old photograph first. He gasped. Staring at the gray-orange image of himself as a toddler and a woman, this was the woman in his dreams. She was pretty with dark hair, dark eyes and a small dimple in her chin.

He had always wondered where he got the dimple in his chin; it was often the only difference others could see between the two oldest O'Donovan brothers.

In the photo, the woman, his mother, wasn't smiling.

He set the picture aside and picked up what looked to be a baptismal certificate, issued by St. Peter and Paul Cathedral for a William David Callahan, birthday, June 15, 1879. *June?* All these years, his father lied to him about another aspect of his life. Every February 15, they celebrated his birthday, and his father knew it wasn't really his birthday. He dropped the paper and clenched his fists.   His father was listed as David O'Donovan, birth mother, Melissa Callahan, adoptive mother, Caroline O'Donovan. He sighed.

Date of baptism, *October 4, 1881.*

Will returned to his father's study with the baptismal

certificate in hand. He knocked three times. His father opened the door. "Will?"

Will stepped into the room and shut the door. He held the paper up in front of his father's face.

"Why would Roman Catholic High School accept me with this birth certificate? They must know that I am illegitimate."

His father's head lowered and he spoke softly. "Come in." He motioned for Will to sit by the fireplace. "I donated generously to the building fund. They agreed to accept you with this birth/baptismal certificate."

Will gasped. Now, he understood all the times that he had been passed over for an important task despite his academic excellence. Now he understood why the principal had always acted uncharitably toward him.

"So you *bribed* them?"

"It was not a bribe. I explained that this was an exceptional case and they should allow you to attend. It was a brand new school; they agreed because they needed the money."

Will released a long, exasperated sigh and ran his hand through his hair. "So the school staff knows I'm illegitimate?"

"You do not need to keep using that term."

"That is what I am. Who else knows?"

His father's head bowed down, as if in prayer. "Only the principal knows, to my knowledge."

Will rapidly blinked his eyes to remove the tears. This was too much information to think about.

Back in his room, he knelt down. "Dear God, help me to make sense of this. Why have You allowed this?" Again, his eyes watered, but he blinked the tears away. Crying would not make him legitimate any more than praying would.

His eyes were drawn to an envelope addressed to "My darling boy, Will." *A letter from her*. He traced the scripted letters that she had written to him when she knew she was dying and needed to find him a place to stay.

Will wasn't ready to read her message yet. He gathered up the tintype and slipped the other items in his dresser drawer and headed to Kathleen's room.

***

Several knocks woke Kathleen from a restless slumber. She sat up and stretched. "What is it?"

"May I come in, Kat?" Will's voice held an urgent tone.

"Yes."

Will opened the door.

"What time is it?" Kathleen squinted at the clock on the mantel.

"Nine p.m."

Kathleen sighed. "Where have you been, Will? Mama and Papa were worried."

Will had a photograph in his hand.

"What is that, Will?"

He didn't respond; instead, he stared blankly at the photo.

"Is anything wrong?"

"Mama is not my mother."

Kathleen's mouth opened and she stared intently at him. "So they finally told you?"

"The family Bible has John's name listed before mine. I questioned it."

"I see. That does make sense." She paused. "I have a faint memory of when you came to our home, but it wasn't until recently that I understood the whole story. I urged Mama and Papa to tell you that you were adopted."

Kathleen glanced at the photograph in his hands. "May I?"

He held out the tintype and Kathleen took it. The woman in the photo was pretty, although not in a sophisticated upper class way. She looked familiar. Little Will had the slightest expression of annoyance written on his face and Kathleen couldn't help but grin. "She's very pretty...and you were a handsome boy."

With a shrug, he said, "I still cannot fathom it. I still cannot believe what Papa...did."

"What do you mean? What did Papa do?"

"That Papa...well...if you know...."

"Know what? What did Papa do?"

"Kat, Papa is my *real* father."

"W...w...hat?" Kathleen sputtered. "No, Will. You must be mistaken. Mama and Papa brought you up and took care of you. They adopted you."

"Kat, he and a servant, Missy," he held the photo in her face, "they were...together...he is my real father."

Kathleen's chest tightened and her mouth fell open. Looking at Will's face, staring at his features, of course, he was Papa's true and natural son. Why had she not realized it before now?

When she glanced at Will, his eyebrows were raised and he was staring at her, incredulous. "You mean...you didn't know?"

Shaking her head, she said, "I knew you were adopted. I was only four so I vaguely remember when you came to live with us. But I certainly didn't know that Papa was your true father. I thought...well, it doesn't matter what I thought. I was foolish not to see that you are more his child than I."

"I cannot believe it. That he could stoop so low as to..."

"He's not like that anymore, Will. He's a good man..." She stopped, realizing that she was defending her father.

"Sounds like you've already forgiven Papa."

Kathleen shook her head. "I haven't. Not yet."

Will cleared his voice. "Did you know that I was discerning a vocation to the priesthood?"

She gasped, a smile forming. "A vocation to the priesthood would be a beautiful gift to this family. And, I dare say, I'm not surprised."

"That's what Papa said, but it's obvious that I'm mistaken. God could not be calling someone like me. How can I even consider a vocation?"

"The manner in which you were conceived is not your fault. Why are you blaming yourself?"

"I'm not, but I'm illegitimate."

"That's ridiculous. The circumstances of your birth are less-than-ideal, but you are a full-fledged part of this family. Besides, no one else knows."

"You're wrong. People whisper. Gossipmongers have a difficult time forgetting. My baptismal certificate lists my real mother's name."

Still, as much as she tried not to show it, Kathleen was nearly dizzy with shock. Papa engaged in illicit activity? It was so foreign a concept to her that she had a hard time believing it. But staring at Will, there was no denying that he was definitely Papa's son.

18

The post-Mass lunch each Sunday at the O'Donovan house was the highlight of Luke's week. When he walked inside the house this beautiful and sunny day, he was greeted with the faint but tantalizing scents of bacon and coffee. Jane welcomed him.

Luke ascended the stairs and knocked on Kathleen's door. He waited for a few seconds. The door swung open. Kathleen scowled, then sighed. She had her robe on. "My shoulder has healed. There's no need to examine me today."

"Very well," Luke said. "How are you feeling?"

She let out a winded sigh. "What do you wish me to say? That I'm doing fine? Well, I am fine."

Luke straightened, but did not attempt to step into her room. She was correct. Her shoulder and bruises had already healed well when he examined her last week. He lowered his head. "Very well." She had already closed the door when he offered, "I shall be downstairs if you need me."

"I shall not need you. Thank you. Good-bye," was her curt response through the closed door.

Luke understood her abrupt manner and, in fact, felt he deserved it, if one considered his responsibility and the guilt that he continued to carry.

Kathleen had physically healed well, but he suspected it would take a long time to recover emotionally. He couldn't imagine a worse scenario for a young girl than to be assaulted by a man she trusted. Gentlemen were not supposed to use the fairer sex to feed their lusts and discard them. Luke was grateful that she had had the foresight to injure him so he would stop. Kathleen could have been left with child.

***

After lunch, Luke joined David, Caroline and the older boys as they gathered in the parlor. Will, John and Pat were sitting on the sofas near the fireplace. David and Caroline were at a couch near the window. Luke sat in an arm chair beside them. The older man always looked at his wife with adulation and rapt attention, almost as if no one else were in the room. David caressed his wife's shoulder and held her hand. It was obvious that this couple was very much in love and Luke was envious.

David glanced at Luke. "How about a game of chess?" David had already stood up and was motioning for Luke to join him at the chess set situated between the two sofas lining the fireplace. Should Luke tell David that he was the chess champion of the 1892 graduating class of the University of Pennsylvania? Should he tell him that he knew the book "Chess Exemplified" better than he knew his medical textbooks from college? Yes, that would be the proper and fair attitude. "David?"

The older man didn't respond.

"Sir?"

"Yes?"

"I ought to inform you that I was the 1892 University of Pennsylvania chess champion."

"Oh?"

"Perhaps you will decide not to play against me."

"Nonsense. I haven't lost a game since I was fourteen."

"Very well. White or black?"

"White. I prefer to move first."

Two hours later, David still possessed his king, queen and a few pawns. His sons and his wife had shouted with glee when David had finally captured Luke's rook and groaned loudly when Luke had captured David's queen. Success in chess depended on staying ahead of your opponent, so Luke focused on anticipating David's four or five possible moves.

David was an extraordinary competitor as most players had never lasted this long against Luke. But the older gentleman was now down to a few pieces. Luke still had all his major pieces with the exception of his knight and his rook.

All of a sudden, a female cleared her throat behind him. He turned to find Kathleen standing at the doorway, watching. The vision of her in a blue and green dress, her hair cascading down her shoulders, jolted him and his mouth fell open. For a moment he couldn't think of any rational thought.

When he tried to focus on the game again, his mind became

foggy. Within minutes, David had captured his queen. Luke shook his head to refocus and finally cornered David's king, uttering "Checkmate!" They shook hands.

"Dr. Luke, Papa has never lost!" Will exclaimed.

"Yes, I can understand why. He's a fine player."

"I should like to play against you." In the cacophony of the voices praising Luke's win, Kathleen's words were so quiet, Luke wasn't sure that he heard them properly and he turned to face her.

"I should like to play against you," she said, raising her voice. Kathleen was still standing in the doorway of the parlor.

"Kat, Dr. Luke is a better player than me. I should think that you do not have a chance against him," David commented.

She ignored her father and made eye contact with Luke. "I should like to play against you."

Luke's eyes narrowed. He was faced with a dilemma. He most certainly would win, but how competitively should he play against a female? Of course, Kathleen was not just any female. She was a girl he hoped would return his affections one day. Perhaps he should not agree.

"I should like very much to play against you, Kathleen, but I must be going." Standing, he walked toward the door.

"Are you afraid to compete against a woman?"

He raised his eyebrows and turned to face her. "No, I..."

"Then I should like to play against you."

He sighed and returned to his seat in the parlor. "Very well."

"There is only one rule," she said.

"And what is that?"

"You must be honest in your playing."

"Pardon me?"

"You may not let me win. You must play honestly and as competitively as you did against my father."

Luke gulped and cleared his throat. His cravat seemed to be cutting off his airway. Had it become excessively warm in this room?

David finished setting up the pieces on the board and asked, "Luke, white or black?"

"I shall let Kathleen decide."

"White," she said.

"You may move first then, Kathleen," Luke offered.

Luke could not seem to concentrate. He could not believe that Kathleen had captured his bishop. Usually, he utilized his bishop excessively and without it, he had to resort to other less versatile pieces. His mouth narrowed into a thin line and he took a deep breath as she considered her next move. He set his mind to focus, trying his best to ignore her: her holly green eyes, her soft pale skin, her shiny golden hair covering her shoulders.

She slid her queen four spaces, took her hand off the piece and exposed it to his knight. David groaned out loud. Luke studied her face and her eyes were staring at her queen. She glanced at his knight and, sighing, realized her mistake, but now it was too late. He cornered her king, called "Checkmate," and she placed her king on its side. With a smile, she said, "Good game, Doctor."

"You play extremely well for..." Luke stopped.

"For a what?"

"I...uh..."

"I play extremely well for a girl?"

Luke gulped and loosened his cravat.

"I couldn't concentrate," she said. "Besides, I let you win."

"What? You said we needed to play honestly."

"I said that *you* needed to play honestly."

Luke stepped back and frowned. This girl was becoming unpredictable.

***

Kathleen sat and smugly considered the game she had just played with the young doctor. She wanted to see what sort of character he was, would he allow her to win, or would he play to win like he had done with her father?

She didn't want to admit it, but she told a white lie: she didn't lose on purpose. Her concentration was poor these days, and Luke was indeed an excellent player.

***

David escorted Luke to his carriage. "Luke, might I ask you a question?"

"Of course."

"Is there something you would like to ask me about my daughter?"

Luke stared, his mouth open, although he couldn't find any words. Could this man read his mind? Finally, he stuttered. "I...don't know what...you mean."

"I've been watching you interact with my daughter. The way you look at her, it seems that you might be, shall I say, fond of her?"

"I...don't know what to say."

"Let me make it easy for you."

"Easy for me?"

"Do you have feelings for my daughter?"

"Uh...well, I..."

"I can see how you stare at her, like she's a prize you'd like to win. You love her, don't you?"

Luke sucked in a breath, his mouth slackening. "Is it that obvious?"

"Probably not to her. But it is to me. Besides, Jane and Caroline have also noticed how you stare at Kat. They are both keen observers."

Luke took a deep breath, then exhaled. With a nod, he admitted, "Yes. I've loved her practically from the moment I first met her."

David patted him on the back and smiled.

Luke continued. "I cannot ask your permission to court her yet...she is still healing emotionally. I intend to wait as long as I have to, if she is agreeable."

"I can't speak for Kat, but you have proven your good character on many occasions. You have my blessing to ask her whenever you feel the time is right."

"Thank you, David." He paused. "A few months ago, I had just about garnered my courage to ask you when Karl stepped in."

David sighed. "I wish you had asked her first."

19

Yesterday, for the first time in many months, Will chose not to attend Saturday morning Mass at St. Vincent's. Saturday Mass was not compulsory, but Will regretted not going. He missed the peace and joy that Mass and the Eucharist always gave him.

He couldn't face God, not yet. In the past few days, prayer did not come easily. His anger remained: with his father, with God. He needed to go to confession. Knowing that their parish priest heard confessions Saturday afternoon, Will had asked his father if he could take the carriage into town for a short time.

At the church, there were two people in line for confession. When it was his turn, he confessed that he had spoken harshly to his father. Fr. Morrissey, recognizing his voice, had said, "Will? I didn't see you in Mass this morning. Is anything wrong?"

So much for anonymity. "No, Father." Will explained that he hadn't been feeling well and this had impacted his prayer/sacramental life. Fr. Morrissey advised him to think of others and to give others the benefit of the doubt. Fr. Morrissey then gave him his penance and said the prayer of absolution.

Earlier today, Will had watched curiously as his sister and Dr. Luke played chess. She obviously was not feeling herself. What else would explain the challenge of a girl to a man who had just won against their father, a man who hadn't lost a game in recent history? She played well, but she was no match for their father and would be no match for Dr. Luke. Dr. Luke appeared to be distracted and fidgety, his eyes shifting from the board to Kat.

Will waited while his father saw the doctor out, then met him in the foyer.

"Papa?"

David looked up, his eyes soft in anticipation. "Yes, Will?"

"May I speak with you in your study?"

"Of course."

The two settled in chairs in front of the fireplace. "Papa, I'm sorry for being curt with you last week."

"I understand why you were upset. You had every right to be angry with me."

Will heaved a sigh. "Like it or not, this is who I am. I'm going to need to become accustomed to my new identity."

"You don't have a new identity. You are the same person you have always been."

He remained silent.

"You must remember that even though I did something wrong, something beautiful came forth from that."

Will wanted to retort that he certainly didn't feel beautiful now. But he didn't.

His father continued. "I accept your apology." He stood up and placed his hands on his son's shoulders. His father then hugged him so tight that Will had difficulty breathing. He stepped back. "I love you, Will. I hope you can forgive me for what I've done."

Will nodded and left.

***

That night after supper, Will knocked on Kat's door and asked if she wanted to play a game of chess with him in the parlor. She stood in the doorway, giving the offer some thought. She finally said, "Yes, I would like that very much."

As they passed by their parents' room, their door was slightly open. They heard their father speaking, "He likes Kat. He plans to ask permission to court her in the future."

Kat whispered, "Wait."

"He's a good man, David."

"Yes, he is."

Will leaned close and whispered, "What man are they talking about?"

"Shhh. I don't know."

Her father's voice. "I wish I could've known what sort of man Karl was or I wouldn't have given my permission. I feel like a fool." He paused. "Luke is a fine gentleman." Kat gasped.

"He says he will wait as long as is necessary," their father's voice said.

Will stepped back. Dr. Luke liked his sister?

"I can't believe it!" Kat whispered and leaned against the wall of the hallway. "Why would he want to..." Kat took hold of his shirt and pulled him toward the staircase. "Come on, Will."

"Come on?"

"Let us pay a visit to the good doctor."

"What?"

"I'm going to tell him what I think of him asking to court me!"

"Wait, Kat, no. If you don't want to court him, just say no when he asks."

"Why does he like me? Why would he want to court me? I will tell you why. He feels sorry for me. Take me to see him."

"Not until you promise you will be charitable. He's a good man."

"Good man or not, I should like to speak with him."

"After all he's done for you?"

"He's a doctor. I'm his patient. That's where it ends. I'm not a piece of chattel to be auctioned off to the highest bidder."

"No one is auctioning you off. Papa just said..."

"Come."

Will sighed and followed his sister outside.

***

In the carriage, Kathleen formulated what she would say to the young doctor. How dare he speak of courting her! The only possible reason he would want her was because he felt sorry for her; but she would not accept his or anyone else's pity.

At Luke's house, Will assisted Kathleen down and they approached the door to his office. Will stood on the edge of the porch behind her. She banged loudly. Luke opened the door and gasped. "Kathleen? Is everything all right?"

"Yes, but I need to speak with you...now!"

"Kathleen, it's...uh....a pleasure, but, as you can see, I am ...otherwise occupied. I can't...what I mean is...I don't have time to...I'm pleased that you're up and about, but I must...tend to an injured girl...may we speak another time?"

"An injured girl?" In her self-centered quest to see — and accuse — Dr. Luke, Kathleen never considered that he might be occupied, but he was, after all, a physician. She immediately recognized that she had been cold and callous. "May I be of some assistance?"

Luke's eyebrows lifted as if, before her offer, it hadn't occurred to him that her arrival was fortuitous and that she could help. He nodded. "By all means, please." To Will, he said, "Would you be so kind as to wait at the carriage?"

"Certainly."

Luke opened the door, "Come in. Please do not be alarmed, but there is a seriously injured girl in my examining room. I'm trying to tend to her wounds.

He opened the door that led to the examining room. Kathleen stepped inside. A young girl lay on her side on the table, moaning and bleeding from multiple lacerations on her face. A blanket covered her. Her exposed arms were soiled and bleeding. As they reached the table, the girl vomited on the table and it dripped down onto the floor.

"I can clean that, Dr. Luke." Kathleen turned on the faucet, filled a basin with water and wiped up the mess. Luke was silent as he examined the girl on the table. Kathleen didn't want to stare, but she watched as Luke folded down part of the blanket. The girl's blouse was torn and she was bleeding from several wounds.

All of a sudden, she became quiet.

Luke leaned close to Kathleen and whispered. "I don't know how she ended up on my porch. I don't even know her name. I've telephoned the Pennsylvania Hospital to have an emergency carriage on standby. I will be taking her there for future treatment. Her injuries are likely too severe to handle on my own."

"Who could have done such a dreadful deed?"

"I don't know," he said, another sigh escaping his lips.

Kathleen stared at the bruised and beaten girl. She was a pretty, big-boned girl, with ample breasts and wide hips.

Luke tenderly cleaned her wounds, but the girl remained unconscious.

"Kathleen, would you mind asking Will to ride to St. Vincent's to see if Fr. Morrissey is available for the Last Rites? This girl does not have long, I'm afraid."

She hurried out to the carriage where Will was sitting, his head bowed, his lips quietly moving.

"Will, can you hurry to St. Vincent's and get Fr. Morrissey? Tell him it's urgent."

"Yes, of course."

Will left immediately, his voice rising as he tried to get the horse to gallop quickly.

Back in the exam room, Luke checked the girl with his stethoscope and, even though she was unconscious, he still warmed the bottom of it before placing it on her chest to listen. "Her heartbeat and pulse are weak. I wish there was more I could do for her."

Within moments, Father Morrissey had arrived, along with his crucifix, holy oil and holy water. He set them up next to the girl, who remained unresponsive.

Fr. Morrissey recited prayers, blessed the girl, anointed her and turned to the group behind him, asking if they would recite the Litany of the Saints with him.

Afterwards, the priest offered a blessing to the three and blessed the young girl again. "Tragic for this sweet lass to be so mistreated."

"Do you recognize her, Father?" Luke asked.

"No, I don't."

Luke escorted the priest to the door. "Thank you, Father."

Kathleen and Will walked with him to the carriage then Will took the elderly cleric back to the rectory.

On returning to the examining room, Luke leaned over the girl.

Was she awake?

"What?" he whispered into the girl's ear.

Kathleen joined him and marveled at the tenacity of this young woman who was fighting for her life and who seemed to have a strong will to live. With her eyes still closed, the girl managed to say, "My...father...hurt me...father hurt me."

With that declaration, the young woman's head bobbed to the side, and her body became limp. Kathleen drew in a breath and stepped back. She glanced at Luke who had blanched at the words.

"Is she...gone?"

Luke felt the side of her neck. His head lowered and he nodded. "Deus misereatur animae...may God have mercy on her soul." He covered her body with a blanket.

Without looking up, he crossed the room to the telephone on the wall. He cranked the side of it and picked up the earpiece. "Operator, this is Dr. Peterson from Germantown, phone number GER 132. Can you connect me to the Pennsylvania Hospital, please?" He was silent for a moment, his head lowered. "Hello. This is Dr. Peterson from Germantown. If the emergency carriage has not already left, I will need a coroner's carriage to pick up the body of a young woman who has just died from her injuries. Yes. Yes. An hour? Thank you."

He turned to face Kathleen. "An hour until the carriage arrives." Luke returned to the exam table and tenderly caressed the young girl's battered face. "Requiescat in pace."

Kathleen could not get this young girl's last words out of her mind. If what the girl said was correct, her father had beaten her to death. Fathers were supposed to protect, love and care for their daughters, not beat them to death.

Suddenly, her father's distraught face came to her mind. She hadn't spoken to him since he contacted the police. He did not respect her wishes, but he had only been trying to protect her. Her father was a kind, gentle and good man. She blinked the tears away.

Luke cleared his throat. "Would you care for some tea? My housekeeper has gone for the day, but I think I can manage."

"No. I should be going."

"Kathleen?"

"Yes," she said, facing him.

"I'm not sure what precipitated your desire to visit, but I'm very glad you did. I am grateful for your assistance."

"I was happy to help."

"Did you want to speak to me?"

"No, no, everything is fine. Good day, Dr. Luke."

"Good day, Kathleen."

***

As soon as Kathleen left, Luke placed another phone call, this time to the police. An officer took information from Luke over the telephone, but informed him that, without knowing the girl's identity, it would be difficult to find and prosecute the father.

***

On the way home, Kathleen said little, and Will didn't prod her. She was sucking in her breath as she tried not to cry. Will couldn't fathom what would possess a man to beat anyone, let alone this young woman, in such a violent manner. First, his sister, now this girl. What was wrong with some men?

"I need to see Papa," she said.

Facing her, he nodded. "We'll be home in less than ten minutes."

Will wondered what made his sister change her mind so suddenly and want to see — and talk to — their father. Until now, she had been so angry with Papa for calling the police. Anytime they were near each other, the tension was thick enough to make anyone in the vicinity steer clear.

***

When Kathleen and Will returned home, they were greeted by frantic parents with worried expressions. Jane was scowling. Baby Maureen was in her mother's arms as they all stood in the spacious foyer.

"Where have you been, Kathleen?" her mother asked.

"I asked Will to take me... somewhere."

Her mother handed the baby to Jane, stepped forward and placed her hands on Kathleen's shoulders. "You haven't left this house in over three weeks. You've rarely left your room. All of a sudden, you were gone and we were sick with worry!"

"I'm fine, Mama. I just...we went for a carriage ride."

"Carriage ride? Where?" her father asked. She looked at her father. The anger and resentment that she had felt toward him had dissipated. Papa was a loving, caring father who was devastated that she had been assaulted. She hated that he contacted the police against her wishes, but he only did so because he loved her and cared for her. She fell into his arms and embraced him. "Oh, Papa, I love you." She began to cry.

"Shhh, Kat, it's fine. Why are you crying?"

Kathleen stepped back. "I'm sorry I haven't been speaking to you."

He caressed the side of her face. "I'm happy that you're talking to me again."

She nodded.

Her father whispered a few words into her mother's ear, then she watched her mother nod her assent. The older women and Will left the room, leaving Kathleen and her father standing awkwardly by the staircase, with neither making a move to leave the room.

"Kat?"

"Yes, Papa?"

"I'm sorry. I know you asked me not to contact the police, but...I just felt so helpless....and I love you so much, I couldn't stand to see you hurting."

"I know, Papa. I don't care anymore." Kathleen's eyes began to tear. "It wasn't your fault. It was mine. And now...." She hesitated, then she began to weep and he took her in his arms.

"Shhh...It wasn't your fault."

Kathleen stepped back. As she wiped her eyes, her father handed her his handkerchief. She said, "I know you were trying to do what was best for me."

"Perhaps someday you'll understand when you have children of your own."

Children of her own? Kathleen could no longer envision getting married or having children, not now, perhaps not ever.

20

Luke helped to place the dead girl's body into the back of the coroner's carriage.

His next telephone call was to the hospital. Again, he thanked God for this invention. He wouldn't have to send a courier to the hospital. He merely had to pick up the handle and talk.

"After the coroner is finished with her, send her body to Kollock Funeral Home. I shall pay for her burial costs." No one seemed to know this girl, so the likelihood of her father receiving punishment was nearly non-existent; while he requested an autopsy be done, the coroner would likely do a cursory one. However, he was thankful that the girl would not have to be buried in an unmarked grave in Potter's Field.

He took two cash bills from the envelope he kept in his office and prepared to visit the funeral home later this evening. Placing the envelope back on the shelf, he recited a prayer of gratitude for David's generosity which had kept four different families from going hungry this month.

Finishing his paperwork, Luke ventured into the kitchen to see what Mrs. Bradley had left for him to eat in the icebox. A plate covered with a napkin likely held his dinner. He lifted it, took off the napkin and nodded, satisfied: cold ham, potato salad and a fresh green salad. He devoured it, surprised at the intensity of his hunger.

***

When Kathleen was preparing for bed, she thought of Luke and of his desire to court her. To love meant to burn with passion, didn't it? At least that was how love was portrayed in the popular novels and plays she often read. She had "burned with passion" for Karl and yet he was a cruel man who had mistreated her. In retrospect, there had been tell-tale signs about his character, but she had been too blind to see them.

As for Dr. Luke, she liked him very much. In fact, she could state that she felt affection toward him. But to burn with passion? And how important was passion in considering a prospective beau? Her mother might have wisdom about that.

Knocking one time, she called, "Mama? Are you awake?"

She heard, "Yes, Kathleen, come in."

Kathleen entered her mother's room to find her mother in the rocker by the dresser, baby Mo in her arms nursing. She caressed the top of her baby sister's curly head.

Her mother spoke. "Are you prepared to become Maureen's godmother tomorrow morning?"

"I am indeed. Mama?"

Her mother looked up. "Yes?"

"I have a confession to make."

"A confession?"

"I overheard you and Papa speaking of Luke's desire to court me."

She frowned. "We did not intend for you to hear that conversation. And if it means anything, Luke did not approach Papa. Your father approached Luke."

"He did?"

"Yes. Your father could tell that he is fond of you. I've been a little too focused on the baby these days, but even I could see his eyes light up every time you walked into the room. Luke understands that you're not ready to court anyone yet."

"I was angry that he was even considering it. I asked Will to take me to his office, but there was a gravely injured girl there. As it turns out, he needed help and I was able to assist him. Unfortunately, the girl died."

"The poor dear."

"According to the girl's dying words, her father caused those injuries."

With a gasp, her mother replied, "How sad and tragic."

"Yes, but it made me realize how blessed I am to have Papa."

The baby started to cough, so her mother moved the infant to her shoulder to burp her.

"May I ask you a question, Mama?"

"Of course."

"Did you love Liam, my real father, at first sight?"

Her mother pursed her lips to consider. "Probably not, but he was easy to love: kind, caring, always thinking of others. I soon grew to love him."

"And what about Papa?"

She laughed out loud. "I did not like Papa at first. In fact, I despised him."

Kathleen drew in a breath. "That cannot be true."

"It is. Papa used to be a very callous, superficial man. I don't remember much in the months following Liam's death — except your birth — but about a year later, I realized that he had changed. His conversion to Christ brought out what was good in Papa: his generosity, kindness, selflessness. I only began to truly love him then."

"It's difficult to believe Papa was ever anything but a good man." She hesitated. "Mama, I like Luke very much, but I do not feel the same attraction to him that I felt for...I do not burn with passion."

Her mother's face flushed. "Sweet, one does not need to 'burn with passion' to engage in a happy, holy marriage. And love is not just burning with passion. Love is a choice that spouses make every day of their marriage, for the good of each other and for their children."

"Do you burn with passion for Papa now?"

Her mother's already blushing face deepened in color. "Well...I..."

Kathleen leaned close.

The older woman finally spoke in a whisper. "I love your father more than words can ever express." Mama straightened, her face losing its blush. "I can only hope that you find a man who loves you as deeply as your father loves me."

"Thank you, Mama. I am not ready to court anyone yet, but I see no reason why Luke and I cannot develop a friendship."

***

The following day was beautiful, warm and sunny. On the way to Mass, Kathleen traveled in the open Cabriolet with her mother and father, the baby and her three youngest brothers.

Will and John rode together in the Columbus rig.

The two carriages pulled in front of the church and everyone got out. Papa assisted Kathleen out first, then handed the baby to her and helped Mama step out of the carriage. Little Maureen was quiet and content in Kathleen's arms and she relished holding her.

***

Karl stood behind the ice wagon half a block away on the opposite side of the street from the small parish church. The horses neighed and snorted as they waited for the iceman to return.

Most families were creatures of habit. The O'Donovans would be at Mass this morning. Karl was as certain of that fact as he was that the sun would set this evening.

His heart started to race upon seeing the open carriage with Kathleen. Refusal or not, she was still the most beautiful girl he had ever known: lovely, still reachable, dressed in a green and white skirt and blouse with fashionably full sleeves, her blond hair pulled up under a green hat.

***

The sun was beaming through a group of brilliant red maple trees to the left of the church. Kathleen squinted and pulled her bonnet over her eyes. Behind her, she heard, "Good morning, O'Donovan family," and turned to see Luke's smiling face.

"Good morning, Luke."

"A mighty fine day for a christening."

"Indeed," Kathleen responded. Luke was smiling; his brown eyes behind his small glasses were warm and welcoming. He was wearing a light overcoat and a bowler hat, which gave him an air of sophistication and made him seem more mature.

The family, after Mass, along with Luke as guest, gathered around the baptismal font in the front section of the church. Kathleen held baby Mo and stood beside Will as they answered questions for Maureen, then promised to assist their parents in raising this child in the faith.

As the last prayers of the christening were recited, Kathleen continued to hold her baby sister. Although it had been a month since her injury, her shoulder started to throb.

Her parents were speaking with Fr. Morrissey so she waited until her mother could take the baby from her.

In the meantime, Luke asked, "Are you in pain?"

"No, but my shoulder feels sore if I hold her in one position."

"Would you like me to take her?" Luke offered.

"Yes." Kathleen carefully handed the baby to him.

Kathleen stared at Luke. Most men tended to hold infants like they would break, but Luke carried her sister so comfortably, it was as if he had been doing so for years.

Her parents invited Luke to a celebratory lunch back home. Luke gave the baby to her mother, then he offered to take Kathleen home. She glanced at her parents for their approval.

"That's fine, Kat. You may ride with Luke. Mama and the boys will be following behind you."

Luke helped her into his carriage and he climbed in beside her. Kathleen noticed that he was careful not to sit too close to her. On the one hand, Kathleen wanted to know more about him, but on the other, she felt awkward and wasn't sure what to say so she remained silent.

After a few moments, Luke spoke. "Beautiful christening. You are a radiant godmother."

Kathleen blushed. This was the most blatant compliment he had given her.

Another ten minutes passed. Luke didn't fill the silence with idle chatter and she appreciated that. Kathleen stole frequent glances at the young doctor. He was not only pleasant looking but what struck Kathleen even more were his kind eyes and gentle manner. Occasionally, he pushed his glasses up on his face. As she stared at him, he turned to look at her. Upon finding her watching him, he smiled awkwardly.

Luke broke the silence. "Thank you again for helping me with that young girl. You are a very capable assistant."

"I was happy to help. I still cannot believe her father beat her to death." Kathleen sat back against seat. There was no denying Luke's genuine care for others, although Kathleen wondered whether it was possible that she was misreading him. Did he have a hidden temper or another side to his personality? Did he have a dark secret in his background?

She released a sigh and, as she did so, he turned. "Are you feeling well?"

She nodded. "I'm fine, just daydreaming."

"Ah. Daydreaming is one of my favorite activities."

"Oh? What sort of things do you daydream about, Luke?"

"You'd probably think they were silly."

"I promise not to laugh."

"About finding the cure to a deadly disease, about being able to help someone who is hurt...about having a wife and children."

Kathleen's eyes widened. A man who daydreamed about a wife and family? What modern gentleman did that?

"And you? What do you daydream about, Kathleen?"

She thought for a moment before responding. "I daydream about being able to feel safe again...."

He nodded sympathetically.

"I used to dream about having a husband and family, but I'm afraid to do so anymore."

"You will feel safe again."

"I hope so."

21

One day the following week, Luke stood at the small sink in his office and scrubbed his hands longer than necessary. As the cool water cleansed them, he became mesmerized by the rush of the water. There was no running water at his aunt and uncle's farm, no luxury of allowing it to run over one's hands. Hot buckets had to be brought to the bathroom for a bath, although he recently purchased an indoor flush toilet for them. Life was so simple at the farm: new life a reality, death another, yet harsher, reality.

"Luke, it's just a chicken. I'm not asking you to kill the dog or a person. This chicken doesn't have feelings." His uncle held it high in the air and the chicken squawked and frantically flapped his wings back and forth. "This bird is going to be on our dinner table this week. All you need to do is..."

Ten-year-old Luke felt sick at the thought of chopping the chicken's head off. "Please don't make me do this. Don't make me kill the chicken. Please!"

"Very well, boy, I won't. Go on inside the house."

The desire to keep living things alive was the main reason Luke became a physician. He recalled the words of the Hippocratic Oath, *First do no harm.* As a doctor, Luke followed this philosophy, no matter who his patient was.

As for his aunt and uncle, he didn't have the opportunity to visit them as often as he'd like, now that he had a medical practice, but he thanked God for this kind and caring couple who taught him that people — and not things — were to be most appreciated in life.

The office bell jolted him back to reality. It was early and he wasn't scheduled to see patients for at least an hour.

He parted the curtains to see a tall stocky man on the porch by his office door. The man pressed a bloodied cloth around his wrist. There were thick red droplets flowing from the wound. Opening the door, Luke welcomed the man inside.

"Doc? Can you help me?"

"Of course, come in. He motioned for the man to follow him to the examining room. When Luke took the cloth from the man's wrist, he could see a long, jagged gash that would need extensive stitching.

"How did this happen?"

"I was hitching up the harness from the horse to the carriage and something spooked him and the fool animal took off. Of course, so did my wrist caught with it."

Luke cringed. Given the circumstances, this man was lucky to have his hand still attached.

"Name's Nate Finner. I've seen you at Mass on Sundays."

"Nice to make your acquaintance, Mr. Finner." Now that he mentioned it, this man did look familiar. "I wish it could have been under better circumstances. This looks painful."

"I don't care about pain. I care about being able to work. Got a job at the rubber factory twelve hours a day. Need my hand to do everything there. I'm already late. Been looking for a better job to support my wife and ten children, but there isn't much available."

As Luke washed, then stitched the man's wound, a thought occurred to him. He needed a hired man, someone to do chores. He certainly wouldn't mind waiting until this man's hand healed.

"Mr. Finner?"

"Yes, Doc?"

"I have a proposition for you."

Luke then offered Nate the job.

With wide eyes, the man replied, "You're offering me a job to work for you?"

"I am. And you don't need to start for two weeks. But that's only if you quit your current job. I will pay you whatever wages you'd be losing. If you give your wrist at least two weeks to heal, you should be ready to work."

The man pursed his lips and nodded. "I live three blocks away. I could stay at home with my family at night?"

"Of course. If I need you, I could always come for you."

The man smiled widely. "Yes, I would be most happy to

work for you, Doc. Thank you."

"Now, what do you make at the rubber factory?"

"Seven dollars per week."

Luke finished wrapping up the man's wrist, then took out his wallet and handed Nate a ten dollar bill and four ones. "This is to make up for your lost wages for the next two weeks."

"I can't take it for doing nothing."

"I insist. I can deduct fifty cents off each paycheck in the future until it is paid back."

"If I accept this, then I'll report for work tomorrow."

"No, Mr. Finner. This wound could get infected and you could lose your hand if you don't allow it to heal."

"Nate, call me Nate. Very well, Doc....and thank you."

He opened up the door and followed Nate onto the porch. "Remember what I said."

"Yes, I will."

Nate walked down the street, turning to wave, a wide smile across his face.

The clopping of a horse and carriage close by made Luke turn toward the noise. Jesse, the O'Donovans' servant, was riding up in the smaller carriage and pulling the reins to stop.

Luke rushed outside. He asked Jesse what was wrong and the young man informed him that "Mr. O'Donovan needed him straightaway."

***

As Kathleen stirred in her bed, it seemed extraordinarily quiet. Checking the time, her eyes widened when she saw that it was already nine a.m. She hadn't heard any commotion earlier. Usually, the younger boys were noisily racing in the halls as they got ready for school. This morning, however, silence reigned. Concerned, she took off her nightcap and quickly got dressed.

Her parents hadn't yet brought up the topic of college. She was aware that she was already too far behind, despite having read her anatomy book every day. She had no desire to return to nursing school and, in many respects, it was a relief.

For the past week or so, she actually had begun to feel close to normal. Even the throbbing in her shoulder was nearly gone.

Downstairs in the foyer, Kathleen looked through the window to see Dr. Luke speaking to her father on the porch. Her father's shoulders were slumped and he had a frown on his face. Dr. Luke's mouth was pursed and his right hand was on Papa's shoulder. She opened the door. "Luke? Papa?"

"Quickly, Kat, out here." Her father shoved past her and pulled on the door.

As the door creaked closed, Kathleen saw that a red sign had been nailed to it. "Quarantine. Scarlet Fever."

"Scarlet fever?"

Papa nodded. "Tim and Kev have the rash now. Luke already knows that you, Will, John and Pat had it when you were younger." Luke's mouth turned up ever so slightly as he saw her, but he was pale and his coat was unbuttoned. Papa continued. "Your mother is trying to keep Mo inside our room. Perhaps the fever can bypass her."

"As I said before, scarlet fever is an airborne illness, David. But it certainly couldn't hurt."

"Why doesn't Mama take the baby elsewhere, say, to Aunt Elizabeth's?" Kathleen leaned toward the two men.

"Quarantine. She isn't allowed." Luke stared at the ground.

Kathleen addressed her father. "Is there anything I can do?"

"Assist Jane. I've sent Will and John to do some errands."

"Yes, of course." She glanced at Luke. He smiled, then tipped his hat. "I shall check back later this evening." He walked to his carriage and got in.

"Luke," Kathleen called.

He pulled on the reins to stop the horse as she rushed toward the carriage. "Yes?"

"The boys will be fine, won't they?"

"Children have resilience. It's the baby I'm worried about."

"Can babies get scarlet fever?"

"Yes, but your mother is nursing, so I'm hopeful that it will provide enough protection against the disease."

"You look fatigued. Were you up in the night delivering a baby?"

"No, just too many late nights. Good day, Kathleen."

"Good day, Luke." She stepped back and waved as he rode down the laneway.

***

Later that afternoon, Kathleen assisted Jane by placing cool compresses on the foreheads of Kev and Tim. Tim was sleeping, although restlessly.

Kev cried as she put the cool cloth on his head. "I want Mama. Kat, can't I see Mama?"

"Not now. She is taking care of the baby."

Her brother seemed placated and finally settled, despite the crying coming from Mama's room. The baby had developed a high fever shortly after Luke left this morning, but she seemed to be fine, nursing and sleeping most of the day. That is, until an hour ago. Baby Mo had been screeching for an hour.

Kathleen knocked then opened the door to her parents' bedroom. Her mother was pacing the far side of the room with the baby in her arms. "Mama, Papa, can I give you a break and walk with Mo?"

Because of the high-pitched wailing, her parents couldn't hear her. "What?" her father asked.

She walked to him. Leaning close to his ear, she asked, "Do you want me to walk with Mo?"

"I've already tried taking Mo from her, Kat. Mama wants to rock her and try to nurse her."

"Should we send Jesse to get Dr. Luke?"

"We haven't seen any signs of the rash yet."

Finally, the loud piercing cries of the baby had ceased. Kathleen and her father turned to see her mother carefully lowering herself to the rocking chair by the window. Kathleen calmed somewhat, all of a sudden realizing how much on edge she had been from her sister's wailing. She and her father stepped quietly toward the rocking chair. As they got closer, her mother gasped and stared. Looking down, Kathleen could see the baby's neck and cheek had the characteristic red rash.

"It's all right, Caroline. She is going to be fine," Papa patted Mama's shoulder.

"None of our children ever had the rash this young, David, and she's burning with fever." She paused. "Kathleen, ask Jane to bring some chipped ice and a cloth...quickly, please?" Mama's voice with filled with urgency.

"Of course."

Kathleen had already entered the hallway when she heard, "Oh no!" She turned, pushing the door back open. The baby was convulsing back and forth as her mother tried to hold her.

"I'm going to get Luke!" her father rushed past her, knocking into her arm. Jesse appeared in the hallway in a nightshirt. Izzy in her nightgown came out of her room and stood behind him.

"Did you want me to fetch Dr. Luke, Mr. David?" Jesse asked.

"No. It'll take longer for you to get dressed. Just come help me hitch the horses and I'll go."

With all the commotion Jane, who was still dressed in her day clothes, came out of Kev and Tim's room. "Miss Kathleen, what's going on?"

"Baby Mo is having a convulsion."

"Good Lord. I'll get the ice chips." Seeing Izzy, she said, "Izzy, come help."

"Yes, Ma'am."

Kathleen peered into the room and the baby had stopped convulsing. Her mother now rocked her.

Rushing down to the kitchen, Kathleen watched as Jane and Izzy chopped the ice like they were in a race. The bowl was quickly filled. Jane stopped and held it out to Kathleen. "Take this up to your mother." Jane reached for a cloth on the table and put it on top of the bowl. "Quickly, Miss Kathleen. We'll stay and chop more."

Kathleen rushed back up to her parents' bedroom, carefully holding the bowl of ice to her chest as if they were diamonds to be treasured and protected.

The now quiet hallway was, in many respects, worse than one filled with screaming. It was an uncomfortable, awkward silence that held little promise; only heartache. Kathleen shook off the feeling and stepped into her parents' bedroom. "Here is the ice, Mama."

"She stopped convulsing, but she's burning up. And she's just vomited her last nursing."

Kathleen placed the bowl of ice on the table beside the rocking chair. "How can I help, Mama?"

"Pray, Kathleen." Kathleen looked down at baby Mo, her body limp and her face and neck red and blotchy like it was sunburned. After crying for most of the afternoon, the baby was now silent and Kathleen wished she would make noise and give them some indication that she was going to get better. Inwardly, she prayed.

Just then, the baby started to violently convulse again, her mother trying to hold onto Baby Mo's small body. Suddenly, it was over. The baby became still and limp like a rag doll.

Kathleen's mother tenderly took off the baby's wrappings. "Jesus, Mary and Joseph, please help Maureen," she prayed as she carefully sponged the baby's small body with cool cloths. The rash had expanded down her chest and into her groin. Expecting to hear her sister cry, Kathleen steadied herself against the bed post. Baby Mo remained limp and unresponsive. Kathleen held her breath as she studied her sister. Her tiny body was so still. *No, it couldn't be.* Kathleen's eyes began to water.

"Miss Caroline?" Jane and Izzy came into the room. Jane crouched down in front of Kathleen's mother, who continued to caress her baby with a cold cloth.

"Miss Caroline?" The servant whispered in Mama's ear.

Finally, her mother turned toward Jane.

"Miss Caroline, you can stop putting the cold cloths on her. She's gone, Ma'am."

"No, Jane. She's just starting to cool down. See? Her skin is lukewarm. And that's what we need to happen."

"Miss Caroline, Little Miss Maureen has passed." Jane wrapped up baby Mo in a linen blanket as the now quiet infant lay still on her mother's lap.

Kathleen felt a sob creep up the back of her throat, but she stifled it and held her hand to her mouth. Her mother was staring down at the baby in her arms. Mama pulled the baby close and began to rock.

"Oh, Mama," Kathleen began to sob. Her mother stared straight ahead.

"There, there, Miss Kathleen." Jane embraced her.

Kathleen turned to see Will, John and Pat lingering in the doorway, their faces etched in grief. The boys stepped back to allow Papa and Luke to come into the room.

"Caroline!" Kathleen ran to David. "Baby Mo is gone, Papa. She's dead."

His eyes widened. He drew in a breath, then exhaled, "No."

***

After David's exclamation, quiet sobbing of the women followed. Luke walked around Kathleen and David and tentatively approached Caroline. He knelt before her as she rocked the baby. She had begun humming a soft lullaby.

"Caroline?"

He waited for her to make eye contact. When she didn't, he quietly called her name again. He reached out to touch the baby and she jerked back, saying, "Don't."

Luke pulled his hand back and stood up. She whispered a few words that he couldn't hear. He leaned close to her face. "Pardon me?"

"She's cool now. She's much better. She's not fussing."

"That's good. Shall I take a look?"

Caroline's haunted expression was so incredibly sad that Luke had to blink to remove his tears. She handed the baby to him. "After you've finished, please wrap her in the blanket and return her to me so that I may rock her," she said, her voice a monotone. "She's been so fussy."

"Of course." Luke gently placed the baby on the bed. He could already tell from her still and graying face that she was gone. However, he felt for a pulse and listened to her small chest with his stethoscope. He was medically certain the baby had passed. "Requiescat in pace, little one," he whispered. Her little mouth puckered, her eyes closed; baby Maureen looked like she was sleeping — a forever slumber. He caressed the side of her face, then swaddled and placed her gently in Caroline's arms.

Behind him, Kathleen wept. Jane and Izzy were wiping their eyes. Will and John were quiet and somber. Pat was crying softly. David's eyes were watering.

Luke addressed David, but his words were meant for the entire family. His voice cracked as he tried to contain his own emotions. "I'm...so very sorry for your loss. If there is... anything I can do, please let me know."

David nodded and held onto Kathleen who was now sobbing into her father's shoulder. David rubbed her back. The older man's jaw was rigid, his lips pursed.

Luke should have returned to the O'Donovans earlier. But another emergency kept him busy until an hour ago, when David showed up at his door, frantic. Once again, he felt responsible and guilt rose in him. If he had returned earlier, perhaps he could have saved the baby. Maybe he could have figured out a way to keep her temperature from rising so high.

Watching the scene, Luke felt like an intruder. He wanted to stay and console the grieving family, but he had no right to do that. This family needed to mourn in private.

As he walked through the doorway, Kathleen called out to him, "Wait, Luke. Don't leave." He stood in the hallway as she approached him. She wiped her eyes with her handkerchief. "Why? Why did she have to die?"

"I cannot answer that. Infants usually don't contract scarlet fever, especially if the mother is nursing. But Maureen was tiny and sometimes different strains affect babies more intensely than older children." Kathleen began to sob again, her cheeks a trail of tears. He pulled her close. "Shhhh. There, there." He allowed her to cry while he whispered soothing words.

22

Kathleen stared, mesmerized by the orange glow of the oil lamp. Her heart ached and she choked back another sob as she sat on the edge of her bed. In the three days since the baby had died, Luke had spent virtually every waking or free moment with her family. Luke became a soothing presence in the household.

When Luke wasn't comforting Kathleen, he was assisting her mother and Jane in preparing the baby's body for burial. Her parents could have employed the local mortician to do so, but Mama couldn't bear to have anyone else take care of her tiny daughter's body.

How could someone so young be gone? And why would God take her baby sister so soon after being born?

Even before the recent tragedy, Kathleen had made the decision not to return to nursing college. There would be an exorbitant amount of work she would have to accomplish to catch up to the rest of the class. Kathleen had decided that while she would enjoy working with and treating children, she would not be able to handle death well. As well, she no longer wished to tolerate Nurse Schmidt.

As she continued to watch the dancing flame, her eyes began to close and she jerked her head up to stay awake. She didn't want to sleep because when she slept, she still saw Karl's face. In addition, waking from sleep was like losing Maureen all over again and it seemed disrespectful to her sister's memory to forget, even in the lulling forgetfulness of slumber.

The distant bells of the grandfather clock in the foyer downstairs chimed and Kathleen listened. Eight o'clock. Her stomach growled. She had eaten little in the previous three days. And now hunger became an enemy to her grief. She reached across the bed for her robe and wrapped it around herself. Opening the door, she stepped into the silent hallway.

Kathleen pressed an ear to her parents' bedroom door and

listened. Last night her mother quietly sobbed, but tonight there were no sounds. Kathleen wasn't sure whether she preferred the quiet sobbing or the eerie silence of mourning.

She crept down the back staircase to the kitchen. Halfway down, she heard voices. At the bottom, she could see the now familiar scene of Jane standing, while her father and Luke sat at the table in the middle of the large kitchen, one oil lamp spreading light to the area. Both men stood as she entered the room.

"Not able to sleep, Kat?"

"No."

Luke pulled up a chair and held it out for her. The men then sat.

"Would you like some tea, Miss Kathleen?"

"Perhaps a small cup, Jane." The older woman poured some tea into a cup for Kathleen. The heat seeped through the cup and warmed her cold hands.

"I ought to be leaving now, David." Luke rose from the chair.

"Why don't you stay the night? Jane, would you prepare one of the guest rooms in the east wing?"

"Of course, Mr. David." Jane hurried up the back staircase.

"Well, I am tired, so I may accept your offer to stay for the night. I left a note on my office door that I'm here in case anyone is in need of a physician."

Kathleen sighed and absentmindedly caressed the top of the oak table. It was peculiar that she didn't seem to notice much these days, but the shock of losing baby Mo was still so fresh and painful. She looked across the table at Luke. He offered a sympathetic smile. "How are you feeling?" he asked.

"Sad. Like I want to cry all the time."

"I know. This is the most dreadful aspect of being a doctor. When someone dies or is hurt or..."

"The most awful aspect of being a parent too," Papa said.

Kathleen nodded. David leaned in and put his arm around his daughter.

Moments later, Jane returned. "Your room is ready, Dr. Luke. It's the third room on the left past the main staircase. It's the only room with the door open."

"Thank you, Jane."

David stood up. "I need to occupy my mind with something other than mourning so I'm going to my study to read."

"G'night, Papa."

"Goodnight, Kat," he said, kissing the top of her head. He headed up the main staircase. Jane picked up the empty cups and plates. "Will you need anything else, Miss Kathleen?"

"I don't think so, Jane. I'll be going to bed shortly."

Luke and Kathleen sat silently in the dimly lit kitchen. Her eyes were drawn to the pantry door and her heart quickened. She straightened. It had been five weeks since her injury. It occurred to her that here she was, alone again with a man in the very kitchen where the incident took place. And yet Kathleen was unafraid.

"I've made a decision about college, Luke."

"Oh?"

"I will not be returning. The instructor, on the first day of school, said, 'Only hearty women should be nurses.' Well, I am not hearty and I cannot deal with death so easily."

"No one handles death easily. It's one of the aspects of the medical profession I find particularly challenging." He paused. "Do you find anatomy and biology interesting?"

"I do, actually. I've been reading my textbook."

"Would you consider a compromise?"

"What sort of compromise can there be?"

"What if I were to train you to be my assistant?"

"Assistant? You mean a job?"

"More like apprenticing. With the knowledge you already have, I would be happy to train you to be a medical assistant."

"Truly?"

"Truly."

Kathleen sat back in the chair and considered Luke's proposition. "No college?"

"No college. Just my training. Then, if you felt comfortable doing so, you could work alongside me."

Kathleen offered the subtlest of nods. She liked Luke and she knew that he liked her. "Would that be appropriate?"

"Of course. Mrs. Bradley and Nate are there all the time,

lest anyone think we might be doing anything other than work."

Kathleen felt warm with a blush. "Oh, I didn't mean that. I just wondered whether I would be qualified enough."

"I would teach you anything you didn't know."

"May I think about it?"

"Yes, take all the time you need."

Her stomach growled. Kathleen felt another warm blush.

"Have you eaten recently?" Luke asked.

"No."

"Let's see what we can find for you here in the kitchen."

"I'm not really hungry."

"Your body says otherwise. I know you are grieving, but you must eat."

He walked over to the table by the window and lifted a towel. A half-eaten loaf of bread sat underneath. "Ah, bread, food for the soul." He reached for a knife and began cutting. "Do you know where Jane keeps the butter? Perhaps the icebox?"

She shrugged her shoulders.

"Well, I'm sure it is delicious without butter."

As he placed one piece in her hand, his fingers brushed her palm. It was awkward, although it wasn't an unpleasant sensation. Luke took a bite, some of the crumbs falling to the table. "Tasty, but going stale."

She chewed and swallowed, but it could've been paper for all she cared. They were silent for a moment as each finished a slice of bread. Luke cleared his voice and spoke softly.

"I lost my youngest sister when she was four."

"How dreadful."

"It was devastating for our entire family. I was only six at the time."

"What happened?"

"I don't remember much about that day. I was too young, I guess. My aunt tells me it was a tragic accident." He hesitated. "About a year later, my parents died in a fire, but they were never the same after Sarah died. I lived with my aunt and uncle, a very kind and loving couple. My brother, Zach, stayed with another aunt."

Kathleen's heart ached for young Luke. To lose three members of an entire family seemed an unfathomable tragedy. She whispered, "You must miss them very much."

He nodded, but remained silent.

"I know my baby sister was only two months old, but I miss her terribly, Luke. And I was so selfish. In the weeks after my injury, I didn't spend much time with her." She blinked away tears and lowered her head.

"You needed to heal." He reached across the table and covered her small hand with his large protective one. She did not cringe nor shrink back. Instead, she welcomed his hand like a long lost friend.

***

That night, sleep eluded Luke. He couldn't imagine a more difficult and challenging three days.

Yet the last few moments in the kitchen with Kathleen were like a ray of sunshine amidst the darkness. Admittedly, he blurted out the offer to train her without thinking about it. Of course, part of him wanted to be around her all the time, but he also wondered whether he would be able to focus and concentrate on his patients.

As he closed his eyes, the disturbing image of the stillness of a small baby and a sobbing mother made him toss and turn. He took out his rosary and began reciting the powerful prayers. At the fifth sorrowful mystery, sleep finally came.

23

Surprisingly, the cemetery was a pleasant location. Fresh flowers and fallen maple leaves dotted the graves. The group of twenty mourners gathered around a small hole, a dirt mound to one side, a tiny casket to the other.

Mama's weeping and Aunt Elizabeth's soft cries were making it difficult for Kathleen to control her own emotions. Jane and Izzy remained at home with Kev and Tim. They were no longer contagious, but they were still too ill to attend.

It caused Kathleen anguish to think of her baby sister's body being placed in the ground. The child's sweet eyes were closed for eternity and her tiny body would soon be buried in a cold and unforgiving ground.

The priest finished the prayers. The tiny casket was lowered into the ground, a few shovelfuls of dirt thrown onto it.

Kathleen glanced past the priest to the gravestone of her real father, and the words: *Liam Francis O'Donovan 1854-1877, beloved husband of Caroline, loving father of Kathleen.* Death had claimed her father when he was only twenty-three. Her mother had told her that Liam wasn't really gone, not while Kathleen was alive, because part of him remained in his only child. And yet she felt no real connection to this man.

Luke's hand caressed her shoulder. "Kathleen?"

She turned and faced him. "Yes?"

"May I escort you back to the carriage?"

She nodded. As she and the others left the grave site, she caught sight of her mother and father. Both walked slowly, arm in arm, chins lifted, her mother occasionally blotting her eyes with a handkerchief. And with one backward glance, Kathleen stared at the small hole and even smaller casket and bid a somber farewell to her only sister.

***

Karl lurked behind a group of red maples in the distance and glared as the family walked away from the grave site in their dark suits and black gowns.

It afforded him a rather pleasant opportunity to watch

Kathleen. He was grateful to whatever caused the baby's death — either a god or sickness. He found out about the death only last night. A frequent patron of the saloon had shared the information about the quarantine at the O'Donovans, and the subsequent death. It was not an unlikely circumstance after a scarlet fever outbreak, although he had been unclear who had actually died.

He watched as they departed, a mass of black humanity moving slowly away from the grave.

***

Will turned and stared at the miniature coffin. He said a prayer that baby Mo would be held in the arms of Jesus and Mary. Following Pat and John, he turned and watched his parents speak to their parish priest. Fr. Morrissey did not possess a mean bone in his body: his manner was always kind and gentle.

As they rode home, Will found himself envying the elderly priest. He envied all priests, who possessed the gift of being *in persona Christi,* in the person of Christ, officiating at Mass, baptizing infants, hearing confessions, consoling the bereaved.

Upon arriving, Will went straight to his room. His family and Dr. Luke were downstairs having a meal but he wasn't hungry. He decided to read *St. Augustine's Confessions.* The more he read, the more he was inspired. It wasn't until he read *"Our hearts are restless until they rest in thee"* that he knew what he had to do.

He wasn't sure of the protocol with the mourning period, but he decided to again pursue information on the priesthood and seminaries in the Philadelphia area.

Will drifted off into a deep sleep and only woke when his father knocked. "Will, are you all right in there?"

"I'm fine." Opening the door, he said, "I apologize, Papa. I should have come down but I was restless and started reading that book you gave me, *Confessions.*"

His father stepped into his room and closed the door.

"And?"

"I became engrossed...."

"It's a compelling read."

"It is. My heart has been so restless since acquiring the knowledge that I'm illegitimate."

Papa lowered his head.

"But I'm convinced."

"Convinced?"

"Of my vocation. I want you to arrange that meeting with your friend, Monsignor Flaherty, about my desire to enter the seminary."

David pressed a hand to his chest and his mouth widened in a smile. "This is excellent news, Will. Although I know that grieving families are expected to withdraw from society for a certain number of months, this may be an exception to that rule. I will contact Monsignor about setting up a meeting sometime in the new year."

Will nodded. "That would be fine, Papa."

His father's expression was a mixture of grief and joy; the eyes which had been etched in grief all day now showed hope. The smile on the older man's face was so wide that Will was grateful to give his father a momentary reprieve from mourning.

Will continued. "I am not certain whether I'm holy enough, but I believe God is calling me. And who am I to question God?"

"That's right. With all that's happened: Kat being injured, the baby's death...it's easy to lose hope. But where there's life, there's always hope. Your desire to be a priest..." David stood up. "It's most extraordinary. I've been praying for you."

Hugging him tightly, Will then pulled away. "No matter how much I tried to forget, I still felt God calling me. And I know that I must be obedient to that call."

"Son, the circumstances of your conception have nothing to do with you or with your desire to be a priest."

"I feel unworthy."

"If anyone feels unworthy, Will, it's me. I made the mistake, one that nearly drove the only woman I've ever loved away from me. Missy and I..."

"I would rather not hear...."

"I do not intend to share any sordid details with you. I wanted to tell you that after that night, I tried to pretend it never happened. Then Mama nearly died birthing John. Jane called a wet nurse to feed John. That day, Missy showed up. I hadn't known she had given birth. Of course, I hardly saw her or you, even though you were in my house. I later found out from Jane that they tried to keep you away from me. You looked like me, even at that young age. I didn't truly know about you until Missy became sick."

Will nodded.

His father continued. "Just before...Missy...died, she brought you to us — you had just turned two — but you screamed and cried because you did not want to be here."

Will grinned. "I don't remember that."

"One night, after you had fallen asleep, I couldn't take my eyes off of you and I realized that even though I made a mistake, God took that opportunity to create something good and precious from it. And that is you, Will."

"That's what Jane told me."

"Jane is one of the smartest people I've ever known." David placed his hand on his son's shoulder. "I shall schedule the appointment with Monsignor Flaherty in the new year."

"Yes. I would like to apply to seminaries in the spring."

"That should give us plenty of time." David hugged his son.

"Papa?"

"Yes."

"Thank you for taking care of me and providing for me all these years."

"No need to thank me, Will. It is my duty and I am happy to do so. I'm very proud of you." He turned to leave. "Continue to pray about your vocation, Will."

"I will, Papa."

"And I shall also pray about it. In the meantime, study the catechism."

"Thank you."

"No, Will, thank *you*. You've been an exemplary son and I'm very grateful to God for you."

Inside his room, Will reached inside the nightstand and lifted the envelope that his mother, "Missy," Melissa Callahan, had written to him. He now had a great desire to read her letter.

My Dearest Will,

I will have been gone from the earth for many years when you finally read these words. I have asked Mr. David and Miss Caroline to take care of you and I am confident they will do so. Miss Caroline is a kind woman and I am certain she will be an affectionate mother to you.

I do not know what they have told you regarding how you were conceived. Many called you illegitimate. However, you have been a great gift to me and to the world and becoming your mother made me want to become a better person. If anyone tries to convince you that you were an accident or somehow less pleasing to God because of these circumstances, they know less of God and more of gossip.

Until recently, I did not hold God or my faith in high esteem. I have returned to the sacraments and I shall spend my last days in the company of the sisters at the Sacred Heart Convent. They have already welcomed me as one of their own.

My Sweet Will, I believe that God has great expectations and plans for you. This gives me hope for your future.

"Today if ye will hear God's voice, do not harden your heart..." Hebrews 3:15 *Listen to God's voice, Will, for He has a special plan for you. I will miss you. Be well and pray for me, as I will pray for you.*

Your Loving Mother
July 27, 1881

Will folded the letter and placed it back into the envelope. He turned down the oil lamp. *Listen to God's voice, Will, for He has a special plan for you.* There didn't seem to be much room for interpretation. His mother, long dead, was telling him to listen to God's calling.

After reading the letter, he was filled with more questions than answers. His mother returned to the sacraments? Why is it that he initially thought so little of her? He should never have judged her so harshly. She gave him life and she has been praying for him, from heaven, all these years.

But why would the Almighty create Will in such an immoral circumstance and allow him to live...yet allow his baby sister, created in love, to die?

As he drifted back to sleep, he promised his late mother and God that he would continue to pray and "listen to God's voice."

24

Black ribbons and closed drapery communicated that the O'Donovan house continued to be one of mourning three weeks after the baby's death. Dark clouds above were threatening to unleash a torrent of precipitation on this cool and cloudy day in November.

Jesse was waiting to take Luke's carriage to the barn when he arrived.

When Luke had seen the family at Mass half an hour ago, Caroline and David, their faces still slack with grief, held their heads high and appeared pleasant and polite when speaking to fellow parishioners.

The official mourning period, in his opinion, sometimes dragged on too long, but it was Luke's belief that these periods did, in fact, assist the family in the grieving process. The local community and neighborhood expected little of mourning families.

He knocked quietly. Jane's smiling face greeted him as the door swung open. "Dr. Luke, please do come in. Miss Caroline and Mr. David are expecting you. I believe they are upstairs. Miss Kathleen's in the parlor, though."

Just the mention of Kathleen's name made his heart skip a beat, and he felt guilty feeling that way while the family was still mourning. He handed Jane his hat and coat and looked up to see Kathleen coming through the doorway of the parlor, looking lovely as usual. When she smiled at him, his pulse quickened.

"Good afternoon, Luke. I trust you are well today?"

"Yes, I am. How are you faring today?"

Her eyes looked downward. "All right, I suppose. My heart still hurts because I miss baby Mo."

"It's normal and natural to miss someone we have loved. How are your parents doing?"

"Yesterday wasn't a good day for Mama. And Papa seems to be so quiet most of the time. He won't play chess or do much of anything, except work and sit in his study at night.

The younger boys often play and forget that we're a family in mourning, and sometimes it's upsetting to Mama to see them act in such a manner." She hesitated. "But I understand how children are."

"It doesn't mean they aren't grieving or that they don't miss their sister. I am certain they do."

"I suppose. My parents have decided to stay in mourning for six months, four of those deep."

"Many families mourn only six weeks for an infant," Luke offered.

"Baby Mo was worth more than that."

"Indeed she was."

After lunch, when the older members of the family gathered in the parlor, Luke bid farewell. He asked Kathleen to accompany him to his carriage outside. As they stepped onto the porch, he whispered, "Have you thought more about my training you to be my assistant?"

"Yes, I have. I should very much like to do so. I haven't yet spoken to my parents about it, but I don't think they will have any objections."

"Shall I speak to them?"

"No, I plan to do so later. When would you like me to start?"

"I was thinking perhaps in a few weeks, the end of this month."

"Yes, I would like that."

She stepped away from the carriage and waved.

***

Up in her bedroom, Kathleen thought about Luke. He was a patient and understanding listener, as he not only had been for her, but for her parents and the rest of her family. His presence at her house now seemed as natural as if he were one of the family.

Could Luke be her beloved? He was compassionate and kind, but this decision was one in which she should reflect with care and without haste.

Three quick raps on her door indicated that Will was there.

"Come in, Will."

"Would you like to finish our chess game?"

She shook her head. "I don't feel like playing chess."

He turned to leave; she called out to him. "Wait."

"Yes, Kat?"

"What is your honest opinion of Dr. Luke?"

His eyebrows lifted. "Honest opinion? A fine gentleman. Why?"

Nodding, she said, "He does seem like a fine gentleman. With all that has happened, I just don't trust my judgment."

"Pray about it. Become better acquainted. He doesn't know that you are aware of his desire to court you, right?"

"No." She paused and lowered her head. "I suppose that was one of my mistakes with..." She didn't even want to say his name. "I was so impatient and self-centered, I hardly prayed at all during our courtship."

"We're all impatient and self-centered, Kat. Pray about this and I shall do the same. You're under no obligation to Luke, but I can tell that he is very fond of you." Will winked and left, closing the door behind him.

Truth be told, she wanted to become better acquainted with Luke before she considered courting him.

Of course, Luke had already proven himself trustworthy; his character was above and beyond that of most gentlemen. She enjoyed his company. Luke had an innate gift of knowing when to listen and when to speak, a talent that Kathleen had always lacked.

Resolved, Kathleen committed to taking her time in deciding whether to court Luke. For now, he didn't need to know that she was aware of his desire.

25

The first official day of Kathleen's training as Luke's medical assistant did not begin on a positive note. It was only the end of November, but near blizzard conditions existed. The snow was blowing sideways, and her father almost gave up on their journey to Luke's and returned home. "Kat, the weather is too bad. Surely Luke will understand."

"I know, Papa, but how shall we let him know? We've already traveled this far."

Her father sighed and continued. Kathleen held her heavy text book against her in the small carriage, protecting it from the elements. She wanted to show Luke that she was keen on learning and had been studying medical terminology. A half-hour later, they arrived on the outskirts of Germantown proper. The snow had finally stopped, so they pulled in front of Luke's place only ten minutes late.

Kathleen entered by the outside office door into the waiting room, a bell signaling her arrival. Luke's examining room door was shut. Mrs. Bradley came into the waiting room from the house foyer. "Dr. Peterson's with a patient, but when he is finished, he will want you to go inside, Miss O'Donovan. May I take your coat, hat and gloves?"

"Thank you, Mrs. Bradley." Kathleen held onto the book as her father helped her to remove her coat and hat.

"Mr. O'Donovan, may I offer you or your daughter a cup of tea or coffee?"

"No, thank you. I must be leaving. I will return this evening around four to pick Kat up." He kissed Kathleen on the cheek and left.

A moment later, the exam room door opened and an elderly gentleman emerged. Behind him, Luke said, "Let me know if that continues to bother you."

"Thank you, Dr. Peterson." The man picked up his coat and hat from the rack in the waiting room, then left.

With a smile, Luke caught Kathleen's eye. "I'm happy to see that you have safely arrived. Quite the morning, isn't it?

Too frosty and wintery for November, if I do say so."

"Yes, it is."

Seeing the book in her hand, he said, "What have you got there?"

"My anatomy textbook."

"Excellent."

He escorted Kathleen into the examining room and office. Outside, Kathleen could see that a tall stocky man with a warm coat and scarf was shoveling the walkway. "Who's that, Luke? He looks familiar."

"Mr. Nate Finner, my new hired hand. He's a good worker. He and his large family attend St. Vincent's."

"Of course. That's where I've seen him. Their oldest is Pat's age, I believe."

He paused, then asked, "Shall I test you on the contents of that rather thick book?"

"Yes. Perhaps we can begin with the cavities."

"Ah, yes. List the cavities first in the dorsal cavity, then in the ventral cavity. State which cavity it is and what it encompasses in the body."

"Oh, that is an excellent question!"

"And I'd wager you have an excellent answer."

"Yes, I do." Kathleen wanted to impress her new teacher. "First, the cranial cavity, the brain; the spinal canal is the spinal cord, the orbital cavity encompasses the eye, optic nerve, muscles of the eyeball, lachrymal apparatus; next is the nasal cavity, the structures that form the nose...." She named every cavity and structure.

"Well done! You know the bodily cavities...perfectly."

***

Loveliness notwithstanding, Luke was impressed with Kathleen's basic knowledge of anatomy and her ability to pronounce the medical words properly. She would prove to be a worthy student, of that he was certain. However, Luke was already encountering the challenge of trying not to be distracted by her presence.

The phone rang and immediately Luke turned toward Kathleen. "Pardon me. I must answer this."

"Of course."

***

While Luke was on the phone, Kathleen stood up and began to peruse the contents on the two bookshelves in the room. She tilted her head and began reading the titles: "The Principles and Practice of Medicine," "Surgical Practices and Procedures," "Puerperal Fever," "Women's Problems and Fertility," "Native Herbs and Remedies." She stopped. Native Herbs and Remedies? *Seems an unusual book among academic textbooks.* She quietly slipped the book off the shelf and paged through it. A small brass bookmark was sticking out of the book and she opened it to the place marked. She read to herself: *Natural Healing Salve recipe...western skunk cabbage... No wonder it smelled wretched.* Kathleen cringed as she remembered the horrid smell, but truth be told, the paste healed the wound on her chin so well that the scar wasn't noticeable. Keeping the book open, she took the small brass bookmark off the page and held it up. Although she had seen similar bookmarks before, this one was beautifully simple and she made a mental note to ask Luke where he had gotten it.

She returned the book. Luke continued to talk on the phone to someone, it would seem, with a skin infection. Kathleen walked through the waiting room to the narrow foyer of the large home. An open parlor was on the other side, or left, of the staircase and Kathleen craned her neck to see a beautiful stone fireplace on the far wall. The room was bright with bay windows facing the front and the back. Stepping into the room, the roaring fire in the hearth urged her closer. Kathleen warmed her hands for a few moments. Returning to the foyer, she passed the stairs to the left, and a small reading room to the right. Didn't Luke tell her there was a bathroom on the first floor? She heard Mrs. Bradley whistling before she saw her down the hall in the dining area. The older woman waved. "May I help you, Miss O'Donovan?"

"The privy?"

"The washroom's right there," the housekeeper pointed to a narrow door that Kathleen had surmised was a closet.

"Thank you." She opened the door, flicked on the light switch and locked the door. This bathroom was one-fourth the size of their sizeable one at home. Here, a basic sink and a modern flush toilet were present, though, and Kathleen quickly used them and returned to Luke's office where it appeared that he had just hung up the phone.

"Sorry, Kathleen."

"No need to apologize."

He opened his pocket watch and clicked it shut, slipping it into his vest. "Patients will be arriving in fifteen minutes. Further training will have to take place with patients. Would you mind asking Mrs. Bradley to bring a light lunch before they arrive?"

"I would be happy to do so."

Kathleen followed the sound of the housekeeper whistling a few rooms away. The tune was quite catchy. Mrs. Bradley was washing dishes at the sink; she turned. "May I help you?"

"Yes. Dr. Luke has asked that a light lunch be brought to his office before patients arrive."

"I shall bring that momentarily."

"Thank you."

On the way back to the examining room, Kathleen stopped at the small reading room in which there were three more bookcases. Kathleen read through the titles. *David Copperfield by Charles Dickens.* "How wonderful! I've never read this one," she said to no one in particular. She took the well-thumbed edition from the shelf and held the book in her hand as she walked through the foyer, then the waiting room, then the examining room.

Luke sat at the desk in front of the window. He brightened as she entered his room. "You went the long way?"

"I did what?"

"The long way." He pointed to a door on the far side of his office. "This door leads to a small storage area, then the kitchen. I wasn't thinking. I should have told you."

"It's no trouble, Luke. I don't mind the extra walking."

Luke stared at the book in her hands. "What have you got there?"

"David Copperfield. I'm going to..." At the mention of the book, he blanched. She continued. "Do you mind very much if I borrow your book?" She began to open the book.

"I...uh..."

She ignored him as the book opened naturally to the middle, a bookmark — perhaps like the one in the Native Remedy book — but no, this was a photograph of a family. The slight, thin father had fair hair and a stern expression. The wife, American Indian perhaps, her expression serious, held a little girl with light hair on her lap. It was hard to see what the girl looked like because the photo was slightly blurred. In front of the man were two boys, the shorter light-haired fellow had a pair of spectacles on his face...she drew in a breath when she realized who it was. "Luke?" She looked up from the photo.

With a smile, Luke sat upright at the desk.

"This is you and your family, isn't it?"

He nodded.

***

Luke's pulse quickened as Kathleen stared at the photo, the only memory he had of his original family. Should he tell her about his heritage? Would she feel differently when she found out?

"Yes, it is."

"You were a handsome little boy. And your family is beautiful."

"My original family, yes, with my parents."

"Your mother..."

"She was Lenape-Delaware."

"I wish the photo wasn't blurred so I could see your sister's face more clearly."

He did not respond, but he also wished Sarah hadn't moved and that the photo had been clearer.

"Beautiful family, Luke. I'm so sorry that your sister died."

"And my parents died in a fire less than a year later. I don't know what would have happened to me if my aunt and uncle hadn't taken me in."

"You ought to frame this and hang it in your parlor."

"My mother was Indian."

"Yes?"

"Does that bother you?"

"Should it?"

Luke relaxed against the chair and shook his head. "No."

They sat in silence as Kathleen stared at the photo, her head tilting from side to side as she studied it. She straightened, as if remembering something.

"Luke?"

"Yes?"

Kathleen walked to the office bookcase, took out one of the textbooks, opened it and brought the book to his desk. "This brass bookmark..."

"That came with the book. I believe it was handmade by a sub-tribe of the Delaware Indians."

"Really? It's beautifully simple."

"It is, isn't it?"

"I should like one of these. They are heavier and hold the place better than a photograph or a thin bookmark."

Luke had to control his urge to give it to her then and there. There would be a better time and place to do so.

***

At the end of the day, Kathleen placed a large stack of files into the tall wooden filing cabinet beside his desk. Luke sat at his desk, jotting down notations.

He finished, stood up and handed the file to her. "This one is finished." His hand brushed hers and he blushed. Kathleen smiled inwardly. Despite his Indian heritage, Luke was as fair skinned as she, which made it difficult to hide his feelings. Sometimes when she spoke to him, he blushed. Other times, she would merely walk into the room, and his whole demeanor brightened.

Kathleen decided this would be an ideal time to talk to him. She remained quiet for a moment, filing the last folder into the cabinet. "Luke?"

"Yes?"

"I know... of your desire to court me."

Luke stepped back, his eyebrows lifting. "You...do?"

"Yes. I should very much like to court you, once the mourning period is over. In the meantime, I would like to become better acquainted."

Luke's mouth fell open. He muttered, "How did you..."

"I overheard my parents speaking about it last month before baby Mo...passed, and...I was still in a bad state, so I became angry that it was even a topic for discussion. I came to you that day when the young girl was beaten to death by her father...to tell you that I wouldn't be interested in courting anyone."

With a nod, he said, "Ah. Now I understand."

"I'm sorry, Luke. I shouldn't have been so contrary."

"No need to apologize. I completely understand. And I am happy to wait until we become better acquainted."

***

David arrived shortly thereafter and took Kathleen home. Luke could see an improvement in organization already, no doubt due to his new assistant.

He stood in front of his bookcase filled with medical texts. He was specifically looking for a book that might help him understand the problems of a patient who had worked for many years in the coal mines. The man was now having problems breathing, so Luke wanted to research lung conditions and maladies. He didn't have any books focusing on lung issues, so he took out his general practitioner's manual, turned off the light in his office and went to the large parlor across the foyer.

Settling into a chair beside the fireplace, he opened the book and began to read. He could hear Mrs. Bradley whistling the tune of the *Battle Hymn of the Republic* as she worked in the kitchen. She blared it with such gusto that Luke felt like getting up and marching. Of course, he wanted to celebrate for other reasons, not the least of which was Kathleen's willingness to "become better acquainted."

***

In the ensuing weeks, Kathleen genuinely enjoyed spending time with Luke, as well as learning from him. He had so much knowledge to share and his enthusiasm for wanting to help others was inspiring. Of course, Luke was a more pleasant and patient teacher than Nurse Schmidt. She shuddered just thinking about that woman, although in the grand scheme of things, Nurse Schmidt had not been the worst person who had ever entered Kathleen's life.

When Luke examined a patient, he would carefully explain what he was doing. This, Kathleen was sure, was not only for the patient's benefit but also for hers. Thinking back, this was one of the aspects that she really appreciated about Luke when she was injured. Luke didn't treat her like an unconscious body. Nor did he treat others that way. He spoke calmly and professionally to each patient, nodding and affirming them in a way that illustrated he cared about them as unique persons. Each time he warmed the stethoscope or spoke gently to a youngster, these scenes settled in a warm and substantial place in her memory...and in her heart.

26

A blast of frigid December air blew in as Kathleen and Will entered the foyer of their home. They took off their hats and coats, brushing the snow from them, and handed the items to Jane who frowned at the puddle of slush on the floor.

"Sorry, Jane. If you hand me a towel, I'll clean it up."

"Never you mind. But can you and Mr. Will take off your boots?"

"Very well." Kathleen and Will leaned against the wall in the foyer and pulled their boots off.

Jane motioned for the pair to proceed into the parlor. "The fire's nice and hot. I'll send Lucy to bring both of you some warm tea, if you'd like."

"Thank you, Jane; tea would be wonderful." She paused, lifting her head to enjoy the smell of bread, cake and cookies wafting up through the basement kitchen. "You and Lucy must be baking for Christmas."

"We are doing a bit of baking, yes."

Kathleen and Will entered the parlor to find both her father and Patrick in concentration, staring at the chessboard and neither saying hello.

"Hello Papa! Hello Pat!"

Pat raised his hand but stared at the board in front of him. Her father said a quiet, "Hello, Kat."

"What am I? The Christmas goose?" Will teased. Finally, Papa and Pat looked up. "Will, I didn't see you."

Pat smirked. "If you were the Christmas goose, we probably would have noticed you."

"Ha ha," Will retorted. "Don't mind us, we're just here to enjoy the heat of the fireplace." Both her father and Pat returned their attention to the board as Will and Kathleen warmed their hands.

Kathleen relished the heat of the roaring blaze as her black dress soaked in the warmth. It was difficult to believe that Christmas was less than a week away.

Of course, this year's festivities would be low key, as it had only been two months since baby Mo's passing. The decorations would be sparse, the tree smaller and the meal not as extensive. Some mourning families' homes were devoid of all decorations. As well, mirrors and windows were still covered and there weren't any trees or gifts. While she understood the reason, she also felt it was important for her younger siblings to celebrate the season, so she was grateful that her parents had decided not to take an extreme approach. Kathleen often found herself welling up with excitement even though there were still moments when melancholy took over. She also still experienced the occasional nightmare. However, Christmas and the start of a new year, 1897, brought hope for her growing friendship with Luke.

She turned to Will. "I enjoy the Christmas season!"

"Kat, it's not technically the Christmas season until next week, on Christmas Day."

"I know. But I do so look forward to the baking, the decorations — however few — not to mention the gifts."

Staring at the blue and orange flames in the hearth, Kathleen decided not to mention that her favorite part of this year's festivities would be Luke's presence with their family on Christmas Eve and Christmas Day. He would remain at their home for Christmas day, barring any medical emergencies or births. Luke's struggling medical practice was now thriving, especially since Papa recommended him to all his local clients. Unfortunately, now that he had so many patients, he was unable to take the long trip to Lancaster County to visit his aunt and uncle for the holidays.

"Miss Kathleen, Mr. Will, I've got some warm tea for both of you," their part-time servant said.

Kathleen couldn't help but smile at Lucy's entrance into the room. The tall and pretty servant always wore a happy expression and Kathleen marveled at the widow's determination to raise her large brood of children.

"Checkmate."

Her father's voice behind her was accompanied by Pat's groan.

"I was so close, Papa."

"So close?"

"To capturing one of your pieces."

"Good game, son. You're improving."

"Maybe I shall ask Dr. Luke to teach me."

Her father cocked an eyebrow. "Perhaps *I* shall ask Luke for a rematch soon." Papa reached over the board to pat his son's back, then he winked at Kathleen and left. Pat moved alongside his older sister and brother. Will leaned down and, with the poker, rearranged the burning maple, then added another log.

"Will, can you give me a few chess lessons?" Pat whined, his voice high-pitched.

"Another time, Pat. John's better than I. Why don't you find him?"

"He never seems to be available. Besides, I just need to be able to capture one of Papa's pieces."

Pat glanced at Kathleen. "Kat, you play well for a girl."

"What do you mean 'for a girl'? Girls can do many things better than boys."

"Come on. Please play chess with me?"

"I'm not anywhere near as competent a player as Papa or Luke. Besides, why do you need to capture just one?"

"Papa said if I could capture just one of his pieces before he won the game, he'd allow me to drive the Columbus carriage to church." He shrugged his shoulders. Patrick, who had turned fourteen recently, would soon surpass both older brothers in height so he certainly would be tall enough to drive.

"Very well, let's sit and I shall see if I can help you."

Pat's mouth fell open. "Gee, thank you, Kat."

Since Kathleen said yes, Will decided to remain and assist as well.

***

At dawn on Christmas Eve, Will knelt beside his bed and whispered his morning prayers. He wished he could speak immediately with Monsignor Flaherty about what needed to be accomplished to enter the seminary. But he willed himself to be patient.

Looking out his window, the oak tree, devoid of leaves, now held a thin layer of snow. The pond had frozen and there was a white dusting of snow like powdered sugar sprinkled on it.

Father Morrissey recently asked Will to serve as one of the main acolytes for Midnight Mass and had instructed him to arrive at the church by 11:30.

He opened the door and descended the back staircase to the kitchen.

"Morning, Mr. Will."

"Morning, Jane. Morning, Lucy. What time does Isaac's train arrive?"

"Two o'clock. You don't mind picking him up? Jesse could do that, you know."

"Not at all. I'm looking forward to seeing him again."

"Izzy can't wait to see her older brother. He makes me proud, Mr. Will."

"I can understand why. Graduating from high school early and taking pre-med, you have many reasons to be proud."

A short time later, Will welcomed Isaac at the train station and they chatted in the carriage. Isaac was a handsome young man and, like Izzy, his olive complexion made him look like a Spaniard.

"How do you find college?"

"I'm doing well. The courses are difficult, though."

"I imagine they would be in pre-medicine."

***

Luke checked the time and decided that he would get his carriage ready for the short jaunt to St. Vincent's for Midnight Mass. He gave Nate the evening off since it was Christmas Eve.

Since Luke lived close by, he rarely brought his carriage to church. However, he planned to follow the O'Donovans home afterwards, so he decided to make an exception and bring it now. Of course, he also wanted to surprise Kathleen and show her his brand new buggy, complete with electric lights. He got in and clicked the reins. The scent of fresh leather, the shiny metal trimming and the smooth wheels made Luke grateful that he had waited to pay for this rig in cash. As he rode up, there was no sign of the O'Donovans, so he pulled his carriage to the lot beside the church and tied the reins to a nearby post.

A few carriages began arriving and soon, the O'Donovans' Columbus carriage pulled up beside him; David and Will got out.

"Happy to see you, Luke. Merry Christmas." David shook Luke's hand.

"Merry Christmas, David, Will."

"Merry Christmas, Dr. Luke. Papa, may I go inside to prepare?"

"Of course, son."

Will headed into the church while David stood and chatted with Luke.

"David, what do you think of my new carriage?"

The man turned and stared. "Beautiful rig." He studied it, rubbed the seats. "Congratulations."

"Thank you."

David peered down the dark road. "If they don't arrive soon, Jesse will not be able to find a parking spot in this lot."

Luke nodded.

Several long minutes passed before Luke eyed the other carriage arriving with Jesse at the helm. David pointed to guide the servant to park across the street.

Luke's heart picked up its pace when he saw Kathleen's face through the window of the enclosed carriage.

Jesse steered the carriage to an area across the street and got down to help the family out. Luke rushed to Kathleen's side and assisted her out. "Merry Christmas."

"Merry Christmas, Luke!" Like most members of the family, Kathleen continued to wear black, but the color notwithstanding, she looked ravishing. Her hair was pulled up under her black hat.

Luke greeted each member of the family, and whispered to Kathleen, "Before we go inside, I must show you something."

"What is it?"

On the way to his new carriage, Kathleen chattered on for a few moments before Luke turned to her and pointed toward his vehicle. "Do you notice anything different about my carriage?"

The parking lot was lit with gas lamps but it took a minute for Kathleen to notice. "You've finally bought a new carriage! It's wonderful!"

"Do you like it?"

"I do! It's lovely."

***

The only aspect of St. Vincent's Church that Karl found tolerable was its close proximity to several homes and alleyways. The brick was cold on his back. Despite the frosty air, his palms inside his gloves were sweaty and his heart pounded as he waited for the O'Donovans to arrive.

He watched as carriages entered the lot beside the church. He had an excellent view from the alley.

A new Columbus Phaeton carriage pulled into the lot with the new doctor, who had obviously gotten himself a new rig. He didn't like the man; he looked like a child going through puberty with his smooth face, his slight form and his childish blond hair. The carriage was a nice one, though, and Karl savored the scent of new leather floating past him. The good doctor hitched the reins to a post.

Looking up, Karl noticed the O'Donovans' smaller carriage riding up with Kathleen's dear old dad and her brother. The doctor approached the pair and they chatted, although Karl could only hear bits and pieces of the conversation.

Several moments later, the Cabriolet pulled up. He squinted to see who was in that carriage but when the good doctor sprinted across the lane, he could guess why. His fists clenched as he saw that hick doctor assist Kathleen onto the stepping block. They came toward him and Karl backed into the shadow of the alley. He couldn't hear exactly what they were saying, but the way he talked to her, the way he looked at her — Karl was no idiot. He knew what that gentleman was doing. Either way, Kathleen wouldn't — couldn't — fall for a mealy-mouthed weakling like that doctor.

He waited for all the people milling about to enter the church. Once everyone was inside, the parking lot became deserted with horses snorting occasionally, their breath visible in the cold air. The only human left outside was the servant who remained with the Cabriolet parked across the street.

Karl leaned forward, his head peeking out of the alley, and watched the young servant, who was sitting in the driver's seat of the carriage facing away from him.

Emerging from the alleyway, Karl walked toward the doctor's carriage. The people in the church sang an exuberant rendition of *Joy to the World*.

The leather scent filled the frosty air. New carriage? Well, that could be fixed in one fell swoop. With the strains of "Repeat the sounding joy" echoing from the church, Karl took out his hunting knife and holding his hand above his head, he stabbed and pulled the knife through the seats with a long X. The cushion material burst forth through the leather like a fat lady's belly being released from a corset.

Yes, that would do just fine. Karl wished he could relieve himself on the carriage cushions too. But since he had to get into the rig to do so, he decided not to chance it with the servant present across the street. He left, satisfied with his destruction.

***

Luke hadn't been this happy in years. Mass had been beautifully celebrated. He and Kathleen followed the rest of the O'Donovans as they congregated in the parking area near the church. It was indeed a time of celebration. A soft snow had begun to fall.

Kathleen leaned down toward her younger brothers. "Come and see Luke's new carriage, boys!"

She pointed. Luke followed as the two youngsters ran ahead.

"Is this yours, Luke? Golly, what happened to the seat?" Kevin was gaping at the carriage seat which, under the gaslight, looked like it had yellow balls on it. As Luke inched closer, his heart sank. Someone had taken a knife to his beautiful new carriage and ripped the leather seat.

"Good gracious, Luke! Who could've done such a thing?"

Kathleen put her hand on his arm.

"I...don't...know."

David soon joined them. "This is terrible, Luke. As if those troublemakers don't have anything better to do on Christmas." He placed his hand on Luke's shoulder. "I shall pay for new seats for your carriage."

"David, you really don't..."

"My Christmas gift to you. It's going to be difficult riding back to the house in that condition."

Will stepped forward. "I can probably sit at the side of the ripped area, Papa, and bring it home. John can squeeze in the Cabriolet. Kat and Luke can go home in our Columbus."

"Very well."

In the darkness of that Christmas night, as he rode home with Kathleen, Luke couldn't rid himself of the feeling that the perpetrator wasn't a random hooligan.

***

Arriving at the O'Donovan home after Mass, Luke still couldn't shake the uneasy feeling. But he was determined to smile and enjoy the time with Kathleen and her family. Jane, Izzy and Isaac had joined the others in the parlor as they all exchanged gifts. Luke was amazed at the energy of the youngest children, despite it being two a.m.

During the hustle and bustle of the exchange of presents, Luke sat on the couch beside the piano. The tree was a six foot Balsam fir that filled the room with crisp evergreen scent. Tinsel and glass balls adorned the branches.

Kathleen, after opening a gift of silk scarves, sat down beside Luke. She must have seen Luke looking at the tree because she commented, "We normally get a ten foot tree. This one is quite small, but we are, after all, still in mourning." She handed him a medium-sized box. "This is for you, Luke."

Opening the box, he chuckled when he saw what was inside: *The Hunchback of Notre Dame* by Victor Hugo. "Wonderful. I don't own any books by Hugo."

"I know. I was paging through this at the bookstore and I thought it would be an activity we could do together."

"Together?"

"I read one page; you read the next."

"Of course. Now it's my turn." He lifted the flat gift from his pants pocket. "This is for you."

Kathleen's mouth fell open. "It's wonderful!"

"You don't know what it is."

"I don't care. I shall treasure whatever it is that you have given me."

She ripped off the paper and opened the flat box. Kathleen's expression went from curiosity to delight and she squealed. "This is perfect, Luke." She held up the brass bookmark that she had admired when she was assisting at his office. "Is this the same bookmark?"

"It is. I hope you don't mind."

"Mind? Of course not. It's lovely!"

Luke handed her a larger rectangular gift. "One more."

"Another? Why, Luke, you shouldn't have!"

Tearing open the wrapping, Kathleen gasped. The top of the small wooden box was an exquisite carving of a deer, trees and a lake.

"This is beautiful. Where did you get it?"

"My grandfather carved it for my grandmother."

"How can you give me such a sentimental item, Luke?"

"Because I truly want you to have this."

"I shall accept it happily then."

Kathleen took Luke's hand. Her soft smaller hand felt like the perfect fit in his as she pulled him off the couch and towards her parents, who were sitting on the sofa beside the fireplace.

"Mama, Papa, look what Luke gave me." She held out the box and the bookmark. "Luke's grandfather carved it for Luke's grandmother."

"Beautiful piece. Was he Indian, Luke?" David asked.

He offered a slight nod. "Both my grandparents were from the Delaware tribe."

David's eyebrows rose. "Luke, you look like you have as much Indian blood as I do."

"I know that people can be prejudiced; that's why I haven't volunteered the information before."

"Understandable." David patted him on the back. "It doesn't...well, we don't care what your background is."

"Thank you, David." Luke didn't — or perhaps couldn't — understand why prejudices existed at all, whether it be against persons of another race or class. Luke firmly believed that all human beings were created in the image and likeness of God; skin color and heritage made humans different and unique, not worse or better than another.

***

The next day, after an uneasy sleep, Luke tried to greet Christmas day with the joy that he should feel in celebrating the Savior's birth. He was with Kathleen and her family so that made him immensely happy. Caroline's cousin, Elizabeth, her husband, Philip, and their daughter arrived for the festivities. Luke had already met Elizabeth when Caroline came to the office for a routine check-up several weeks previous. Elizabeth had blond hair and was a large woman in more ways than size. While standing in the foyer, she laughed loudly at a comment of David's while her husband, a tall, thin man with graying brown hair, stayed by her side and smiled, but kept silent. David turned to Luke, "I'd like to introduce Dr. Luke Peterson. Luke, this is Caroline's cousin, Mrs. Elizabeth Smythe, and her husband, Mr. Philip Smythe."

"Yes," Luke said, "I had the pleasure of meeting Mrs. Smythe several weeks ago at the office."

"That's correct," Elizabeth said. "Your house looks so spacious from the outside, but your office reminds me of a simple country doctor's office, not like the offices at the Philadelphia Hospital with their high ceilings and fresh paint."

Luke smiled awkwardly and held his hand out to Philip, who had a slack handshake for a tall man. "Pleased to make your acquaintance, Dr. Peterson."

"Please call me Luke."

"Luke."

David continued the introductions. "And Alice, their lovely daughter, is in the parlor with Kathleen."

Alice, as tall as Kathleen, giggled and laughed frequently,

and Luke could see the family resemblance. She looked like an interesting combination of her parents and was naturally pretty.

After supper, the men gathered in David's study. David offered them cigars, which Philip accepted and Luke politely declined. Before David closed the door, he invited Will and John to join them. The young men's eyes lit up at the prospect of being invited to be part of the circle of "men."

Closing the door, David announced, "Gentlemen, fair warning. My wife has asked me to play the violin when we emerge. I'm not the world's best player and I do not pick it up often, but Kat has agreed to accompany me on the piano. I tried to tell my wife we were a family in mourning, but she so wisely reminded me that music soothes the soul."

Philip puffed on his cigar. "David, Luke, what is your opinion of President-elect McKinley? He seems a fine chap with excellent ideas."

"Yes, he does."

Luke added, "I must admit that the whole 'front porch' idea was brilliant."

Philip nodded. "Agreed. Although I would never have voted for Bryan since he does not have the maturity for such a high office."

Will and John contributed little to the conversation, but Luke could tell from their satisfied and grinning expressions that they were happy to be amongst the *men*.

***

A short time later, the men, women and children gathered in the parlor. Tim first recited "Cradle Song" by William Blake. Kevin then gave a dramatic rendition of "Minstrels" by William Wordsworth and Luke found both boys' readings quite entertaining.

David set up a stand with sheet music. David and Kathleen whispered and murmured. Kathleen shook her head and frowned a few times and her father did the same.

Putting his violin under his chin, David began playing upbeat fiddle music. The children and adults were soon clapping and stomping their feet. David played rather well and Luke could not hear any indication that the music was off beat, flat or sharp. Kathleen was also a talented pianist. At one point, she caught her father's eye and he winked.

After nearly ten minutes of upbeat music, David walked over to where Caroline sat and whispered in her ear. She nodded and he returned to his music stand.

David began to play a slow, soft melody. The older man played it as if he had done so many times before. Luke wasn't familiar with the song, but it was moving and soon the adults were dabbing their eyes with handkerchiefs.

When he was finished, Caroline held her hand out to take the instrument from David. She set it carefully, almost reverently, on top of the piano. She leaned in to kiss her husband. Feeling like he was intruding on a private moment, Luke glanced away. The way they interacted, however, made him want to keep staring.

Finally, Caroline said to David, "Thank you for allowing my soul to sing after the sadness of these past few months." The two embraced.

***

After Elizabeth and Philip left, Luke suggested that he and Kathleen take a stroll outside. Her preferred place on a brisk evening was in front of the fireplace. But she agreed, since it would give them private time to converse. The gas lights lit up the area and a light coating of snow sparkled like tiny diamonds. Ice crystals floated in the air. Kathleen shivered and pulled her coat closer.

"That was the most fun I've had listening to poetry and music," Luke said. "Kevin and Tim read extremely well. And you and your father make a great duet."

"We don't play very often. As the only musicians in the house, it does afford us enjoyable time together. I like playing piano, but I don't practice enough to be especially proficient."

"It sounded exquisite."

"Papa used to play that last song when Baby Mo was fussing and she would settle down. She evidently enjoyed Papa's playing."

"I'm certain she did. What is the name of that song?"

"Oft in the Stilly Night."

"Lovely, sweet song."

"That was my real father's favorite song as well." She paused. "Of course, it seems odd to say 'real father,' because Papa seems like my 'real' father."

"And your late father's name was..."

"Liam."

"Ah, Lee. I understand now. Your father likes to call people by monosyllabic names."

"Indeed, although he has never shortened my mother's name, unless he calls her 'love.'"

With a smile, Luke nodded, but remained silent.

"I almost forgot to tell you. Margaret is with child!"

"That's excellent news."

"She is due to deliver in May."

A few moments passed as Luke stared up at the black sky. "The glory of the stars is the beauty of heaven; the Lord enlighteneth the world on high." He turned to face her. "Sirach 43:10."

"A beautiful verse, Luke."

"The stars also remind me of the Scripture verse where God tells Abram that his descendents will be more numerous than the stars in the sky. Some day I hope to have that many descendents. I grew up virtually an only child and I pray my home will be filled with many children."

Kathleen stepped back, her eyebrows lifting. *A man who hopes and prays to have a houseful of children?* Luke certainly was different from the gentlemen she had known.

"I cannot imagine being an only child. When I was younger, especially with so many brothers, I used to dream of running away to a quiet home."

"You could have run away to our home; it was very quiet."

With a smile, Kathleen watched as Luke spoke in quiet puffs of air. "Come," he said, "let's walk to the back yard. I think we might be able to see more stars." At the side of the house, near the stable, Luke pointed. "That's the constellation of Ursa Major, sometimes called the Big Dipper. Do you see how those stars look like a pot?"

"Yes, I do."

Luke walked, lifting his chin at the sky as if he were studying it. He nearly ran into a lamp pole beside the clothesline. "Watch out!" Kathleen pulled on his arm to stop him. He chuckled. "I might have seen different stars had I run into that pole."

"Yes, that's true," she said, smiling, then she pointed to the brightest star in the sky, just above the horizon. "What star is that, Luke?"

"That's not a star. It's Venus."

"Venus? It's very bright."

"Yes, it is. Venus just passed through Aquarius and will be setting soon so we won't be able to see it again until sunrise." He paused before continuing. "I can stare at the night sky for hours, especially when so many stars are visible." Luke turned toward her. "I want to teach you about the stars and the constellations."

"I would like that." She paused. "Luke?"

"Yes?"

"I would like to thank you for being such a patient teacher. I'm grateful to have something with which to occupy my time besides reading. Will and John are engrossed in their studies, Papa has his business, and the younger children attend school. Jane, Lucy and Izzy bake and clean. Mama reads and embroiders. Sometimes, I feel lonely and without purpose in our big house. I often feel alone, like my destiny is calling me forward and, without purpose, I cannot proceed."

Tilting his head upward, Luke pointed. "When I was a youngster and feeling lonely, I would gaze at the stars. I don't know why it consoled me, but it did. I missed my sister, I missed my brother who I only saw at school, and, of course, I missed my parents, who by that time were gone."

Luke gently took hold of her hand. "If you're ever lonely, all you'll need to do is to stare at the stars and know that I'm looking at those same stars with you and be assured that I am thinking of you." Then he gazed upward, his breath visible in the cold air. Kathleen's pulse was racing, her heart beating quickly. Luke's soft features, his small glasses perched on the bridge of his nose and his kind, gentle spirit...any persistent doubts had dissipated. This *was* her beloved.

***

Karl's appearance at his father's house on Christmas evening had little to do with family obligation and more to do with Karl's gift to himself: a trip to visit his favorite hussy, Pearl, the slight green-eyed girl who could be Kathleen's twin.

After dinner, he rode his horse to the brothel. Karl wondered how the doctor liked his 'new and improved' carriage. He snickered.

He pulled up to the area near the whorehouse and was disturbed to find carriages crowding the area in front of it. He tied the rein to a post. Entering the building, he asked for Pearl and he was told that she was "otherwise occupied."

Karl scowled. "How long?"

The middle-aged madam glanced at the clock. "Half an hour. Christmas evening has been busy."

"I will wait for her."

"Suit yourself, but we have other girls." She waved her hand and pointed to a group of unoccupied females in their shifts.

Shaking his head, Karl was filled with disgust that these scantily clad girls strutted around with their tempting gazes. Then again, whores had little decency. He fidgeted in his seat and studied the madam. She had probably been attractive in her younger days, but now? The woman wore too much face paint in a vain attempt to cover her deep wrinkles, sagging cheeks and disappearing lips.

He kept himself occupied by counting the pink and blue flowers in the parlor's wallpaper.

"Sir, do come up," Pearl finally called from the top of the stairs. Karl hadn't noticed anyone leaving.

On the second floor, Pearl stood in the doorway of a spacious room and stepped aside to allow him to enter.

"My, my. Do you ask for me every single time?"

He nodded.

"Why, pray tell? Do I look like someone you know?"

This girl was too inquisitive.

"Yes, you do, if you must know."

"Someone you loved?"

"Perhaps."

"Well, I can be anyone you want. What is this girl's name?"

"Kathleen."

"Then I'm no longer Pearl. I'm Kathleen...what's her last name?"

"O'Donovan."

The girl's eyebrows lifted. "The wealthy O'Donovans of the O'Donovan Mercantile?"

With a nod, Karl replied, "Yes."

"Very well. Call me Kathleen."

The interaction took less than ten minutes and Karl gave the girl a bonus coin for her fine performance.

27

February 15th came and passed with no fanfare for Will. His parents had offered to celebrate his birthday this year on the same date, but Will insisted they wait until his actual birthday in June. It would be peculiar celebrating in June, but it *was,* after all, his true birth month.

His father had finally arranged a meeting with Monsignor Flaherty after school and before supper the following Wednesday.

"Will, are you ready?" His father tapped the door open.

"Yes, Papa."

"Catechism questions memorized?"

Will scowled in a moment of panic. "Memorized?"

His father winked. "Just teasing you, although you should have your Baltimore Catechism memorized at this age."

"Of course."

St. Michael's Parish was in the Kensington Section of Philadelphia, a twenty minute ride from their home. The sky was clear, the air cold and unmoving.

When they reached the church, his father steered the carriage to the side of the road and pulled on the reins to stop Gent. They got out and tied the reins to the post. As they walked towards the church, Will lifted his head and studied the building. It was similar to St. Vincent's in its Italian Renaissance design but, unlike their church, this one had two spires reaching toward the sky. A clock adorned the taller spire and red bricks covered the front.

"Papa?"

"Yes?"

"May I visit the Blessed Sacrament after our meeting?"

"Of course. Remind me to ask Monsignor."

To the left was a smaller, three story building with a similar red brick façade and an arched doorway. His father climbed the steps and knocked while Will waited on the sidewalk. An elderly heavyset woman with white, pulled-back hair answered the door. "May I help you?" She pulled her wool sweater close as the cold air swept in through the open door.

His father spoke. "Permit me to introduce myself: I'm David O'Donovan and this is my son, William O'Donovan. We have an appointment at 4:00 p.m. with Monsignor Flaherty."

"Pleased to meet you, gentlemen. I'm Mrs. O'Reilly, the housekeeper. Come right this way." She led them through a foyer to a waiting room. "I will take your coats and hats. Please wait in here for Monsignor."

They sat down in the arm chairs by the window but soon heard, "Please come this way." Mrs. O'Reilly took them through a wide hallway lined with chairs where Monsignor was waiting for them. The priest was younger and taller than Will imagined he would be. He looked to be in his mid to late forties, with graying temples, and was dressed in a cassock with small glasses similar to Dr. Luke's spectacles on the bridge of his nose. Also like Dr. Luke, this priest had kind eyes and a caring smile. "Good day, David. Good day, Will, it's a pleasure to see you again."

Will politely offered his hand and the priest shook it firmly. "You don't remember me, do you, Will?"

Shaking his head, Will said, "No, Monsignor, I don't."

"Will, first, I will need to discuss a few matters privately with your father, then I shall come out and invite you to join us. Would you please wait here in the hallway?"

"Of course."

His father and the priest went into the office, the door closing. Will sat in one of the chairs nearby.

Will studied his surroundings. The high ceiling was painted a dull white. The walls were adorned with sacred images. Directly across from him, on the outside of the priest's office hung an image of the Sacred Heart. Above the priest's door was a crucifix. He stood up to take a closer look, then he heard his father's angry voice: "That's absurd!"

Inching toward the door, Will heard his father and Msgr. Flaherty speaking. Then he could hear the priest tell his father to lower his voice. His father's voice bellowed.

"This is outrageous. Will is my son and he is accepted as

my son in every manner. I am listed as his father on the baptismal certificate..."

"Yes, David, but we also listed his birth mother's name."

No response from Papa.

"He is, for all intents and purposes, your son and is viewed as your son, but when a person is born illegitimate, the manner of birth cannot be changed."

"Surely you are jesting!"

"I'm afraid not. When you informed me of Will's interest in entering the seminary, I retrieved the baptismal registry and his birth mother's name is, in fact, listed. But the name also says William David Callahan, not O'Donovan. Have you changed his name legally?"

"Yes, we formally and legally adopted him and had his name changed; he is listed as my natural son and included in my legal will....and he is, most certainly, my blood offspring. We have only ever referred to him as William David O'Donovan."

"In the eyes of the Church, the circumstances of his birth determine his legitimacy or illegitimacy. Unfortunately, adoption does not take away his status at birth. Canon Law states that illegitimates cannot enter the priesthood."

At the door, Will drew in a breath; his shaking hand covered his mouth as he continued to listen.

His father's voice blurted, "This is nonsense. Will is a fine, devout young man who has never given me a moment of grief."

"David, I am hopeful that in this particular case we can obtain a special dispensation for Will to enter the seminary. But first an extensive investigation must be carried out and there are no guarantees."

"Who gives this special dispensation? Let me talk to him."

"His Holiness Pope Leo XIII. There is protocol that we must follow before any dispensation can even be considered. Allow me to research this and I will keep you informed."

Will straightened and turned away from the door. He held his hand to his chest to calm the rapid beating of his heart. Could it be true? Could it be that, because of his beginnings, he would not be able to serve God as a priest? And, if so, why would he feel such a strong call? He backed away from the door and knocked into a small table. A gaping hole of emptiness tore through his soul.

Will needed both men to understand that this *was* his calling, and that he would do anything — and everything — to fulfill his vocation. For several moments, Will could not hear anything as he stood facing the closed door. Finally, he heard the priest's voice once more.

"If you will recall, I was able to obtain for you and Caroline a special dispensation since you were Caroline's brother-in-law and your affinity was considered too close."

"Yes, I remember. But this?"

"This will most certainly be more difficult. The Canon Law regarding illegitimacy is in place because of...well, genetics. The line of thinking is that children born out of wedlock tend to repeat their parents' mistakes."

"Monsignor, with all due respect, I am a changed man."

"Yes, that is an important point we shall mention in our application for dispensation."

Suddenly, the conversation ceased and the door opened. Monsignor Flaherty stepped back in surprise. His mouth softened in a smile. "Come in, Will."

Will felt a warm flush on his face.

The priest opened the door. When Will entered the room, he avoided eye contact with his father. "Take a seat in here," Monsignor pointed to a chair near a desk. He finally glanced at his father; the man's face appeared pale, his mouth pursed.

"I couldn't help but hear the conversation. Are you angry with me, Papa?"

"I'm not angry with you." He shook his head. "I'm angry at myself. I should have known there would be long-term consequences to my immoral behavior."

The priest's quiet voice responded. "That's in the past, David. I shall do my best to phrase it in such a way as to strongly recommend this dispensation. This is an ideal case for one."

He turned toward Will. "Did you...hear... everything?"

"Enough. I heard that the Church says that I cannot become a priest because I'm a bastard." Both his father and the priest winced. "And a source of scandal. That's about as plain and clear as it can be."

"Will," the priest said, "it will be necessary to obtain a special dispensation in order for you to enter the seminary. It doesn't necessarily mean that you cannot become a priest. It just means an investigation will need to take place, then a recommendation will be made. The Pope will then consider all the facts. And it could take up to two years."

"Two years?" Will sunk back in his seat and sighed.

"Unfortunately, yes. It could take less time, but that is unlikely."

"Is it possible that a special dispensation *won't* be granted, Monsignor?" Will didn't want to think of that possibility but he had to ask.

The priest got up and stood beside Will's chair. "Yes, but if God is truly calling you, the dispensation will be granted. I firmly believe that."

"What shall I do until then?"

"Pray, continue to discern, attend daily Mass and adoration when you're able." Facing David, Monsignor Flaherty said, "I should like to meet with Will on a monthly basis. Perhaps the third Saturday of every month?"

"Yes," David responded. "Will, is that acceptable to you?"

"That's fine. I often attend Mass at our parish on Saturday morning."

"You can attend Mass here in the morning at seven and we can meet afterwards. Or, if you prefer, our meeting can be at one p.m."

"I would prefer to attend Mass in my home parish, Monsignor. But can't we start right away?"

"Next Saturday is the third Saturday."

"Oh, yes, thank you."

"Then one p.m. every third Saturday of the month. David, you will need to accompany him the first two or three appointments so I can compile the information I will require for the application."

"Of course."

"And, Will," Monsignor Flaherty said, "your father tells me you've read *St. Augustine's Confessions*?"

Will nodded.

"Excellent discourse. Don't be discouraged. If God is truly calling you to a priestly vocation, then He will still be calling you in another year or so. If you'll just wait in the hallway, I need to discuss another matter with your father."

Out in the hallway, Will sat cross-legged. All of a sudden he realized he was gripping the arms of the chair. He relaxed his hands. This time, he could not hear any conversation inside the office. The priest finally opened the door. Before his father stepped out of the office, he handed the man an envelope. "This should cover expenses, Monsignor. If you should need more, please let me know."

As they turned to leave, Will reached out and touched his father's arm. "The church, Papa?"

"Oh, yes, Will would like to visit the church. Is it locked?"

"Yes, but you can come this way, then I'll let you out at the front and open the church for you."

"Thank you for all you have done." Will's father shook the priest's hand.

28

The March winds blew briskly against Kathleen's face as her father steered the horses on the road to Germantown and Luke's home. She shivered and pulled her coat closer to her body, thankful for the warm cakes in the bag in front of her.

Leaning her head to one side, she peered up into the sky at the white clouds and wondered whether snow was on the way. Snow seemed to have been on the ground continuously since before Christmas.

"Papa?"

"Yes, Kat?"

"In a month, it will be six months since baby Mo passed."

"I know," her father's voice muttered.

"I should like to court Luke."

"I know that, too."

"And?"

"You have my blessing. He's a fine gentleman."

"Thank you, Papa."

As they pulled in front of Luke's place, Kathleen's heart started to race. She enjoyed working with Luke. While she was sorry she had quit nursing school, she was grateful to have an opportunity to help others and, at the same time, become better acquainted with Luke.

Each day they were together, Kathleen had made it a point to learn one new detail about him. He hadn't, as yet, caught on to what she was doing. So far, she had discovered that his favorite author was Charles Dickens, but he also enjoyed reading books by Mark Twain and Tolstoy. Together, they enjoyed reading *The Hunchback of Notre Dame*, although enjoy was not the correct word. That dark story was a challenging one because of the difficult circumstances of the main character, Quasimodo.

Recently, she discovered his penchant for angel cake, so early this morning, Jane had helped her bake two small cakes.

Luke came out to greet them and assisted Kathleen out of the carriage and onto the stepping block. "Good morning.

What have you got there?" He pointed to the bundle under her coat.

"Angel cakes."

"Delightful! We shall have that for our mid-morning break. Thank you, Kath." Turning to her father, Luke said, "David, I can bring Kathleen home this evening. I had hoped she could stay and help me with filing after the last patient leaves."

"Yes, that's fine. I hope you will join us for dinner. Caroline and Jane would think me impolite not to invite you."

"Of course. I would be happy to accept your invitation."

After waving goodbye to her father, she accompanied Luke across the porch. They went in through the main door and entered the foyer. To the left, a fire blazed in the parlor's fireplace. Luke took her coat and hung it on the rack by the door. "I thought you might like to warm yourself by the fire for a few minutes."

"Yes, thank you, I would."

He strolled toward the kitchen with the warm cakes as Kathleen followed the warmth of the fireplace in the parlor. The spacious and bright room was her favorite room in this house. Hardware floors, wooden chairs, a comfortable sofa and a brick fireplace gave the room a rustic atmosphere.

Luke's voice behind her said, "Warm enough?"

"Afraid not, but that's fine. I'm ready to work."

He held open the door from the foyer to the waiting room and allowed her to step inside. She walked ahead to his examining room/office and nearly gasped at the tall and numerous files piled on his desk. He pointed. "This is what we shall be doing when the last patient leaves."

"Would you like me to do that now?"

"No. Mrs. Thayer will be along momentarily."

"Very well." She continued staring at the various folders and items on his desk. The disarray told her that yesterday (when Kathleen had not been present) had obviously been extra busy or perhaps there were emergencies. Luke's office usually appeared more organized and neat.

***

On the way to the O'Donovan's, Kathleen's chatter was music to Luke's ears. It was cold in the carriage, but they had dressed warmly. Mrs. Bradley, God bless her generous soul, had placed both of their coats near the fire for a time before they'd left. Luke recited an extra prayer that his kind and thoughtful housekeeper would live and work for him until she was 100.

"Did you hear me, Luke?"

"Sorry...no, I didn't."

"I was saying...since it's near the end of the mourning period for baby Mo..."

"Yes?"

"We should...well, I think we should officially begin our courtship."

Luke cleared his throat to avoid laughing out loud. He had planned to confirm his desire with David later this week and expected Kathleen's father to give the courtship his hearty blessing. Then he planned to ask her. But it meant a great deal to him that she had brought up the topic first. "Of course. I had planned to speak with your father later this week, but I can do so today."

"Excellent!" She slid closer to him in the carriage and let out a satisfied sigh. Turning toward him, she was quiet, but the corners of her mouth lifted in a wide smile.

29

Kathleen could hardly contain her excitement the Saturday before Palm Sunday. The snow had finally disappeared. It was a beautiful spring day, with clear blue skies above, and a cool breeze blowing. Luke would be arriving at any moment and would be spending the day with her and with her family.

Officially, it would be their first full day together as a courting couple. In actuality, it wouldn't be much different from their growing friendship over the last six months.

Aside from her father and brothers, Luke was the kindest man she ever had the pleasure to know. She could tell that he had been restrained in his affection toward her, respecting the mourning period.

"Miss Kathleen?" Jane asked through the door.

"Yes, Jane?"

"Dr. Luke is downstairs waiting for you."

"I'll be down immediately."

Kathleen fixed her hat to her head and tilted her head from side to side as she studied herself in the mirror. "Yes, this will do just fine."

***

Luke was downstairs in the foyer, his hat and riding gloves in his hands, his foot tapping as he waited. When he saw Kathleen descend the stairs, he blinked his eyes. She was a vision of loveliness. As much as she looked beautiful in any shade of black or gray, today she was dressed in a fetching green blouse with puffy sleeves and a yellow and green-patterned skirt with matching hat and gloves. Her bright eyes and wide smile made him want to keep staring.

"Hello, Luke! Isn't it a fine day?"

"Uh...it is," he managed to say.

"Might we take a walk before lunch? I do so relish these spring days before the heat of summer sets in."

Luke held his arm out and Kathleen took hold of it.

The two walked toward the pond near the maples and oaks in the distance. In the sky, numerous clouds drifted slowly, like staggered ships. A flock of honking geese flew overhead in a V formation. Buds already appeared on the trees and tulips had already popped through the soil in the front of the house. It was a beautiful day, filled with promise.

"Luke?"

"Yes?"

"I've been so excited all morning."

"I cannot lie...I have been happy and carefree as well."

"And yet...."

He looked at her with a pinched expression. "And yet?"

"With baby Mo gone, I feel guilty."

Relieved, he responded, "It's normal to feel melancholy that you lost your sister, but also comforting to embrace hope and happiness."

"Mama and Papa are still grieving. I notice certain ways they look at each other or sometimes Mama will stare at the photograph we had taken after baby Mo was born and she'll become pensive for a moment."

Luke nodded, but remained silent.

"But when a day is as beautiful as today, I feel so hopeful, despite the sadness."

"When you feel hope, anything is possible." Luke looked down at Kathleen, who was smiling and her eyes were bright. Her back was against the tree. A narrow sunbeam was peeking its way through the thick oak leaves and landed like a halo just above her head. Squinting, she raised her chin and stepped closer to him.

Luke reached out and caressed Kathleen's cheek. Pulling her close to him, he kissed her forehead. "You know how I feel about you, Kath."

With a slight nod, she stepped back and looked up at him. "You are fine, honorable gentleman, Dr. Luke Peterson. You are the kindest man I have ever met. And I am happy that you feel this...affection toward me."

"Affection?"

He kept his hands on her shoulders. "I love you, Kathleen. I have only refrained from saying so out of respect for your parents and the mourning period. I have felt this way for a very long time."

"Truly?"

With a nod, he said, "Truly."

***

Will stepped onto the porch and immediately halted when he observed Dr. Luke and his sister beside the oak tree. Dr. Luke leaned in to kiss his sister's forehead. He turned away, awkward that he had intruded on their private moment. They spoke quietly to one another, then embraced.

Will coughed loudly to communicate that he was there. They stepped away from one another, his sister turning crimson and Luke straightening, clearing his throat.

"Will."

"Dr. Luke."

"Have either of you seen John? He's nowhere to be found in the house."

"No, we haven't seen him," Kathleen said.

"Very well. I shall check out back."

***

Will lazily strolled off, his arms swinging back and forth, his head turning and smiling at his sister and Dr. Luke. He wouldn't be surprised if they were talking marriage in the near future. He also knew, as surely as he knew himself, that Dr. Luke was the kind of man who would love, protect and care for his sister.

Heading toward the barn, Will heard no sounds, except for chickens clucking. He walked around to the back of the barn, then gasped, his hand at his open mouth. "What in the world..."

John and Izzy were locked in what Will could only describe as a passionate – and highly inappropriate – kiss. They broke apart and Izzy's skin flushed as red as it was able, while John wiped his mouth and cleared his throat. "Do you need something, Will?"

"Uh...I don't suppose I do." He immediately turned and followed the path back to the front of the house. As he passed Luke and Kathleen by the tree, he avoided eye contact.

Will ran into the house and up the stairs to his room. While he was not surprised to see Kat and Dr. Luke at the tree in the middle of a chaste kiss, he was highly disappointed that John and Izzy were attached in an inappropriate kiss. Should he tell Papa?

No wonder John and Izzy kept out of sight. If their parents or Jane knew, none of them would be happy. What was John thinking? Izzy was a servant. In addition, the girl was not Catholic. She was beautiful, but everything taken into account, she was not the sort that John ought to be marrying. John might be only six months younger than Will, but he was obviously several years less mature.

He should speak to his brother at the first opportune moment and try to convince him that he ought not to be romancing the servant's daughter.

Will heard thunderous footsteps then two quick, hard knocks at his door.

Good, he thought. *We shall take care of this quickly.*

"Will, I need to talk with you...now!"

Opening the door, Will stared. John wore a distinct frown. His brother stepped inside the room and closed the door. "You need to promise me that you won't tell anyone what you just saw."

"Why should I promise that?"

"Because it's none of your business."

Will sighed. "You are my brother. It is my business."

"No," John leaned in close to Will's ear and hissed, "this is none of your damned business. Stay out of my affairs."

Will glared at John. He couldn't believe that his brother could stoop so low as to become involved with a servant. Then a realization hit him and he winced. Papa was with a servant and that is why he was alive.

"Promise me," John demanded.

"I shall not promise anything. Besides, you said to stay out of your affairs. I shall do so, but I must inform Papa that you are...I don't even know what you call being with Izzy."

John's face softened. "Promise you won't say anything...I will tell Papa in my own time. Promise me."

Will scoffed. "She's a servant, John."

"I don't care. I love her."

Will did not respond.

"Stop worrying about me." Without waiting for a response, John left the room.

Will shook his head. *If being in love makes you that foolish, that's another good reason to become a priest.*

30

Looking at his reflection in the mirror, Karl lifted his chin and tilted his head from side to side. Without needing to shave, his morning preparation time was less than ten minutes. His already full black beard and longer hair changed his appearance so much that even he did not recognize himself. He had recently left his job at the saloon for employment as a farmhand only a quarter mile from the O'Donovans. Lower class work clothes, beard, long hair and right down the road. Life was going in the right direction and even his father had no idea where he was.

This was his first day off in many weeks, and it was a fine, sunny spring day, so he had great plans. First, he would ride over to St. Vincent's and watch her family enter the church. He wouldn't have to stand behind any carriages or in any alleyways because he would be dressed as a farmer, a wide-brimmed hat on his head, a thick beard covering his face.

Near the church, Karl got off the horse and tied the reins to a post. He acted as if he were searching for something in the saddle bag and not merely waiting.

That's when he noticed the hick doctor ride up with his carriage. Karl scoffed, then smiled, remembering when he slashed the new carriage cushion seats last Christmas. The man-boy appeared to be glancing in the direction of the road and, thankfully, not toward him. At that moment, the doctor smiled, his gaze directed to the area in front of the church. What in the...Karl's mood darkened.

The O'Donovan caravan arrived and the doctor nearly knocked over another gentleman as he rushed to greet them. Karl's hands gripped the reins so tightly that his nails dug into his palms. The stupid doctor put out his arm and Kathleen took hold of it. Karl gritted his teeth. Were they courting? No, it couldn't be. But why else would they be arm in arm and her smile so wide? How could she fall for such a lame excuse of a man?

Just wait, just wait, he calmed his burgeoning anger and

composed himself momentarily. *Just wait.* Finally, they all went into the church. Crossing the street, he paced the walkway. Another carriage pulled up and a family hastily got out and went inside. From the church came a hearty rendition of *Let All Mortal Flesh Keep Silence.*

Returning to his horse, he untied the reins, hopped on and kicked his spurs deeply into the horse who ran faster as Karl's anger increased. He finally stopped at the laneway of the O'Donovans' house.

No family members would be here, only the servants, if any. He rode into the forest and tied the animal to a tree. He crept to the side of the house, listening. All was quiet. He waited. That's when he saw another carriage pull up with the older female servant and an elderly couple.

"Goodbye, Jane."

"Goodbye, Henry, Clara. Thank you for bringing me home."

"Happy to do so. Tell Izzy to get well soon."

"I will. The poor girl has suffered from croup since she was a baby. I do believe she's on the mend, though."

Karl remained in the forest, watching and waiting. He hadn't seen the other two servants, but learned one of them was ill. After waiting twenty minutes, he stepped out of his hiding place. That's when the same servant emerged from the back door, now dressed in a white and gray outfit, with a basket of clothes. She proceeded to the clothesline.

He quickly returned to the forest until he was out of sight. Waiting until she turned her back, he found a place that was closer to the front of the house. Then he burst out of the forest like a bullet and was on the porch within seconds. He saw no one. His shoes were covered in mud, so he roughly brushed the dirt from his boots using the shoe brush on the ground. He slowly turned the knob and was pleased to find it unlocked. He stepped into the foyer and listened. A barking type cough came from the second floor. Creeping up the staircase, he turned right and quietly walked through the hallway, trying to determine which room might be Kathleen's. He knew from seeing her at her window that hers was either the end room or next to end. He opened the last door to his right. Feminine, lacey decor, yellow and pink wallpaper, hope chest, vanity with mirror. *Yes, this must be it.*

His hands were trembling as he caressed her bedspread, captivated by the knick-knacks on her bedside table. And her lamp. His heart picked up its pace when he recalled her fear of the dark. It would be too difficult to take this lamp with him. Instead, he moved it to the floor behind the trunk. She would panic for a moment; and that would be good enough for now.

Turning, he saw her nightgown hanging over the bedpost. He yanked it off and held it to his face. Breathing in her scent, he thought, *Yes, this is perfect.* He had to quash his compulsion to rip to shreds every piece of clothing she had. He must wait.

As he stepped forward to leave, he heard footsteps approaching. He ducked into the closet, the door remaining open slightly, as he heard someone enter the room. He held his breath. The older servant stood beside the bed, her hands on her hips. "Now, Miss Kathleen, where is your nightdress? I told you before I left for morning service that you were supposed to leave it on the post." The woman sighed, then left.

Relieved, the nightgown over his shoulder, Karl came out of the closet and listened. He heard her speaking to the other servant. "I'll bring you some honey and lemon water in a few moments, Izzy. I need to check on the cinnamon loaf in the oven."

Karl opened the door a crack to see the older servant approach from the other hallway and come in his direction. He backed away from the door and heard her go down the back staircase. He waited one minute, then rushed through the hallway and out the front door. Within seconds, he was on his horse, Kathleen's nightgown safely tucked away in his bag as he headed back to Germantown and his favorite brothel.

When he arrived, the brothel was deserted. The madam answered the door. "I'd like to see Pearl."

"She's sleeping."

He paid the woman three times the usual amount.

"I'll go wake her."

Karl then took out the nightgown, bunched it up and held it behind him. Moments later, he was told to come upstairs. Pearl met him in the hallway.

"Hello there. I'm Pearl." She opened the door to a room and they went inside.

"Pearl, it's me, Karl."

With wide eyes and a seductive smile, she said, "The beard is very...becoming. And the clothes...well, you look like a farmer." Karl took the nightgown out from behind him and held it in front of her. "Put this on."

Her eyebrows lifted. "You want me to wear this when we're..."

"Yes," he handed it to her.

She took him by the hand and walked with him, her hips swaying, to the bed. He didn't like when she acted like a whore. He wanted her to act like she was a good girl, but frightened, afraid of him.

His fists were already clenched as the whore's thin green dress fell to the floor.

"The gown. Put...it...on...now!" He felt like yelling, but kept his voice down. He prided himself on his control.

She did as she was told, then he threw her on the bed. He no longer saw the whore. Now, the only face he could see was Kathleen's. His fists clenched, his jaw hardened, the volcano of anger he had been storing inside for months finally erupted. He grabbed her head and slammed it against the headboard once, twice, three times. Her face contorted, her mouth was open but no sound came forth. She finally released an ear-piercing scream, and he only let go of her head when a sting like a hot poker burned into his arm. He turned to find the madam pointing a gun at him. "Get your sorry ass out of here before I shoot lower. If I ever see you here again, I *will* kill you. Get out!"

He took off, droplets of blood falling to the floor as he ran down the stairs.

***

His arm on fire, Karl swore for the entire trek back to his horse. He hoisted himself onto the mare and rode along the street. That bullet needed to come out. He stopped a few blocks away and got off. He tied the reins to a post. Looking around, the street was deserted. *Everyone is at church or the whorehouse.* That's when he noticed the MD on a rickety sign outside the doctor's house. The house or office was likely vacant with that stupid doctor at Mass. Maybe he could just break in, find a proper tool to remove the bullet and leave a mess. Yes, that would be his preference.

Behind the home and office was a modest yard that bordered a thin woodsy area. The back door had glass panels above the knob. He knocked in case a servant was home. No response. In his pocket, Karl kept a thin hair pin to pick locks, but with the pain in his arm, he had no time to pick the lock. He used the butt of his gun to shatter the glass and opened the door. He stepped into a large kitchen, a table directly in front of him. He sat down at the chair. The small hole in his arm was dripping blood onto the hardwood floor. Lifting his head, he saw a doorway straight ahead and he rose again to pass through a storage room of medical supplies. He walked further into the doc's examining room and began pulling drawers open. In one, he found an instrument resembling a small knife. *Yes, this will do just fine.* He sat down on the chair, pulled his shirt up and studied his left arm. The bullet was just above and on the inside of the elbow. He clenched his jaw and braced himself as he jabbed the small knife in and tried to remove the bullet. He groaned and grunted, but nothing came out. "Damn it!" He pitched the knife across the room.

***

After Mass, Luke accompanied Kathleen to her family's carriages. Jesse was waiting with the Cabriolet.

"Luke, will you be coming for lunch?" Kathleen had tilted her head and was looking up at him.

"Of course."

"Pardon me? Doctor?"

Turning, Luke saw a young man, his hand holding an envelope in front of him.

"Thank you." He opened it and found this letter inside:

Dr. Peterson,

One of our girls is in need of immediate medical assistance. The note on your door indicated you would be at church...and this is why we sent a boy to deliver the message instead of one of our girls. Please come immediately. Life or death.

Sincerely,

Madam Violet Lavender

He turned to Kathleen, who was a young lady of gentle nature, so Luke weighed his words carefully. "A girl has been hurt. I'll need to tend to her injuries. I shall come to your house as soon as I am able."

"Of course, Luke."

He bid a hurried farewell to Kathleen and her family, then jogged to his carriage. He rode off toward his house and thought of the girl "in need of immediate medical assistance." He suspected the usual problem.

As he pulled up to his stable, he noticed a horse tied to a post across the street, unusual for a Sunday morning. He quickly tied his horse to the post in front of his house, leaving the carriage there while he went in to his office to get his medical bag. Stepping onto the porch, he took out his key, opened the office entrance and entered the waiting room. Just as he grabbed his bag, he heard a clicking sound behind him.

"Don't move."

Luke drew in a breath. "P...Please, a young girl needs my immediate help."

"Take this bullet out...now!"

Luke slowly turned, his bag in his hands. The voice sounded vaguely familiar. Now facing the man, Luke could see that he was dressed in farm clothes, had dark hair, dark eyes and a full black beard. He was probably tall but was currently hunched over.

The man's gun was pointed at Luke, his blood dripping onto the hardwood floor.

"I'd like nothing better than to shoot you right now. If you want to live, remove this damn bullet from my arm."

Dear God in heaven. It's Karl. This was not a safe situation. *Think...think.*

The gun still aimed at Luke, Karl motioned for him to go into the examining room. Luke kept glancing back at the barrel of the gun and the man's rigid — and pained — expression. Karl shuffled slowly, his feet dragging. Luke dropped his bag onto the floor and pointed to the chair beside the examining table.

"Sit...down," he told Karl.

Karl lowered himself onto the chair and took off his shirt. Karl was the definition of broad-shouldered and he possessed well-developed muscles that would allow him to easily hurt Luke, never mind the gun. "Take this it out....now!" He lifted his left arm up.

Luke clenched his jaw. Studying the area, it looked like the bullet had lodged itself just above the elbow, but had not grazed the bone. "How did you get this?"

"Shut up."

Luke's legs felt weak. He didn't trust Karl, but what other option did he have?

Opening his medical drawer, he took out a small scalpel. He would need to excise the wound and extract the bullet. Despite the Hippocratic Oath, he fought the impulse – no, urge – to plunge the knife into the man's chest.

He washed the wound with alcohol and Karl gasped, spat out a swear word and yanked his arm away.

Banging and yelling at the exterior office door startled both men, their heads turning toward the door.

"Get rid of them, whoever they are."

Luke gulped and straightened. He stepped into the waiting room, starting to close the door of his exam room. "Keep it open so I can see you!" Karl hissed.

Luke went to the outside office door and opened it slightly. A girl in face paint and a low cut dress bounced in place. "Doctor? Did you receive the message? Please hurry!!"

"Yes, I will be along shortly."

"Hurry, please!"

He closed the door and joined Karl again in the examining room. Luke turned on the electric lamp near the table and looked closely at the wound. When Luke touched the man's arm, he jerked it away again. "Hold still."

Karl mumbled something.

Luke was concentrating and hadn't fully heard what Karl had said. He ignored him. Then the man grabbed Luke's arm with his free hand.

"I hear you and Kathleen are courting? Well, isn't that sweet? I bet my dear Kathleen is happy with a small, insignificant and weak man like you." Luke did not respond and continued focusing on removing the bullet, but Karl repeated, "You're nothing but a spineless coward."

Finally, Luke stood up, looked away, his jaw grinding, his hands balled into fists. Luke heard the click of the gun behind him. "Finish the job or I'll kill you. Is that what you want?"

Luke turned and faced Karl. He leaned over and studied the area again, moving the electric lamp closer. He cut a small area to excise the bullet; Karl grunted and groaned but remained still. Then Luke washed it again with a cleaning solution.

Looking up, Luke could see the back door's glass had been smashed. He turned his attention back to his 'patient.' Luke made a conscious choice not to stitch the wound. He wouldn't have time and, God forgive him, he hoped the area would become infected. Luke glanced at the telephone.

"Don't even think of telephoning the police. Not now...not ever. If I find out you called the police, I will return and kill you."

Luke placed a bandage on the wound and straightened.

"Help me get on my horse."

At this point, it was Luke's greatest desire to treat that poor girl at the brothel. However, he felt obliged to do whatever the man asked in order to stay alive.

As Luke assisted him onto his horse, Karl said, "Just a piece of...friendly advice: I am not finished with Kathleen. She would never be happy with a weakling like you. Break off the courtship. Or...you...will be sorry. I promise..."

Luke's entire body tensed, then he straightened. "Leave her...us alone. I've repaired your arm; now leave us alone."

"You can never...make Kathleen happy. Break off the courtship now...or...I'll..." Karl hadn't finished his sentence when he rode off.

Relieved, at least momentarily, Luke quickly returned and grabbed his bag. Leaving his horse and carriage, he ran the three blocks to the brothel. He couldn't think about Karl now...he must get to the brothel. Arriving at the brownstone building, the madam was waiting for him at the front entrance.

"This way, Doctor." The heavyset madam pulled him along the foyer and up the staircase to a large room on the second floor, the floor Luke surmised was where the girls brought their "customers." The room was lavishly decorated with red-patterned wallpaper and mirrors everywhere. Luke shuddered. A girl on the bed moaned and he thanked God that she was still alive, especially considering the disarray of the bed. The headboard was covered in blood spatter and two scantily clad girls were holding a towel to the injured girl's face and head.

"Pardon me," he said to the two girls. He set his bag on the floor, leaned over and took the towel off the girl's head. Blood trickled from several wounds. He must first stop the bleeding. Once that was accomplished, he could begin stitching up the wounds.

"I need a wash basin, a clean cloth and clean water." He paused. "It must be clean water...if you have to boil it, do so quickly." Luke took off his suit jacket and rolled up his sleeves. Leaning down, his glasses slipped a little and he pushed them up on his face. As he was trying to diagnose her condition, his stomach growled and it was only then that he realized that, other than the Sacred Host, he hadn't eaten since dinner last evening. The Eucharistic fast and the "emergency" of Karl in his house meant that he had had no time for food.

He discovered there were three major lacerations in the

girl's blond head and, one by one, starting with the largest wound, he was able to control the bleeding, then stitch the lacerations. By that point, the girl had slipped into unconsciousness — perhaps from loss of blood — but her pulse continued to be strong.

Turning to the madam, he asked. "What happened to this girl?"

"A customer. I shot him. Don't expect he'll return."

Luke drew in a breath. *This is Karl's handiwork.*

The water was brought to him and he set to work. Once he finished, he checked for other wounds. It was only at this point that he noticed the girl was wearing an unusually modest white nightgown with pink embroidery hiked up above her waist. He pulled the nightgown down to cover the bottom half of her body. Then he tried to wake her. "Miss?"

She roused and moaned.

"Her name's Pearl."

"Miss...Pearl..."

"Doctor, when can we take her back to her room? This room needs to be cleaned and ready for customers." Hands on her ample hips, the madam's eyebrows were lifted, waiting for a response.

"We can take her now, but we shall have to be careful not to move her head. She may have a concussion. She will need to be roused every few hours."

"Of course."

He held a bottle out to the madam. "This is laudanum for pain, ten to twenty drops, and only two or three doses."

The madam took the bottle and placed coins in Luke's hand.

"And I should like to see her in two weeks, unless she worsens."

"Fine."

"Will you be filing charges against the man who hurt her?"

"No."

"No? But — "

"With all due respect, I'm running a business and I need to make this room presentable."

Luke now faced the two girls in short, scanty shifts. "Would you have a fresh nightgown for...Pearl?" He pointed to the injured girl on the bed.

"Her clothes are in her room," one of the girls said. With her wide, brown doe-like eyes and smooth skin, she looked too young to be a 'working girl.' "But I don't recognize that one. One of her customers must have given it to her."

Behind them, the madam said, "That farmhand who hurt her, he brought it with him. I saw him carrying it behind his back."

Luke nodded, then assisted the women in carrying the girl to the third floor, a small room devoid of furniture except for a cot, dresser and mirror. As soon as they arrived at the room, the girls left. Luke quietly pulled open a few drawers until he found a nightgown. It was plain and frayed at the collar, sleeves and neck, but it appeared clean. Removing the soiled — and obviously well-made and expensive — nightgown, he dressed the girl with a clean gown and pulled the covers up to her chin.

He checked her pulse and heart rate. Both were steady and strong. Satisfied, he turned to leave, then paused. He took his rosary out of his pocket and put the beads in the girl's palm and closed it. Luke made the sign of the cross. "Mary, keep her in your protection. Help her to leave this way of life. Hail Mary, full of grace..." He finished the prayer and returned to the second floor room to collect his bag. The door was already closed; his bag was on a chair in the hallway.

On the way home, he stopped at Nate's house. The man was outside working on his carriage. "Nate?"

"Yes, Dr. Luke?"

"I know it's Sunday and I apologize for taking you away from your family, but could you take a few moments and come with me to my house? I would appreciate it if you could feed and water my horse while I'm cleaning up."

"Of course." The man followed Luke home.

Once there, Luke checked his watch to find it was already 2:20. After cleaning up, he went to his carriage, which was where he left it at the hitching post. Nate stood beside it.

"Thank you, Nate. There's quite a mess in my office and at my back door. Do you have a moment to tidy those areas?"

"Of course." The man frowned. "But who would..."

"Don't worry. Everything's fine. Clean it for me, please."

"Very well."

"Thank you."

Luke was soon on his way. Too many thoughts were turning like a whirlpool inside his head. How could Luke protect Kathleen from that vile man? Break off the courtship? Did that deranged man think he had a chance with Kathleen? Karl had already threatened to return and hurt Luke if he went to the police. Knowing that his father was the chief, he couldn't go to the police. What other options were there?

Luke was suddenly filled with dread. Could Karl have been the vandal who ripped his brand new carriage seat last Christmas?

Kathleen's pretty face came to his mind. His carriage did not matter. Kathleen and her safety, however, did. Should he ask David's permission to marry her right away? And, if so, would David ask the reason for his haste? He and Kathleen had only been courting a month. He clicked the reins and rode quickly.

31

Kathleen paced back and forth on the front porch. She knew that Luke was treating an injured girl, but would it take this long?

***

Karl slumped over, but he did his best to steer the horse back to the farmhouse. Once there, he fell off the horse, wrapped the reins around the post and stumbled up the stairs to his room. He was feeling sick to his stomach and the floor seemed to be moving. But he didn't care about the pain. Now that the bullet was out of his arm, discomfort was minimal. He hated that he had lost control and beat that whore. He hated that he had to ask that stupid doctor for help. Karl should have just killed that boy doctor after he removed the bullet. However, his aim would have been less-than-precise with the nausea and blood loss. If that poor excuse of a man knew what was good for him, he would break off the courtship now. Kathleen deserved a real man.

***

Kathleen shielded her eyes from the afternoon sun. As soon as she caught sight of Luke's new carriage and the bright yellow MD at the front, she nearly jumped off the porch in joy, and ran toward the carriage.

"Luke! How is that poor girl?"

"I think she will survive. She took a bad beating, though."

Jesse came and walked Luke's carriage to the stable.

Taking hold of Luke's hand, Kathleen walked him to the porch.

Luke's face seemed pale and he was blinking excessively. "I had to return to my house to get cleaned up. I'm sorry to have missed the luncheon." He rubbed his arms, despite the warmth.

"Jane saved you a plate of food. I'll take you to the kitchen." On the way there, Kathleen asked, "What sort of wretched man would do something like that?"

Luke seemed to be forcing a smile.

"And remember that poor girl last autumn who was beaten by her father?"

"I do."

"What is wrong with the men in this world?"

***

Absolutely, thought Luke, as he tried not to react when Kathleen asked who could have harmed the girl. He had blurted out that the girl had been beaten and wished he had kept that information to himself. He didn't want to lie to her, but he couldn't bring himself to tell her about Karl. Kathleen had recently shared that she had stopped having nightmares. What would the knowledge that Karl had threatened him do to her peace of mind?

Would Kathleen be disappointed that Luke treated Karl? Perhaps he should have tried more diligently to refuse. With a gun aimed at his chest, however, there wasn't another option. Luke didn't want Kathleen to think that her beau couldn't take care of himself — or her. No, he decided, he could not have done anything differently. And he would keep the information — and the perpetrator's name — secret for the time being.

In the basement kitchen, Luke sat at the table and ate his lunch, with Kathleen chattering on beside him. She was such a bright light in his life right now that between the good food and her presence, his mood definitely was improving.

Jane came down the back staircase. "Dr. Luke, I would have brought your lunch up to the dining room. You don't have to eat here in the kitchen."

"I don't mind, Jane. It's cozy down here."

With a chuckle, her hands on her hips, Jane addressed Kathleen. "What did you do with your nightgown, Miss Kathleen? Before I left for Sunday service this morning, I told you to leave it on the bed post."

"I did, Jane, like always."

"Well, it wasn't there when I went for it this morning."

"That's odd. Maybe it slipped off the post."

"Hmmm. Maybe."

"I'll check later. That's one of my favorite gowns to wear

for bed. Mama bought it for me in Boston; it has delicate pink lace embroidered around the collar."

Luke froze. Could it be? He shook his head. Many stores sold nightgowns with pink lace.

***

Luke left after dinner that night. He had acted peculiarly, fidgety and anxious all afternoon. Kathleen supposed that treating injured and ill people might be difficult on his nerves, but then again, she had seen him in action with his patients and he always seemed relaxed and confident.

In her bedroom, Kathleen relaxed in the arm chair by the window sill and began to read. It soon became difficult to see the words as dusk was quickly bringing darkness to her room. Standing, she immediately went to her bedside table to turn on her oil lamp. She squinted in puzzlement. Maybe it *was* there, but why she couldn't see it? She felt around, then stared. Her oil lamp was most definitely not on her table. With an annoyed sigh, she thought, *Those brothers of mine! Where did they move my lamp?*

In the hallway, she yelled, "John, Will, Pat, what have you done with my oil lamp?"

Will immediately emerged from his room. John and Pat met the pair in the hallway.

"This isn't funny. You know I need my lamp."

"Kat, I didn't do anything with it," said Will. "Give me a minute and I'll get my lamp so we can look."

John and Pat traded glances and shook their heads.

Kathleen returned to her room, John and Pat following her. Will stepped into the room, his lamp lighting up the area. The four of them searched, and it didn't take long before John, on the other side of the room near the fireplace, announced, "It's over here, Kat." He lifted it up from behind her trunk.

"Whatever is it doing there?"

"I don't know," John said.

"Well, no matter, you found it. But if I find out any of you hid this on me, I shall tell Mama and Papa."

"Kat, we already told you...we didn't do this," Will offered.

"Very well then. Thank you for finding it, John."

When her brothers left, Kathleen set the lamp down on her bedside table. Jane or Izzy wouldn't have moved it. They usually didn't clean on Sunday and, when they did, they rarely moved items across the room unless they asked permission. Besides, Izzy was still in bed with the croup.

Kathleen changed into a nightgown and remembered Jane mentioning that her other gown hadn't been on the post. She knelt beside her bed and looked under it: nothing except for a few dust particles. In her closet were only dresses. She yanked open dresser drawers and moved articles of clothing around. That nightgown was indeed missing. *What could have happened to it?*

32

After Will arrived home from Mass that Saturday morning, he worked with Jesse to pack six additional crates for a delivery that Papa would be making later that afternoon in Gladwyne. Only his father, the servants and John remained at home. The rest of the family was visiting next door at his aunt and uncle's house. Will had asked John if he wanted to engage in target practice out back, but he had declined. John seemed distant and sullen, especially in the last six months since he had moved into his own room, and since he and Izzy had been spending time together.

Will decided to ask his father if he could accompany him to Gladwyne. Upstairs on the main floor, the door to the study was closed. Will knocked and opened it. "Papa?"

"Yes, Will," he said, from where he sat at his desk, "what can I do for you?" He looked up briefly, then went back to writing on a paper in front of him.

"I should like to accompany you on your trip today. Would that be acceptable?"

The older man stopped writing and lifted his head, smiling. "I'd be delighted! Do you remember when you and John would come with me on short jaunts many years ago?"

Will nodded and smiled. He recalled those Saturday afternoon trips when he and John were ten or eleven. He couldn't remember why they had stopped.

***

At the end of the day, Will and his father returned home. Papa remained in the barn for a few minutes with Jesse.

As he walked toward the basement kitchen door, Will could hear sobbing. Was that Izzy? The tone and intensity of her weeping saddened Will. Had someone died? Opening the door, Will could see Izzy's back as she crouched down in the corner near the pantry, her shoulders bobbing as she cried. Jane was at the table in the center of the kitchen kneading dough.

"Jane?"

"Yes, Mr. Will?" Jane didn't look up.

"Why is Izzy crying?"

The older servant sighed, picked up the dough and plopped it in a large bowl. She covered it with a towel and made her way to the faucet to wash, then dry, her hands. She turned to Will.

"Never you mind about Izzy, Mr. Will." Jane was scowling. *What is wrong with Izzy?*

"Izzy," Jane said. "If you want to make noise, do so in your room." Jane grabbed her daughter's arm and pulled her up the stairs. Will had never heard such a sharp tone from the older servant nor had seen her so angry.

What was going on? He took an apple and, eating it, sat at the chair for a few moments. That's when he heard the banging of a door upstairs on the main floor. He jumped up and headed upstairs via the main staircase. As he stepped into the area behind the grand staircase, he heard shouting from his father's study.

"What in God's name were you thinking?" Papa's voice yelled, loud enough for anyone on the property to hear.

"I love her," John screamed back.

"What do you know of love?"

"I know plenty. I know the way I feel."

"If you loved this girl, you would not have been fornicating!"

Will gasped and nearly dropped his apple. Fornicating? *Dear God in heaven. John and Izzy.* He should have known.

"Scandal...do you know what that word means?" His father drew out the word "know" emphasizing the 'w' sound.

Will could not hear a response. Quiet murmuring followed for several minutes. Then Papa's voice: "Marriage? Are you serious? You are 17. How do you propose to support your 15-year-old wife?"

"I can get a job. I can work for you."

"Work for me? You don't reliably handle your chores at present. What makes you think I will hire you?"

No response.

"I cannot believe that you had the audacity to do this in my house." His father shouted the words "my house."

"It wasn't technically in the house."

"John, so help me..."

"It was in the barn..."

"You ungrateful..."

"The apple doesn't fall far from the tree, does it?"

Will heard a slap. This time, Will's half-eaten apple did fall out of his hand and onto the floor. With a gasp, his eyes widened. Did Papa just slap John's face? Papa had never raised a hand to any of his children. Picking up the fallen apple, Will's eyes blinked tears away.

"Go to your room. I will deal with you later."

Will ducked into the parlor as John opened the study door. His brother ran through the foyer and up the stairs, taking two at a time, not looking back. John turned left at the top and raced towards Izzy's room. Will sighed.

Will could hardly feel the stairs under his feet as he climbed them. He was still shaking. Since John had turned left, he did the same and surmised both Izzy and John might be in Izzy's room. When he got to the young girl's room, he knocked. John opened the door. Will couldn't even look at him, at either of them, and kept his gaze downward.

"What?" John asked, his tone angry.

"What's going on?"

"None of your beeswax."

"John, listen to reason."

"I don't care about reason. Leave us alone."

"Scripture says, *Flee thou youthful desires, and pursue justice, faith, charity, and peace, with them that call on the Lord out of a pure heart.*"

"I don't care what Scripture says. Mind your own business, Father Will." He said "Father" in a high-pitched voice.

Will's mouth fell open. He brought his eyes up and stared at his brother. Will barely recognized John, whose mouth was pressed together in a frown. He looked past his brother to see Izzy wiping her tears with a handkerchief. John closed the door and Will stepped back to avoid being hit by it.

Shaking his head, his shoulders hunched over, Will inched

down the hallway to his bedroom. By the time he reached his door, he could hear his father's footsteps followed by Jane's, behind him. Turning, he saw his father and Jane at Izzy's door. Jane went into the room. Papa's voice bellowed, "Out of there!" Papa pulled John by the arm toward his brother's bedroom and, once there, closed the door. Neither his father nor his brother looked at him, but Will could tell both were angry.

Pray for John. Pray for Papa. Although he wanted to listen to what was going on, he knew what he needed to do. Back inside his room, he got down on his knees and prayed the rosary, trying to focus on the joyful mysteries as Papa yelled two rooms away. Every time his father raised his voice, it hurt Will's soul and he found himself on the verge of tears.

By the end of the rosary, his father's voice seemed muffled. A deep penetrating melancholy gripped Will's soul. His eyes watered and he blinked away the tears. In a moment of realization, he knew the source of his sadness: sin, the kind of sin that separates us from God. He felt sadness that John had allowed his passions to take over, that his brother had given into lust rather than worked for continence and chastity. He wiped his eyes, and continued his efforts to pray.

***

Kathleen's first indication that all was not well in their house was that Jane was not present to greet them when they stepped inside the foyer. The second was her father's booming voice floating down from upstairs. She turned to her mother, who had stopped to listen.

"Kathleen, could you assist Tim and Kevin in removing their jackets? I'm not sure where Jane or Izzy are."

"Of course, Mama."

Her mother quickly ascended the stairs and, exchanging words with Jane at the top of the stairs, said, "Good gracious, no!"

"Yes, Miss Caroline, I'm sorry to say it's true."

"What's going on, Kat?" Pat asked, his head lifted upward, staring.

With a shake of her head, she said, "I don't know, but it

doesn't sound good, whatever it is. Until we find out, I think it best to keep Tim and Kev occupied in the parlor."

"How about a rousing game of chess?"

"That will only keep us busy. We need to entertain Tim and Kev."

"You could play piano."

"Somehow I don't think that would be a good idea."

"Let's play marbles." They turned to see Kevin behind them, his eyebrows lifted, waiting for an answer. Marbles wasn't Kathleen's favorite game, but she knew Pat, Tim and Kev would enjoy it.

"Kev, where are your marbles? I'll get them for you."

"On my dresser, in a brown cloth bag."

Kathleen quietly crept up the stairs. Coming from John's room, she heard Papa's raised voice...and was Mama crying? But she also heard sounds of weeping from the other side of the hallway. Were Izzy and Jane sad too?

Passing John's door, Kathleen straightened her shoulders. She heard the words "scandal" and "fornicating." She drew in a breath. Who was involved in this scandal?

Tap, tap, tap, she heard as rain began to dance on the roof. A downpour. The window at the far end of the hallway near her bedroom was open and the wind was splashing rain on the sill and floor. She raced to shut it before it caused a major flood. The window was stuck and rain poured in and soaked the front of her skirt. Behind her, she heard, "Let me try, Kat." She stood aside so her brother could close it. With some grunting and pushing, he finally managed to shut it, but now his pants and shirt were wet. "Thank you, Will. Sorry. Now both of us are wet."

"I don't care. Glad to help."

She turned to listen as muffled shouts emanated from John's room.

"What is going on?"

Will lowered his head.

"Do you know something, Will?"

He blushed.

"Well?"

"It's not for me to say, Kat." He paused. "Where are the others?"

"Downstairs in the parlor. Pat, Kev and Tim are going to play marbles. Want to join in the fun?"

He shook his head. "I'm going to make sure the other windows upstairs are closed, then I shall return and remain in my room."

"Very well."

Why was Will so somber? She opened the door to the boys' room beside the now closed window. She scooped up the bag of marbles, then returned to the hallway. She passed John's room again and heard his voice, "We're getting married whether you like it or not!"

Oh dear. Marriage? Who did John wish to marry?

"Kat? Where are the marbles?" Kev called from the bottom of the steps.

"Yes, Kev, I'll be right there." Her curiosity was piqued and she wanted to listen. However, she rushed down the stairs and handed Kev the marbles. He scurried into the parlor and sat in the middle of the floor with Tim and Pat. Leaning down towards Pat's ear, she whispered, "I shall return momentarily."

Pat nodded.

When Kathleen stepped into the foyer, Jane was coming down the stairs. Her face was pale, her shoulders slumped and her usual pleasant expression was replaced by...was it sadness? Anger? Why would Jane be sad or angry?

The servant headed down the back staircase to the kitchen.

Kathleen's curiosity got the better of her. She went upstairs to the young servant's room. Perhaps Izzy would know what was going on. "Izzy, it's me."

No response. It sounded like Izzy was crying. Kathleen held out her hand again to knock and before she could do so, Izzy opened the door.

The poor girl's eyes were red, her cheeks shiny with tears. "Yes, Miss Kathleen?"

"May I come in?"

"I don't feel well right now. I would prefer..."

Kathleen ignored her and pushed the door open. "What in the world is going on with John? And why are you so sad?"

The girl shook her head, then dropped to the floor in a heap, crying. Kathleen joined her, placing her arm around her. "Now, now, it can't be all that bad."

The girl continued to sob.

Then, as if everything fell into place, Kathleen understood. She had heard the words *scandal* and *fornicating,* and John had said *marriage.* Izzy was crying. John was yelling. Could it be?

"Izzy, were you and John...doing what I think you were doing?"

She offered the slightest of nods.

Kathleen moved back and stared, her hand at her open mouth. "You and John were..."

Another subtle nod.

"I don't believe it. You were..."

"We are in love, Miss Kathleen. We were just expressing that love...in the barn when Mama found us."

"Stop. I cannot listen anymore." Kathleen slapped her hands against her ears. This couldn't be true. Izzy and John? Izzy was only fifteen and John seventeen. And not only was there a romance, but they were engaged in...Kathleen shook her head to rid herself of the thought.

Kathleen reached out to pat Izzy's back. This was indeed a serious situation.

Izzy remained on the floor and lifted her chin. Her eyes, glassy and wet, sad and intense. "We love each other." Izzy stood up and Kathleen followed. The young servant fell into Kathleen's arms and wept on her shoulder. "Thank you, Miss."

Her arms encircled Izzy in a gesture of support. She was concerned for both her brother and this girl. Her parents would never approve of such an arrangement, but she couldn't voice those concerns.

Kathleen held Izzy at arm's length. "I must go check on Tim and Kev. Will you be all right?"

She sniffed, then nodded.

Kathleen left the room, closing the door behind her. She returned downstairs to stay with her younger siblings.

***

Later that evening, at the request of her parents, Kathleen tucked Tim and Kev into bed and read them a short bedtime story. After they were settled, she walked slowly to the staircase. Will was sitting on the top step, a rosary in his hands. She sat down beside him as he quietly finished.

At the sign of the cross, she whispered, "Do you remember when you, myself and John snuck out here while everyone was asleep as we waited for St. Nicholas to arrive?"

"I do. I also recall Papa discovering us and telling us that St. Nick would not make his entrance until everyone in the house was in bed."

Raised voices emanated from the parlor; Will and Kathleen straightened and tilted their heads to listen.

John was shouting. "We are getting married and you can't stop us."

Their mother's soft and garbled tone.

Their father's voice was loud and slipping dangerously close to anger. "We can stop it now. You are both too young."

John's voice was strangely high-pitched. "We love each other and you cannot stop that."

His father's tone was elevated but controlled. "Love is a great deal of work. Love gives. Love means suffering."

Kathleen could not hear John's response.

"How do you plan to support your fifteen-year-old wife, John? You have not yet finished secondary school!"

"I intend to leave school and get a job. Besides, what would be the harm of me marrying Izzy and us remaining here? She could continue working as a servant."

Kathleen and Will traded surprised glances. Kathleen was still in shock that her younger brother had any romantic affection for Izzy, let alone that they had been intimate.

Now their parents and Jane were talking at the same time, so Kathleen couldn't understand what was being said. But the tone and words stated that a romance between the two would not be possible, at least for the time being.

The doors to the parlor were opening and Kathleen and Will quickly backed up and out of sight at the top of the stairs.

"Go out to the barn and clean up the manure. Then you may go to bed," their father instructed.

"What? Am I your servant now?" was John's tart reply.

"As a matter of fact, yes, you are. You need to understand what it's like to actually work for a living. Every day after school, you shall be working alongside Jesse as my new hired hand. And since you are an apprentice, you will be paid with free rent and food."

"What is this nonsense?" John asked.

"Do as I say."

Kathleen and Will heard John stamp his feet across the foyer. It sounded like he punched the wall before heading out the front door.

Jane's voice said, "Mr. David, Miss Caroline, I will send Izzy to my cousin's tomorrow after you return from church."

"I'll have Jesse drive her to your cousin's house after lunch."

"That would be fine, Mr. David."

"Jane?"

"Yes, Mr. David?"

"I'm so sorry for this. I want to apologize that our son has taken away your daughter's innocence."

"Yes, Jane...we...are sorry." Mama's voice was cracking.

Jane replied in a no nonsense voice. "Miss Caroline, Izzy did exactly what she wanted to do. They are both to blame." Jane turned and left, presumably for the kitchen downstairs.

Kathleen leaned out of the shadow upstairs. Her mother and father stood silently, their gazes downward, their shoulders sagging.

"David, John is... so angry with us right now."

Papa raised his voice, "I'm angrier. Our son was dishonest, taking advantage of a young girl, not to mention committing mortal sin." He paused. "Having him work here and sending Izzy away, it's a solid plan...if this is true love, then it will still be love in a year or two. If not, it will be over in a few months."

Will motioned to his sister that they should return to their rooms.

33

When the O'Donovans arrived that Sunday at St. Vincent's, Luke immediately sensed their anxiousness. They couldn't know about Karl, could they? Even Kathleen seemed to be forcing a smile when he assisted her down from the carriage. The older children and adults wore pinched expressions; the younger boys seemed oblivious to their older siblings' tension.

After Mass, Luke understood the reason when Kathleen took him aside and quietly explained the "scandal" of John and Izzy. In light of the difficulties present at the O'Donovan House, the two decided that Luke should return to his house instead of coming for their usual post-Mass luncheon.

Knowing they wouldn't see each other for the rest of the day, Luke listened as Kathleen chattered on about a variety of topics. He just stared at her sweet green eyes and listened. He could gaze at her all day and be content. Her golden hair was pinned up and she wore a lavender dress with matching hat and gloves which he decided made her look even lovelier than usual.

Each day brought new promise of their relationship. For Luke, seeing Kathleen became as important as breathing. And when he *was* finally able to spend time with her, it passed like a few moments. As his love for her deepened, so did his worry and anxiety; Karl remained a dark shadow that always followed them.

"Come on, Kat. We're leaving," called David, as he also waved to Luke.

"Goodbye, Luke. I shall see you tomorrow at the office!"

"Goodbye." He tipped his hat and left, wondering how he would pass the time until he saw her again.

***

The following Saturday, Monsignor Flaherty welcomed Will and his father into his office at the rectory. The priest asked Will to wait for a few moments while he interviewed his father. Once that was completed, it was Will's turn to speak to the cleric. He nodded as his father passed him. Papa leaned in and whispered, "I told him about John and Izzy," before continuing to the waiting room.

When Will entered the priest's office, he said little at first, waiting for the priest to ask questions. "Do you want to get started on the next lesson, or do you want to talk about what happened on the weekend?"

Will felt the warmth of a flush on his cheeks. He nodded. "It was partially my fault."

"Now, Will, how could their actions be your fault? John and the young servant made their choice."

"I should have told Papa about them. Maybe they would not have...sinned."

"Your brother is the one at fault, Will, not you."

Will dropped his gaze and stared at the floor. "And I'm so ashamed of John. I can't even look at him."

When Will looked up, the priest was nodding. "Listen to yourself, Will. Where is the charity in your last sentence?"

"Pardon me?"

"The charity. You talk about your brother as if he is a vile creature that disgusts you."

Will's eyebrows narrowed. "Well, he does..."

"Let me ask you this: do you love your brother?"

Will sunk back in his seat and nodded. "I suppose."

The priest shook his head. "Not good enough. Do you love your brother?"

"Well, yes, but what he did was wrong. It was a mortal sin."

"Will, if you aspire to be a holy priest one day, you must not sit in judgment of any person, no matter what he or she has done. When a penitent comes into confession, you must be *in persona Christi, in the person of Christ.* Be open, loving and forgiving; condemn the sin, but never the sinner. You need to separate the two. You must see Christ in every person, sinners and saints alike."

Will was at a loss for words. Shaking his head, he rubbed his brow.

Monsignor was correct. Will had so much pent-up anger and resentment that he'd forgotten that John was not only his brother, but his oldest friend, one to whom he owed his unconditional love.

"Have you prayed for your brother?"

"I...uh...yes, I have, but probably not as fervently as I should be."

"And are you fasting?"

"No."

"Pray and fast for him, Will. Pray and fast for your entire family. That will help in preparing you for a lifetime of service. And you should also know your catechism. Now, let's get to the lesson, shall we?"

***

Regrettably, Karl had missed two Sundays of watching Kathleen and her family at church since he had to work on the farm. This Sunday, despite the warmth, he dressed the part of an upper class gentleman and not a farmer. The heavy beard still allowed him to appear incognito. Even his own father hadn't recognized him as the older man's buggy passed by.

He had borrowed his employer's smaller carriage, dressed in fine clothes and parked the carriage in the lot beside the church. He tied the reins to the post and lingered behind a group of gentlemen mulling about in front of the church. He hoped they would remain for an additional few moments because he wanted just one glimpse of Kathleen.

Karl was rewarded a few moments later. When the O'Donovan carriages rode up, Kathleen looked happier and lovelier than ever, and the good doctor had not arrived or waited at the front of the church for her. Maybe the stupid doctor was not so stupid after all. If he knew what was good for him, he had already ended their courtship.

As the O'Donovans passed by, Kathleen's father said, "Will, remind me to invite Father Morrissey to your graduation from Roman Catholic next Wednesday."

"Yes, Papa."

Karl smiled inwardly. He nearly laughed out loud. He knew where he would be next Wednesday.

34

Will glanced at the time and nearly panicked. As usual, he had woken early. However, he spent most of the time in prayer or rehearsing the short speech for his commencement later this morning. All of a sudden, he realized that he still needed to take a bath and get dressed.

Yesterday, the family had celebrated Will's 18th birthday on his actual birthday, June 15th. Pat and Kev had inquired as to why his birthday was being celebrated in the summer. Papa had told them an outlandish story about peacocks and ink wells with everyone bursting out laughing. Will understood that Papa did not want to lie, but he also did not want to share the truth with his youngest sons.

He grabbed his towel, opened the door and nearly ran into Kev and Tim running through the hallway. "Whoa!"

The bathroom door was closed so he knocked. "John? Kat? Papa? Who's in there? I need to use the toilet." No response.

Within a few moments, there was a click and John opened the door. His hair was wet and his robe was slightly open at the front. "Why the impatience, brother?" he snapped.

"I have to go."

"Tie a knot in it."

Will sighed at his brother's crass language. *Charity*, he kept repeating to himself, *charity*. He hurried in and used the bathroom, then took a quick bath. Will had been shaving once or twice a week for about six months, but as he stared at himself in the mirror, he realized that he would soon have to begin shaving every day. He shouldn't complain. There were more deserving things about which to complain, like the poor being hungry, or suffering, or war. So he mixed the shaving cream, lathered it on his face and carefully ran the razor over his cheeks and neck.

After breakfast, Will returned to his room and dressed. Although he wanted to proclaim it to the world, no one except his family and Monsignor Flaherty knew of his desire to enter the priesthood. He had already applied to St. Joseph's College and was accepted, so while he waited for the investigation for the dispensation to be completed, he would bide his time at St. Joseph's studying philosophy.

Will had interacted little with John since 'the incident' six weeks previous despite the fact that they had traveled together on the train every morning. John went out of his way to sit apart from Will. Following Monsignor's advice, though, Will acted charitably toward John, even though John seemed annoyed or angry with everyone most of the time. In addition, he could see dark circles under his brother's eyes. When John wasn't at school, he was working for their father. Will had occasionally suggested to Papa that he give John a few days off but his father replied, "He does not have to work on Sunday, which is more time off than many hired hands get."

***

Kathleen hummed with excitement. This month had turned out to be a most eventful one. On the first of June, Margaret had given birth to a bouncing baby boy, nearly eight pounds, Joseph Stephen Quinn. Best of all, Margaret and Stephen had asked Kathleen to be the boy's godmother at the christening next weekend. When they asked her, she blinked back tears of joy as well as tears of regret that her other godchild, her baby sister, was now gone.

She was disappointed that Luke would not be able to join her for Will's graduation today. He had told her that he would be attending a medical seminar until four p.m., but he promised that he would arrive in time for the celebration afterwards.

Her heart continued to sing. Then she eyed the letter from Izzy on her bureau. The poor girl's tone sounded desperate, like she was trying to convince herself of the reason for John's unresponsiveness over the past three weeks. Kathleen hoped that her brother would not break the young servant's heart, but she surmised that might be what was happening.

***

Will waited for his brother in the carriage, tapping his foot and glancing frequently at his pocket watch. Both boys had to be at the school early for the commencement.

John finally emerged and said, "Good, you're driving. I need a day off."

At first, the brothers remained silent. The clopping of the horse was muffled by the dirt laneway.

Will finally broke the silence. "How have you been?"

"Damn tired. All I do is attend school and work from sun up to sun down, and I don't foresee that will change any time soon."

Will was sorry he asked. He noticed something, though. "John, can you say a sentence without using the word 'I' in it?"

"What?"

"Every time you speak, you say I. *I've* been tired. All *I* do. *I* don't foresee."

John shot him a sharp glance. "You asked me how *I* — let me repeat — how *I* was. How do you expect me to answer without using the pronoun I?"

Will pressed his lips together. "Have you ever asked yourself what is best for Izzy? What is best for her soul?"

"You're going to be a priest. How do you know what's best for her?" John spoke through his teeth with forced restraint.

Will cleared his throat. "Fornication is not what is best for her."

"Cease your chatter, Will. I've heard enough."

Will fell silent. His brother's face seemed to have a permanent frown etched in it.

Finally, they reached the beginning of Center City and the cobblestone streets intensified the horse's clopping. This might be his only opportunity for the next few weeks or months to say how he felt. "I love you, John."

"What?"

"I love you. You're my oldest friend and I don't want to lose you."

John scoffed. It was not the reaction Will was looking for.

With a sigh, Will said, "I don't care what you've done or how you treat me, I will always love you."

This time, his brother neither frowned nor smiled. Instead, John lowered his head.

Will steered the horse and carriage to a livery stable three blocks away. He pulled inside the building and got out. Taking a few coins from his pocket, he gave them to the attendant. Parking would be minimal near Broad and Vine and the livery stables in that area would be fully occupied.

John then got out, and the two made their way to the school. John had to report to the gymnasium and Will would need to proceed to Room 105. At the path to the gym, John stopped and mumbled, "I love you too." Will stopped and stared, but John continued and held his hand up in a slight wave. A smile slowly formed on Will's face.

***

After the commencement, Will posed for a photograph with his class, then met his family at the cafeteria for a light lunch and refreshments.

Later on, Will would have an opportunity to indulge in some of his favorite foods, courtesy of Jane. Aunt Elizabeth, Uncle Philip, Alice, Dr. Luke and a few others had been invited.

***

It was a simple task for Karl to disguise himself and blend in with the crowd attending the commencement. Today, he dressed as a lower class gentleman in a worn suit he picked up at a consignment shop nearby. Most of the ceremony was spent with Karl going back and forth outside. Thankfully, no one paid any attention to him.

The O'Donovans were easy to find. Kathleen looked quite pretty and again, that hick doctor was not present. This was the second time that Karl had seen Kathleen without that doctor around. His pulse quickened. Had he called off the courtship? Was the man-boy so easily led around by the nose?

Kathleen stepped away from her family and walked by the

refreshment table. The area was crowded and he passed behind her, close enough to touch her. He nearly brushed against her, but decided against it. That would happen in good time. Her luscious *Essence of Violets* perfume was intoxicating. He wanted to take her right there, but he knew he needed to be in control...always in control.

***

Luke rode up to the O'Donovans. John was taking a leisurely stroll on the grounds. He always looked twice because the two brothers were so similar in appearance. However, Will's gait held more of a bounce and when he studied the young men closely, he could tell the difference. Besides having a dimple, Will had slightly more curl to his hair and a wider jaw.

Jesse took Luke's carriage to the stable. Before going inside, Luke approached John. "Good day. How did the convocation go?"

"Fine. Will's short speech went well."

"Your parents must be proud."

"I suppose so."

Kathleen's voice called to him and he turned. Her eyes were bright as she rushed to greet him. She glanced at John, then focused her gaze on Luke. "No one told me you had arrived."

"Good afternoon, Kath."

"I missed you." Kathleen gazed at him, her eyes bright with affection, her mouth upturned in a smile. His heart skipped a beat. Did she become prettier every time he saw her?

"Dinner shall be served shortly. Let's go inside, shall we?" She took his hand and they went inside.

35

The Germantown post office was situated two blocks from Dr. Luke's house and across the street from the rubber factory. Will's father made the trip every few days since there was no postal delivery to their house, which was outside the city. Today, Will accompanied him.

After collecting the mail, the older man scanned the letters. At one point, he sighed and Will craned his neck to see who the letter was addressed to. *Mr. John O'Donovan,* in feminine script. It didn't take a genius to figure out the sender. As his father thumbed through the rest of the mail, he frowned.

"What's wrong, Papa?"

"This letter is addressed to Kat. Who would be sending her a letter? This isn't Izzy's handwriting; it's familiar but...I can't quite..."

"I don't know."

His father stuck the rest of the letters inside his coat pocket, then slapped Kat's letter against his palm. He stared at the envelope. He flipped it over. "I know Kat may become angry with me, but I must open this."

Will nodded in agreement, but Kat would be madder than a skunk if she knew Papa was opening her mail.

His father ripped open the letter and Will leaned in to read it with him. The two gasped. It wasn't signed, but both suspected who had sent it.

My dear Kathleen,

I just wanted you to know that I was extremely pleased to see you at your brother's recent convocation at Roman Catholic High School. You probably don't remember seeing me, since I look quite different than the last time you saw me. Your pale purple gown matched your fragrant "Essence of Violets" perfume. But my favorite dress is the blue gingham you often wear to Mass.

I was overjoyed that the boy doctor wasn't with you.

Good. I hope your courtship with that weakling has ended. If it hasn't ended, I trust you will do so soon. That man-boy would not be able to protect a dumb animal, let alone a young lady such as yourself.

I will be watching you always. Just when you least expect it, you will see my face because someday, I will come back to collect my prize.

Your Devoted Admirer

Before Will could say anything, his father muttered, "That son of a..." With clenched fists, he began ripping the letter.

"Papa, don't!"

His father ignored him and continued until the letter and envelope were ripped into a hundred pieces, the wind scattering them in every direction.

"You're not going to tell Kat about this, are you?"

"And neither are you, son."

"Shouldn't we have given the letter to the police?"

Papa sighed. "It's not signed. We wouldn't be able to prove it was Karl." Then he paused, rubbed his hand over his eyes and took a deep breath. "On second thought, you may be correct. Sometimes my Irish temper gets the better of me. Come, let's pay Luke a visit before we return home."

"Is Kat there?"

"No, she is not there on Friday."

"Are you going to tell Dr. Luke? If this was Karl —"

His father cut him off. "The letter was written by Karl. There's no doubt, Will."

"Well, the man threatened Kat to break off the courtship."

"No, I'm not going to tell Luke. That fine gentleman does not need intimidation. He needs encouragement."

***

At his desk, Luke jotted down notations on two different patients. He finished with Mrs. Henkel's file. The hearty woman was to be admired. She had given birth earlier this week and was already doing farm work, despite Luke's admonition that she rest at least one additional day.

The open window carried a warm breeze and the scent of

summer into the room. It smelled like a few neighbors were mowing their lawns on this beautiful day.

Luke glanced up and was pleasantly surprised to see David and Will ride up in front of his house. He set his quill pen down, covered the ink well and went out to meet them on the porch by his office door. David seemed to be forcing a smile and Will was avoiding eye contact.

"David, Will, is anything wrong?"

David answered. "Uh...no. We just stopped by for a visit."

"I see."

"Luke, do you carry a gun?"

"Pardon me?" The truth was that he had *never* carried a gun and had no plans to do so, but he wondered why David asked the question. "Uh...I..."

"Luke, you must carry a gun at all times, especially when you're with my daughter."

"I'm uncomfortable with guns. There is a fairly new gun left by Dr. Mayfield, but I certainly don't carry one on me."

"What?" David reddened with anger. "How do you expect to protect my daughter without a gun?"

Luke shook his head. "Can I not protect her without...the use of a weapon? I have an aversion to firearms."

David, his dark eyes intense, stared at Luke then placed a hand on his shoulder. "I have no idea why you have this aversion, and I know guns can accidentally injure people, but I beg you to consider carrying one. For Kat's sake."

Luke sighed. Truth be told, he had no idea why he despised guns so much. He reasoned that it was probably because firearms caused destruction and not healing. But he also had no idea what precipitated David's interrogation of Luke's gun use or lack thereof.

David said, "Ever since Karl hurt Kat, I don't for one minute trust that he is gone. I believe he will return some day."

Is it possible that David knows about my treating Karl?

"Luke, could we step inside for a moment?"

"Of course."

"Will, wait at the carriage."

"Yes, Papa."

Inside the waiting room, David cleared his throat.

"Luke, I would like to know what your intentions are for my daughter."

"For your daughter?" Why would David ask that? He must know the answer.

"Eventually — and hopefully — marriage, at some later date. In fact..."

"What are you waiting for?"

Luke scowled. Was David a mind reader?

"Uh...I...I'm just waiting an appropriate time. I planned on asking you for permission when the one year anniversary of the baby's death had passed."

David appeared to be cringing. "Of course. No need to wait, though. I give you permission to marry Kat as soon as possible."

"As soon as possible?"

"Yes. Do you love my daughter?"

"Very much so."

"Then there's no reason to wait. Ask her now...today. It's early July. Would October be an acceptable month for a wedding?"

Luke's jaw nearly dropped to the floor. He could barely speak. Given the opportunity, Luke would have married Kathleen yesterday. "Yes, if Kathleen is happy with that." Luke wanted to jump for joy. David had made it easy for him.

"She will be. I assure you. Now, let's talk about protecting my daughter."

"David, aren't there other ways to protect her rather than a loaded gun? Like asking the police for help?" Of course, even as Luke said it, he realized that, given the fact that Karl's father was the chief, they would likely be no help at all.

"Luke, you're as tall as I. Perhaps five feet eight inches? You're on the thin side. And Karl's father is the chief of police. Do you think we can count on them? No, I don't think there's a better way to protect her. Besides, if you want to marry her, you must allow me to teach you the fine art of firing a weapon."

Luke sighed.   Truth be told, aversion was not a strong enough word. He loathed any sort of firearms. As a medical doctor, he saw the destruction they could cause. But he loved Kathleen and would do anything to marry her. "I...very well." He walked to storage area behind the examining room, reached up to the top shelf and took out a box with a gun and ammunition. David took it from him. "Nice piece, Smith & Wesson long cartridge, 32 first model hand ejector. Looks brand new. You say this was Dr. Mayfield's?"

"Not sure if it was his, but it was left here."

David slipped two shells into the chamber. "There." David handed it to him and stared as Luke held it in the palm of his hand. "Have you ever even fired a gun, Luke?"

"I...well, I..." With a sigh, he shook his head.

David put his hand on Luke's shoulder. "Before this day is over, I am going to teach you how to fire a gun properly."

Luke wanted to shout that he wasn't going to fire this gun. But he didn't. David *was* correct. What Luke couldn't tell the older man was that Karl had said that he "wasn't finished with Kathleen." He couldn't share his suspicions that Karl had slashed his carriage cushion. He didn't want to worry him. But if there ever came a time when he needed to defend Kathleen, he recognized that he must learn how to fire a gun correctly.   He hadn't the faintest idea how to load, aim or shoot a firearm.

"Keep this with you at all times."

Luke nodded as he took the gun and placed it in his inside pocket. The gun burned his pocket and felt like a rock against his chest. Luke straightened.

"Are you finished seeing patients?"

"Yes. On Fridays, I...uh...have appointments only in the morning." The gun hung heavy, pulling the left front of his coat downward.

"Do you have time to visit our home?"

"Yes, I just need to finish making notations on several files. I can join you later this afternoon."

"Good. As I said, before this day is over, I will teach you the fine art of how to use a firearm. And don't forget to bring ammunition with you."

"Uh...yes, of course." Luke took off his glasses, closed his eyes and pinched the bridge of his nose. He put his glasses back on.

"I'm going to ask Monsignor Flaherty if the beginning of October might be available. I would like him to co-officiate at the wedding, which will take place at the Cathedral in Philadelphia."

"Please allow me to get down on one knee and ask your daughter properly before you contact Monsignor Flaherty."

"Of course."

***

Kathleen was thrilled to hear that Luke would be visiting this afternoon. Besides seeing him three times a week at his office, she also saw him the better part of the weekend with the family.

When he arrived, she and her parents met him in the foyer. Before Kathleen could say anything to him, Tim and Kev took hold of Luke's hands and pulled him toward the parlor. "Come on, Luke, let's play marbles," said Kev. Kathleen tried to be patient with her brothers but this was, after all, her beau, not their playmate.

Luke glanced back at her and smiled. He stopped and crouched down to the boys' eye level. "Fellows, I would enjoy a game of marbles with you. But, I need to speak to your sister first, then your father wants to teach me how to fire a gun. Then — and only then — I would be happy to play a game with you."

"Don't you already know how to fire a gun, Luke?" Tim's sweet voice asked.

"No. But your father is going to teach me."

Kev dropped his gaze, then said, "Even I've shot a gun before. Why haven't you?"

"Boys, leave Dr. Luke alone." Papa gave Kev and Tim his sternest look. The two boys finally ran off toward the parlor.

"Luke, would you like a cup of tea?" asked Mama.

"No, thank you."

Kathleen took Luke's arm. "Let's take a stroll outside. It's a beautiful day."

Luke nodded to her parents and allowed Kathleen to take him outside.

"What did you wish to speak to me about?"

"Let's stroll over to that tree over there, by the pond."

"Very well." They walked in companionable silence, but Kathleen continued to wonder about the reason for his desire to speak to her. He took hold of her hand as they strolled across the lawn.

"Luke, didn't you say you grew up on a farm?"

"Yes."

"Why do you not know how to use a gun?"

"I don't care for guns or anything that causes destruction."

Kathleen didn't respond.

When they reached the tree, Luke's hand began to tremble. And was he blushing? *What is wrong with him today?* Then his shoulders squared. He lifted something small from his pocket, took hold of her hand, then bent down on one knee. "Miss Kathleen Emma O'Donovan, I love you with all my heart. Would you do me the honor of being my wife so that we may raise children and grow old together?"

Her mouth fell open, her heart raced and, for a moment, she was speechless. Could it be true? She expected a proposal, but not this soon.

"Well?" Luke leaned forward, as he remained on one knee.

"You've already asked Papa's permission?"

"Uh...yes, we've discussed it."

"And he said yes?"

"He did."

"Then yes, yes, yes! I would be honored to be your wife!"

He placed the ring on her finger but it was too loose.

"This was my great-aunt's ring. It will need to be refitted."

The ring was beautifully simple: eighteen carat gold with a small emerald set in the middle. "It's lovely, Luke!" They embraced and Kathleen stepped back. "A late November marriage, before Advent or shall we wait until spring?"

"Do you wish to wait?"

"Well...no, but we shall need time to plan a wedding."

"Does October sound acceptable? I've always enjoyed autumn weddings."

"In less than three months? This is most unusual."

"Autumn nuptials would be ideal, don't you agree?"

Kathleen didn't need to think about it any longer. A fall wedding would indeed be lovely. "Yes, that would be wonderful!"

The news was then shared with the family, who reacted as excitedly as Kathleen. Papa patted Luke on the back. "Congratulations, Luke." He embraced his daughter. "Congratulations, Kat. Now I must take your fiancé to the firing range."

Kathleen pouted. "Do you have to go to the range right now, Papa?"

"Yes, Kat. John and I are going to teach Luke how to fire a gun."

"Yes, I know. But..."

"No buts. If this man is going to be your husband, he needs to learn how to defend you."

"Papa, why would Luke need to defend me?"

Her father avoided eye contact.

"Is there something you're not telling me?"

"Kat, I'm just worried about you and, quite frankly, over-protective since you were injured."

She winced at the word "injured," then straightened. "Papa, that wretched man is gone. We shall never hear from him again."

"Kathleen," Luke said, "as much as I despise guns, your father is correct that I should learn how to use one properly."

She stared at Luke and, as her betrothed said the words, she wondered whether he was trying to convince himself.

***

The firing range was basically part of the field between two forested areas on either side and behind the house. David brought Luke to a tall oak tree near a wooden structure with cans set up about ten feet away.

John stood straight and fired, then set more cans up. It was good to see the young man doing activities other than chores. He turned toward David and Luke.

David held his palm out. "Hand over your gun, Luke."

Luke gave it to him, happy to have it out of his coat.

"First, I'm going to teach you the basics of handling a firearm. Then I'll show you how to fire it. John's job this afternoon will be to stay with you while you become accustomed to this fine piece and perhaps give you a short lesson on how to clean and maintain your gun, which is as important as knowing how to fire it." David lifted, caressed and turned the gun as if he were admiring a piece of expensive jewelry. "John is an outstanding marksman, almost as good as I," he said, winking at John.

John ignored his father's comment.

"We have some tin cans set up. As a beginner, it's better to have targets that are close. Once you know how to shoot the gun, you can shoot cans farther away."

"Also," he continued, "I believe this piece has quite a bit of back action. You can get hurt if you're not expecting it."

He held the gun in front of Luke and began pointing to the different parts. "This has an exposed hammer, checkering on the spur here, a smooth trigger, black hardcover grip, a fine nickel-plated finish. In order to put the bullets in, you need to pull forward on the ejector rod and swing out the cylinder. It's double action, so you can shoot two ways. The barrel is short," he ran his finger along it, "just over three inches long. It has a tiny rear sight and a blade front sight and it's actuated by this spur."

David was speaking too quickly for Luke to fully understand, but he patiently nodded. "Of course, it's best to have this sort of gun already loaded with ammunition. Once you've shot it, you can eject the cartridges like so," he pulled something and the bullets flew out, unused. David crouched down, gathered up the bullets and quickly loaded them again.

"Now," he said, "to shoot it, hold the gun up, look through this sight here, eyeball the target, then fire."

Then he gave it to Luke, who held it in his palm and stared, his hand now shaking. He hated even touching it.

"Luke?"

Luke cleared his voice. "Uh...yes, of course."

"Come on, Luke, hold the gun straight out." His uncle stood behind him and cupped the gun with his hand. Luke didn't want to hold the gun. He didn't want to shoot it either. His uncle pulled the trigger for him and the gun fired and snapped back against the boy's chest. Luke became hysterical and started to cry. "Please don't make me fire it again. Please, please!"

"Very well, Luke. Run along and do your chores."

Luke held the gun in front of his face. For a moment, he felt dizzy and lightheaded. He shook his head. *This is ridiculous.* A gun was only as dangerous as the person using it. All he was going to shoot was a tin can ten feet in front of him.

"Hold the gun far enough in front of your face that the back action won't hurt you or your glasses."

Luke nodded and stretched his arms almost straight out. He gulped and was finding it hard to breathe.

"Go ahead, fire," David commanded him.

His hands shaking, Luke held the gun extra firmly to try to quell his trembling hands. He slowly pulled the trigger. It looked like the bullet flew ten feet over the cans.

David's eyes narrowed. "Hmmm. Too high. At least you shot it. Still, it seems odd you never learned how to fire a gun."

Luke nodded. "I was a nervous child." *And I'm a nervous adult as well.*

"Well, don't worry. John will have you shooting the tin cans in no time." David again winked at his son and patted him on the shoulder, but the young man stiffened and remained unresponsive to the older man.

"Luke, I'm going to leave you in John's capable hands."

"Very well."

David walked off.

Luke loaded the gun once more with five additional bullets. It took a while, but John didn't sigh or act impatient as he tried to do so. "Keep trying," he said. "Take your time."

Standing with his arms outstretched in front of him, Luke

fired three times, but none came close to any target. He set the gun down and wiped his brow with his handkerchief. He still felt sick to his stomach and nearly retched.

John stared and shook his head. "Are you ill, Dr. Luke?"

"Fine...I'm fine."

"It doesn't make sense how you can be a doctor and not be able to keep your hand still enough to shoot a gun."

"I can assure you when I'm using them for medical reasons, my hands are quite still."

"You really despise guns that much, Dr. Luke?"

"Yes."

"Why?"

"I don't like killing any creature."

"But we're not killing anything now. I'm just shooting that tin can. Watch." John held the gun up, pointed it, cocked it, then pulled the trigger. *Ding*, the bullet found its mark in the first tin can.

"Now, you try. Here, you hold it and I'll talk you through it..." Luke held the gun. "Eye up the target...that can in the middle, the one with the red paint on it...cock it here," he pointed, "and pull the trigger." Luke hesitated. "Luke, go ahead, pull." Luke did as he was told, the gun fired and the bullet hit the can with a ding. All of a sudden, he became breathless.

"Are you all right?"

He nodded.

"You did a good job."

Luke fired about ten more times, rarely hitting anything. John said, "That's probably enough practice for now."

Luke ejected the cartridges and put the empty gun back in his jacket and picked up the spent casings on the ground.

The young man put his gun in his holster and raked his wavy dark hair with his hand. John blinked, then rubbed his hands down his pant legs. After a few moments of silence, John cleared his throat. "Uh... Dr. Luke?"

"Yes, John?" Luke leaned forward to listen.

"May I... speak honestly with you?" The young man spoke softly.

"Of course."

"You won't tell my parents?"

"No."

"I...well...I...I love Izzy."

Luke offered the slightest of nods.

"I'm not sorry for what we did."

As a physician, Luke tried not to be judgmental. It was more difficult, however, when it came to people who were closer to him. *Help me to give John good counsel, Lord.* "Well, John, one of the disadvantages of engaging in those sorts of...behaviors before marriage is that it easily leads into habit. For example, I find continence difficult, but it would be challenging if I actually engaged in the act and then tried to stop. Do you understand what I'm saying?"

"You've never...been with a woman?"

"No."

With wide eyes, the young man stared as Luke continued.

"That's not to say I haven't been tempted. All men are. But I keep busy. I stargaze. I read." He hesitated, trying to formulate the best words.

"True love is sacrificial. If you really love Izzy, it's best to wait for further activity until you can be married."

"Some of my friends have already been...with a girl. They say that every man sows his wild oats before marriage. Some have been to the brothel."

Luke drew in a breath. "I can say from my own experience that not every man 'sows his wild oats.'"

John nodded. "My father told us we have to try to be perfect...but I know I'm never going to be perfect so why should I try?"

"All human beings are called to be saints. In his letter to the Romans, St. Paul says, 'to them that love God, all things work together unto good, to such as, according to his purpose, are called to be saints.'"

John leaned his shoulder against the oak tree. "I miss Izzy. But if she was here, with me, I would want to...well, her body is so beautiful. That's all I can think about."

"John, our bodies and souls make up who we are. You cannot separate them."

John remained silent and kept his eyes focused on the ground.

"Do you know of a priest you might be able to speak to about these spiritual matters?"

"I do not wish to speak about such matters with a priest. You're a doctor."

"What about discussing this with your father?"

"No. I know now that Will came about because my father was 'with' a servant. Papa told Will that while he did something wrong, something good came out of it. Initially, I wanted Izzy to become with child. I thought if she carried my child, my parents would have to consent to our marriage."

Luke pressed his lips together, but remained quiet to allow the young man to continue.

"Izzy sent me a letter saying she could not possibly be with child. The more I thought about it, the more I realized that this is the way it should be. I'm only seventeen but I'm so fatigued every night, I fall asleep as soon as my head hits the pillow. And my father doesn't seem to be open to giving me much time off. Not yet."

"Being occupied with work is not necessarily a negative thing. Your father is a wise man to keep you busy."

"Luke!" Kathleen strolled over to him. "How is the gun education coming along?"

"You'll have to ask my teacher."

John's normally frowning face broke into a wide smile. "He's learning."

"Show me." Kathleen pointed at the cans in the distance.

"I'd rather not, Kath."

"Come on, Luke, you can do it," said John.

Luke took out his gun and one cartridge from his pocket. Focusing and trying to remember all the steps, he clicked open the cylinder, put one cartridge in, then shut it. He eyed up the target and took a deep breath. Firmly holding on to the grip, Luke pulled the trigger. Ding, it hit the can on the far right.

"Excellent, Luke! You hit it!"

"Good job, Dr. Luke. That's the first time you hit the target on the first shot."

"I have excellent teachers," he said, not wanting to admit that he had been aiming at the can on the far left.

36

Kathleen busied herself with a new process for alphabetizing files that she had begun the previous week. Luke now had so many patients that files needed to be ordered for easier access. At present, Luke was waiting for one last patient before he finished his work day. Looking at the time, Kathleen tapped her foot impatiently and was slightly annoyed that the woman was already late.

There was a knock at Luke's office door. Kathleen opened it to find a young woman dressed in a plain brown skirt and blouse, her blond hair pulled up under a small hat. Kathleen surmised the girl to be middle to lower class. However, she looked similar enough to be Kathleen's relative.

"I have an appointment. May I come in?"

"Of course. I believe he's waiting for you. Are you Miss Smith?"

"I am."

The door to the examining room was slightly ajar, so Kathleen knocked, then announced, "Miss Smith is here."

"Thank you." Luke greeted the woman and welcomed her into the examining room. She waited to see if Luke wished her to join them, but when he did not call on her, she guessed that her assistance wasn't needed. Instead, Kathleen placed the files back in the cabinet and joined Mrs. Bradley in the kitchen.

***

"Good afternoon, Miss Smith."

"Good afternoon."

"What is your ailment?"

She held out her hand, his rosary beads in her palm. A spark of recognition. *The prostitute who had been injured by Karl.* Her appearance made her look almost normal, dressed as she was in modest clothing and wearing no face paint. She could easily be anyone's sister...or wife.

He waved his hand to indicate no. "I want you to keep the rosary."

She shook her head. "I appreciate all that you did for me, Doctor, but..."

"Pearl...is it?"

A subtle nod indicated it was.

"Might you consider leaving the... brothel?" Luke didn't even like saying the word.

With a sigh, Pearl stared out the window. Shaking her head, she said, "I wasn't able to 'work' for three weeks after Karl hurt me. I shall need to work three more months just to pay for the time I was unavailable to 'entertain.'"

"You knew this man by name?"

Pearl avoided eye contact, although she nodded. "He used to be a regular. I don't imagine I shall be seeing him again."

I certainly hope that is true, Luke thought.

"If and when you wish to leave that way of life behind and join respectable society, I can assist you."

"Assist me? There's not much you can do. This is the only life I have known."

"The only life? You're a young woman. Surely you have a family?"

Nodding, she said, "My parents and brother died when I was 11; there was no one to take care of me. I started working as a servant. The man I worked for...he took advantage of me. After that, I ran away and I learned I could make money pleasing men. And, except for the most recent incident, the gentlemen are mostly kind. I...don't... mind it so much."

Luke winced. It was plain to him that the girl was lying to herself. "Look, I can give you money to pay back the madam. I can give you money to help you start a new life."

She sighed deeply. "No. But I do appreciate the offer. And thank you."

"I was doing what I was trained to do."

"No, I don't mean that. Thank you for looking at me with kindness rather than lust or disgust."

Luke felt the warmth of a blush, then cleared his throat. "If you need help, I am here to assist."

She went to leave, then stopped. Her back to him, she said, "Are you...married?"

With a slight smile, he said, "I'm engaged to my lovely assistant, Miss Kathleen O'Donovan."

She gasped and slowly turned toward him. Her face was paler than when she'd arrived. "Kathleen O'Donovan of the O'Donovan Mercantile?"

"Yes."

"And when, pray tell, is the happy day?"

"October 2nd."

"Congratulations, Doctor, and thank you again."

***

The coins clinked in the ceramic jar, then Karl headed up an old staircase beside a wall with peeling paper. He was told to proceed to room four on the second floor. He knocked and a rather buxom young woman in a corset opened the door.

He had found this lower class brothel in Center City by accident. The rooms were small and this prostitute smelled of liquor. After trying for several minutes, Karl couldn't continue. He swore. She pleaded with him. "Honey, it's fine. This happens all the time. Some men have trouble getting things going. You don't need to be..."

Karl cut her off and glared at her. "Shut up." He had never had any difficulty "getting things going." It was obviously this girl and these dismal surroundings.

As he was getting dressed, he felt the girl touch his arm. He swung around and slapped her so hard, her body knocked into the vanity table. She began to cry.

He ignored her and left.

Damn these third class whores. He needed to see Pearl, but the madam had warned him not to return. Karl had last visited that brothel several months ago, when he was in his farm clothes and a longer beard. Of course, he was too smart for that small-minded madam. First, he purchased a pair of plain clear glasses. He visited a barber, had his beard trimmed short, his hair cut and he purchased a fine suit and expensive gentlemen's top hat (on his father's credit) at Lit Brothers. Standing in front of the mirror at the department store, he turned his body from side to side, admiring himself. With his changing appearances, he was certain the madam would never recognize him. Now he was prepared to visit Pearl.

When the madam answered the door of the brothel, he spoke with a southern drawl. "Ma'am, I would be mighty obliged if I could spend some leisurely time with one of your girls. My preference is thin blondes."

"I have just the gal for you. Her name is Pearl."

Karl just about jumped at the name. "My my, that sounds like a lovely name. How much for a half hour?"

The madam quoted the price. Karl handed her the money. She went off, he supposed, to tell Pearl she had a 'new client.'

When the madam returned, she said, "Pearl is ready. Top of the stairs, second door to the left...oh, and leave your gun at the door. New policy."

Karl clenched his teeth. He didn't like leaving his gun anywhere, but did as he was told.

Pearl was waiting for him at the doorway of her room. "I hear you're a fine southern gentleman. Come on in." Pearl looked just as he remembered her.

"Thank you, Ma'am."

Staring, she squinted. "Do I know you? Have we met?"

Karl shut the door. He took his coat off and hung it on a hook behind the door. "Well, Ma'am, yes, we have." He removed his hat, then his glasses and turned to face her. Winking, he said, "Karl Wagner, at your service, my dear."

Pearl gasped and stepped back. She reached into her dresser drawer and pulled out a gun. She pointed and cocked it. "You were told not to return. You put me out of business for three weeks. I'll be paying Violet back for the next three months for what you did to me."

"Now, Pearl. I shouldn't have hurt you. But I've tried a few of the brothels in Cheltenham and one in Center City...and they're just not the same. No one is like you." He tried to sound as nice as he could, but he wanted to use his fist to show her that was no way to talk to a client.

Pearl didn't move; the gun was aimed at his chest.

"You know, Pearl, I already paid."

"Fine. But you will not be getting what you came for. Instead, perhaps you might be interested in receiving new information about Kathleen O'Donovan."

Karl's head jerked up. "What sort of information?"

She held the gun high. "Information...instead of what you came here for."

"And what if I say no?"

"Trust me. You will want this information. It's that or me shooting you. And I really don't want that mess to clean up."

With a scowl and an angry sigh, he said, "Very well. What?"

"Kathleen O'Donovan and Dr. Luke Peterson are engaged to be married on October 2nd."

He stiffened. "What? That's a lie, whore." He stepped toward her and she kept the gun trained on him, her finger ready to pull the trigger.

She smirked. "I heard it from the doctor himself."

"There's no way she's marrying that..." He barked out a nervous laugh.

"Think what you want. They're getting married on October 2nd and you cannot do anything about it. Now get out! If I ever see you again, I will shoot. Out!"

Karl clenched his fists and, had that stupid whore not been holding a gun to him, he might have taken what he paid for. Instead, he turned around, went downstairs, picked up his gun at the door and quickly left.

Kathleen and that hick doctor hadn't called off their courtship after all. Not only that, they were to be married in less than three months. Karl could not fathom what Kathleen saw in that 120 pound weakling with the ugly glasses and the baby face. Was she so stupid that she could prefer *that sort* over him? And how could that sissy refuse to listen to Karl's admonition to break it off?

As Karl rode home, it occurred to him that it was Kathleen's fault he "couldn't perform" earlier. In fact, it was her fault that he had hurt that whore. It was her fault that he couldn't think of anyone but her.

No invitation would be forthcoming. Nevertheless, Karl planned to be present for the happy nuptials.

***

After three hours of constant studying, Will had a headache. Monsignor had asked him to memorize the section in the Baltimore Catechism on Holy Orders, but he wanted to show his full commitment by memorizing the entire catechism.

Two knocks on his door were followed by John's voice. "Will? May I speak with you?"

"Come in."

John opened the door and sat comfortably on Will's bed. He swung his legs without speaking.

"What do you need, John? I'm busy studying."

"May I travel with you to your appointment today?"

Will pushed the book up on his desk and sat back in his chair to face John. His brother hadn't said much to him since his graduation. Although Will had attempted to engage him in conversation, John had always answered curtly with one or two words.

"Of course." Will wasn't one to be overly curious, but he wondered what would entice John to want to accompany him. "Why do you want to go?"

Lowering his head, he said, "Papa has given me the rest of the day off. I would like to visit St. Michael's Church."

"Why?"

Without responding, John asked, "Is Papa coming with you?"

"Not this time."

John released a long sigh, lifted his chin and stared at Will, but did not speak.

"What's the matter, John?"

"I would like to speak to a priest, preferably not one that I see on a weekly basis."

"Really?" If there was any possibility that John wanted to go to confession or talk to the priest about moral matters, Will had an obligation to encourage it. "Of course. In fact, you may take the entire hour if you need it."

On the way to St. Michael's Church, thinking that perhaps this would give him an ideal opportunity to interact with his brother, Will asked John questions and, again, received curt responses. He finally surrendered and quietly prayed for John.

At the church, Will and John walked to the rectory. John

said little and Will didn't prod him to speak. Will knocked, then waited for the housekeeper to come to the door. Today, however, the priest answered the door. When the cleric saw the two brothers standing side by side, his eyes became wide. He welcomed them into the foyer. "Good afternoon, Will. This must be your brother, John?"

"Yes, may I present my brother, John O'Donovan."

The priest held his hand out and John shook it. "A pleasure to finally meet you, John. The two of you do look very similar."

John did not respond, so Will spoke. "Monsignor, my brother is wondering if he might be able to talk to you first."

"Of course, come right this way."

The three walked to Monsignor's office and the priest motioned for John to enter his office.

"May I visit the Blessed Sacrament while you speak to John?"

"Yes, please do. There are several women cleaning this afternoon, so the church is open."

"Thank you, Monsignor."

Walking next door to the church, he opened the wooden door of the archway entrance and entered. He had already attended Mass at St. Vincent's this morning, but he hadn't had the chance to pray before the Blessed Sacrament.

Will was already grateful that his brother desired to speak with a priest. He was additionally thankful that his brother had come along as it provided him this unexpected opportunity to spend more time with Our Lord.

Two women were polishing statues to his left. Thankfully, they did their task with quiet reverence. Will wouldn't have known they were there except that Monsignor had already informed him.

He genuflected and knelt at the communion rail in front. He blessed himself, rested his elbows on the rail and clasped his hands in prayer. He heard shuffling beside him and opened his eyes to observe the women quietly leaving. Will was now alone. He prayed for his brother, his other siblings and his parents. Despite the worries of the day, his soul was filled with peace.

The Holy Sacrifice of the Mass was Will's preferred prayer as he actually became a living tabernacle after Communion. However, adoration in front of the Blessed Sacrament, in the true presence of Christ, was an activity he wished he could participate in more frequently. He silently recited the Act of Adoration:

O my Jesus, in union with all the Angels and Saints, I adore Thee in this Most Holy Sacrament, in which Thou art concealed for the love of me; I adore Thee as my Lord and my God, my Creator and my Redeemer.

In recent months, he had begun reciting St. Francis's vocation prayer:

Most high, glorious God, enlighten the darkness of my heart and give me, Lord, a correct faith, a certain hope, a perfect charity, sense and knowledge, so that I may carry out Your holy and true command.

Peace, joy and love filled his entire being. He closed his eyes. Again he felt God's call not just with ambiguity, but with certainty. There was neither earthquake nor lightning, just the quiet, true presence of Christ.

It seemed only a moment or so before Monsignor tapped his shoulder. He looked up at the priest who was staring quizzically at him. "Will, we're finished."

The priest turned to John, whispered some words, then John left. Monsignor Flaherty leaned down and spoke gently. "Will, you are absolutely radiating. Your face is as bright as an electric light."

Will felt a flush creeping up his neck and onto his cheeks. "Is it?"

Inside the office, Monsignor sat down and Will eased himself onto the chair opposite the desk. Checking his pocket watch, Will had a difficult time understanding how thirty minutes could have passed without his knowledge. The experience made him more resolved to follow, with fervor, his true vocation. When he had asked God for a sign, he received the question from Fr. Morrissey and other hints of affirmation along the way.   With every passing day, with each hour, Will felt his vocation to the priesthood with his entire mind, soul and body. This, he believed, was God's will for him.

The priest perused Will's written work from the previous week, then looked over his glasses at him. "This is excellent work." He jotted down more notes and lessons for the upcoming week, and for the next ten minutes, reviewed important aspects from the catechism.

37

Kathleen squinted as she studied the gowns that Jane removed from the closet. With only a month before the wedding, there was still much to be done.

The servant removed the linen covers and carefully placed the dresses across the bed.

Mama pointed first at the white satin and lace gown. "I wore this one at my first wedding." She then lifted up the intricately designed cream-colored lace gown. "This I wore at my...second wedding."

In light of the modern styles that featured large puffy sleeves and high waists, these were not "in fashion," but Kathleen didn't care.

"Kathleen," her mother said, "you are nearly the size I was when I wore this dress," she said, pointing to the first gown. "You are welcome to wear either dress for your own wedding or, if you would like, your father and I will purchase you another one."

Kathleen glanced from dress to dress. She could tell that her mother wanted her to wear one of these.

"If you were me, which would you choose?"

Mama tightened her lips and stared, then lifted each one and held it up. She pointed to the white satin and lace gown she had worn at her first wedding to Kathleen's father, Liam. "This one."

Kathleen smiled. "Then this is the gown I shall wear."

"Miss Kathleen, this is a fine, fine choice."

Jane held it up to Kathleen. "I might need to take a half-inch off at the bottom, so try it on, Miss Kathleen."

"Yes, all right." The two women helped Kathleen take off her skirt and blouse, leaving her corset and shift in place. Jane slipped the dress over Kathleen's head and buttoned up the back. Her mother then lifted Kathleen's long hair out and smoothed it down her back. The future bride turned and studied herself in the mirror. Luke would be pleased. In fact, so would her real father, if he were alive. Papa would also be happy since he would be walking her down the aisle.

"Why, Miss Kathleen, you look lovely in that gown!" Jane's smile was wide.

Her mother blinked back tears.

"Mama."

She pulled Kathleen close and held her for several long moments. Then she stepped away. "I can't believe my little girl is getting married." Her mother lowered her head and began to cry softly.

"Shhh," Kathleen whispered as she stood beside her.

"I'm sorry. I'm very emotional these days." Mama wiped her eyes with her handkerchief, then straightened. "You look so lovely, Kathleen."

Jane stepped in. "Let me take this off so I can make the adjustments, Miss Kathleen."

After the two older women left the room, Kathleen went to her window. Peering out at the beautiful end-of-summer day, she breathed in deeply. Just beyond the pond, Jesse was mowing the lawn and the scent of fresh, earthy grass, combined with clean hay, wafted by her window.

Kathleen contemplated what life would be like once she married Luke next month. There was much to anticipate. She had always dreamed of a honeymoon to Atlantic City. At least once per summer, her family would travel to Atlantic City for several days of beach fun. Earlier this year, Luke had been invited but had been unable to attend. Disappointed, he'd promised that one day they would go together. She had asked him last week about a honeymoon, and he had told her that he wouldn't be able to take any time off.

***

Luke waved to Kathleen as he rode past her and Will to the front hitching post. The pair ran to greet him. Luke emerged from the carriage and embraced Kathleen, then he shook Will's hand.

"Luke, you're early!"

"Yes."

"Come, I need to speak with you."

"Is anything wrong, Kath?"

"Well..."

They walked hand in hand to the oak tree. With a sigh, Kathleen leaned close to him. "Are you sure we can't embark on a short honeymoon? Every newly-married couple is doing so these days."

"Oh...uh...like I told you the other day, business is picking up and I don't want to risk being away for any length of time." He didn't want to share with her the real reason he opted for no honeymoon.

Embracing her, he kissed the top of her head. Her hair smelled of roses. "Besides, I can carry you over the threshold of our home. I'll plan some beautiful surprises for you."

She relaxed against him. "Very well. No honeymoon." Kathleen forced a smile, but her head hung low and her shoulders were slumped. Luke could tell that she was trying not to show her disappointment but it was evident to him.

"Will you promise me that one day we can enjoy a holiday in Atlantic City?"

"Yes, love, I promise." *Some day.*

38

Inside the foyer, Papa met Kathleen and Luke. "Kat, would you mind if I spoke privately to your fiancé?"

"Privately?"

"Now, now, some things are better discussed outside the gentle ears of a young lady."

"Yes, I suppose so."

Luke kissed her forehead. "I don't think we shall be long."

"Very well."

In the parlor, she played piano quietly as she pondered what her father and fiancé might be discussing.

***

"Kat tells me you're too busy to take a honeymoon?"

Luke winced. He wasn't too busy. He just didn't think going on a honeymoon was the best idea given his last interaction with Karl, and the man's assault on the prostitute and his suspicion that he might have wrecked his new carriage cushions last Christmas. Although four months had passed without incident, Luke felt safer and more comfortable in a familiar environment.

"My medical practice has been picking up."

"You will be taking one day off for the wedding, correct?"

"Yes."

"And you always take off on Sundays."

"Unless there is an emergency."

"When Kat was little, all she would have to do is look at me with those big green eyes and say, 'Please, Papa,' and I'd give her whatever she wanted. I want to do this for her and for you."

"I don't know what to say, David."

"Say yes. Just one overnight trip. Let's give Kat what she wants, a honeymoon. All the upper class couples take honeymoons these days."

"That's what Kathleen said. I'm just not sure this is the best..."

"It's my gift."

What was Luke supposed to say to his future father-in-law? Then again, perhaps David was right. It would only be an overnight visit. What could happen in one night? He nodded. "Thank you."

"How about we surprise Kat with a honeymoon in Atlantic City?"

"Atlantic City?" Luke would have chosen a venue closer to home, but Kathleen would be excited with this gift, and he really wanted to make her happy. "Fine, that would be fine."

"Oh...and one more thing, Luke." David reached into his drawer. "I had this made for you." In his hands was a leather holster. "I noticed that you carry your gun in your coat. Not the best place for it."

Nodding, he said, "Thank you, David. This will surely make it easier to carry."

"Yes, it will."

He strapped it around his waist, and slipped the gun inside, still uncomfortable with carrying a gun.

***

After supper, Kathleen accompanied Luke to his carriage. He was quiet, but not his usual quiet. He seemed distracted.

"Luke?"

"Yes, love?"

"What were you and Papa talking about for so long in his study?"

He chuckled nervously. "Wedding preparations."

"Why the secrecy?"

"Do you trust me?"

At first, she scowled. Whenever he didn't want to share information with her, he usually asked her that question. She was annoyed, but she did trust him.

"Yes."

"I shall explain in due time."

"Very well."

***

After Luke left, Papa asked Kathleen to come to his study. The window was open, the sun shining on his desk. This room reminded her so much of Papa, the scents of wood and pipe tobacco filling every crook and crevice of the masculine room.

"I cannot believe that, in just a few weeks, you'll be a married woman."

"I know; hard to fathom." She paused. "Papa?"

"Yes?"

"Tell me what you were like when you were my age."

"I'd rather tell you what your real father was like. Lee was a fastidious man and a very moral gentleman. In those few hours before he died, he must have had a premonition that he would die. He made me promise to marry your mother, to protect her, to financially support her and his unborn child."

"Me." Kathleen looked past Papa at a framed photograph he kept on his desk. It was a photo of Papa and his brother, Liam. She stood up, walked to the desk, and stared at the photo up close. Smiling, she found it peculiar that the brothers looked so different. But she could definitely see part of herself in this fair-haired man with a shy smile. In his last moments on earth, her real father thought only of Kathleen and her mother. For the first time, she felt a connection to Liam, a man whose face she had only seen in photographs.

"Of course, I had already fallen in love with your mother."

Kathleen placed the photo on the desk and returned to her chair. "Really?"

"But she despised me."

Kathleen laughed. "That's what Mama told me. It's hard to believe Mama felt anything but love toward you."

"Well, she had every reason to dislike me, considering my licentious behavior. We were 'married' for over a year and a half before we actually entered into a sacramental marriage."

"Obviously Mama grew to love you?"

"Yes. But I had changed. My faith had become an important part of my life."

For Kathleen, these revelations seemed like a story from a novel. She had only known her parents as affectionate and loving toward one another. And their open affection wasn't limited to each other; it extended to their children as well, which was unusual, especially amongst her friends.

"Once your mother realized she loved me, we met with Monsignor Flaherty — Father Flaherty at the time — and we scheduled our sacramental marriage ceremony. Until we honestly made our vows before God and then acted on those vows, we weren't married in the eyes of God and in the eyes of the Church."

"I see."

"Our marriage took place in the rectory since your mother wasn't Catholic at the time. You were about a year and a half old. When we walked in, you said, 'Papa, dark?'"

Kathleen leaned in and took her father's hand.

"You were a precious child, Kat."

"And you have been a most wonderful father. Your brother would have been proud of you. I am proud of you. Thank you for your honesty, Papa. I love you." She kissed his cheek.

***

Upon returning home, Luke went through the back door to the kitchen, poured himself a glass of water, then headed up the back staircase to the upstairs. In his bedroom, he took off his new holster with the Smith & Wesson inside, placed it on his beside table. His jacket and tie were next and he hung them in his closet. Smiling, he thought of David's offer to pay for and arrange a honeymoon in Atlantic City and, although he was concerned, he hadn't seen hide nor hair of Karl in many months and hoped that the man had left the area.

Luke was too happy at present to think about Karl. Tomorrow, he would move many of his belongings from this closet to the attic to make room for Kathleen's clothes and items.

And in less than a month, he would be a married man. Were most prospective grooms this joyful?

***

In her room, Kathleen reflected on this information about her father. How could an upstanding, righteous and devout man like her father have a sordid history? Mary Magdalene had a similar history and she became a great saint. Kathleen understood Papa's occasional comment that many of the local people had a difficult time forgetting the past. But she had no

idea it was *his* past to which he was referring. Will was a
product of her father's past, but Kathleen could not imagine
the world without her brother. Everything happened for a
reason and she truly believed that every human being was a
gift created by a loving God.

39

The second day of October couldn't arrive quickly enough. After a restless sleep, Kathleen woke and sat up in bed. Joy filled her soul and heart. In less than three hours, she would be joined to her beloved forever.

She removed her night cap and ran her fingers through her hair. Rays of light were beaming through the window. Birds were chirping gaily in the trees, their leaves just starting to turn red, yellow and orange. Nothing could — or would — ruin her joyous mood.

In the past few weeks, she found herself daydreaming about children. Luke would be a wonderful father and hopefully their union would be a fruitful one.

Descending the staircase, she met Jane in the foyer.

"Miss Kathleen, you look like a ray of sunshine today!"

"I feel like one. Today is my wedding day! Can you believe it is finally here?"

"No, I can't. It seems like yesterday you were just a wee baby. I remember your Mama on her wedding days. You look very much like her. But I can see some of Mr. Liam in you, too. You have his smile."

"Thank you, Jane."

***

Izzy stood beside Jane and handed her mother the pins as she helped Kathleen style her hair.

"Miss Kathleen," Jane said, "Dr. Luke will think that you are a most stunning bride. I have no doubt about that."

"Luke told me he thinks that I am stunning in any dress."

"I agree wholeheartedly with my mama," Izzy joined in.

"Miss Kathleen, I need to check on the roast in the kitchen. I'll return momentarily."

"Certainly, Jane."

When the older servant left the room, Kathleen could not control her curiosity any longer. "Izzy?"

"Yes, Miss Kathleen?"

"You must be so happy to be home!"

"I am. I haven't seen John yet. I've missed him so much."
She nodded, then turned away. Whimpers, like the sound of a
quiet cat came from the girl.

"Izzy, what's wrong?"

"My mama said that we should forget about each other.
I'm a servant and John is an upper class gentleman."

"Upper class maybe, not sure about the gentleman part."

"I...love...him."

Kathleen nodded, although in actuality, she had no idea
what to say to the young servant. Izzy was beautiful and John
a most handsome gentleman; she understood the physical
attraction. But marital love between them?

"John and I, we're going to...what I mean is...some day,
we're going to be married."

"I see." In truth, Kathleen wasn't so sure.

"We're trying to obey the rules of not spending time alone.
But after being away from each other for four months, I have
realized that all I want is to be with John. When I am with
him, I'm not a servant. He treats me with respect."

"Treats you with respect? Truthfully, Izzy, if he respected
you, he wouldn't have...well, he wouldn't have insisted you
and he..."

Izzy pinned up the bustle of Kathleen's dress but made no
response.

Kathleen continued. "Izzy, I want you and John to be
happy. If you both still love one another after a couple of
years, then get married."

"I only wished to make John happy. That made him
happy."

"I suppose it did. But that act is meant to be within
marriage. And it has led to consequences...you were sent
away and John has been working day and night."

"We have already pledged our lives to one another."

Kathleen sighed. Did Izzy have heartbreak in store for her?

***

Will was in the front yard when John and Jesse rode up in
the small carriage. Izzy burst through the door and ran to
John, who smiled awkwardly. "It's been so long!" Izzy's eyes

were bright, her smile wide. As Will studied John's pinched expression, he wondered why his brother didn't seem happier at having been reunited with Izzy.

"Hello," John said. He embraced her, then held her at arm's length. John seemed to be forcing a smile. "Izzy, you are a sight for sore eyes."

Izzy's expression turned to one of adulation, as if John held the answers to all the important questions in life.

"Let's take a walk by the pond over there." Then turning to Will, he said, "Would you act as our chaperone?"

With wide eyes, Will nodded. "No, I don't mind, John. I should be happy to do so." *John is asking for a chaperone?*

The two of them strolled off to the tree. John gently placed his hands on Izzy's shoulders and caressed the side of her face. Will felt he should turn away; instead he watched.

John kissed her forehead, then murmured words to her. All of a sudden, Izzy stepped back, her hand to her mouth; her eyes wide. Was she crying? Finally, John hugged her and stroked her hair.

Jane called from the porch. "Mr. Will, you best be getting ready for your sister's wedding." Jane shaded her eyes with her hand to look in the distance at Izzy and John.

"Yes, I shall be there momentarily." Will, as chaperone, could not leave until John and Izzy separated. So he waited.

Staring, he saw Izzy nodding. John wiped her cheeks and kissed her forehead once more. The couple embraced, then Izzy broke off and ran past Will into the house.

John remained by the tree, staring off in the distance. Checking the time, Will decided he better return to his room to get dressed.

Moments later, two firm knocks sounded at his door. *John.* Will was just pulling his trousers on. "One moment." He swung the door open. His brother waited in the hallway, his dress clothes draped over his arm. "May I dress in here? We don't have much time to talk and I need to speak with you."

Will allowed John to step inside before he closed the door.

John talked as he removed his clothes. Will faced the window. The rustling behind him suggested John was dressing. Will reached for his shirt and put it on. It was quiet for a moment. John then cleared his voice. "Will?"

"Yes?"

"Thank you for helping me to see that I was selfish. I'm sorry for not listening to your advice."

Could Will's ears be deceiving him? Was his brother thanking him and apologizing?

"You may already suspect it, but I went to confession with Monsignor Flaherty. He gave me absolution, but as part of my penance, I needed to apologize to all parties involved. First, and most importantly, I asked Izzy's forgiveness. A few moments ago, I apologized to Jane. She tried to place most of the blame on Izzy, but I wouldn't allow that. Izzy was trying to please me and I took advantage of her."

Will nodded.

"Then I asked forgiveness from Mama. She cried."

"What about Izzy? You haven't written to her for months."

"I tried to apologize to her in a letter, but...I wrote it ten times and could not find the proper words."

"So you don't love her?"

"On the contrary. It's precisely because I do love her that I told her we are not going to engage in intimate activity reserved for married couples. I'm trying to discern the right path for me, just like you are."

"The right path?"

John continued. "I had a conversation with Dr. Luke first, then I spoke with Monsignor Flaherty. At first, it was difficult to hear what the priest had to say. But these past five months have been the most excruciatingly difficult and...as challenging as the time has been, it also helped me to realize that I'm not ready to support a wife and child; not yet. I'm only seventeen."

"But Izzy was crying."

"Not because she was sad. She told me that she felt wrong doing what we did, but she was afraid she would lose me."

Will nodded. "Do you still love her?"

"I love her more than I can express. Both Dr. Luke and Monsignor explained to me that true love is sacrificial, not selfish. And, of course, you were right, although I don't know why I'm surprised, Father," — he drew out the two syllables of the title — "Will." John's eyebrows were raised but he was smiling.

Will laughed in return.

"Now, the last apology will be the most difficult. It's why I have been procrastinating. I need to speak to Papa. Would you accompany me?"

"Are you sure you don't want to apologize privately?"

"No. I would appreciate the support."

"Very well."

Before they reached their parents' bedroom, Papa had opened the door. The top of his shirt was unbuttoned and his cravat hung loosely around his neck. He sighed.

Will stood behind John. "Boys?"

"Papa," said John. "I should like to talk to you."

Their father's eyebrows lifted. "I'm a bit busy..." The older man stared at John, then he glanced at Will.

"This will just take a moment."

"Very well." Their father opened the door wide. He stopped trying to tie his cravat and looked up.

John remained silent, his eyes blinking rapidly.

Papa's head tilted forward, his eyes staring intensely at his two oldest sons. Will nudged John closer to their father.

"Papa?"

"Yes, John?"

"I want to ask for your forgiveness for engaging in sin on your property, for disobeying you and for disrespecting you."

Papa's eyes widened. "Why...how...did you..."

"After months of backbreaking work, I'm not angry anymore; mostly fatigued. Will said something to me on the way to his graduation..." Papa turned to Will and winked.

John continued. "Then I spoke with Dr. Luke. He advised me to talk to a priest. I felt uncomfortable speaking to Father Morrissey, so I went with Will to visit Monsignor Flaherty two months ago. I finally went to confession."

"But you haven't been to communion."

"I needed to make reparation first. Monsignor said for my

penance, I should ask forgiveness from all the parties involved. He said I also needed to intend never to take part in that sin again. Eventually I want to ask Izzy to marry me."

"Marry you?"

"Perhaps a couple years from now."

"I see. Who knows what might happen in the meantime?"

"I love her, Papa. I want to marry her."

"Well, son, nothing is etched in stone. But I think what you have done is courageous and I'm proud of you." Papa hugged John.

"Papa?" John stepped back.

"Yes?"

"After the wedding, I would like to suggest that Izzy be sent to Kat's and Luke's house instead of Quakertown."

With a nod, Papa said, "I'm sure Kat and Mrs. Bradley would appreciate the extra help, especially if Kat is going to assist Luke in his office." He paused. "Now, we've got a wedding to attend."

40

From their expressions, an outsider would have thought that the women were preparing for a battle instead of a wedding. Kathleen tried to scratch her nose. "Miss Kathleen, stop moving or you'll get this needle stuck in you."

"Sorry, Jane. My nose itches."

"That means you're going to get into a fight."

Shaking her head, Mama said, "Posh, Jane, that's superstitious."

Jane scoffed and continued stitching.

Mama stared at Kathleen in her wedding dress. Jane was scowling as she made a last minute adjustment to the shoulder. The lace and satin, now over twenty years old, had ripped slightly after Jane had already buttoned the hundred silk buttons on her back. Adjustments needed to be made with the dress in place.

Once Jane finished, she exclaimed, "Miss Kathleen, your cheeks are flushed and you've been smiling wide all morning. You don't need any rouge to be a beautiful bride."

"Thank you, Jane."

"We'll be right back with the veil, Miss Kathleen, Miss Caroline." Jane and Izzy left the room.

With a nod, Kathleen turned toward the window. She couldn't keep still with anxiousness and excitement.

It was unusually sunny and warm for October. Jane had already taken the curtains down to wash them.

Kathleen peered out the bare window. The sky was robin's egg blue; no clouds dared to ruin the otherwise perfect weather.

Her hope chest, which had belonged to her mother, sat near the window, packed and ready to be delivered to Luke's house later in the day. The next hour would be her last moments as an unmarried woman.

Kathleen faced her mother. "Mama?"

"Yes, sweet."

"Did you wish to speak to me about anything?" Jane and

Izzy had left them alone for a reason. "Like...about the wedding night?"

Her mother lowered her head, a sigh escaping her lips.

"Mama, I'm nervous about...marriage and children."

Mama cleared her throat, then closed her eyes. "Most brides are...tentative, even anxious. I was."

"Truly?"

"Truly." Her mother nodded, a flush creeping across her cheeks. "Your father, Liam, was a patient and kind man, but..."

"But?"

"I shall only tell you this: be selfless, not selfish. Give your husband your entire heart, soul and body."

The door swung open and Jane and Izzy returned, cutting their mother-daughter dialogue short. Her mother lifted out a piece of jewelry from her skirt pocket and held it in front of Kathleen. A small blue and white cameo was nestled in her palm. "Your father had this made before you were born. He had planned to give it to me at your birth, but he passed away before doing so." Kathleen studied the smooth blue cameo with intricate etching of a mother and child on a pearl and gold base. "It's beautiful, Mama."

"Look at the back."

"COD with love LOD July 15, 1877. It's lovely. How did my father know the date?"

"He didn't. I had that engraved after you were born." She paused. "I wanted you to have this as you walk down the aisle." Her mother was now blotting her eyes.

"Mama." Kathleen hugged her mother until the older woman took her by the hand to the mirror. Kathleen stared at her reflection. The bodice of the dress was made of satin and pearls, had a V neck design with lace sleeves, and a plain white satin skirt with a lace overlay. She embraced her mother, Jane and Izzy. Her mother put the veil on her head and over her face.

Kathleen elevated her skirt so as not to trip, and hurried out into the hallway. "Slow down, Miss Kathleen," Jane pleaded.

"I'm excited, Izzy! I want to get to that church and marry Luke!"

Outside, there were four carriages, their Cabriolet and three additional vehicles that Papa had rented. He had also hired three additional drivers.

When she reached the Cabriolet, she was surprised to find it decorated in white roses. "How lovely!" she said to Jane and Izzy. "Did you do this?"

"Yes, we did, Miss Kathleen," Jane said. "We had to hide it at the side of the house so you wouldn't see it until now."

Her father squeezed her hand. "Kat, you look absolutely beautiful."

"Thank you, Papa."

Papa, Jane and Jesse assisted the bride from the stepping block into the carriage. Then Papa helped Mama in and she took the seat beside her husband.

The trip to the Cathedral was longer than she would have liked. Their small church would not be able to accommodate the large number of invited guests. Of course, her father insisted on having the reception at the posh and luxurious Walton Hotel at Broad and Locust Streets.

It was a most spectacular day, not only because it was the day she would be joined with her beloved, but because it was simply picture perfect. Kathleen couldn't imagine a more ideal day.

***

The first in the O'Donovan four-carriage caravan stopped in front of the cathedral. A crowd had congregated on both sides of the street.

"We'll wait a few moments, Kat, until the others have pulled in behind us."

Kathleen wanted to leap out of the carriage. Knowing that was neither ladylike nor proper, she relaxed in the seat and scanned the crowds on either side of the street. Most of the people were in formal clothes for the wedding and Kathleen recognized a few distant relatives and her father's clients.

***

His back against a tree, Karl waited in an area across the

street from the cathedral. He had visited St. Vincent de Paul Church earlier this week to find out the precise time of the wedding. In doing so, he discovered the wedding would be taking place at ten a.m. at the cathedral in Philadelphia, rather than at the church in Germantown.

The Cabriolet rode up with the pomp and circumstance of a royal wedding, decorated with white roses and the rider, whom he recognized as the O'Donovan servant, was wearing a top hat. He scowled and clenched his fists. Karl wanted nothing better than to ruin this happy day. Kathleen had rejected him. Worse was that she'd chosen a weakling as a husband. He had no idea yet what he meant to do, but he would wait and watch, then decide.

Today Karl dressed in his finest clothes, his beard still full and trimmed, with a top hat, just for the occasion. He wanted to blend in. As he scanned the crowd, there were at least ten other gentleman dressed in similar fashion.

***

Jesse's friendly face, along with Jane's and Izzy's, appeared alongside the carriage to assist Kathleen and her parents.

Papa emerged first, then Mama. Together, David and Jesse assisted Kathleen onto the stepping block while Izzy and Jane kept the bottom of Kathleen's train off the ground. Looking up at Jesse, Kathleen thought the young servant looked handsome in his formal morning suit and top hat.

Inside the church, Kathleen took a few deep breaths. Her parents were close by and her bridesmaids, Alice and Margaret, with their rose-colored gowns, waited. Will then escorted Mama down the aisle.

The doors opened and the organist played "Ode to Joy."

Her father had made the right choice of venue for the wedding; this cathedral was beautiful and radiant, from the marble floors to the polished wooden pews.

Papa leaned over and whispered, "I love you, Kat. I pray that you and Luke will have many years of happiness."

"Thank you, Papa. I love you, too."

The congregation stood and turned to face the bridal party. Alice and Margaret slowly walked down the aisle.

Her father nodded to her, then held up his arm. She took hold of it and they began walking down the aisle. She was thankful to have the veil over her face as she blinked away the tears. A year ago, she couldn't imagine having a normal life, let alone a wonderful new husband.

Luke was standing straight with a huge grin on his face. His brother, Zach, was taller, dark-haired and didn't look like Luke. Zach stood beside Luke as best man. Andrew, Luke's cousin, was a short, stocky man, who stood to Zach's left.

***

Luke turned and stared as Kathleen and David made their way down the long aisle of the cathedral. The sight of his bride took his breath away and he could not think any rational thought other than *Thank you God, for my beloved*.

***

When they reached the front, her father kissed the top of Kathleen's veiled head, shook Luke's hand, then joined her mother in the front pew. Together she and Luke stood in front of the Monsignor Flaherty and Father Morrissey and made their vows in front of God and witnesses.

Afterwards, the bride and groom emerged from the cathedral. Kathleen's veil had been lifted from her face and rested beautifully on her hair. She had little time to think before the photographer motioned for them to assemble on the steps with the two bridesmaids and groomsmen.

The bridal party posed for several photographs with family, friends and guests.

Luke escorted Kathleen to the wedding carriage. She stopped and stared at the flowers adorning the closed carriage. The white roses that were on her family's Cabriolet had been transported to this new carriage and additional pink, yellow and green flowers added. Jane, Izzy and Mama assisted her into the vehicle. She carefully sat down and Luke got in to sit beside her. The scent of roses, carnations and other fragrant flowers made Kathleen dizzy with happiness.

Luke craned his head as he looked out the small window. "Looks like the other carriages are decorated with flowers too."

"It's beautiful. Where did Papa get all these carriages?"

"We're actually riding in our wedding gift from your parents."

Kathleen squealed with joy. "Truly?"

"Yes. I told your father that we would be fine with just the one carriage. But it's hard to say no to your father."

"I know that to be true."

"He insisted that we have a larger carriage with more room for — shall we say — additional members."

"Additional members?"

"The pitter patter of little feet?"

"Oh, of course." She blushed.

"And there's one additional prize you'll receive later."

"Oh, do tell!"

"It wouldn't be a surprise if I told you now."

"Oh, Luke." She leaned in and kissed him on the lips. Within the privacy of their closed carriage, Kathleen and Luke kissed in unrestrained affection.

41

At the Walton Hotel, the newly-married couple proceeded across the large reception room to the table decorated and reserved for them and the bridal party. Kathleen's normally frugal father had splurged for the occasion and the tables were set with French lead crystal glasses, porcelain china and polished silverware. The seats were covered in white linen and bows and each table held a vase of a dozen pink and yellow roses, Kathleen's favorite colors.

She and Luke stood beside the table, along with her parents, her attendants, and Luke's brother, cousin and aunt as they received guests. Luke's Aunt Edna, who stood beside Kathleen and Mama, was a vivacious woman who embraced the young bride just before they began receiving guests. Dressed in an elegant green gown, the white-haired woman was in her late sixties and slight in stature, but she moved with the agility and grace of a younger woman. Her eyes were kind and Kathleen surmised the woman could not have a mean bone in her body. Luke was fortunate to have had this woman raise him. Unfortunately, Luke's frail uncle had not been able to travel because of ill health so he was not in attendance.

Kathleen saw Mrs. Bradley's smiling face and half-expected the woman to whistle a happy tune for the occasion. Jane, Jesse and Izzy had already taken their seats.

In the carriage earlier, Luke had embraced his new role as husband, kissing her most intimately. She blushed thinking about it. Although she was anxious, she looked forward to more of Luke's affections as the day progressed.

Her mother approached her.

"You are a lovely bride, sweet."

"Thank you, Mama."

The older woman turned and stared at Papa. "Your father seems rather fidgety. He can't seem to remain still."

***

Kathleen was absolutely ravishing and she seemed so

happy to be marrying that boy-man. Karl could see no sign that she was nervous or anxious. Her eyes were bright and she had a perpetual smile plastered on her face. All Karl could think of was wiping that stupid smirk away. He still hadn't come up with a final plan to destroy her day. But he would eventually, when he was certain it would be foolproof.

In fact, Kathleen's doting father seemed to be the one who could not keep still as he questioned the waiters and workers. Karl wouldn't get caught. He was too smart. He had avoided the receiving line successfully then ducked into the men's room for an hour.

So Kathleen was happy. Wasn't that nice?

***

Luke barely touched the food on his plate. It was tender goose with a cream sauce and it smelled delicious. He was hungry but too excited to eat. He noticed that David was not sitting during the meal. The older man walked over to a tall broad-shouldered server, and patted him on the back. The man turned and David nodded and smiled. Then he stepped back and appeared to be scanning the room.

"Luke," Kathleen said, "you normally have a robust appetite. Do you not like the food?"

"It's very tasty. With the wedding and all the excitement, I do not have much of an appetite."

"Me neither." Despite her words, she continued staring at him so he made an effort to eat a few bites.

This aside, Luke couldn't contain his curiosity any longer. He put his fork down, returned his napkin to the table and excused himself.

Approaching his father-in-law, he said, "David, what are you doing?"

"I'm... checking to make sure everyone is an invited guest."

"Couldn't you have hired someone to do that?"

"I'd rather do it myself."

"And why wouldn't everyone here be an invited guest?"

"You've heard of lower class people trying to get a free meal?"

"And so what if they did? You often help these people and would probably welcome them."

David considered that. "I suppose you're correct." He paused. "It's none of your concern, Luke. This is your wedding day. Enjoy yourself."

Luke hesitated, considering David's command. Then he said, "You are acting in a most peculiar manner. Why?"

David pulled at his collar. "I'm just being...overprotective."

"Overprotective of Kathleen?"

"Well...yes."

"I still don't understand, David. Isn't that what I'm supposed to be doing? The gun education?" He opened his jacket and pointed to the gun and holster.

"Yes, but..."

"But what? If you know something, you must tell me."

With a long sigh, his new father-in law said, "Very well. Karl sent a letter to Kat three months ago telling her that he has been watching her...and that he would eventually 'claim his prize.'"

"What?" Luke whispered, his heart now racing. "Why didn't you tell me about that letter? Did you bring it to the police?"

"No, because my Irish temper got the best of me. I ripped it to pieces."

Luke groaned.

"Besides, I didn't want Kat to know...and you're a poor liar."

Stepping back, Luke scowled. "That's why you pushed the marriage."

"I already knew you wanted to marry Kat. You are trustworthy and have virtue and morals. I'd rather her married to you than have that deranged lunatic sending her letters."

With a shake of his head, Luke said, "Well, that's troubling. Karl threatened me shortly before that. He showed up at my office and demanded I remove a bullet from his arm or he'd kill me. And he told me if I called the police, we would be sorry. He said he wasn't 'finished' with Kathleen."

"Good heavens! Why didn't you share *that* information with *me*?"

"The same reason you didn't tell me about the letter. I suspect Karl is also the one who ruined my new carriage cushion."

"Surely I'd recognize the man," said David.

"Not necessarily. He looked quite different when he showed up at my office: a heavy beard, long hair, farm clothes."

David stared across the hall at another tall broad-shouldered man, dressed in a fine coat and trousers, speaking to a waiter near the men's room. "Who is that man over there?"

The two men walked briskly to the tall gentleman. David patted the man on the back and he turned. Neither David nor Luke recognized the man.

"Pardon me, sir, may I ask your name?"

"Mr. Winston Hemphill," the man answered with a southern drawl. "I'm one of the managers of this fine hotel. I was just here to observe the reception and to see if you might need anything."

"Of course. Thank you."

David turned to Luke. "I'm going to send a telegram to the hotel in Atlantic City and inform them that your privacy is important. If anyone happens to inquire, I will request that they do not divulge your room number or that you're even at that hotel."

"A good plan, David, but I wonder whether we should cancel the honeymoon."

He shook his head. "This is Kat's big surprise. I want her to be happy."

***

That was close. Karl had been standing in the reception hall near the men's smoking room when he saw Kathleen's father and the weakling doctor walk toward him. He immediately turned into a narrow hallway. Karl knew it was only a matter of time before they discovered that he was not, in fact, an invited guest.

Karl waited until the Kathleen's father and the hick doctor were facing away from him, then he left, but not before he heard that the happy couple would be spending the night in Atlantic City. He nearly choked on his drink when he heard that interesting bit of news, because he now had a plan.

Taking his horse to the stable, Karl paid the liveryman a few coins to keep his horse for the next two days. He then caught the trolley to the ferry at Market Street and bought a ticket for the next train to Atlantic City.

***

Luke returned to the table and took another mouthful of lukewarm goose. He tried to savor it. He refused to allow anything to ruin the happiest day of his life. Swallowing the food, he wiped his mouth with a napkin.

A short while later, the string quartet began playing a waltz. Luke leaned close to his bride and whispered. "I love you very much, Kath." Luke stood up and bowed to his wife. "May I have this dance, Mrs. Peterson?"

"Of course."

"Just a warning, I'm a rather clumsy dancer."

"I know. We shall take it slow."

42

When Luke and Kathleen arrived at the O'Donovan house after the wedding reception, the blushing bride went upstairs to change her attire. With Izzy's assistance, Kathleen dressed in a yellow and green skirt and blouse.

It was only four o'clock, but Kathleen was hungry again. Jane had a large buffet waiting for the guests and Kathleen enjoyed spending time with her extended family and having an opportunity to chat with her new 'in-laws.'

Zach, Luke's brother, was taller and had dark hair. Although they didn't look much like siblings, Zach's voice sounded like Luke's and he was chattier. Andrew, his cousin, was a quiet man. Aunt Edna was a small woman who was gentle and kind. Kathleen promised her that she and Luke would visit their farm in the near future to meet Uncle Henry.

Kathleen's friend and bridesmaid, Margaret, had already been reunited with baby Joseph whom she happily held in her arms. Margaret and her husband had hired a nanny to care for the baby during the wedding and reception.

Once dinner was over, Papa invited the entire family to come outside to bid goodbye to the happy couple.

Her father announced loudly, "May I have everyone's attention? I will be taking Kat and Luke to a secret location momentarily. We invite you now to say a proper goodbye to the newlyweds."

Kathleen squealed. "Papa, wonderful! I adore surprises! I thought we were just going back to Luke's house." Kathleen turned to Luke. "Did you know about this?"

"I did."

For several minutes, she and Luke hugged, thanked and bid farewell to everyone: Aunt Elizabeth, Uncle Philip, her cousin Alice, Aunt Edna, Zach and Andrew, Margaret, her husband and baby Joseph, the O'Donovan siblings, Jane, Izzy, Lucy...her last goodbye would be to her mother.

Luke turned to chat with his brother and cousin which gave Kathleen a moment of privacy with her mother.

"Kathleen, I hope you have a wonderful time with Luke."

"Do you know where we are going?" she whispered.

"I do, but I want you to be surprised."

The two women embraced and Mama kissed her cheek.

"Be happy, Kathleen. That's all a mother could ask for. And Luke is a fine, fine gentleman."

"I know."

In the carriage, with her father in the driver's seat above them, she turned to Luke. "I don't have a bag packed."

"Izzy packed one for you."

"And what about…"

"Don't worry. Your father and I have a grand plan."

"Sounds like a great adventure."

"It is most certainly a great adventure."

"How long will we be gone?"

"Only one day…I must return to see patients."

"It's more than I expected."

***

When Karl arrived in Atlantic City, he pushed to the front to disembark and nearly jumped off the train. He had been racking his brain for the past two hours trying to remember which hotel Kathleen had said her family visited. There were only four or five upscale hotels in the city and he would bet a year's wages that the newlyweds would be staying at the hotel she had mentioned last year.

At a souvenir shop, he bought a hotel guide and scanned the names of the hotels. Three-quarters down the list, he saw the name, Seaside House Hotel. Bingo. That was it. He was certain. The pamphlet described it as "close to the beach."

Now all he needed to do was to inquire of the desk clerk whether Dr. and Mrs. Peterson were staying at the hotel. He walked up to the desk. Karl explained that he was a friend of Dr. and Mrs. Peterson and would like to send his greetings. The clerk gave a sympathetic smile. "I'm sorry, sir. I'm not at liberty to divulge any information about our guests."

Karl bit on his lip to keep from frowning. "Thank you."

He prided himself on his high intelligence and knew, without a doubt, that the happy couple must be staying here.

Looking at his watch, he figured that he had about three to four hours before they would arrive. He left the hotel, purchased a writing tablet, envelopes, a pencil and a sharpener at a pharmacy. He returned, folded a clean sheet of paper, then wrote "Dr. and Mrs. Peterson" on the outside of the envelope. He watched the clerk until he saw that the man was overwhelmed with guests, then Karl made his move. "Excuse me, I have a delivery for Dr. and Mrs. Peterson." The clerk hurriedly took it, looked down at the register, then slipped it into the compartment for Room 3A. He smiled inwardly. All he needed to do now was to wait.

***

Luke parted the curtain of the carriage just in time to see David pulling up to the Market Street Ferry station. Luke got out and the two men assisted Kathleen out and onto one of the stepping blocks in front of the station. Looking up, Kathleen's eyes widened. "Papa! This is where we come to take the ferry to Camden, then the train to the shore!"

"Yes, Kat. Have a pleasant honeymoon. Surprise!"

***

Kathleen squealed and turned to Luke. "We're going to the shore! To Atlantic City?"

"Yes, we are, love."

Kathleen embraced her new husband. "We're going to my favorite place!" Turning to her father, she hugged him. "Thank you so much, Papa!"

They boarded the ferry and Kathleen felt as if she had been walking on air for most of the day. She had not only married the most wonderful man in the world, but they were also going to Atlantic City for an actual honeymoon!

Beside her, Luke stared out the window of the fast-moving ferry crossing the Delaware River to Camden. She removed her hat and placed it on her lap. Luke reached for her hand and squeezed. His smile seemed torn between joy and anxiety.

"Luke, is everything all right?"

"Yes, of course, my dear."

"You are not a very convincing liar, husband."

"Now, now, I'm fine. Really." He squeezed her hand again.

Kathleen regarded Luke. He patted his waist, seemingly for the gun and holster that were now a common part of his clothing. She knew that the only reason he did so was because of Papa. Sometimes her father could be overprotective and, last year, she had resented it. Now she understood it.

***

The ferry docked in Camden where the young couple boarded the train to Atlantic City. They arrived an hour later and a hotel carriage was there to greet them.

"Are you Dr. and Mrs. Peterson?" the driver asked.

It would be difficult becoming accustomed to being called Mrs. Peterson, although it made her feel more grown up.

"Yes, we are, thank you," Luke offered. The man got down and placed the two bags onto the rear of the carriage. Then he held open the door. Luke assisted his wife inside.

"You are traveling to the Seaside Hotel, Dr. Peterson?"

"Yes."

***

The lobby of the Seaside was open and bright. David had told Luke that this was where they usually stayed in Atlantic City. David had also shared with him that the Seaside Hotel was a long-time client of David's company.

They stopped by the registration desk and gave their names as "Dr. and Mrs. Peterson." The clerk handed Luke an envelope. He didn't open it, nor did he show it to Kathleen. "Dr. and Mrs. Peterson" was barely legible on the outside. David had telephoned the hotel to inform them that no one was to know where they were staying.

Luke kept his face and manner relaxed. Leaning his head toward the clerk, he asked, "Do you happen to remember who left this for us?"

"No, sir. I just arrived five minutes ago. The man who had been on desk duty has left already."

Luke clutched the letter so tightly that he was starting to crumple it. He lifted his chin and scanned the room. Should they turn around and leave? No, he decided, perhaps this was a wedding message or gift. Kathleen was staring at the high ceilings of the foyer and the artwork so Luke took that opportunity and quickly opened the envelope. Inside, there was a blank sheet of paper. No congratulations. No message. Then again, a blank sheet of paper in an envelope was a message; he just wasn't sure what kind. Luke's hands were shaking slightly as he placed the paper back into the envelope and into his coat pocket.

She looked at him and he forced a smile.

"Is... something wrong, Luke?"

"I..." Shaking his head, he said, "I'm happy to be with my lovely new bride."

She responded, "I cannot believe it, Luke! It is my wedding day and I am with my favorite person in my favorite city! Can life get any better than this?"

Luke certainly hoped it would. He took her hand. He couldn't disappoint her now.

***

When her family visited the shore, they typically stayed in a more spacious room on the other side of the hotel because it accommodated their large family with four bedrooms, a sitting room and a parlor.

This suite, however, was quite roomy for only two people. There were numerous windows with white shades and drapery pulled to each side. Modern electric lights had already been turned on inside the room and a massive four poster bed jutted from the left wall. Blue and yellow flowered wallpaper matched the bedspread and curtains.

The bellboy, a young man around Will or John's age, pointed to a sign on the wall. "This room is equipped with electric light...read the sign for safety."

Luke indicated that they would, then hurriedly shoved some coins into the boy's hand and saw the bellboy to the door.

"Thank you, sir. Good evening," the young man said.

Luke closed the door.

Kathleen embraced her husband from behind.

He turned and welcomed the gesture, pulling her into his arms. "Do you know how much I love you?"

"Yes, I do, Dr. Peterson."

"I almost forgot!" Luke opened the door, took her by the hand into the hallway, then swept her off her feet and carried her over the threshold. "I would have been remiss in my husbandly duties if I had forgotten to do this."

"Indeed," she laughed, as he placed her down.

She glanced at the table near the window. A bottle in a metal bucket, with two small wine glasses nearby, was neatly placed there. "Luke, is that champagne?"

He crossed the room and read the card. "Congratulations. All our love, Mama and Papa."

"How wonderful! Since alcohol makes me sleepy, let's save it for later."

"That would be fine."

Kathleen's gaze lifted. "The bellboy told us to read the sign. It's a bit high for me."

Luke returned to her side. He read the sign out loud. "*This room is equipped with Edison Electric Light. Do not attempt to light with match. Simply turn key on wall above door.*" He grinned. "I imagine some poor souls actually try to light a match on these dandy electric lights?"

Kathleen held her hand to her mouth to stifle her own laugh. Luke reached to the right of the room's entrance and opened a door to find the bathroom. "Private bathroom," he said, craning his neck, then turning the switch on. "A private bath with an electric light. Our dreams have come true." He clicked the light off.

She chuckled nervously. Somehow she wasn't sure she wanted to use a privy that was so close to their bed.

Luke took hold of her hand and walked her to the balcony. He pushed aside the drapes and opened the double doors. The sun was close to setting on the horizon and the deep blue of the ocean contrasted with the red-orange of the sun.

"This is such a breathtaking view!" Kathleen exclaimed. Dusk was approaching and a few people dotted the shoreline. The calming swish of the waves made Kathleen want to jump from excitement. She breathed in deeply. "And just smell that ocean air. Isn't it exhilarating?"

"It is."

"May we take a short jaunt along the beach? Please?"

With a deep sigh, Luke nodded. "Of course."

Kathleen picked up her light jacket and opened the door. She stood at the threshold, waiting for Luke. He remained on the balcony, looking down.

"Luke?"

"Yes, I'm coming."

He picked up his hat and took one last glance at the room. "This is a lovely room. I must thank Papa."

***

Luke could not rid himself of the uneasy feeling that made his stomach twist in knots since receiving the envelope at the registration desk. Was it possible that Karl had followed them here? Before he shut the door, he scanned the room. His gun safely in his holster, his hat in his hands, only their two bags remained, along with the champagne from his in-laws.

***

Earlier, Karl had studied the layout of the third floor. He discovered there was a small unlocked — and mostly unused — closet to the right of the staircase. This was where he planned to spend the next two hours. The main staircase was in the center of the floor. Room 3-A was an end room with a balcony facing the beach.

The closet door was open a crack. He saw them when they arrived, his heart pounded so loud in his chest that he wondered whether they could hear it. Less than half an hour later, they were leaving their room. Either they were the fastest lovers this side of Philly or they hadn't yet consummated.

As they passed by his door, Kathleen was so close that he nearly lost control and reached out to touch her. He willed himself to be patient. He must stay in control.

He heard them speak of going down to the beach. Perfect. He waited an additional five minutes to ensure they were actually gone. Then he looked up and down the hallway, slipped out of the storage closet and nearly ran to Room 3-A.

He took out the small metal hair pin he always kept for times like these and, within five seconds, he had opened the door and stowed away inside. He could smell her intoxicating perfume, *Essence of Violets,* and breathed deeply.

Turning off the lights, he crossed the large room, parted the curtains slightly and stared down at the beach below. There was a balcony and, from his vantage point, Karl could see a fire escape ladder on the other side of the balcony. Yes, that would do fine for an exit when he was finished.

There they were, the happy honeymooning couple, arm in arm, walking toward the boardwalk on the way to the beach.

Out of the corner of his eye, he saw a metal bucket and bottle on a table in front of the window. He lifted the bottle, popped the cork, the beige liquid bubbling onto the table. Then he poured some in one of the glasses and downed it. He picked up the card, *"Congratulations. All our love, Mama and Papa."* *Oh how sweet*, Karl thought, as he ripped up the paper and left it in a heap on the table. He yanked the bed covers off and threw them on the floor, then he returned to the window. Looking down, Karl saw Kathleen and that man-boy as they continued their stroll. He sat in the chair beside the window and drank their champagne.

***

Luke was finding it hard to walk on the beach since his shoes were not made for walking on sand. Kathleen was proceeding slowly, so she might also be having the same difficulty. They lingered close to the water but far enough away that the water didn't reach their shoes. Finally, he suggested they return.

"Not yet, Luke." She shivered, and Luke pulled her closer to him. She pointed at the sun setting over the water. It transformed the sky into an explosion of orange and pink casting the color onto the normally blue-green water.

Luke as yet couldn't rid himself of his anxiety. Now, though, he had the uncanny sensation of being watched. As Kathleen was staring at the sunset, Luke was studying the few spectators on the beach for anything out of the ordinary. The sun was setting. As the colors faded, so did his ability to see others clearly.

Kathleen continued walking. Breathing in deeply, she said, "Isn't that ocean air wonderful?"

"It is."

"Did I tell you this was my favorite place in the world?"

"At least a hundred times today."

"I'm sorry, Luke."

"No need to apologize, love. It makes me happy when you are happy."

Luke glanced back at their hotel and wondered whether his wife might be putting off their intimacy. He nearly blurted out that she need not worry about that, if there were any concerns on her part. As much as he anticipated their consummation, he would not barrel ahead without taking her wishes into account, especially in light of her assault the year previous.

"It is getting dark. I suppose we should return, Luke."

***

Karl had relaxed in the chair, his feet propped up on the low table. The sun had gone down and the room was becoming dark. He stood up, moved the curtain and stared down at the beach. It was too difficult to see anyone clearly. Jumping up, he grabbed the bottle, poured the rest of the contents over the stripped bed, and tossed the bottle into the middle. Karl wished he could clearly see and enjoy his destruction, but he wouldn't chance turning the electric lights back on.

A clicking noise at the door made Karl jerk his head sideways. Were they back so soon? Damn!! He flew out onto the balcony, leaving the door wide open, climbed down the fire escape and onto the roof of the first floor veranda. He was so close, but he wouldn't be able to remain there. He jumped the ten feet to the hotel's veranda, then onto the street below.

***

At the door to their room, Kathleen waited as Luke put the key into the doorknob and opened it. She was feeling slightly anxious, but happy all the same. Resolved, she wanted to make this a memorable evening for her new husband.

"Didn't we leave the lights on? I distinctly remember

leaving them on so it wouldn't be dark when we returned." Luke felt around at the entrance for the switch and clicked on the light. Luke gasped and roughly pushed Kathleen out into the hallway.

"Luke, whatever is going on?" He tried to shut the door, but she forced it open and moved past him.

"Good gracious! What in the world happened here?" Their bed covers were strewn all over the floor and a bottle had been dropped in the middle of their bed. The metal bucket was empty and the glasses were on the floor. The door to the balcony was open. "Luke, what...how..." Kathleen began to cry. "Who could have done such a dreadful deed?"

***

Luke knew very well who had committed this crime, although he would never be able to prove it. He just thanked God they weren't in the room while that lunatic was there. The balcony door was wide open. "Wait here, Kath." Luke stepped onto the balcony and peered out. It was dark so he couldn't see much, except for a few areas near the street lamps. Looking over the side, he could barely see the cloth fire ladder. No doubt that had been Karl's escape route.

He escorted Kathleen downstairs to the registration desk and demanded to know how someone could have gotten into their room and created such havoc. Luke was normally calm and patient, but after the stress of the day, he was anything but. The clerk agreed to call the police. While the manager tried to convince them to take another room, Luke was adamant. He didn't want to disappoint Kathleen, but he refused to stay there or in Atlantic City.

A bellboy was sent back up to their room to retrieve their bags. Luke sat in the lobby and tried to console his wife, who was no longer sobbing, but still blotting her eyes with her handkerchief and pinching her lips to keep from crying. "I don't understand, Luke. Why would someone do this?"

Lowering his head, Luke avoided eye contact. Finally, he heard her say, "What is going on, Luke? I demand you tell me. Please."

He nodded. "Yes, very well."

Luke proceeded to tell her about Karl's gun shot wound, his threats, the suspicions about his ripped carriage seat, the letter to her father, and the blank letter today. Her eyes grew wider with each revelation. Scowling, she asked, "And why did you and Papa keep this information from me?"

"Kath, your father and I did not want you to worry. You had just stopped having nightmares."

Her shoulders relaxed as considered this. "And you think... Karl did this?"

"Yes. But I don't think we shall be able to prove it. This is why we should leave. I'll send your father a telegram saying that we shall be returning late this evening. I hope we haven't missed the last train back to Philly."

Now his wife was physically shaking on the lobby couch.

The hotel manager on duty, anxious to make amends to the couple, sent the telegram without cost, and another hotel employee bought their train and ferry tickets back to Philadelphia. Luke looked at his pocket watch. "It's 7:00. Hopefully, we'll be able to return by 10:00 p.m."

A police officer arrived and interviewed them but, as Luke suspected, the officer confirmed that it would be hard to find out who actually perpetrated this crime. He reminded Luke that vandalism was not a serious crime. Luke handed him the envelope with the blank page he received earlier. The policeman did seem hopeful that there might be fingerprints left behind by the criminal on either the letter or in the hotel room. However, if the man had no record of criminal activity, it would be unlikely he could be connected to the crime.

The train to Camden was sparsely occupied and when they had settled into their seats, Kathleen broke down and wept.

***

With a puffed out chest, Karl felt an overwhelming sense of satisfaction to know that he had ruined the happy couple's "honeymoon." Before he jumped down onto the veranda, he had watched as the electric light in the room went on. He could hear the distant sounds of husband and wife lamenting their discovery. But Karl couldn't enjoy their anguish as the stupid doctor would probably be checking the balcony at any moment and he didn't want to be discovered. Karl calmly walked across the street to the Albion Hotel, which was currently closed. From that vantage point, he could get a better view of the front entrance of the Seaside. He knew Kathleen and that man-boy would be leaving soon. He bided his time on a small gazebo several feet behind the gas lamps. In darkness, he waited and watched.

Within an hour, he was rewarded with their departure. He nearly shrieked with happiness.

To celebrate, he headed for the nearest brothel. He didn't need to return to the farm until Monday, so he owed it to himself to spend a day or two relishing the ocean air. Since the happy couple was on the way home, he might as well enjoy the town.

He hastened up the street toward the center of town and searched. It didn't take long before he found what he was looking for a garish-looking, noisy establishment. Karl waited and watched four different men go into the house.

He knocked. A large buxom woman with too much lip rouge answered the door. "Yes?"

"Is this a brothel? May I pay for a woman?"

"Come on in. You're new, aren't you?"

"Just visiting the area."

"Three dollars. Pay me, then you may proceed to the girl's room."

He handed her the money. "I prefer thin blondes."

Pocketing the money, she replied, "Room 303, third floor, her name is Honey."

"Thank you, Ma'am." Karl did his best to act polite, but he abhorred most madams with their heavily made up faces and sagging bodies. He went up one flight of stairs, passed over a small landing, and took another staircase, seeing girls on the way who looked too young to be whores. Shrugging, he continued to Room 303. He knocked and a girl answered. She was a blonde, but not as thin as Karl would have liked. Still, she would do. It was time to celebrate.

43

When the ferry arrived at the Market Street dock, Luke sheltered Kathleen by holding her close to him and urging her forward until they reached the exit.   David was waiting for them as they disembarked. When he saw them approach, he opened his arms. Kathleen ran to her father and began to whimper.

"Shhh, Kat." He turned to Luke. "This is the hotel's fault."

"The manager was very apologetic, agreed not to charge you and offered to give us a complimentary weekend."

"A little late for that, isn't it?"

"Yes."

"They called the police?"

"Yes, but it's unlikely much will come from it."

***

Karl was pleased with "Honey."   So much so, that he offered to pay her three additional dollars to spend more time with him. She agreed but soon there was pounding at the door and the large madam's piercing voice. "Time is up, sir. Honey has another client waiting."

But Karl wasn't yet finished. He continued until the girl began to resist and pushed him away. This, after he already gave her three more dollars! When she shoved him aside, he backhanded her, then began punching her. She cried out and, all of a sudden, two men were yanking him off the bed.

"Thank you, Officers," the madam was saying. Karl turned to see a policeman placing handcuffs on his wrists and another standing beside him.

"You're under arrest."

"I paid her for additional time."

"You assaulted her," the officer was pointing. Karl slowly tilted his head. Honey's mouth and chin were bleeding.

"Since when does it matter how I treat a harlot?"

"Look, buddy, you don't know me, do you? I'm the new police chief here in Atlantic City. I don't tolerate anyone being assaulted on my watch; that includes prostitutes.

You're going to be charged with assault and battery."

"But my father is the police chief of Germantown."

"I don't care if he's President McKinley, sir, you're going to jail."

The next two hours were a blur for Karl. He was taken to the Atlantic City jail for arraignment. He asked if he could contact his father. Surprisingly, the chief unlocked his prison cell and brought him to the phone. Karl dialed the number of his father's place of employment, the police station.

After a moment, his father answered. "Hello?"

"Hello? Father, this is Karl. I'm in jail in Atlantic City."

For a long moment, there was no response. Then he said, "I'm not helping you, Karl. I told you that last year. Goodbye."

Click. Did his father just hang up on him?

Rage filled every crook and crevice of his body. His father wasn't going to help him? His father always gave him what he wanted.

***

For Kathleen, the familiar scents of her childhood home — spices, a hint of cigar smoke, oak paneling — consoled her. Her mother, dressed in a nightgown, greeted her with an embrace.

"I cannot believe it. Are you both all right?"

Luke stepped forward and kissed her mother's cheek. "We're fine, but we couldn't stay at the hotel."

"Well, you're safe now," Mama kept her arm around her.

"Miss Caroline, I can prepare one of the guest rooms so that Dr. Luke and Miss Kathleen can have some privacy."

Kathleen shook her head. "That's not necessary, Jane. Luke and I can sleep in my bedroom."

"Very well, Miss Kathleen. The bedding is clean and I hung the curtains in the room before I went to bed."

"Thank you, Jane."

***

Later in her bedroom, Kathleen changed into a nightgown. Instead of putting on the special nightgown she had planned to use at the hotel, she pulled out one of her usual — albeit plain — nightgowns. She needed the soothing comfort of normalcy.

This was the last place she thought she would be at this moment. She tried not to dwell on Karl and his now revealed presence in their lives, but she couldn't stop thinking of him.

With a sigh, she turned up the oil lamp. She took out a nightshirt for Luke and hung it on the bedpost. Her eyes were already closing from exhaustion. Somehow, though, she wasn't ready to give in to the possibility of seeing that wretched man's face in her slumber.

The smell of an autumn breeze drew her to the window as she sank into her favorite arm chair. Despite all that had happened, this was where she felt safe, looking out at the night sky and "Luke's stars," as she now called them. It was a cool cloudless evening and countless stars twinkled like diamonds above. Kathleen's head bobbed as she tried to stay awake. Determined, she straightened, leaning against the window sill. Her head lowered, her eyes closing. Kathleen finally surrendered and went to bed. She laid her head against her pillow, the fresh scent of lavender soap lulled her and she drifted off to sleep.

***

In the study, Luke and David discussed the escalating danger presented by Karl. Luke could not rid himself of the awful feeling that Karl had been in their room, poured champagne on their bed and vandalized their belongings. He took his glasses off and rubbed his eyes, then opened his mouth wide in a yawn. The grandfather clock in the foyer bonged twelve times.

"Luke, go ahead upstairs. You must be exhausted."

Nodding, he returned the glasses to his face, then ran his hand through his hair. He bid David goodnight and ascended the staircase, his hand on the smooth banister.

As a new groom, Luke had normal desires and found himself looking forward to their eventual consummation. *Patience*, he told himself. It wouldn't happen tonight — or likely anytime soon.

This was certainly not the place he envisioned spending his

wedding night. Of course, he had already been prepared to wait for the physical expression of their vows, even if Kathleen were willing. His wife didn't need that additional stress. He carefully turned the knob. It quietly clicked open, then he closed and locked it. Once inside, he noticed that the oil lamp was bright so he lowered it to a flicker. Smiling, he noticed that she had hung his night shirt on the bed post. He quickly took his clothes off and slipped his nightshirt over his head. The lamp's subtle glow revealed his wife sleeping in the middle of the bed, her breathing even. All inhibitions were gone, her eyes closed, her features relaxed. He knelt beside her and stared. His heart beat rapidly; he never realized that he could love another human being with so much passion and intensity. He now understood how someone could die for another; for in that moment, if anyone tried to harm her, he could, without hesitation, sacrifice his life defending her...and someday, their children.

Children. One need not be a doctor to know that marital intimacy would need to take place for children to be conceived. *Patience,* he reminded himself.

Just the thought of their children, the fruit of their love, was enough to set his heart racing again.

As Kathleen slept, she drew in a breath and his heart skipped a beat. How was it that his heart could feel so full knowing that Kathleen loved him? Of course, he would like nothing better than to crawl in beside her but he would not be able to accomplish that without waking her. He brought an arm chair next to her bed. He took off his glasses and placed them on the nightstand. Lowering himself to the chair, he reclined slightly, putting his feet up on the edge of the bed.

His physical desire was not dissipating as fast as he'd like. *God, bless and protect my wife, help me to be patient, grant me a patient and chaste heart...keep us united as one...*

***

Kathleen gasped in her sleep and sat up. That awful man had returned to her nightmares. She began to hyperventilate, despite the soft light of the oil lamp. Luke gathered her into his arms. "Shh...I'm here, love. Breathe slowly."

She took a deep breath in and released it. Luke caressed her hair and kissed her forehead. Soon, she was breathing normally. "Thank you. I..." She glanced past him at the chair beside the bed, then at the undisturbed area of the bed. "You slept in the chair?"

"I didn't want to disturb you."

"You're my husband. You belong in bed with me."

With a sigh, he agreed. "I suppose you are right."

She lifted up the covers and he climbed in beside her. He welcomed her into his arms. She laid her head on his chest and relaxed against him. Soon, she was drifting back to sleep.

She found herself in a field of long grass. In the distance, she could see Luke and they ran toward each other. Before she reached him, however, Luke turned into Karl and grabbed her and began laughing, a loud hearty cackle. No, no, no!

"Shhhh, it's fine."

She clung so desperately to Luke that she was afraid to let go. He stroked her damp hair away from her face.

"You won't ever leave me?"

"No, love, I will never leave you. You're my wife, forever." Then his soft voice said, "Let's recite the St. Michael the Archangel prayer." He made the sign of the cross, and together they recited the prayer of protection in Latin. Afterwards, Luke caressed her face until she drifted back to sleep.

***

The sound of a single distant rooster crowing woke Luke. It was still dark outside. He hadn't slept much with his wife's gasping and startling most of the night. However, he hadn't minded. He'd gladly give up any sleep if he could comfort her.

He drifted off again, but it seemed only moments passed before he woke. This time, he got up and watched the sun rise.

***

Later that morning, Kathleen and her new husband attended Mass with the O'Donovan family. Kathleen, who sat between Luke and her mother, was fidgety and anxious. Her brothers were excited to see her in the morning, but were naturally inquisitive as to why she and Luke had returned early. Papa had told them there was a problem with the hotel.

Luke kept taking hold of her gloved hand and squeezing it gently. At the ambo, the priest read from Genesis, Chapter 2: 21:

"Then the Lord God cast a deep sleep upon Adam; and when he was fast asleep, he took one of his ribs, and filled up flesh for it. And the Lord God built the rib which he took from Adam into a woman and brought her to Adam. And Adam said: This is now bone of my bones, and flesh of my flesh; she shall be called woman, because she was taken out of man. Wherefore a man shall leave father and mother, and shall cleave to his wife, and they shall be two in one flesh. And they were both naked: to wit, Adam and his wife and were not ashamed."

The two shall be one flesh. Kathleen felt one spiritually with Luke — although admittedly, they hadn't yet become one flesh physically. To be naked and not ashamed? Kathleen didn't understand how one could be without clothes and be unashamed. *Such inappropriate thoughts for Mass.*

After Mass, Jane, Izzy and Mama came to Luke's house to help Kathleen organize her belongings.

In her and Luke's bedroom, Kathleen stood beside the bureau and unpacked one wicker basket of petticoats, shifts and nightgowns. Someone — most likely Jane — had already hung new curtains and had made the bed with new flannel sheets and a bright blue and yellow quilt. Kathleen's trunk and other possessions had been delivered on Saturday while they were enjoying their reception. If only she could go back to the overwhelming joy of yesterday instead of the unease she experienced now. At first, she had been angry that Luke and her father had kept Karl's antics from her. But now? She preferred being blissfully ignorant over knowing that Karl was out there and had been watching her for many months.

***

Later that evening at the O'Donovan's, Luke enjoyed spending time with his in-laws. However, he was anxious to return home to prepare for patients the next day. Each time he suggested to Kathleen that they take their leave, she shook her head to indicate she wished to remain. Mrs. Bradley, Izzy and Nate would not be there until the morning. Was Kathleen nervous about being alone for one night? He was about to suggest they bring Izzy along when Kathleen finally agreed to leave.

***

Kathleen was having so much fun with Pat. While her brother's chess game had improved immensely, she was still easily able to win. Her mother asked her to play piano and she obliged. Luke seemed insistent on leaving earlier and every ten minutes or so, suggested they return home. While Kathleen was with her parents and siblings, she felt safe and distracted, but she finally acquiesced.

44

Upon entering the foyer of their home, Kathleen stood at the bottom of the stairs. "Are you coming to bed, Luke?"

"In a short while." Luke's eyes followed his wife as she went upstairs to the bathroom. He heard the water running in the tub. Looking upward, he envisioned her preparing for the bath and immediately regretted doing so. The visual image of his wife in a state of undress was not one he ought to be dwelling on if he wanted to patiently wait for consummation.

Sighing, he proceeded to the back door to ensure that it was locked. He cringed recalling the mess that Karl had created when he broke in many months ago. He closed all the windows and locked the front door. As he passed the smaller downstairs bathroom, Luke decided to use it. He had no idea how long his wife would take. He finished and went upstairs.

In his — their — bedroom, he couldn't help but smile at the new decor. While it wasn't overtly frilly, it certainly reflected Kathleen's own tastes and preferences and, for that reason, he had been pleased with the design.

Luke removed his clothes and pulled on his nightshirt.

His wife was taking an extraordinarily long time. Perhaps this was her usual routine. He made certain the oil lamp was lowered to a flicker to keep the room from darkness.

***

After the bath, Kathleen put on her nightgown. Since misplacing her favorite cotton nightdress last year, Mama had bought another — nearly identical — one for her, white cotton with delicate pink lace around the collar. She chose it because she thought Luke would like it best.

The disquietude about their unfortunate honeymoon in Atlantic City notwithstanding, Kathleen had already decided that she desired to be Luke's wife in every way. She might even be uncharacteristically bold in her willingness to become "one flesh" with Luke this evening. The previous night, she knew that he had been 'ready' for their union, but in his patience and kindness, he'd gently soothed her and had protectively embraced her as she'd tossed and turned most of the night.

Most importantly, this was her duty as a wife and she did not wish to delay any longer. She turned down the bathroom's gas lamp.

In the bedroom, Luke was sitting up in bed when he saw her standing in the doorway of their bedroom. He had already lit the oil lamp and, for that, she was grateful.

The soft light danced on his fine features. His gentle expression made her pulse quicken, for it was his heart and his gentle, kind manner that made him so desirable. God had blessed her with a most wonderful husband.

"You left the oil lamp on."

"How could I not?"

"Thank you."

"Besides, it's symbolic."

"Symbolic?"

"Yes."

"Why?" She did not move toward the bed.

"In the 16th century, painters would typically paint a light or lamp in their artwork to signify Christ's presence."

With a nod, she sighed. "That's lovely."

He turned to place his glasses on the night table. She took that opportunity to take her gown off, hastily putting it at the bottom of the bed. She quickly climbed in. His brown eyes stared intensely at her.

"You are so beautiful."

"Luke, I love..." Before she could finish, her husband pulled her flush against him. When he kissed her, she kissed him back, fully. In that moment, she longed to be one with him in that most intimate marital embrace. Peace, then joy, settled in her soul as the two became one flesh.

***

When it was over, their hearts were beating rapidly in unison. Kathleen was overwhelmed, despite the initial awkwardness. Unshed tears filled her eyes.

Luke whispered, "Shhh."

"We are one flesh and now married in every respect."

He blinked his own glossy eyes. "Yes, we are." He kissed both of her eyelids, her salty tears coating his lips.

They lay quietly for a few moments before Luke whispered, "Thinking back to the first time we met...did you ever imagine that you'd be my wife?"

"Certainly not."

"Do you know how difficult it was to look at you as a patient, to see your unclothed body and, with utmost respect, to give you the modesty you deserved?"

"I imagine most difficult."

"It makes me want to stare at your body for the remainder of the night...instead of sleeping."

A blush warmed her face.

He gently caressed her neck, then trailed kisses to her mouth. "I love you, Mrs. Peterson."

"I love you too, Dr. Peterson."

They fell asleep in each other's arms.

***

Kathleen's eyes opened as she roused. Thankfully — and miraculously — she had slept without nightmares. Outside, it was dark, although a rooster squawked in the distance. The faint flicker of the oil lamp would soon be outshone by daylight. Lifting her head, she propped herself up on her elbow and stared at her husband's face in slumber. The most minute, ash blond hair came through his smooth skin in small patches, his eyelashes were surprisingly long and his shoulder length dark blond hair fanned the pillow. He looked youthful, even vulnerable, without his glasses.

She reached for her nightgown at the bottom of the bed and put it on. She gently laid her head against his chest and, content, drifted back to sleep.

***

Luke awoke to a bedroom bathed in bright sunlight. He squinted and blinked. It took a minute to gather his wits to remember that the most beautiful moments of his entire life happened a few hours previous. It took great control not to sob out of happiness. He was thankful that he could now gaze upon his wife's beautiful body without limitation. Kathleen was his, now and forever. God willing, children would come soon. The dark shadow that followed them would hopefully be gone from their lives and they could continue on with their happy life together. For now, he focused only on blissful thoughts. Luke couldn't imagine any problem that couldn't be solved.

Kathleen's head was on his chest, the quilt covering them both. She sighed in her sleep. Luke kissed the top of her head. He was dozing when gentle knocking on their door woke him. "Dr. Peterson?" It was Mrs. Bradley's voice. "A message was just delivered for you."

Not wanting to wake Kathleen, he deftly crept out of bed, easing her head onto a pillow. He pulled on his robe, went to the door and opened it. "Mrs. Bradley," he whispered, "thank you." He felt a hot blush on his face. He had no idea why he was embarrassed. He was a physician, for goodness sakes, and now a married man.

Mrs. Bradley handed him the letter. "You're welcome, Dr. Peterson."

He opened it and saw that it was a message from Mr. Stott, informing him that Mrs. Stott was in labor. He quickly dressed. Mrs. Stott was pregnant with her fifth child and the labor would likely be fast. He jotted down a note in pencil to Kathleen at the bottom of Mrs. Stott's letter: *Must go, be back as soon as possible. I love you...*

Kissing the top of her head, he fought the urge to crawl back in bed with her. She stirred, turned on her back, and with a sigh, fell into a deep slumber. Luke stared, and in the bright morning light, saw pink lace at the collar of her nightdress. His jaw clenched as he lifted up the blanket and pulled it down slightly. There was no mistake. The nightgown she wore was identical to the one the prostitute had worn when beaten by Karl.

Shaking his head, Luke knew that it could not be a coincidence. He didn't want to ask his wife about it now since Mrs. Stott was waiting for him.

Luke vowed to get to the bottom of it when he returned.

***

Since his father refused to help him, Karl had no money for legal counsel. He was convinced that after explaining to the judge that it was only a whore, they would realize a mistake had been made and allow him to go free.

But that was not to be the case. Despite his explanation, he was found guilty by the judge and sentenced to ten months in the New Jersey State Penitentiary in Trenton. He could not fathom that he had been arrested, let alone found guilty. Not only had he been arrested for assault, he had also been charged with solicitation, both sentences to be served concurrently.

He sat on the floor of the prison carriage on his way to Trenton. Two prisoners traveling with Karl informed him that the new Atlantic City police chief had been a frequent visitor to that brothel and "would no longer tolerate violence against working girls."

Karl would have ten months to consider how he would seek vengeance against Kathleen, whose presence in the city was the reason he was at that brothel. Yes, everything that was wrong was Kathleen's fault...and one day, he would exact his revenge.

45

Mrs. Stott's baby was quite obliging; the infant was born a mere one hour after Luke arrived. The Stotts were now the proud parents of a seven pound baby girl, their third daughter and fifth child. Luke admired the young couple and prayed that his and Kathleen's marriage would be as fruitful.

Returning home mid-day, he resolved to privately ask Kathleen about the nightgown. He stood in the foyer, listening. It was quiet; even Mrs. Bradley's pleasant whistling tunes seemed absent today. Then he heard laughter from upstairs and he followed the sound.

In their bedroom, Mrs. Bradley was standing on a chair, Izzy and Kathleen handing her boxes to put inside Luke's small closet.

"Hello!"

They all turned and Kathleen rushed across the room to greet him. "I'm so glad you're home! I've missed you, dear husband."

Her terms of endearment were like music to his ears. "And I, you."

"Dr. Peterson," said Mrs. Bradley as she stepped off the chair, "I wonder whether it might be acceptable for Mrs. Peterson to put some of her boxes and crates into the cellar."

"The cellar?" At the mere mention of the word, Luke began to perspire. He pulled at his collar.

"Uh...I think that would be fine. I've never been down there. Is there room?"

"Yes, there is a great deal of storage."

"Wonderful," exclaimed Kathleen. "Then we don't need to keep rearranging these boxes. We can just move them down to the cellar."

"Do you think you might be able to carry these boxes down to the basement?" Mrs. Bradley stood in front of him, her head tilted forward.

Luke blinked rapidly and his heart pounded. He couldn't go to the cellar; he simply could not. He had no idea why, but just the thought of entering that room below the ground made him nauseated. Perhaps he suffered from claustrophobia?

What excuse could he give? "Well, I really do need to fill out Mrs. Stott's charts before I do anything else. Perhaps Nate can do it?"

"Mr. Finner won't be returning until four p.m."

"Could it wait until then?"

"Yes, that would be fine."

***

Later that evening, when Mrs. Bradley and Mr. Finner had left for the day and Izzy had retired to her attic bedroom, Luke waited in bed for Kathleen. Again, it was nearly thirty minutes before she emerged from the bathroom. If Luke didn't have a pressing matter to discuss with her, he wouldn't have cared.

He turned the oil lamp on full light. Only his office had electricity, although he made a mental note to research costs of installing electric lights in the rest of the house.

When Kathleen finally entered the bedroom, he nearly gasped because she was wearing the same white cotton nightgown with the pink lace around the collar. Luke forced a smile and made every effort not to appear concerned.

"Kath, where did you get...that nightgown? It's...lovely."

"I knew you would like it. This was the nightgown that went missing last spring. Remember? It was the same day you were late because you were called away to help that poor injured girl."

Yes, of course he remembered. He attempted to sound nonchalant. "Oh...uh, yes. And you somehow were able to replace it?"

"Yes, Mama found another nightdress just like it two weeks ago at Gimbels! I was so happy because it is my favorite kind to wear at night...and now I see you like it just as much!"

He turned down the oil lamp as they settled into bed. But Luke could only relax when that nightgown was off her body.

46

The Petersons' first Christmas as a married couple was spent in nearly identical fashion to the previous year. Kathleen and Luke attended Midnight Mass, then traveled behind her family's carriages to spend the night and following day at her childhood home. This year's ten-foot Balsam Fir tree with plentiful festive decorations was a contrast to last Christmas's small tree and minimal decorations.

Just after gifts were opened after Midnight Mass, though, Luke was called to deliver a baby and didn't return until mid-day. Kathleen was disappointed, but accepted that this would be the life of a physician's wife.

***

Snow clouds filled the sky on the Feast of the Epiphany, Thursday, January 6, 1898.

Just before Mass, Luke and Kathleen, with Izzy riding in the back seat, headed to St. Vincent de Paul Church to meet the O'Donovan entourage. After Mass, they would all be traveling again to the O'Donovan house for the Feast Day celebration.

Upon arriving at the church, Izzy nearly jumped out when she saw John and Will ride up in the Columbus. Izzy was even more beautiful when she was happy. She and John had officially become a "courting" couple on New Year's Day, much to the chagrin of local upper class society.

From her parents' demeanor, Kathleen guessed that they were not overjoyed, but accepted John's choice. Papa and Mama ignored the murmurs of polite society.

After Mass, Tim and Kev asked to ride home with her and Luke. Kathleen was happy to oblige and thankful that her father had gifted them with a fine family-sized carriage that would accommodate children in the back seat. Izzy traveled with John and Will in the Columbus carriage.

A sparkly mist of snow lay on the ground, but it was a brisk and windy day and Kathleen stuffed wool blankets around her brothers. She and Luke had their own blanket to keep warm.

***

Luke relaxed the reins as another carriage traveling in the opposite direction passed. He couldn't remember a time when he was more peace-filled and satisfied. Marriage was blissful at best, challenging at worst, although the difficulties were miniscule compared to the joys.

Frankly, Luke was disappointed that Kath was not with child yet. Of course, they had only been married for three months and Luke understood, probably better than most people, that these delicate processes take time. Luke hoped — and prayed — Kathleen would become with child soon.

***

As their carriage pulled up to the O'Donovan house, Jesse was ready to assist them down and take the carriage to the stable.

Inside the foyer, Jane brightened when she saw Izzy. The young servant was scheduled to stay with the O'Donovans for a few days. To eliminate any possible temptation for the courting couple, Izzy would be staying in her mother's room and John would be staying with Will in his room.

"You look lovely today, Miss Kathleen. I'll take your coats."

"Thank you."

Her parents came from the parlor to greet them. Mama embraced her while Papa spoke. "We just received word that the Mutual Automatic Telephone Company will be installing a new telephone line in this area. We are getting a telephone in the spring! We no longer have to wait for Bell."

"Papa, that's wonderful!"

"Good news," said Luke. "Then at least we'll be able to call one another."

"Yes, I know someone who is quite happy, especially now that her eldest is living away from home," he winked at Mama, the corner of her mouth lifting in a smile.

Tim pulled on her skirt. "Kat, do you think Mama or Jane will let me eat the king's cake now?"

"No, Tim. The king's cake is for later in the day, and after we have taken the decorations down."

Tim scowled. "Darn."

"It is good to wait for things because when you finally get to eat it, it will be sweeter and more enjoyable."

"I would like it more if I had it now."

"Silly boy." She pulled her brother close. How could Tim already be six years old?

Kevin was carrying on a fine conversation with Luke about the clay marbles that she and Luke had given him for Christmas. As usual, Kev was talking a mile a minute. Luke was smiling and nodding as the boy chattered on about how much he liked the swirly marbles the best.

Tim and Kev scurried off to the parlor, leaving Luke and Kathleen together in the foyer.

"Luke, I enjoyed the way you spoke with Kevin and listened as he rattled on excitedly about the marbles we gave him."

"His exuberance is quite contagious."

"Indeed it is."

***

Will enjoyed his family's Epiphany celebration. Everyone gathered in the parlor.

Luke, Kat, Izzy and the rest of the O'Donovan siblings were playing a game of musical chairs. Kat played piano; the chairs were set up behind her. It was down to two chairs and three people circling the chairs: Kev, Izzy and John. His parents and Jane were sitting on the sofa watching while any siblings who had been ousted from the game milled about in front of them.

Loud knocking of the door interrupted the game, and Kathleen stopped playing. Kev groaned. "Don't stop, Kat!"

Will touched his brother's shoulder. "Be patient, Kev. You can finish the game shortly."

Jane stood up and went to answer the door. From the doorway, she called, "Mr. David, Mr. Will, Monsignor Flaherty is here."

Will's eyebrows came together. He couldn't imagine what would bring the priest out here on a feast day.

Papa stood up. Will followed his father into the foyer and greeted the priest, still dressed in his coat. "Monsignor, Happy Epiphany. Jane will take your coat..." Jane moved forward to collect his coat, but the cleric held his hand up.

"No. Thank you, Jane. Happy Epiphany, David, Will. I cannot stay long so I shall keep my coat on. I wanted to inform you of the news as soon as possible. This came by courier late last night, but I couldn't leave it until after all the Masses."

"What news?"

"The Holy Father, Pope Leo XIII, has read the documents of investigation and has requested a private audience with Will to discuss the dispensation. He has given the date of April 22."

"A private audience? What does that mean?" Papa asked.

"The Holy Father wishes to speak to Will personally," the priest said, nodding toward Will.

"Is...that a good thing?" Will managed to ask.

"It means that Pope Leo has not rejected your request for special dispensation...that he wants to interview you face to face. It is a positive step in the right direction."

Will's heart raced and his hands began to shake. What if the Pope thought he was unworthy? What then? What sort of questions would the Holy Father ask?

Papa patted his back. "This is good news, Will."

"What if I don't answer the questions properly?"

The priest reassured him. "Will, you shall do fine."

"How shall I prepare for such an important meeting?"

"Prayer and fasting. Besides, you have three months. We shall meet more frequently. Do not worry."

"I will travel with him as well, Monsignor."

"That would be prudent, David. He may have questions for you as well." The priest put his hat on. "I must be leaving."

"Monsignor, might I ask you to give my family a blessing before you go?"

"Oh, yes, of course."

Will assisted his father in gathering the family into the foyer. The priest made the sign of the cross and said, "Come Holy Spirit, come fill the hearts of Thy faithful and enkindle in them the fire of Thy love. May Almighty God bless you all, in the name of the Father and of the Son and of the Holy Ghost."

They all replied, "Amen."

***

After the decorations had been taken down, Jane brought out the Epiphany "Three Kings" cake, not surprisingly Tim's favorite dessert. It also became the "Going to Visit the Pope" cake.

***

Karl kept to himself in the state penitentiary, but spent his days and nights plotting and planning. He scratched another mark on the wall. 178 days left.

47

During the final days of January, no matter how many hours Kathleen slept, she always seemed to crave more. She often felt overtired when she had her monthly, but she hadn't had her monthly in nearly five weeks, since before Christmas.

It was difficult for her to believe that she and Luke had already been married for nearly four months. Until now, she had continued helping out in his office because she enjoyed working alongside her husband.

However, as she pulled herself out of bed, she was doubtful that she would be able to assist him today. Her body begged for more sleep. In addition, she felt nauseated, but she dressed as quickly as she was able. As she was buttoning up her blouse, she knew she would not be able to stifle her nausea. She ran to the bathroom, leaned over the toilet and vomited. She pulled the string to flush it and sat down on the floor. Nausea, no monthly, fatigue. Could she be with child?

Mrs. Bradley would be assisting her elderly brother this week and, unfortunately, could not arrive before 10:00 a.m. Izzy agreed to cook breakfast, although she wasn't as skilled a cook as Mrs. Bradley or Jane.

When Kathleen descended the back staircase into the kitchen, Izzy was at the stove frying eggs. The coffee was brewing. As the scent of coffee wafted past her, Kathleen felt like retching. She took a deep breath.

"Miss Kathleen, you don't look so well," commented Izzy.

"Oh, I'm... fine, Izzy."

The nausea seemed to pass so she sat down to eat. Izzy gave her an egg and she ate it hungrily. However, her nausea soon returned, followed by a tingling at her mouth. Finally, she ran to the nearest trash bin and spilled the contents of her stomach. For the moment, she felt better.

When she turned back toward the stove, Izzy cracked two more eggs into the sizzling pan.

"You sit right down, Miss Kathleen." Izzy was lowering her onto the chair.

Instead of protesting, Kathleen agreed and sat for the moment.

"Not feeling well, this morning, Kath?" Her husband stood in the doorway between the hallway and the kitchen, smiling as if he possessed some sort of secret. The learned doctor probably knew what Kathleen already suspected.

She shook her head. Izzy served Luke a large breakfast of fried eggs, bacon and potatoes. Kathleen then watched her husband sit down and eat with gusto. If it were possible, he wore a smile the entire time. When he was finished, he whistled as he rinsed his plate and coffee cup. He turned and kissed the top of her head.

"You should go back to bed, love. You look fatigued."

"I wanted to help you in the office."

"Don't worry about that. You need your rest."

Kathleen nodded, then stood. She walked alongside her husband to the foyer. He kissed the top of her head and, moving his lips close to her ear, he whispered, "You haven't had your monthly flow since before Christmas, correct?"

"Yes."

"And you're nauseated."

"I am."

"Your breasts are tender."

She blushed and lowered her head.

"Although it's still early, I believe you are carrying our child."

With a nod, she said, "I suspected."

"It's wonderful, Kath. I cannot stop smiling. I just wish you didn't have to feel so poorly."

Kathleen stepped away, grinning. "It's fine."

"You are happy, though?"

"Very much so. Until we're certain, though, let's not share the news with anyone. Let this be our secret for now."

"I agree, love. But don't tell me I have to stop whistling and smiling."

"I won't. You'll have to harmonize with Mrs. Bradley's whistling band."

"Yes, I will. Now...back to bed with you."

"Yes, Doctor." Despite the queasiness, a smile formed as she protectively touched her stomach.

***

A few weeks later, in the downstairs examining room, Luke listened to Mrs. Findlay's chest with his stethoscope. The elderly woman was one of those incredibly hearty souls. At eighty-five years of age, she continued to be a hardworking farm woman whose only impediment was that she was stone deaf and had to use a tin horn. Her face looked like one of those dried-up apple dolls and she rarely smiled, although when she did, it was a toothless one. She was a good person who loved and was loved by many. But she sat on the table, back hunched over. When he made eye contact with her, she was staring intensely at him.

"Well, Doc?"

Leaning close and speaking into her tin horn, Luke said, "Your heart seems as steady and strong as a few weeks ago, Mrs. Findlay. But if you're concerned, please visit my office anytime, and I'll take another listen."

"Thank you, Doc."

Luke turned and washed his hands at the basin, allowing the elderly woman privacy to button up her blouse. He dried his hands on a towel, then turned and assisted the woman off the table.

He accompanied the woman out. These were the times he missed his capable assistant, who was now resting comfortably though vomiting into the toilet when she wasn't sleeping.

He tidied up the waiting room and made his way to the kitchen.

In the hallway connecting the storage room to the kitchen, Luke floated on the aroma of roast beef and fried potatoes. He inhaled, his mouth watering. The tantalizing scent of his favorite meal had hung in the air for the past two hours.

Mrs. Bradley stood at the stove, stirring a pan of potatoes as she whistled a song he wasn't familiar with. She stopped and turned to greet him. "Afternoon, Dr. Peterson. Supper's almost ready. I don't think Mrs. Peterson will be joining you.

She was downstairs half an hour ago and looked rather green." The woman paused. "She's not been feeling herself these days....it seems." She cocked an eyebrow; her mouth turned up in a smile.

With Kathleen's obvious pregnancy symptoms, it wasn't going to be easy keeping it a secret much longer. He'd suggested to his wife that by the end of the month, two weeks from now, they should tell her parents.

"Would you mind preparing a plate for my wife? I'll bring it up to her before I eat my dinner."

After trying to convince Kathleen to eat, Luke gave up. He knew she was feeling ill, but she would have to force something down soon, for the baby's sake.

Back in the kitchen, Luke scooped up the last bit of potatoes and beef off his plate, then glanced out the side window to see Nate opening the cellar doors and going down the stairs. Immediately, his pulse quickened and he began to sweat.

"Dr. Peterson, is something wrong?"

He shook his head. "No." Just the thought of anyone going into that storage cellar made him anxious. It was nonsense and childish, much like his gun aversion, but he seemed to have that fear conquered, at least in part. Of course, he hadn't actually fired a gun in many months but, at David's insistence, still carried one in his holster and ensured it was cleaned every few months.

Basements and guns. Cellars were easily avoidable and, up until his dealings with Karl, so were firearms. Luke understood why he disliked guns, but he had no idea why the very thought of going into a basement made him sweat and hyperventilate.

Staring off toward the back staircase, Luke remained silent. Mrs. Bradley took his plate and asked him if he wanted apple pie. He declined. "Save me a piece for later."

Luke was extremely happy that his wife was with child. But with each day, he worried more about her and their unborn baby. Pregnancies could be precarious. Most ended naturally with a healthy baby. He thought about the maternal-infant mortality rates, then shook his head. With modern methods of delivery, that rate was low. There was no denying that deaths still occurred, however.

From this point forward, Luke resolved to offer prayers of protection for Kathleen and their unborn child.

***

That Sunday, during Mass, Kathleen nearly fainted a few times and, despite the chill, felt warm. She sat several times, even when others were standing.

"Shall we leave?" Luke asked, his voice filled with concern.

"I shall be fine."

Luke had become quite an attentive husband who catered to her every need. Sometimes his help was welcomed; other times, he seemed overprotective.

After Mass, Kathleen waited for Luke to answer medical questions from two patients, trying not to be annoyed that they had bothered him on Sunday. She understood emergency cases, but most of the time, they asked about ways to cure the winds or boils or other non-life-threatening conditions. With a sigh, Luke finally returned and they were on their way to her parents' house. Kathleen sat back in the carriage, trying to quell the nausea that had returned. Nothing, however, could cease it from coming. "Stop now, Luke!"

"Whoa." He pulled the reins and maneuvered the carriage to the side of the road. Kathleen leaned over and vomited onto the ground. Luke rubbed her back sympathetically. "All better?"

"Not quite." She finished her task, then sat back in the seat. "I'm sorry, Luke. I couldn't stop it."

"No worries about that, love. Besides, it's a normal occurrence when a woman is with child. Shall I continue riding?"

She nodded. "My parents will be expecting us."

Kathleen was torn between excitement and awkwardness. She and Luke had kept her pregnancy secret for the past month, although she had wanted to tell her mother as soon as she and Luke suspected she was with child.

"Come, shall we? You'll want to tell your parents our news," Luke held his arm out and Kathleen took hold of it. They walked into the house with the others and settled in for a post-Mass luncheon.

Papa approached the pair, hugging Kathleen and shaking Luke's hand.

After the typical greetings and hugs from her siblings, Kathleen entered the parlor on the arm of her husband and with Kev and Tim jumping about. "David and Caroline, Kathleen and I have news that we would like to share with you...privately."

Her father looked concerned, his eyebrows in a scowl. Her mother cast a worried look toward Kathleen.

"Mama, Papa, there is no need to worry."

The older woman embraced her daughter and kissed the side of her face. "You look so beautiful today, Kathleen. You are absolutely glowing!"

"I don't feel beautiful. I've been fatigued and sick."

"Oh?" She held the back of her hand to Kathleen's forehead.

"Not that kind of sick." Kathleen smiled.

Her mother glanced from Luke to Kathleen, her mouth slightly open. Her father's eyebrow was cocked quizzically.

Luke spoke. "We are...expecting a child in October."

Her parents stared, their mouths agape. Then her father shouted, "Wonderful news!" He kissed the side of Kathleen's face. Her mother smiled and stepped in to embrace her.

Crossing the room, Papa took out a couple of cigars from the box on the mantel and offered one to Luke.

He shook his head, "No, thank you."

"Well, I'll smoke yours for you!"

Her mother quietly stood beside Kathleen, her eyes filling with tears. "I'm so happy. Our house needs a baby now more than ever."

48

The night before their journey, Will had suggested to his father that they arrive in New York City three hours before their boat's departure, in order to visit St. Patrick's Cathedral.

It was a beautiful, breezy and cloudless day. The entire family had gathered on the front lawn to say goodbye. Will had already bid farewell to Kat and Luke the previous night.

Will lifted his head to allow the sun's rays to warm his face. His mother's voice, "Will, now did you remember to pack your toothbrush?"

"Yes, I remembered. I also didn't forget my Italian book. I wish to be able to say 'Thank you, Holy Father' in Italian."

"And do you know how to say that?" she asked, her eyes smiling.

"Grazie, Santo Padre."

"That's very good, Will."

His younger brothers were chasing each other around the group. Pat stepped forward. "Keep a journal so you can tell us all the details of your trip."

"Of course."

They caught the train at the Germantown depot, traveled two hours northeast, then took the ferry to Manhattan. They stored their luggage at the Cunard Line building, traveled by streetcar to St. Patrick's Cathedral, then returned an hour before the ship's scheduled departure time of 3:00 p.m.

Will and his father lingered with the rest of the passengers on the deck of the Lucania as it floated away from New York City. The skyline reminded Will that there was a huge world beyond his home. The Lucania was a large passenger ship with all the amenities of home. They passed the Statue of Liberty; Will stared, wide-eyed until it became a speck in the distance.

His father nudged his arm. "Time for dinner in the second class dining room."

He nodded and followed his father. Although they were recognized as upper class and usually took first class by both train and boat, his father chose to buy second class rooms. "No need for us to travel in such luxury," he had said. "Second class cabins are fine." Will agreed. As they sat down for dinner, they were served by pretty cabin maids. Dinner was a choice between spring lamb or roast turkey, boiled rice, mashed turnips, cole slaw and tapioca for dessert. It was tasty food and Will ate it quickly.

"Will, slow down. You'll get indigestion."

"Sorry, Papa."

Back in their second class cabin, there were two single beds lining opposite walls of the small room and a mirrored bureau in between the two with a pitcher and basin. They would have to use the public washroom and shower outside their berth. Their room did not have a porthole, which disappointed Will.

The five days of the voyage passed quickly, except for a case of seasickness during the halfway mark. Will and his father attended Mass on the ship, and the following day, they arrived on the coast of France and boarded a train for Rome. They had a comfortable second class cabin with two seats that converted to beds for nighttime.

Two days later, on April 20th, they arrived in Rome. They checked into their modest hotel. His father wanted to sightsee, so they hired a footman with a horse and carriage to take them first to the Coliseum, then to the Pantheon and Castel Sant'Angelo. Will especially enjoyed the outdoor artworks and paintings that seemed so plentiful on the streets and outer walls of the buildings.

The following day, they toured the Sistine Chapel and Will stared at the awe-inspiring painting by Michelangelo on the ceiling, savoring the moment, although he was surprised at the numerous naked bodies included therein.

"Papa, why are there so many naked bodies in the Sistine Chapel's paintings?" he whispered.

"Not sure, Will, but it could be because the naked body is beautiful."

Will felt a hot blush.

"What does Genesis say about Adam and Eve and their nakedness?" Papa asked.

"They...covered up."

"Only after they sinned. Adam and Eve were naked in the garden; they weren't ashamed and had no need for clothes. It was only after they sinned that they wanted to cover themselves. Why do you think that is, Will?"

"I don't know."

"Because with sin, it was difficult for Adam to look purely at his wife and vice versa. Because of sin, lust entered their hearts. Therefore, they needed to cover up their bodies."

"So it is possible for a husband to lust after his wife?"

"It *is* possible, but in a holy, sacramental marriage, not as likely. I have experienced lust and I have experienced love. There is most certainly a difference."

Will winced. His father's lust had produced him. Bringing it to the forefront of his mind made him melancholy, but he squared his shoulders. "That lust produced me, Papa."

His father's head hung low. "But isn't God most wonderful to produce a holy and virtuous son from that moment of sin?"

Will knew that his father was trying to make him feel better, but it still hurt his soul to know that he was not conceived as the result of a holy marital bond like his siblings.

After their tour of the Sistine Chapel, they stopped by the Vatican bookstore. Will purchased postcards, as well as holy cards with the St. Michael prayer that had been composed by this Pope, and which the Holy Father requested to be recited after every low Mass. He purchased a package of ten, then he obtained a copy of *Divinum Illud Munus*, the Holy Father's encyclical on the Holy Ghost, in English.

The next morning, the day Will had been waiting for, had arrived. He and his father attended Mass at dawn at St. Peter's. He offered up the Mass for the intentions of his family and that he would have the grace to accept whatever decision the Pope made. The two then breakfasted at a local restaurant. Will could only manage a few bites of a croissant and a half cup of coffee before he thought he might be sick.

"Will?"

He looked at his father.

"I will be beside you the entire time."

"Thank you, Papa."

"This is my journey too. Your discomfort, the reason for the special dispensation, it's my fault and I shall move mountains to repair it for you. You deserve that."

Will sat rigid and straight in the seat. He closed his eyes and breathed in deeply, then exhaled.

It was Will's desire to be present at the Vatican at least an hour beforehand. Of course, he always preferred to be an hour early rather than a minute late. "Should we leave now?"

"Already? Yes. You remind me of my brother."

"I do?"

"Yes. Lee always had to be at the train station an hour before boarding. Me? I would always arrive just as the train was pulling away."

They were escorted into the Vatican offices and a grand lobby. The winding staircase seemed wide enough to accommodate ten to twelve people across. At the information desk, Will's father spoke to the man behind the desk. His father tried to manage a few broken Italian words before the kind man stopped him.

"No worry. I speak English. You have appointment?"

His father answered. "Yes, sir. One o'clock with the Holy Father."

"Name?"

"I would like to introduce, William O'Donovan, my son. I'm David O'Donovan."

"Yes. Take the staircase to the second floor and one of the sisters will escort you to the waiting room of the Papal office."

When they reached the second floor, a youthful sister in a black and white habit nodded and escorted them to the waiting room for the Papal office.

When the time came for their appointment, the same sister came and accompanied them to the Papal Office. When they entered, Pope Leo XIII was sitting in a high-back chair. He was a small, very elderly and frail-looking man with a kind expression. A folder of papers sat on his lap. A taller priest with dark eyes and sparse gray hair, who was dressed in a black cassock, stood beside the Pope. Will's father handed the papers to the priest who introduced himself. "I am Father Giuseppe Gallo, the Holy Father's assistant," he said with a slight Italian accent. "May I present to you his Holiness, Pope Leo XIII."

Will knelt before the Pope and kissed his ring; his father followed suit. The tall priest now spoke in Italian. "Vi presento il signor William David O'Donovan che cerca dispensa speciale per accedere al sacerdozio e suo padre, il signor David O'Donovan."

The Holy Father smiled and nodded, then spoke Italian to his assistant who then interpreted for the two.

"You desire holy priesthood, young man?" The taller priest interpreted the Holy Father's words with an Italian accent.

"Yes, very much so, Your Holiness. I believe it is my calling."

The Pope did not wait for his assistant to interpret and said, "Good, good." Then he spoke quiet words in Italian to his assistant who continued to translate. "That is good, no hesitation. And you were born illegitimate?"

Will sensed his father cringing beside him, although even Will wasn't accustomed to that term. With a nod, he lifted his chin. "Yes, sir."

The Pope then spoke in Italian, with his assistant interpreting. "I have read all the materials sent to me by Monsignor Flaherty. My advisory council has recommended that I not grant this dispensation, but I wanted to meet with you personally to decide."

Will felt his eyes beginning to well up. After this long trip, was the Pope going to refuse his request? He blinked rapidly. He would be strong, no matter what the decision. He had already prayed for God's will. Now, he must accept it, whatever it was. "Grazie, Santo Padre."

Again Pope Leo's words were translated for Will. "So why should I grant this dispensation to allow you to enter the seminary and study to be one of the Church's holy priests?"

Will took a deep breath and released it. Monsignor Flaherty had advised him to carefully listen to the Holy Father's question, consider it, then respond. He closed his eyes, lowered his head and reflected. *God Almighty, give me thy grace to respond humbly, truthfully and wisely.*

Lifting his head, Will squared his shoulders and spoke with conviction. "Your Holiness, God is calling me. If this *is* God's will, then I must be obedient. I believe that God has already made His decision." He paused, considering his words. "However, I am obedient to Holy Mother Church first and shall abide by your decision." The last sentence was difficult to say because he sensed the Pope was leaning toward refusal.

While the taller priest was translating Will's statement, the Pope smiled, his brows furrowing, but he said nothing for a moment. Finally, he nodded and spoke. "Be', giovanotto, si questa decisione è già stata fatta da Dio, allora chi sono io per mettere questo in discussione? Concedo la dispensa..."

Will had already understood the gist of the Holy Father's message and his mouth fell open in humble surprise. Given that he wasn't fluent in Italian, though, he waited until the tall priest translated it: "Well, young man, if this decision has already been made by God, then who am I to question it? I shall grant the dispensation."

Will heard his father exhale behind him and felt him put his arm around his shoulder.

"Grazie, Santo Padre, grazie mille." He knelt and kissed the Pope's ring again.

Pope Leo then patted Will's head. In a very thick Italian accent, he said "I shall pray for you, giovanotto. The Church needs holy men. Dio vi benedica." The Pope blessed him.

As they were leaving the Vatican offices, Will asked his father to make a special trip to St. Peter's again so that he could offer a prayer of thanksgiving. He lit a candle and knelt down to pray. The immensity of the special dispensation filled him with joy and gratitude. Someday, Will would be a priest. He blinked back the tears.

Will and his father traveled to the nearest wireless office and sent the good news to Mama and the rest of the family.

49

At long last, Karl was released from the New Jersey State Penitentiary. He was in possession of only the clothes on his back, sore muscles and a few coins. But he was now free. He had spent ten months in prison dreaming of this day and about the first place he would be going. If Kathleen hadn't come to Atlantic City, he would never have gotten arrested. His jail term was most definitely *her* fault.

He walked the short distance to Trenton and, after watching several gentlemen walk by, he stole an elderly man's wallet. *Some men are just plain witless.* He stowed away in an alley between two buildings, and was shocked to see that there was nearly $20 in the wallet...enough for a one-way train ticket, a ferry ticket, and a barber visit where his long beard would be removed. A new tailored suit would also be on the list. He could not wait any longer. His greatest desire was to return to Kathleen.

That evening, he arrived by train in Philadelphia and stayed at a modest hotel on the outskirts of Center City, not too far from Germantown. *Soon,* he promised himself.

***

The hustle and bustle of late summer was one of Kathleen's favorite times of year: plentiful corn on the cob and other summer vegetables and fruit, cooler nights but warm days. Kathleen was nearly seven months along, a large roundness in her stomach showed her pregnancy although, thankfully, her nausea had subsided months ago. She was enjoying this little baby's presence, loving him or her more with each passing day.

A few short months previous, electric lights had been added to the rest of the house. A small hanging light bulb had even been installed in the storage cellar at Mrs. Bradley and Izzy's request since they frequently ventured down there. Luke's reasoning was that he wanted to modernize the home and office.

Will's "going away" party was scheduled for this evening at

her parents' house. He would be leaving on Tuesday for the seminary, and she would miss her brother very much. She was still trying to think of an extra special gift she could give him.

Luke was away for the day at a medical seminar in Philly and planned to return around dinnertime so that they could attend the party together.

Downstairs in the rustic parlor, Kathleen sat on the comfortable sofa near the window. She picked up her book and began to read. These days, she and Luke didn't have much time for reading together. There would be less time after this sweet babe was born. With that thought, she began to nod off and woke up when her unborn baby turned a roll inside her. She sat up and glanced at the clock. Just before five p.m.

She had been having a silly dream about having ice cream and...that's it! Will's favorite dessert was ice cream. She would bring her cedar ice cream freezer with the extra long crank to the party, along with sugar and cream. Jane had one at the house, but Kathleen's cedar one, which they had received as a wedding present, was more reliable and created a thicker, creamier concoction. Now where had she stored the ice cream freezer?

Her stomach was grumbling, so she got up. After visiting the privy, Kathleen went to the kitchen, which was now quiet. Looking out the window, she could see Mrs. Bradley and Izzy hanging clothes on the line. They were quite the pair: Izzy, the young, beautiful, slim girl and the older short housekeeper. They often teased one another and Kathleen enjoyed watching the pair interact.

Kathleen took a piece of cheese from the icebox and an apple from the table. She sat down and ate, then remembered that she had stored the cedar ice cream freezer in the cold cellar. She finished her apple and cheese, and then ventured outside. The exterior basement doors had already been opened and looked like shutters on either sides of a window. It was pitch black except for whatever daylight shone downward. The wooden steps were not steep; on the contrary, but there were many. She held onto the metal banister to her right. Once she made it to the bottom, she would turn on the lone electric light and retrieve the ice cream freezer.

***

Luke clicked the reins for the horse to proceed into a full gallop. The medical seminar's topic was "The Modern Treatment of Burns," but he didn't find it at all helpful so he was thankful it had ended two hours early. When he had tried to share his experience with the use of cold water and natural healing salves to treat second degree burns, his colleagues dismissed his ideas, allowing the older, more established physicians to talk about camphor oil, flour and more 'traditional' treatments. It irked him that patients might suffer because of outdated medical practices.

As he exited the city, the police station to his left, Luke winced as he thought of Karl. He and Kathleen hadn't had any contact with him in eleven months. Could Karl have just decided to leave the area after he ruined their honeymoon? Could he have forgotten about Kat? Unlikely, he decided. The only other possibility was that Karl had died. Somehow, he didn't think that was the case.

He passed the rubber factory to his right. Thinking of Kathleen, his heart picked up its pace. Even after ten months of marriage, the mere thought of her made his heart race and his palms sweaty. In only five minutes, he would be arriving at his house and embracing his lovely wife.

***

Kathleen had only been in the storage cellar a few times. She had found it dusty and damp, so this wasn't her favorite place. Mrs. Bradley and Izzy appeared to be occupied, Nate was away and Luke wouldn't be home for another two hours. There was no reason to wait. Just because she was pregnant didn't mean she was an invalid.

She carefully went down the wooden steps, holding onto the banister. However, the bottom step broke and her foot caved in causing her to cry out in pain. She didn't fall because she had been holding onto the banister, but when her foot slipped through, the wood scraped her ankle. She tried to pull her foot out of the hole, but it was stuck like a thumb in a baby's mouth. She couldn't see, but she felt wetness and burning on her ankle and surmised she'd cut herself because her ankle was now throbbing.

She sat down on the second to bottom step, the cold seeping through her dress into her bottom. She let out a long sigh. She grunted as she leaned in toward her leg and tried once more to pull it free. No luck.

"Mrs. Bradley? Izzy? Hello? Could someone help me, please?"

No response except for a bird chirping in the tree behind her. She couldn't stand up, so she remained seated, every few minutes calling for help.

Finally after Kathleen succeeded in making a particularly long and loud shout, Mrs. Bradley and Izzy came running to the top of the stairs. Her head lifted up and around. The two women's eyes were wide. "Mrs. Peterson, what happened? Are you all right?"

"The bottom step broke and I'm afraid my ankle is stuck in this board. I'm going to need assistance."

Mrs. Bradley and Izzy were soon by her side. "Why were you going to the cellar, Miss Kathleen?"

"To get the ice cream freezer for Will's party."

Mrs. Bradley crouched down and peered into the hole. "I shall need a lantern to see better, but from what I can see, your ankle is bleeding mighty badly, ma'am. I dare say Dr. Peterson might have to stitch this."

"I don't care about that. I just want to get back upstairs."

Mrs. Bradley stood at the bottom near the cellar doorway and stared again at Kathleen's trapped foot. "I'm afraid to use a hammer or something to break the wood, in case I hurt your foot more."

With a sigh, Kathleen said, "This is just plain dumb."

"It may be dumb, Miss Kathleen, but we don't want you to get more injured than you are."

"Yes, I know, Izzy, but this wooden step is hard on my behind."

***

Luke turned left and rode up to the stable beside his home. The exterior doors to the storage cellar were open. He knew that Nate was gone for the day; perhaps Mrs. Bradley or Izzy were down there? Then, as if in response, Mrs. Bradley thrust out of the open doors like a ball from a cannon.

"Come quickly, Dr. Peterson. Mrs. Peterson is hurt."

Luke's heart stopped at the word "hurt" and he was filled with dread. "She's...hurt?"

"Yes, sir. Her foot is trapped in the bottom step."

Luke nearly laughed with relief. In the second or two after he heard she was injured, all kinds of images came to mind. In her condition, there were two people to worry about. So knowing her foot was stuck in the cellar step did not seem serious. As he briskly walked toward the steps to the cellar, he began to perspire, his heart continuing to pound in his chest.

"Kath? What happened?"

"Oh, hello. It's all right, Luke. I'm fine, just trapped."

"Mrs. Peterson's going to need some stitching, Dr. Peterson."

"We'll see about that." He hesitated, then went down the stairs.

"Now that you're home, can you get my foot out of here, Luke? They didn't want to break the wood because they were afraid they would hurt me."

Luke nodded. Izzy and Mrs. Bradley left and stood at the top of the steps as he crouched down in front of his wife. Taking off his coat and loosening his tie, he laid them on the steps beside Kathleen. He stared down at her foot trapped in the hole, but he couldn't see much as the two women were standing at the top of the steps keeping the light from getting to him. "Mrs. Bradley, Izzy, could you move either right or left so I have some light?"

The two women immediately did as he asked.

Luke's hands were shaking, his shirt already bathed in sweat. He imagined it was because he was so close to the cellar. *Why this childish nonsense?* he asked himself. He could already tell that his wife would be fine and that she had only a cut on her ankle. From his vantage point, though, he could also see that it was bleeding and might need a couple of stitches. All of a sudden, he became breathless.

"What's wrong, Luke?"

He shook his head. "Nothing. I was just upset when I heard you were hurt. I'll be fine in a moment." He took a few deep breaths.

"I wish you could get my foot out of here."

"Yes, yes, I will do that." He saw that a small part of the wood had rotted, probably from moisture. Nate would have to fix that as soon as possible. But the main part of the step was still pretty sturdy. It would have been easier had the entire step caved in, but only a narrow piece fell through.

"Izzy, do you know where the hammer is?"

"Not sure, Dr. Luke, but I could sure see if I can find it."

"Yes, please do that."

"I'll help her, Dr. Peterson," said Mrs. Bradley.

"Luke, I feel so stupid."

"No reason, love. This could have happened to anyone."

"Well, not to you. You never come down here."

He pulled at his collar. "Well, yes...I..."

"And I know why. It's not safe!"

Keeping his eyes on her foot and the rotting wood, he wondered whether it might help to use a small saw rather than a hammer. If he were able to saw it about an inch, Kath would then be able to pull her foot upward out of the hole. First, though, he would try pulling it just an inch or so to see if it would move. However, when he pulled on it, Kathleen cried out. "That hurts, Luke. Please stop."

"Yes, of course. I think this will need to be cut."

"I found the hammer, Dr. Luke." Izzy stood on the top step.

"Bring it down. Thank you, Izzy," he said, as he took the hammer from the girl. "Can you see if you or Mrs. Bradley can find a small saw?"

"Yes, of course." The girl sped off.

"I don't think you should use a hammer, Luke."

"You're right, but I didn't want Izzy to think she had retrieved it for naught."

"You're always thinking of others."

He brushed off the remark. Taking out his handkerchief, he tried to stuff it down the hole in order to stop her bleeding. She drew in a breath. "That stings."

"Yes. I'll need to treat that as soon as we get you out of here."

Izzy came down the stairs, handed Luke a small saw and returned to the top of the stairs with Mrs. Bradley.

Luke was perspiring and wiped his brow with the back of his hand. Then he set to work, gently sawing back and forth, until the wood bent about an inch and a half. He gently pulled Kathleen's foot upward. She winced, but then exclaimed, "My hero! Thank you, Luke."

Wrapping the handkerchief around the cut, he said, "Now, let's get you up to the examining room to see how many stitches you will need."

He bent down to pick her up and she said, "No, wait."

"Wait for what?"

"Could you get the ice cream bucket?"

"Kath, can't it wait? Your ankle needs to be examined."

"I'm fine, really I am. And it would be a shame not to get it after all the trouble of me coming down here and getting my foot stuck. It's on the bottom shelf on the far side. Please get it and hand it to Izzy."

He sighed. He felt like he was suffocating in the small area, his hands were still shaking, but he turned. "Where is the light?"

"Just over your head."

As his eyes adjusted to the darkness, he reached up and switched the light on. He wiped the perspiration off his forehead and walked to the shelves. The cedar ice cream bucket was just where she said it would be. He picked it up and walked toward the door. He could see his wife's bloody leg near the doorway and, for a moment, he thought he was going to be ill. He closed his eyes, bucket in hand.

Luke was no longer a doctor, but a little boy in the damp and musty storage cellar of his parents' home.

"Come on, Sarah, let's play cops and robbers!" Six-year-

old Luke peered down into the basement; one of its doors lay open.

"Wanna pway house." Four-year-old Sarah, her blond hair just touching her shoulders, was dressed in a maroon and black dress.

"Cops and robbers is a better game. Come on." He went down the wooden steps first. The only light in the room was a rectangular patch of sunlight from the doorway. His sister followed him and squinted to face the darkness. "It's dark. Wanna go back up."

"Stay with me and play cops and robbers."

"Wanna pway house."

"House? That's a girl's game. I am the cop and you are the robber."

"I wanna be a cop."

"Well, girls can't be a cop."

Young Luke's eyes had now adjusted to the dark. To one side of the steps were shelves with canned goods. To the other side a long table with tools and guns.

It would be fun to play with a real gun. Sarah wouldn't be able to hold the real gun anyway. That's why he had to be the good guy, the cop. He studied the guns and took the smallest one. Picking it up, he was surprised how heavy it was.

Luke wanted to be the hero. He wanted to be the good guy.

"Pretend you're holding up a bank."

"Don't wanna do that."

"Come on, just do it."

"No." When she turned to go up the stairs, he pulled the trigger and yelled "Pow, pow." But the gun slammed back into his chest with a loud pop before he realized it had actually fired. For a moment, he became breathless, his mouth trying to take in air, the smoky scent assaulting his nostrils. And his sister lay face down on the dirt floor near the steps, just beyond the light patch from the doors. He stared into the darkness. She wasn't moving. He cried, "Come on, Sarah. Get up. Get up!" His voice was high-

pitched as he pleaded with her. A copper, metal smell reached his nose. "Please, Sarah, please get up!"

He ran up the steps and bumped into his father. Looking down at Sarah's still form on the floor, he yelled, "What did you do, you stupid boy! You stupid, stupid boy! Get out of my sight!" Picking her up, his father rushed her up the stairs, knocking roughly into Luke, who fell backwards onto the grass. Then Luke heard the haunting sound of his mother's screams, the shock of a woman who had lost her only daughter.

***

Kathleen, her ankle throbbing, watched as her husband stared, unfocused. He gasped, dropped the ice cream freezer, held his hands to his face and began to weep.

"Luke, good gracious! What is wrong?"

With Mrs. Bradley and Izzy behind her asking questions, Kathleen told the two women to return to the house, that Luke would bring her up and not to worry.

Finally, his eyes moist and dark with sadness, Luke came to her, his head hung low and sobbed.

After minutes of prodding, Luke pursed his lips to stop crying. As he told his story, Kathleen also began to weep. In hindsight, all of the signs that he had carried this burden had been present: he had never wanted to fire a gun; never wanted to kill anything, not even a small insect. He never wanted to come down to the cellar.

Kathleen wrapped her arms around him as he sat beside her on the step, his head lowered, his eyes wet.

"I cannot believe what I did. All these years, I didn't remember, couldn't remember."

"It was an accident, Luke. It wasn't your fault."

"I disobeyed a rule. I was not supposed to touch the guns."

"Your father should have kept those guns locked; the basement should have been locked. This is *not* your fault. You were only six years old."

"How will I ever be able to forgive myself? If my parents could not forgive me, then how can I forgive myself?"

"Oh, Luke."

***

Luke finally straightened his shoulders and carried his wife up to his office. He cleansed her wound and stitched it, then applied some natural healing salve. He remained quiet the entire time, but Kathleen kept caressing his arm or face as he treated her.

He assisted her off the table and allowed her to walk. "I don't think it's sprained."

"I agree," she said. "It stings, but I think I shall be able to walk fine."

They were scheduled to arrive at his in-laws within the hour for Will's party, but how could Luke present himself in public, especially now that he remembered how his sister had died? How could he ever forgive himself?

"How can I help you, Luke?"

"I don't think you can, love. Nothing can change what I did."

"But you've forgotten about it in all these years...maybe that was God's gift to you."

"But now I've remembered.   Perhaps that is my punishment. How can I ever live with myself knowing what I've done?"

"You were a child, Luke, a small, unknowing, naïve child. It was not your fault. If anything, it was your father's fault for leaving his gun out."

"I disobeyed him."

"All children, especially young children, disobey their parents."

He considered it for a moment. With a shake of his head, he said, "I killed my dear sister."

"Do you think Sarah would want you to hate yourself? Would she want you to stop living because of what you remembered? You have done so much good in the world, Luke, and you need to forgive yourself."

Pressing his lips together, he nodded. "I know you're right, Kath, but..." He shook his head, "I will bring you to your parents' house, but would you mind if I returned here? I don't think I shall be very good company this evening."

"Yes, of course, Luke."

***

Late in the afternoon, Karl decided that he couldn't wait any longer. He had so many plans for Kathleen. He took a trolley into Germantown, getting off at Vernon Park. He walked to the area behind the man-boy's house. The doctor, Kathleen and a young servant were getting into a carriage. Were his eyes deceiving him? No...Kathleen was most definitely with child. His fists clenched and his jaw became rigid. *Isn't that sweet?*

When he saw them leave, he snuck behind the stable adjacent to and behind the house. He waited. No sign of anyone outside and it didn't look like any servants were inside either. Then again, it was Saturday evening and perhaps the two lovebirds were at the O'Donovan home.

He picked the lock with a straight pin and, while it took a few minutes, he eventually succeeded. He helped himself to a glass of water, leaving the glass on the counter. He went upstairs via the back staircase and found himself staring at a large telescope facing the back window and a short hallway. At the end of the hallway was a spacious bedroom. Peering inside, there were framed photographs on the wall and on the dressers, a four poster bed jutting out from the far wall. Yes, this was most certainly the happy couple's bedroom. He moved the smaller pictures around on the more feminine looking chest of drawers with the mirror, touching Kathleen's brush, smelling her perfume, holding her clothes to his nose and breathing in the fresh scent of laundry soap. There were three hair combs on her vanity, so he took one. He then relaxed on the bed, laying his head against both pillows, regretful that his shoes were not dirtier.

He nodded off and woke with the sound of a door opening and closing downstairs, then heard movement within the house. Panicking, he stood up, pushed the window wide open and jumped down onto the grass. He sprinted across the street and behind the horseshoer's establishment. That was too close. It couldn't happen again.

***

When Luke returned home, he opened the back door and went inside the kitchen. Stopping, he realized that he didn't need his key to get inside. In his grief and distraction, had he forgotten to lock the back door? That was not like him. Shrugging, he immediately headed for his office. Work had always been an adequate distraction for him and he needed to think of others right now and not himself. Try as he might, though, it was too challenging to forget. David had said that he would bring Kathleen home by ten p.m., but Luke was missing his wife desperately and wished she would return sooner. He needed her soothing presence like lungs need air.

He returned several folders to the filing cabinet and went upstairs. Before he knelt down to recite the rosary, he noticed the window beside the bed was wide open, so much so that the warm breeze was flapping the curtains. He closed the window halfway and returned to the bedside, kneeling. "In the name of the Father and of the Son...."

50

Karl leaned against the hick doctor's stable, his foot tapping on this cool Sunday morning in mid-September. He had been out of prison for nearly two months, and had enjoyed being able to watch Kathleen without her or her man-boy husband suspecting he had returned.

Last week, he was able to procure a room at the boarding house beside the rubber factory, within walking distance of the Peterson home. Coincidentally, most of the men living there worked at the factory and now Karl also had gainful employment. He neglected to mention that he had recently been released from the New Jersey State Penn.

In one sense, being in jail may have been a good thing, because it meant that Kathleen and her man-boy husband were now complacent. He liked their complacency and it almost made those ten months in prison worthwhile.

When everything fell into place perfectly, when he had the opportunity to have Kathleen alone, he would finally exact his revenge. Until then, he was satisfied with touching her things and breathing the air in her house.

The happy couple and the pretty servant were chatting as they got into their carriage. He knew from watching their house that the housekeeper and hired hand usually weren't there on Sunday morning. And the young servant always went with them to Mass. So he waited ten minutes then sprinted across the yard to the back door and used his straight pin to break in. He was becoming proficient at getting it unlocked and now it only took a minute. He helped himself to a glass of water from the tap, then placed the glass on its side in the sink.

Karl sprinted up the back staircase to the second floor and to the happy couple's room. Again, he moved items around on both the man-boy's bureau and Kathleen's vanity table. Caressing the bottle of *Essence of Violets* perfume, he sprayed it generously on the side of the bed closest to the vanity — hoping it was, in fact, her side of the bed — then placed the bottle sideways on her vanity, and sat on the side of the bed.

He stayed only a half-hour and, after touching all the items at her vanity and in her closet, he decided he could not leave the house without taking her brush, for it contained her hair. His pulse quickened. Soon...very soon, he would find a way to achieve his revenge. Returning downstairs, he locked the kitchen door with the key hanging by the counter, returned it, then left by the back window.

***

Upon returning home later that day after having lunch with her family, Kathleen longed to sleep in her bed, just for an hour or so. But when she stepped into her bedroom, the air seemed thick with perfume, yet she hadn't worn the scent during her entire pregnancy. Had it spilled? Crossing the room to her dressing table, she saw that the bottle was tipped over. Was she that clumsy? With a sigh, she picked it up; no liquid had appeared to come out. And while her hand-painted mirror was in its usual place, the matching brush was missing. Kathleen sat down on the edge of her bed. The overwhelming scent of her perfume was making her nauseated.

***

"Are you certain you cleaned every glass and dish, Izzy?"

"Yes, Dr. Luke, every glass and dish. I have no idea how this glass got here."

Luke felt his entire body stiffen. Out of the corner of his eye, he noticed the back door knob, which he locked when they left for Mass earlier. He jiggled it and it *was* locked. With a relieved sigh, he said, "Izzy, it's only one glass. Perhaps you don't remember leaving it there? Or maybe Kath got a glass of water before we left."

"Yes, that must be it, Dr. Luke."

"Luke?" Kathleen called from the top of the back staircase.

"Yes?"

"Could you come up here for a moment?"

"Of course."

He met her at the top of the stairs near the telescope at the back window.

"Come with me." She took hold of his hand and walked with him to their bedroom.

"Do you smell anything unusual in here?"

Luke took a deep breath. "It's your perfume, Essence of..."

"Violets, yes. Now smell our bed."

He leaned down toward his side of the bed. Admittedly, his olfactory system was not his most developed, but the quilt did carry the strong scent of perfume. "Did you spill it?"

"I haven't worn it since I've been with child."

"I see." Luke did find it peculiar. However, Kath had been more forgetful recently, losing small things, although recently he had chalked it up to her pregnancy. Now? He couldn't believe anyone could be *that* forgetful, especially his wife.

Izzy stood at the doorway. "Miss Kathleen, will you be taking a rest this afternoon?"

"I'm not sure...can you bring me the quilt from the spare bedroom? This one seems to have been doused with perfume."

With a nod, Izzy said, "Of course." She turned and left.

"Luke, I feel like I'm going crazy. My room smells like perfume and the hand-painted brush my mother gave me for my birthday is missing."

"You're not crazy."

"I'm sure I didn't spill perfume on the quilt and I have no idea what happened to my brush."

"I'm sure you didn't too." The image of Karl's face came into his mind. His arm on her shoulder, he pulled her close.

Izzy brought a new quilt and removed the perfume-laden one. Kathleen settled into bed for an afternoon nap, so Luke went downstairs to his office. Since the revelation of how he accidentally killed his sister, he had stopped carrying the gun he had promised his father-in-law he would. Setting his fears aside, he took the holster and weapon out of his office drawer, cleaned it as John had taught him, and slipped one bullet into the chamber. From now on, he would carry the gun at all times.

51

It was a warm and sunny morning, this second of October, 1898. *One year of marriage.* Luke's in-laws had informed him that they had a special after-Mass anniversary celebration planned. Luke had purchased his wife a lap writing desk and ivory-colored pad. However, since Kathleen had been awake on and off since around two a.m., it was unlikely she would be doing anything but resting today.

As much as Luke wanted to sleep, he had already rested for four hours and decided to get up and stargaze. Luke peered out at the dark morning sky with his telescope, its lens poking out the rear window. He didn't often have an opportunity to gaze at the stars before sunrise and was delighted to do so.

***

Kathleen felt utterly exhausted. Luke told her that the baby could be born any day, but not likely for a few weeks. The nausea had returned with a vengeance. After tossing and turning for most of the night trying to find a comfortable sleeping position, she concluded there were none, not with her large stomach and recurrent need to retch. Poor Luke. Before sunrise, she felt him get out of bed and go into the hallway.

When it came time to dress for Mass, Luke urged her to remain in bed. He kissed her and whispered, "Happy Anniversary."

"Happy Anniversary, Luke. I nearly forgot!"

"No worries, love. We shall celebrate when you are feeling better."

Her husband asked Izzy, who usually went to Mass with them, to stay home in case Kathleen needed her.

Kathleen finally surrendered and tried to sleep. The side of her stomach pressed into the mattress and the baby responded by kicking her. This little gentleman (or little lady) was already strong and had a unique, playful personality.

She rested her hands lovingly on her large stomach, and slowly drifted off to sleep.

***

Sunday mornings at St. Charles Borromeo Seminary began with Morning Prayer and High Mass, followed by a hearty breakfast. Sunday afternoons were devoted to sports and leisure activities after the academics of the previous week. When Mass concluded, instead of going to breakfast, Will chose to remain at the chapel and spend time in adoration. All morning, he had been restless. The only way to rid himself of the feeling was to pray before the Blessed Sacrament. His head bowed in prayer, he lifted his soul to Christ.

***

Kathleen stirred with the familiar tingling at her mouth and tried to get up in time. Instead, she vomited down the front of her nightgown. "Izzy?"

"Yes?" Izzy came to her room, then said, "Oh...I'll clean that, Miss Kathleen." Kathleen then changed into a fresh nightgown, her favorite cotton gown with pink lace on the collar. It was wide enough that she could still fit into it, albeit tight to her form. She hadn't worn it in several months, but it would help her to feel pretty instead of large and cumbersome.

Kathleen lowered herself to a resting position. "I don't think I'll be able to sleep now."

"Would you like some soda crackers?"

"Yes, perhaps so."

"And I'll get you a glass of water."

"First can you help button the back of my gown?"

"Of course, Miss Kathleen."

***

Karl checked his pocket watch. It was 11:10 a.m. Kathleen and that hick doctor would be at Mass for an hour and a half as the 11:00 a.m. Mass was a High Mass. He felt smug in the knowledge that the man-boy and Kathleen knew nothing of his adventures, stealing and moving items in their house. Oh, how he wished he could tell them how much a part of their life he was now. *Some day.*

The last time he saw Kathleen, she had popped out like a large balloon, her tent-like dress hiding her large stomach.

He went to the back door and heard the horse in the barn. It was odd since they had been taking the carriage to church in recent weeks, even though it was close enough to walk. Why then hadn't they done so today?

It only took a few moments before he was able to pick the lock and opened the door. Inside, he went to turn on the tap, but stopped when he heard voices upstairs.

Did they not go to Mass? This was most unusual as even the live-in servant attended Mass with them each week. Footsteps on the back staircase made his eyes search for a hiding place. He ducked into a closet and waited to see who came down. *Ah, the young pretty servant.*

"Izzy," he heard Kathleen call from upstairs, "would you please bring an extra linen towel?"

"Yes, Miss Kathleen." The girl stood at the sink and turned the faucet on to fill a glass.

So my dearest Kathleen is here after all. Was that man-boy husband of hers present too? Listening, Karl heard no other noises coming from either above him or behind him in the office.

Karl concluded that the only two present were the girl and Kathleen. He could not believe his luck. If he could just dispose of the servant girl, that would mean that he had an hour and a half with Kathleen, alone, all to himself. Ah, the things they could talk about...and the activities they could engage in. Yes, this was most fortunate. This is what he had been waiting for. His patience would soon be rewarded.

He quietly stepped behind the young girl. He slapped his hand over her face so she couldn't scream, but the glass and water went crashing to the floor. He slammed her head down onto the table. The girl fell to the floor, her body lifeless and still, a red trail of fluid flowing from under her head. *A shame. She was a pretty girl.*

***

The sound of glass smashing made Kathleen sit up straight. Sometimes Izzy could be so clumsy, but she was a sweet girl so it didn't really matter to Kathleen. "Izzy?" she called. There was no response. Perhaps the girl could not hear her.

Kathleen swung her legs over the side of the bed and listened.

***

Will's restlessness wasn't calmed or soothed by the Blessed Sacrament as it normally was. Then, in the deepest recesses of his soul, he felt the words *Kat is in danger*. The last time he felt those words, he ignored them. This time, he would not. He made the sign of the cross, genuflected and immediately made his way toward the main building.

Once there, he pleaded with the priest in charge. "I must use the telephone to call my sister."

Fr. O'Halloran, a heavyset priest, arched his brows. "Young man, slow down and tell me what is wrong."

"Please, there's no time. Allow me to telephone my sister."

"What is the matter?"

"I don't know. Please allow me to do so." The priest nodded and accompanied Will to the telephone.

Glancing at the time, he knew the Peterson household should be at Mass, but something urged him forward. If he called and there was no answer, perhaps everyone was at Mass and he had no reason to worry.

As he stood by the phone, he tried to remember the number. He had only called his sister once. GER 101? GER 123?

He cranked the handle on the side of the phone and the operator came on. "I'd like GER 123, please."

"Hold one moment, please. Connecting."

The line rang for what seemed like eternity, then a woman's voice answered. "Kat? Izzy? This is Will."

"There's no Kat or Izzy here, young man. You must have the wrong number."

Will's shoulders slumped. He cranked the phone again for the operator. "Operator, could you try GER 101?" "Yes, sir, connecting."

The phone rang, but no one answered it. Again, he cranked the phone to speak to the operator. "Operator, could I inquire as to whether you have a listing for a Dr. Luke Peterson?"

"I'll look that up, but it will be a ten cent charge."

Will's eyes pleaded with Fr. O'Halloran. "Father, it's a ten cent charge to find out my brother-in-law's number. Please. I will pay back the money."

The priest nodded.

The operator said, "The number is GER 132." Will sighed with relief. "Could you connect me, please?"

"Very well."

***

Kathleen heard the telephone screech in Luke's office. As much as she liked having the convenience of a telephone, the sound irritated her like nails on a chalkboard. And who on earth would be calling on a Sunday morning? Her parents and siblings were at Mass.

Why wasn't Izzy answering the phone? Even if Kathleen wanted to rush down stairs to answer it, in her cumbersome and nauseated state, she would not be able to do so.

***

Will waited as the phone rang over twenty times. The operator spoke. "I'm sorry, sir. They aren't answering."

They must be at Mass.

***

Karl listened to that blasted telephone for twenty long rings. He almost answered it, but decided against it. Anything that might alert the police would not be prudent. He was smarter than that. Climbing the stairs, his heart began to race. He had been waiting for this opportunity for nearly two years. He would not ruin his chances now.

***

Instead of Izzy's usual light quick steps, these sounded heavier and slower. Kathleen gasped as the door swung open. Karl stood in the doorway.

Kathleen tried to find her voice to scream, but terror stole the breath from her lungs as he sprinted across the room and was on top of her before she could manage any sound. He slammed his hand on her mouth.

Her heart was pounding, her body trembling. Horrific memories came flooding back.

"My dearest, just when you thought I wouldn't

return...we're finally together." His body covered hers, her hands protectively clutched her stomach.

"Now, I'm going to take my hand away from your mouth and, if you scream, I will kick your stomach so hard, your precious baby will not survive."

A scrambled smattering of thoughts spun around in her mind. How could she let Izzy know? Perhaps Izzy could run and get help. Where was she? No matter what, Kathleen decided, she must try to escape. But to run in her current condition would take nothing short of a miracle.

"Do not make a sound. Do you hear me?" Karl took his hand off her mouth. She kept quiet. "That's a good girl." He lifted himself and sat back on the edge of her bed and patted the mattress beside her legs. "I wanted to inform you that I have been enjoying this lovely bed occasionally for these past two months."

Kathleen cringed and sunk back against the headboard. Her shaking hands were now pushing into the bed.

"Ah, I see you're wearing a lovely nightgown. Isn't that just like the gown that went missing a year and a half ago from your bedroom?"

She pressed her back further against the headboard.

"Yes, my dear, I've been inside this very house every other Sunday morning. I picked the lock of the back door and stole some items. Have you missed your hairbrush? Your hair comb? Mostly, I enjoyed moving items like your wedding photo on the bureau over there."

Kathleen sucked in a breath to keep from crying. This lunatic had invaded their house countless times and they knew nothing of it. But now the lost items, the articles that were moved...it all made sense.

"Of course, you must know that I am responsible for ruining your Atlantic City honeymoon at the Seaside?"

Kathleen stared straight ahead, but kept silent.

"Yes, I thought you and your man-boy husband must have suspected that was my handiwork. The champagne your dear old dad ordered was certainly a fine — and tasty — beverage. And...your wedding...that was such a lovely affair. And now I see there is a little bundle of joy coming soon."

With a fear-filled gasp, Kathleen bit on her lip to keep silent.

"Now, my dear, let me tell you what will happen in the next hour or so. I will finally take what I've been wanting these past two years. Admittedly, it will be more difficult with your rather large and unattractive stomach, but I assure you, I can be very accommodating. Besides, that weakling man-boy of a husband of yours —"

Kathleen cut him off. "Luke is stronger and more of a man than you'll ever be!"

He backhanded her. Crying out, her hand flew to her cheek.

"Now see what you made me do to you?"

***

Luke felt a tapping on his shoulder. Mrs. Findlay, the deaf elderly woman who was in the pew behind him, said rather loudly, "Dr. Luke, I'm going to faint. Can you escort me outside?"

He nodded. Getting up, he exited the pew and accompanied the woman up the aisle and outside.

Luke took out his pocket watch and felt the woman's wrist as she sat down on the top step. Her pulse seemed rapid, but he wasn't overly concerned. The woman was pale, though, and given her age, he wondered whether her heart was in distress.

"Are you having any chest pain or tingling in your arms, Mrs. Findlay?" he asked as he spoke into her tin horn.

She shook her head.

"Do you mind if I check your ankles to see if you're retaining water?"

She held up her skirt a bit, but it was difficult to see whether her ankles were retaining water with her high boots.

"Do your shoes feel tight?"

"No."

"Excellent. Do you feel any better?"

"I do.

He heard a faint cry, then a louder screech behind him. He

turned to see Izzy. She was hobbling toward him, so he ran to meet her. Her hand was holding onto her forehead, and blood dripped down the side of her face. *Kath? Where is Kath?*

"Izzy, what happened?"

"I don't know, Dr. Luke. I was getting Miss Kathleen a glass of water and, all of a sudden, I felt strong hands against my face. I don't remember much after that. I woke up on the floor, I heard Miss Kathleen...crying out...and a man's voice saying that he was the one responsible for ruining the honeymoon. I couldn't hear much after that." Izzy began to weep. "My head hurts so much...but I wouldn't be able to help her like this, so I knew I had to come and get you!"

He quickly did a cursory exam. Izzy had a long and open laceration at the top of her forehead near the scalp and her hands were trembling uncontrollably. He took out his handkerchief and held it to the wound as he walked her back to the front of the church. It would need stitches, but he couldn't stop to do so now. Into the deaf woman's tin horn, he said, "Mrs. Findlay, hold this to Izzy's head."

To Izzy, he said, "Remain here with Mrs. Findlay. And if you feel drowsy, please do your best to stay awake."

The girl nodded. Luke had no time to inform David. He must go *now*. As he ran, he turned and shouted "Tell David and John to come to my house as soon as possible."

***

Should Kathleen just pretend to go along with his "plan"? Should she fight or try to hurt him? She was a slight and very pregnant female and he was an over six-foot-tall, broad-shouldered male. *Dear God in heaven, please help me. St. Agnes, please pray for me.*

"Hail Mary, full of grace, the Lord is with thee..."

"Shut up! Stop that!" he spat.

"Blessed art thou amongst women and blessed..."

He cut her off with a slap to her face. She bit her lip, tears now forming, her hand rubbing her cheek. "Is the fruit of thy womb, Jesus." She bowed her head quickly then looked up to see that Karl had taken out his gun and was now aiming it at her stomach. She stopped.

"Good girl." Keeping his gun pointed at her stomach, he took his coat off, then he started to push up her nightgown.

Please God, not this. Please...

52

It was eerily quiet as Luke rushed to his house. He fumbled to stick the key in the front door knob and it clicked open. Once inside, he drew his gun. Should he stop and call the police? His answer came when he heard his wife's anguished cries for help. He turned toward the stairs, hoping, praying he wouldn't be too late.

***

Karl came down upon her. She was breathless from being on her back, but when he tried to kiss her, she turned her head. Her knee was exactly where it needed to be and she thrust upward. He grunted and fell backward. She pushed herself away from him and tried to stand up quickly. Racing to the door, she stumbled, then reached for the door and flung it open. Kathleen then ran for her life, for her baby's life, reciting the rest of the prayer. "Holy Mary mother of God pray for us sinners now and at the hour of our death. Amen," she said with urgency. She'd nearly made it to the front staircase when Karl yanked her back and slammed her against the wall by her bedroom. His arms felt like steel as he held onto her. In an instant, she bit his left hand and he grunted. She got away again, this time running toward the back staircase, near the open window and Luke's telescope. Karl grabbed her by the hair and swung her around. He held the gun to her head, the gun clicking as he cocked it. Lifting her chin, she saw Luke at the top of the front staircase, gun drawn. *Thank you, God. Thank you for Luke.*

***

Luke was not prepared for the sight before him. Karl, his left fist clenching Kathleen's hair, his gun drawn and pointing at Kathleen's head, her eyes wide and glistening, her mouth pursed. *Dear God in Heaven.* Luke felt every muscle in his body tense and his throat close.

Holding the gun in front of him and moving forward, he pointed it at Karl, his hand trembling like a swaying leaf.

"Oh, the *man-boy* himself has arrived. And, look, he has a

gun. Put that down. You'll hurt yourself. Or, worse yet, you'll hurt someone you love."

Luke cringed.

Karl continued. "Besides, I could shoot both of you before your shaking hands cocked it. Do you even have any bullets in it? See, Kathleen, I told you he's useless. Your hero can't even hold his hand still...."

"Release her, Karl. I don't want to hurt you."

"You can't hurt me, Doctor."

"Leave her alone. She's with child."

Karl smirked. "Sorry, but no. And while I would have liked to have had my way with her, that's of no consequence now. Killing her will give me as much pleasure as the other."

***

Will waited at the main office for what seemed like an eternity. Fr. O'Halloran tried to persuade the young seminarian to return to his room, but he respectfully asked to stay. "I must try Luke's telephone again immediately. Please."

"Go ahead."

Will cranked the phone and spoke to the operator. "Please connect me to..."

***

Luke slowly brought the gun upward, his hand continuing to shake. He glanced at his wife, whose fear-filled eyes and quivering lips were begging him to help her.

Kathleen turned her eyes toward Karl. At that moment, the telephone in his office screeched. It was enough to distract Karl for a split second, and he lessened his grip on her hair. Kathleen pushed him against the telescope at the window, which knocked over and crashed against the floor. She fell to her hands and knees, her back to Karl. Straightening his body in front of the window, Karl pointed his gun at her and prepared to fire. Luke cocked his own gun — with no time to eyeball the target — and fired. The shot ripped through Karl's chest. He fell back, tripping over the telescope which thrust him backwards, arms outstretched, through the open window.

Despite the deafening commotion, Kathleen screamed a

garbled noise. For a moment, Luke couldn't move; he couldn't breathe, and his heart pounded from his chest to his ears. He dropped the gun, its barrel still smoking. Both arms hung limply at his sides. When he was finally able to inhale, the distasteful scent from a memory long past attacked his nostrils, bringing back the painful image of his sister on the cellar floor. He shook his head to rid himself of the reminder.

All of a sudden, Kathleen was hugging him. "You did it! Thank God, Luke!"

Finally, he muttered, "Are...you...all right?"

"Yes, yes, I'm fine." Then as if Kathleen had been holding it in, she began to sob against Luke's chest. "Luke, I love you so. You saved my life! You saved our baby!"

"Deo Gratias. Thanks be to God. You're safe, Kath." She was squeezing him so tightly, he could barely breathe. He removed her hands. "Allow me to go to the window. I need to see for myself." With a nod, she released him.

He walked to the window and peered down onto the ground below. Karl was on his back, his arms and legs twisted, his eyes slightly open. Luke shivered. A pool of blood was slowly seeping out from under the body.

Luke knew that he should pronounce the man dead but, with the amount of blood near his body and the stillness, the man was likely gone.

Returning to his wife, they embraced, her large stomach now safely cradled between them. Kathleen's head lowered and she pointed. "Your telescope is ruined."

With a nod, he responded, "It is easy to replace. You and our precious baby are not." He kissed the top of her head.

Behind them, on the front staircase, David, Caroline and John stood wide-eyed. "Luke killed him, Papa. Luke killed Karl."

Luke glanced back toward the open window. "May God have mercy on his soul."

***

Will was frustrated that no one had answered, so he remained in the office, wondering if he should telephone them again. Suddenly, his soul felt unburdened and the anxiety about his sister had completed dissipated.

***

"Oh dear!" Kathleen exclaimed as fluid dripped from between her legs and onto the hardwood floors, splashing onto Luke's shoes. With all the commotion, it took a few seconds for Luke to realize what was happening. If there hadn't already been enough activity today, it looked like their baby would be making his or her arrival.

"It's fine, love. Your amniotic sac has broken. You're going to have a baby — perhaps today. Come." Caroline immediately came to her daughter's side and assisted Kathleen onto her bed.

Luke asked David to telephone the police first, then to call Will at the seminary to inform him of the day's events. Later, David shared Will's revelation to Luke that he had telephoned specifically because he had felt uneasy all morning. Will told his father that he was thankful that his telephone call had been a blessing that had distracted Karl enough to give Luke the opportunity to shoot.

Kathleen had gone into active labor; her mother staying by her side. Pat took the younger children to Elizabeth's and Philip's, then returned with Jane.

A worried and anxious John held Izzy's hand the entire time Luke stitched Izzy's head wound. Luke had just finished when David peeked into the examining room. "How's Izzy doing?"

"Fine."

"And Kat?"

As if in answer, they could hear her moaning through another contraction upstairs. The older man lifted his head and scowled. Of course, Luke was trying his best to be a physician right now and complete the task. He placed a bandage over her head. "Let me know if you have any dizziness, headaches or other problems, Izzy."

"Yes, Dr. Luke. Thank you."

"No, Izzy, thank *you* for coming to get me even though you were injured."

David moved closer and whispered, "The police officer has arrived. Karl's father has been notified. When you have a moment, you can inform the officer where Karl's body is."

Luke opened his eyes widely. "He's right under the window in the back yard. I didn't move him." With a long sigh, Luke rushed through the medical storage area, into the kitchen and out the back door, with David running behind him. Under the window, the grass and leaves were flattened, a pool of blood the only evidence Karl had been there. However, his body was now gone. A policeman was staring down at the spot. He turned and held out his hand to Luke. "Dr. Peterson, I'm Officer James Murphy. Where did you say the body was?"

"It was right here," he said, pointing under the window. Officer Murphy was a stout man who, given the circumstances, looked rather more somber than his full, good-natured Irish face might normally show. Luke explained that he had shot Karl in the chest while defending his wife, that the man had fallen out the window, but that Luke had not taken the time to pronounce the man dead.

Officer Murphy began walking beside the flattened grass and trail of blood. Luke followed along, staring, incredulous that Karl had somehow crawled away. David was behind him.

The group of men followed the crimson spots on the grass to the area behind the barn.

Birthing moans floated down from the open window and Luke's heart pounded as he felt compelled to return to his wife. But he also knew — and hoped — that the baby would not be coming for at least a few hours. This situation with Karl was not something that could wait. The police officer drew his gun and the three men slowly turned to enter the grassy area behind the barn.

There was blood matter on the grass which led them to Karl's body, now face down. Slowly, the men inched toward him. Again, Karl appeared too still to be alive, but Luke would not make the same mistake twice. Officer Murphy placed his gun back in his coat and crouched down.

"Doc, you want to pronounce him dead?"

Luke knelt down on the grass beside Karl, whose black hair was damp, his skin ashen, his left hand on the grass beside his head. Karl's coat had turned brick red with blood. Luke reached his hand to touch Karl's neck and felt for a pulse. All of a sudden, Karl moaned.

***

Kathleen tried to catch her breath through the next contraction, but she had no time to do so. Jane wiped her face with a cool cloth, but Kathleen shook her head and pushed the hand away. When the contraction subsided, she finally breathed in deeply. Realizing that Luke had not returned, she asked, "Where is Luke?"

"It's fine, Miss Kathleen. You've got a while before your wee baby comes. Your mother and I are here to help you."

"But where...is Luke?"

"He needed to speak with the policeman about Karl's death," Mama said.

It all came back now. Karl. Dead. Relaxing her head against the pillow, she steeled herself for the next pain.

***

When Luke heard Karl groan, he gasped and stepped back. "Dear God, he's still alive." At the same time, Kathleen's painful cry drifted down from the upstairs window.

Karl had lost a tremendous amount of blood, so Luke didn't know whether he would be able to successfully treat the man, but would his physician oath of "do no harm" also apply to this man who had caused them so much pain and heartache? A small interior voice urged him on. Luke was a healer, a physician. Despite everything that had happened, he must try to save Karl.

He glanced at David's face, the man's expression rigid and unchanging. "I'd be happy to put him out of his misery."

Officer Murphy held his arm in front of David. "Mr. O'Donovan, we cannot shoot a dying man."

"The officer is correct, David," Luke said.

David exhaled and, in a measure of remorse, agreed. "I suppose you're right."

It was then that Luke noticed Kathleen's younger brother,

Patrick, standing behind the group and staring at the scene, mouth open and eyes wide. "Pat, check on your sister, please. Ask your mother how she is doing and report back to me."

He nodded. The young man finally left and Luke sighed. He didn't want these images staying in Pat's young mind.

Luke carefully turned Karl over to assess the wound made by his gun, the weapon he never wanted to carry or use. But what should he do? There was another distant cry as his wife struggled through a contraction.

The gaping wound in his chest still oozed blood. Luke pressed down hard on it to stop the bleeding. He felt the man's chest. He suspected that Karl had a collapsed lung. If he performed a tracheotomy, that might assist him in breathing.

The blood coming out of his chest, however, could not be stopped. Luke quickly determined that Karl also had several broken ribs caused by the fall and/or the gunshot wound, although his injuries were likely made worse by Karl dragging himself across the grass. Either way, this man was mortally wounded. He took Karl's pulse again; it was weak and barely measurable. But he continued to place pressure on the wound. Finally, the bleeding ceased, and Luke surmised it was because Karl was gone. The absence of a pulse confirmed he was dead. "May God have mercy on this troubled man's soul." Feeling moisture, Luke glanced upward, his face getting wet, the rain tapping on the barn roof sounded like hands clapping. He stood and approached the group behind him. "He's dead."

The rain now came down in steady drops. Officer Murphy ordered another policeman to stand guard near the body as he ran with the two men into the kitchen. "There will be an investigation and a coroner's inquest, Dr. Peterson. However, we have enough evidence that you shot Karl Wagner to save your wife." He pointed outdoors. "This officer will remain here until the coroner arrives. When the rain lets up, photographs will be taken and other evidence will be removed from the property."

Pat came down the back staircase and called to Luke.

"Jane and Mama say Kat's asking for you, and to come quickly."

He sprinted up the back staircase to their bedroom where he would soon deliver his child.

***

Caroline held Kathleen's hand later that evening. Luke could hear steady murmuring in the hallway. The police had come and gone and Karl's body had been removed. Luke was now able to focus on his wife and soon-to-be born child.

Jane stood beside him at the foot of the bed. Kathleen had already been pushing for half an hour when Luke saw his baby's head crowning. "Come on, Kath, one more push and our baby will be here."

Kathleen moaned and grunted, her wet hair plastered against her face as she pushed. The child slid from her and into Luke's waiting hands. "It's a girl!"

Luke and Kathleen were the parents of a beautiful — and very bald — infant daughter. The proud father cut the umbilical cord; he began cleaning her just in time for her to urinate all over his shirt. "Well now, little one, making messes already, are we?" She responded by heartily crying.

Laughing, Kathleen lifted her head to look. "Is she...all right?"

"She's exquisite."

"May I hold her?"

"One moment, love. We're cleaning her up for you." He tenderly washed the baby's pink skin. Jane handed him a blanket and he wrapped her tightly and kissed her small forehead. "She is beautiful...just like her mama."

Kathleen beamed. Luke placed the tiny baby in his wife's arms and, for one surreal moment, he felt like he was in heaven. His and Kathleen's love was now embodied in this tiny human being.

His wife's expression was radiant as she gazed at their daughter.

To Caroline, he said, "Well, Grandmother, what do you think of your new granddaughter?"

"She's lovely," Caroline said, as she gazed at the baby with tear-filled eyes.

"What name have you chosen for your baby, Miss Kathleen?" Jane asked.

"Luke and I decided that if we had a daughter, her name would be Sarah Maureen Peterson, after both our sisters."

With a happy sigh, her mother said, "That's lovely, sweet."

"Now, Miss Kathleen, once we get this baby fed, you'll need rest. You've been through a lot today."

"May I eat first?" Kathleen asked her husband. "I haven't had anything to eat since last night."

"Of course you may, Kath. Jane, could you run downstairs and make a sandwich for my wife?"

"Right away, Dr. Luke."

Caroline turned. "I shall return momentarily." She opened the door to a flurry of questions about the baby. John and Izzy, Pat and David were waiting. Luke could hear the excitement in the hallway as Caroline closed the door behind her and shared the news.

"And you, Luke. How are *you*?" Kathleen asked.

"Fine...now."

"Well, we have a new daughter...and we shall never have to worry about having that black shadow following us again so those are two reasons to celebrate."

***

Kathleen stared at her husband as she held their child in her arms. He was elated, to be sure, but he seemed reserved, given that she had just given birth to their baby daughter. Of course, this day carried the most beautiful memory of her life and the most terrifying. Was Luke disappointed that their child was a girl?

"Is anything wrong, Luke?"

With a smile, he said, "Not anymore. Everything's perfect."

***

Later, chants of "We want to see the baby! We want to see the baby!" came from the hallway outside their bedroom.

"Luke, can everyone come in and see the baby?"

"Just for a moment...you should be resting."

"I know, but I cannot. I'm too happy."

Luke opened the door and the O'Donovan children began to crowd into the room. Her mother had returned to her bedside, and Kathleen could see her father tilting his head toward her; he winked and smiled widely. A cacophony of mostly young men's and boys' voices prompted Luke to put his hand up again. Kathleen could see that Tim and Kev were in front, trying to shove their way closer to the bed.

"Boys, one at a time, and only for a moment because your sister and niece need their rest." Luke's voice was firm but gentle.

One by one, the O'Donovan boys passed by to fawn over their new niece. John and Izzy came close to see the baby. Izzy looked slightly pale, but the long bandage on the girl's head was a reminder for Kathleen that a special thank you was required.

"Izzy, I am so grateful that you ran to the church and alerted Luke even though you were injured. You saved my life. I'm so glad that you will be fine."

The girl's mouth lifted in a smile, but she was silent.

Instead, John answered, "Me too, Kat. I don't know what I would have done if..." John squeezed Izzy's hand.

Papa was last in line. He kissed her cheek and whispered, "This was certainly an eventful day, wasn't it?"

"Indeed. Isn't your granddaughter beautiful?"

"She is. Your mother told me what you have named her. Beautiful, lovely name."

"Papa, will you telephone Will as soon as possible to let him know he has a new niece?"

"Of course. He will be pleased, very pleased."

When each of her brothers had seen the baby and had left the room, she asked her parents to remain so she could ask them a private question.

"Mama, Papa, I know that it's unusual, but Luke and I have chosen you both to be Sarah's godparents."

Their expressions brightened. "We would be honored to be our first grandchild's godparents." As she studied her mother, however, Kathleen noticed her mouth lift in an amused smile;

and there was something in her eyes, a twinkle that Kathleen hadn't noticed before now.

"Mama, is everything all right?"

"Everything is beautiful, Kathleen, just beautiful."

"We should tell them, Caroline," offered David as he put his arm around his wife. "This day needs more good news."

"Tell us what, Mama?"

Her mother nodded. "Your father and I are expecting a baby in about six months' time."

Kathleen opened her mouth in amazement. "That's wonderful!" Turning to Luke, she said, "Can you believe my parents are having another baby?"

"I believe it, Kath."

"I'm a grandmother and expectant mother at the same time," the older woman whispered as she hugged her daughter.

Kathleen held her mother at arm's length and faced her father. "Papa, I'm so happy. Your baby will be incredibly blessed."

"We're happy, Kat."

"Giving birth to our baby girl and finding out your news is the perfect way for this day to end."

"Amen," agreed Luke.

Epilogue

April 29, 1899

The birth of a new century would begin in eight months and Kathleen greatly anticipated it for more than one reason.

She bounced baby Sarah on her knee in the side yard of her home. The tiny girl laughed and giggled. Her bald head had begun to sprout white-blond hair.

Flowers were in full bloom, the trees were filled with bright green leaves and the breeze was warm and gentle. Mrs. Bradley's enthusiastic whistling drifted forth from the kitchen window and it made Kathleen smile.

Luke called to her from his examining room window. "Kath? Mr. Rutherford said he would be arriving at one o'clock with the new sign for my office door. Have you seen him yet?"

"No. But I've only been outside for a few moments."

"Very well." He winked at his wife, then waved to Sarah. "Hello, little one! How's Papa's girl today?"

Sarah responded by squealing and waving both hands.

Later this afternoon, she and Luke would be visiting her parents and their newborn son, Matthew Joseph O'Donovan, Kathleen's baby brother, who was only three weeks old.

Kathleen had been present for the birth and, for the first time, at her insistence, Papa had also been in the room to witness his youngest son being born.

After experiencing the labor and delivery of her own child, Kathleen was in awe of her 42-year-old mother's strength and stamina. And baby Matthew (or Matt, as Papa was calling him) was a strapping eight-pound boy and another handsome, fair-haired son like Pat and Tim.

John had picked up Isabelle earlier to spend the day at their house, where John would be assisting in her preparation to become Catholic. Isabelle had recuperated well from her head injury many months ago. Excitement was in the air because of the young couple's upcoming nuptials in two months' time. John and Isabelle had requested that everyone call Izzy by her Christian name, Isabelle. Their planned wedding would take place at St. Vincent's next month with immediate family and friends. Of course, the gossipmongers among the upper class had much to say about the mixed-class match, but the family ignored them.

After their marriage, John and Isabelle would be living at the O'Donovan house, while John learned the mercantile trade. The plan was for Isabelle to continue to work at the Petersons' home until she and John started their family, then Luke and Kathleen would have to search for someone to replace her. When the time came, Kathleen would miss the girl's daily companionship and help.

Papa had officially changed the name of his business from O'Donovan Mercantile to O'Donovan & Son Mercantile. Eventually, Kathleen surmised, the business name would be O'Donovan & Sons once Pat, Kev, Tim and Matt were older, if they chose to join their father in the business.

The bells from St. Vincent's rang for the noon hour and Kathleen interiorly prayed the words of the Angelus. When she finished, she thought of Will at the seminary. In three years, he would be ordained to the sub-diaconate. It was difficult but wonderful to imagine there would be a priest in their family one day.

Out of the corner of her eye, Kathleen noticed a woman approaching the porch near Luke's office door. She was dressed in a plain brown dress and she looked vaguely familiar. She approached the woman.

"May I help you?" Kathleen asked the young woman.

"Yes. Is Dr. Peterson in?"

"Yes, but he isn't seeing patients today. Shall I make you an appointment?"

The woman glanced away. As she did, Luke opened the office door. "Ah, Miss Smith. Thank you for coming."

Kathleen stepped back as Luke accompanied the woman inside.

***

Luke shut the door and motioned for Pearl to sit down in the waiting room. The girl did not make eye contact as she lowered herself to a chair.

"Pearl, how can I help you?"

"I'm...leaving the brothel. I need...money."

"Of course." Luke went into his office and pulled some bills from the envelope. He handed the girl three tens. "Will this be enough to get you started?"

The girl's eyes glistened. "That's nearly three months' wages. Yes, it will be plenty. Perhaps I shouldn't take so much, though." She handed one of the tens back.

He pushed it back into her hand. "Please keep it. It is yours." He paused before saying, "What made you change your mind?"

She let out a long sigh. "I'm not entirely sure. I just didn't want to spend the rest of my life doing...that. I want my life to mean something."

He nodded.

"I don't know how to thank you, Dr. Peterson."

"It is my pleasure to help you. I shall pray for you."

"Thank you."

***

Kathleen watched the young woman leave. Was she crying? Did Luke give her unexpected news? The girl turned and approached Kathleen. "Do you know where the nearest church is?"

"I believe St. Vincent's is open. It's three blocks that way." She pointed.

"Thank you." She reached out to touch Sarah's hand. The baby scowled, unfamiliar with this new person, and held onto her mother tightly. "Good day," she said.

"Good day."

An open carriage finally arrived and out stepped Mr. Rutherford, the woodcarver. She called to her husband through his open office window. Luke came out and greeted the man. Sarah started to fuss so Kathleen took a seat on a wooden chair in the yard, bouncing Sarah on her knee.

A half-hour later, Mr. Rutherford shook Luke's hand and left. Luke called to his wife.

***

As Kathleen reached the porch near Luke's office entrance, he turned to face her. "What do you think?"

"That's a fine-looking sign, Dr. Peterson." She lifted her chin and stared at the polished oak that read, "Dr. Luke Peterson." A blue and green hummingbird flew over, then returned and hovered above the sign.

At that moment, Kathleen recalled her dream and the poem/prayer to St. Agnes. She shared the prayer and the dream with Luke:

Now good St. Agnes, play thy part,
And send to me my own sweetheart,
And show me such a happy bliss,
This night of him to have a kiss.

His face was blurry like an Impressionist painting, except with less detail. The man leaned in to kiss her, but his lips only gently brushed against hers. Immediately, Kathleen knew that this was her beloved. She couldn't explain how, but she could tell that his heart was pure and true and good. All of a sudden, the man vanished and in his place was a blue and green hummingbird hovering above her. How would she recognize her sweetheart if she could not see his face?

"Very appropriate, I should say."

"That you should have such a pure and good heart?"

Luke laughed. "No...the hummingbird. In Indian culture, the hummingbird is the symbol of pure love, joy and a celebration of life." He gently caressed her mid-section, which had not yet begun to show her delicate condition.

"Ah...yes, now it makes sense. I was annoyed because I couldn't see your face in the dream. And yet I saw and felt the most important aspect of you: your pure heart and soul."

"I love you, Kath." He kissed her forehead. "I always will."

"I love you, Luke. Thank you so much for this beautiful life and for giving me peace and security again."

"You should be thanking God, love."

"Indeed."

"When are your parents expecting us for dinner?"

"Around five o'clock." In her arms, the baby was closing her eyes, her stomach full from lunch and a long nursing. "But I must put Sarah down for a long afternoon nap. And I think I shall join her."

"In your condition, you'll want to get as much rest as possible."

"I don't mind the fatigue; it's the nausea I don't like."

"But it means that our daughter is settling in very nicely."

"You mean our son."

"I would cherish a hundred more like this sweet child." He kissed Sarah's head, now nestled against Kathleen's shoulder.

"As would I. This is a celebration of life, a new baby for a new century, and a new beginning for *all* of us."

Want to read more about the O'Donovan Family?
A Subtle Grace is the sequel to *In Name Only* (FQP, 2009) although each book is a 'stand alone' book and can be read independently of the other.

Book clubs, contact the publisher for bulk rates and discussion questions: fullquiverpublishing@gmail.com

Did you enjoy this novel? If so, check out the other inspirational novels from Full Quiver Publishing (listed below "About the Author").

Author's Note:
Prior to 1983, illegitimacy was an impediment to the priesthood and receiving Holy Orders. With the promulgation of the 1983 Code of Canon Law, special dispensations for illegitimates are no longer necessary.

For more information on St. Agnes, one of the patron saints of rape victims: (also of chastity, girls, engaged couples, and virgins) http://en.wikipedia.org/wiki/Agnes_of_Rome

Acknowledgements

I am grateful to everyone who assisted in the creation of this novel:

With love and gratitude to my beloved husband, business partner and developmental editor, James Hrkach, for spending many hours discussing plotlines and characters with me. I'm also grateful for his photography and exquisite cover design.

Special thanks to Fr. Arthur Joseph for being the first reader of this novel and for helping me with the spiritual aspects. As well, my gratitude to Fr. Denis Lemieux, for answering early questions about dispensations.

Cheryl Thompson, my copy-editor, thank you for your keen eye and your thorough job.

Krisi Keley, I am very grateful for your invaluable editorial suggestions.

A huge debt of gratitude to Maureen Sullivan-Bentz, RN and to

Rosemary Drziak, RN for assisting me with medical terms and procedures.

Thank you, Shawn Humphrey and Christopher Blunt, firearms experts. As someone who has never picked up a gun, let alone fired one, I am grateful to Chris for answering initial gun questions and, to Shawn, for helping me to create realistic scenes involving guns.

The Arnprior & District Museum's 19th century wedding gown and Victorian sitting room made this cover possible (thank you, Cathy Rodger and Janet Carlile). I am very fortunate to have this resource so close. Special thanks to Kristina Waclawik, our cover model.

Thank you, Christian LeBlanc, for helping me to make the Italian in this book believable and correct.

My wonderful group of beta readers has been indispensible! Thank you: Kathy Cassanto, Karen Murphy Corr, Erin McCole Cupp, AnnMarie Creedon, Krisi Keley, Patrice MacArthur, Laurie Power and Ginger Regan.

And if this book is devoid of typos, it's only because I have a skilled group of proofreaders: Louise Waclawik, Sarah Loten and Kayla Janoska. Thank you!

About the Author

Ellen Gable (Hrkach) is a bestselling, award-winning author of five books. She is also a freelance writer, publisher, editor, book coach, NFP teacher and President of Catholic Writers Guild. When she's not writing, Ellen enjoys spending time with her family, watching old movies, playing trivia games and reading on her Kindle. Originally born in New Jersey, USA, the author now calls Canada her home. She and her family reside in rural Pakenham, Ontario, Canada.

Ellen loves hearing from readers. Please feel free to email her:
feedback@fullquiverpublishing.com

Ellen's books have been downloaded over 500,000 times.
http://www.amazon.com/Ellen-Gable/e/B002LFMXOI/

You can find her:
Blog: http://www.ellengable.com
Facebook: https://www.facebook.com/ellengable
Twitter: http://www.twitter.com/ellengable
Goodreads:
http://www.goodreads.com/author/show/1595635.Ellen_Gable

Books by Ellen Gable

Emily's Hope
www.emilyshope.com
Honorable Mention 2006 IPPY Awards
Amazon Kindle Top 20 Religious & Liturgical Drama

In Name Only
(O'Donovan Family #1)
www.innameonly.ca
Gold Medal Winner 2010 IPPY Awards, Religious Fiction
Amazon Kindle #1 Bestseller Religious & Liturgical Drama
(February - April 2012)

Stealing Jenny
www.stealingjenny.com
Amazon Kindle #1 Bestseller, Religious & Liturgical Drama
(February, June - August 2012)

Come My Beloved: Inspiring Stories of Catholic Courtship
www.comemybeloved.com
Amazon Kindle Top 10 Catholicism

Books Published by Full Quiver Publishing

Angela's Song by AnnMarie Creedon
www.angelassong.com
Amazon Kindle #1 Bestseller Religious & Liturgical Drama
(October - November 2012)

Growing Up in God's Image by Carolyn Smith
www.growingupingodsimage.com
Amazon #2 Bestseller Parent Education

Don't You Forget About Me by Erin McCole Cupp
www.dontyouforgetaboutme.ca
Amazon #1 Bestseller Religious & Liturgical Drama
October 2013